T0157463

Exquisite Folly

By the same author:

The Thomas Dordrecht Historical Mystery Series

Die Fasting [1758]
Great Mischief [1759]
If Two Are Dead [1762]

Exquisite Folly

THOMAS DORDRECHT IN 1765

JONATHAN CARRIEL

EXQUISITE FOLLY

iUniverse books may be ordered through booksellers or by contacting:

iUniverse
1663 Liberty Drive
Bloomington, IN 47403
www.iuniverse.com
1-800-Authors (1-800-288-4677)

Because of the dynamic nature of the Internet, any web addresses or links contained in this book may have changed since publication and may no longer be valid. The views expressed in this work are solely those of the author and do not necessarily reflect the views of the publisher, and the publisher hereby disclaims any responsibility for them.

Author photo by Margery Westin.

ISBN: 978-1-4917-6482-4 (sc)

Library of Congress Control Number: 2015906676

Print information available on the last page.

iUniverse rev. date: 5/8/2015

For Frederick Cookinham

whose support has enhanced the Thomas Dordrecht series from the beginning

The most exquisite Folly is made of Wisdom spun too fine.
—Benjamin Franklin, *Poor Richard's Almanac*

But is it equitable that 99, or rather 999 should suffer for the Extravagance or Grandeur of one? ... Perfect Equity indeed is not to be expected in this World, but surely both Individuals, and legislative Bodies can come much nearer to the Standard of Right and Wrong than they generally do, For, *do unto all Men as you would ... reasonably desire they should do unto you*, is a Precept that has the most full and rational Approbation of the Consciences of ALL MEN.
—Excerpt of a letter from "A.B.C."
New York Weekly Post-Boy, July 11, 1765

Major Characters

*(Historical characters are indicated in **boldface**)*

❖ *Thomas Dordrecht*, 25, a New Yorker with ambitions in the shipping business

Thomas Dordrecht's Circle of Family and Friends:
- *Chastity Pennyman Dordrecht*, Dordrecht's mother, owner of farmland and a tavern/inn, *The Arms of Orange*, in New Utrecht, Kings County, New York
  - o Her eldest son, *Harmanus Dordrecht*, farmer; his wife *Anneke*; their children *Berendina, Hendrik, Willem, Lena*
  - o Her eldest daughter, *Geertruid Dordrecht Kloppen*, resident of Flatbush, NY
  - o The *Floris Van Klost* family, next-door neighbors; including his son-in-law *Engelbertus Hampers*, a first cousin of Thomas Dordrecht
  - o *Lodewijk & Katryne Nijenhuis*, neighbors and close friends of the family
  - o *Wouter & Marijke Van Voort*, neighbors—he the dominie of the town's Dutch Reformed *kerk*
- *Charles Cooper*, Dordrecht's first cousin and close friend, resident in New York City, writer and activist against the Stamp Act
  - o *William & Janna Dordrecht Cooper*, his parents—he a furniture retailer; their elder son, *Rev. Henry Cooper*; their daughter, *Mary Cooper Fitzweiler*
- **Marinus Willett**, friend from Dordrecht's 1758 military service, now an upholsterer and activist against the Stamp Act
- *Benjamin & Hermione Leavering*, employers and friends
- *John & Adelie Chapman Glasby*, employers and friends

- *Baldur Fischl*, friend, German immigrant, proprietor of a Pearl Street music store
- *Cyrus Mapes*, sometime colleague at Castell, Leavering & Glasby, shippers

<u>INDIVIDUALS FIGURING IN *EXQUISITE FOLLY*</u>:
- **John Tabor Kempe**, Attorney-General of New York province
  - **Catharine Kempe**, one of his four maiden sisters, betrothed to Peter Colegrove; their mother, *Abigail Kempe*
- *Aaron Colegrove*, wealthy and prominent New York City merchant, formerly a patron and employer of Thomas Dordrecht—a relationship now mutually disdained. (*See the chart of the Colegrove family tree.*)
- *Mrs. Nugent*, Dordrecht's landlady on Reade Street
- *Henry Tenkus*, unemployed mariner
- *Caesar & Calpurnia*, slaves at Aaron Colegrove's mansion on Broadway
- *Edward* and *Virginia Ramsay*, siblings, friends of Oliver Colegrove
- *Mrs. Herbert Pannikin*, next-door neighbor of Aaron Colegrove
  - *Leah*, her slave girl
- *Willie Martin*, grocery clerk
- **Isaac Sears**, merchant, former ship captain, activist against the Stamp Act
- **John Lamb**, wine merchant, activist against the Stamp Act
- *Lionel Tolbert*, New York City Clerk
- *Marge Williams*, Reade Street resident
- *Captain Ford*, of the CL&G coastal sloop *Janie*
- *Augustus* and *Octavian*, brothers, slaves at Aaron Colegrove's Mamaroneck, New York, estate
- *Reverend Willibald Peacham*, Anglican minister, resident of White Plains, New York
- *Captain Enos Trent*, of the CL&G ocean-going merchant ship *Dorothy C.*
- *Uzal Parigo*, friend, boatswain of the *Dorothy C.*

<u>INDIVIDUALS REFERENCED (BUT NOT APPEARING)</u>:
- *Samuel Low Aldridge*, Philadelphia merchant implicated in the Sproul murder case
- **Colonel Isaac Barré**, Irish soldier and politician

- *Substance Coldcastle*, a horse trader in Hempstead, New York, known to Thomas Dordrecht as the other son-in-law of the Van Klosts of New Utrecht
- **Cadwallader Colden**, acting Lieutenant-Governor of New York province
- **James DeLancey, Sr.**, late chief justice of New York province; eldest son of Stephen DeLancey
- **Captain James DeLancey, Jr.**, merchant, political leader of the "DeLancey faction"
- **General Thomas Gage**, military commander-in-chief in North America
- *Darius Gerrison*, solicitor to Aaron Colegrove; employer of Timothy Colegrove
- **George Grenville**, Whig Prime Minister of Great Britain, originator of the Stamp Act
- **Patrick Henry**, member of the Virginia House of Burgesses
- **Zachariah Hood**, distributor of stamps for Maryland
- **Thomas Hutchinson**, Lieutenant-Governor of Massachusetts
- **Jared Ingersoll**, distributor of stamps for Connecticut
- **Major Thomas James**, artillery commander at New York City's Fort George
- **Sir William Johnson**, British Superintendent of Indian Affairs for the northern colonies
- **Archibald Kennedy, Jr.**, New York-born Captain of *HMS Coventry*
- *Tobius Leendert*, Amsterdam merchant, Dordrecht's employer, winter of 1764-65
- *Jacob Leisler*, late 17th Century New York populist leader
- **James McEvers**, chief stamp officer for New York province
- **Sir Henry Moore**, newly-appointed Governor of New York province
- *Thomas Pennyman*, Dordrecht's maternal uncle and namesake, a London merchant of musical instruments; his daughter, *Anna*
- *Daniel Sproul*, late former partner of Castell and Leavering, the solution of whose 1762 murder brought Thomas Dordrecht to the attention of John Tabor Kempe
- **John Wilkes**, controversial British Whig politician
- *Roderick & Elisabeth Dordrecht Willett*, Dordrecht's brother-in-law and younger sister, resident in Jamaica, New York—he a fictional brother of the historical Marinus Willett

Family Relations of Aaron Colegrove

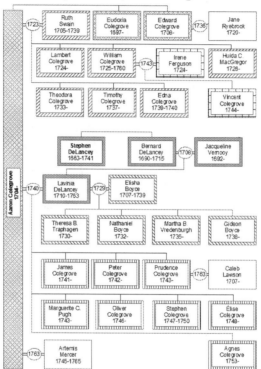

All the characters on this chart are fictional, with the exception of **Stephen DeLancey**, patriarch of the prominent 18th Century New York family.

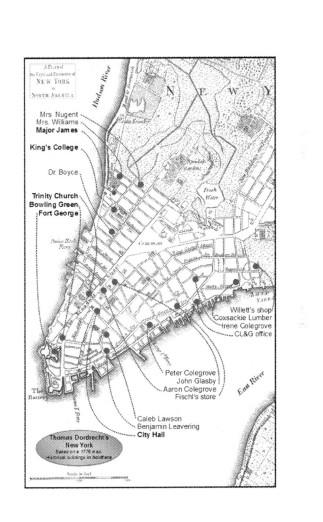

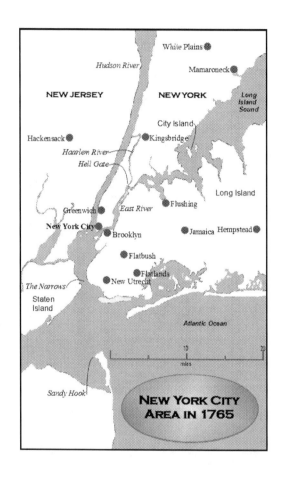

White Plains

Hudson River

Mamaroneck

NEW JERSEY

NEW YORK

Long
Island
Sound

City Island

Hackensack

Kingsbridge

Haarlem River

Hell Gate

Long Island

Flushing

East River

Greenwich

New York City

Hempstead

Brooklyn

Jamaica

Flatbush

Flatlands

New Utrecht

The Narrows

Staten
Island

Atlantic Ocean

10

20

miles

Sandy Hook

**NEW YORK CITY
AREA IN 1765**

Concise Time-Line of the Stamp Act Crisis

- May 28, 1754: A bloody skirmish south of modern Pittsburgh, Pennsylvania, touches off a global war
- September 8, 1760: Montréal falls, ending North American hostilities
- February 10, 1763: Treaty of Paris
- May 7, 1763: Pontiac leads a Native American attack on Fort Detroit
- July 9, 1763: Whitehall deputizes the British navy to enforce customs regulations—ending the long era of "salutary neglect"
- October 7, 1763: The Proclamation of 1763
- April 5, 1764: Parliament passes the Molasses Act
- April 19, 1764: Parliament passes the Currency Act
- November 16, 1764: Pontiac surrenders to the British
- February 27, 1765: House of Commons passes the Stamp Act—to become effective November 1, 1765
- May 15, 1765: Parliament passes the Quartering Act
- May 30, 1765: Virginia House of Burgesses passes Patrick Henry's resolutions against the Stamp Act
- June 8, 1765: Massachusetts legislature proposes Stamp Act Congress
- August 14, 1765: Boston has an orderly riot
- August 26, 1765: Boston has a disorderly riot
- August 26, 1765: James McEvers resigns New York commission
- September 2, 1765: William Coxe resigns New Jersey commission
- September 5, 1765: New York's newspaper proposes November 1 protest
- September 15, 1765: Jared Ingersoll resigns Connecticut commission
- September 16, 1765: Philadelphia has a disorderly riot
- October 7–25, 1765: Stamp Act Congress held in New York City

- October 22, 1765: The *Edward* arrives outside New York harbor
- October 23, 1765: Two thousand armed New Yorkers prevent landing
- October 24, 1765: Stamps landed by the navy overnight
- October 31, 1765: New York merchants sign non-importation agreement
- November 1, 1765: New York has a mildly disorderly riot, which leads to—
- November 2, 1765: —an extremely disorderly riot
- November 5, 1765: Governor Colden surrenders the stamps to the city
- November 13, 1765: Sir Henry Moore replaces Colden, defers enforcement
- November 1765–May 1766: Non-importation agreement holds; ships evade stamp usage; protests continue throughout the colonies
- February 21, 1766: Parliament passes the Declaratory Act, then rescinds the Stamp Act

The critical fact to understand in regard to the crisis, is that the stamp tax was universally regarded in America as entirely unprecedented, entirely unjust, a betrayal and a harbinger of even greater future oppression. That belief was utterly astounding to its imperial creators—who perhaps suffered from "wisdom spun too fine"—because they saw the tax as perfectly mild, fair, reasonable, and patently necessary.

CHAPTER I

Thursday, September 5, 1765—3:30 P.M.

"Take your hand off me, sir! How dare you!"

As I stepped off the gangplank to set foot, once again, upon my native continent, a wave of nausea unexpectedly overwhelmed me. Reeling, I had reached out and taken hold of the one stationary object in the vicinity—the shoulder of a tall, spare, scowling gentleman standing on the quay. Having been so long at sea, without illness, I'd smugly forgotten how I sometimes suffer this relatively mild affliction, which manifests itself in a few minutes of dizziness and disorientation upon reconnection with dry land. *"Mal de terre,"* I'd christened it, though the sailors call it "sea legs."

"I beg your— *Ooh!*" Once again, my legs nearly buckled.

"Well, just sit down on the ground, for— I say, don't I know you?"

Oh no! Woozily, breathing heavily, I focused upon the be-wigged fellow with the youngish face—and groaned again. *Of all people!* "Mr. Kempe!" I exclaimed weakly.

John Tabor Kempe, though but five years my senior, is the attorney general of the royal province of New York. We had had some necessary, but not particularly comfortable dealings with each other three years ago. "Dordrecht! Thomas Dordrecht, no?" he said, frowning.

"Yes sir. I do beg your—"

"Come on, there's a bench just over there." He grasped my elbow, an expression of annoyed dutifulness on his face, and escorted me to it, ten yards away, where I sat with great relief. "Are you going to be ill?"

"I don't think so. Thank you very much, I shall be fine in a few—"

Though his eyes were fixed on the ship's deck and the gangplank, he seemed disposed to make conversation. "You've been abroad, I collect?"

"Yes sir. Over two years."

"Indeed! You were factoring goods for Mr. Leavering, I presume?"

Hmph! Impressive, that he recalled that association. "Only on the first leg, Mr. Kempe. My permanent connection to Castell, Leavering, & Glasby was severed before I left—business conditions being so abysmal— but they arranged for me to market a load of flaxseed in Belfast, which I managed to exchange for a great quantity of finished linens."

"I see."

"Then I proceeded on my own." He looked bored. "The passage I had from Belfast to Bristol was scarier than either trip across the Atlantic. Normally, it's less than two days; for me, it was the worst five—"

"So you spent the rest of your time in England? Did you get to London?"

"I was in London for fifteen months, Mr. Kempe," I replied, feeling my equilibrium returning by the second, "then I went on to Holland, Flanders, and France."

"My word!" He raised his eyebrows, as if reluctantly acknowledging that he was impressed. "Did you have business in all those places, Mr. Dordrecht?"

I smiled ruefully. "I was attempting to *create* business, Mr. Kempe. It is, I'm afraid, far easier said than done."

"Of course. Particularly in these troubled— Will you be resuming employment with Mr. Leavering, then? Is that why you've come back?"

"Would that it were so, sir," I admitted—too forthrightly. "The sad fact is, I've no immediate prospects, once I sell off the few goods I bought in Europe."

"*Ah.*" He grimaced, as if wondering how demented I must be to return in such circumstances. "I say, can you tell me what day your vessel departed? I am most anxious for the latest news from home."

So *that's* what he's doing here! I had to smile: I too was anxious for news from home, but now I *was* home, at long last. Kempe, I recalled, had been born in England. "We departed from Portsmouth on July the second."

"Ah," he shrugged, apparently disappointed. "The *Royal Charlotte* arrived last Saturday, having left direct from London on July sixth."

I had enquired about traveling on the *Charlotte*, but found it well beyond my means. "A faster ship, it appears."

"Yes. Well then, if you'll excuse— Mr. Dordrecht, perhaps you can tell me if you were able to gauge the mood of the— Of at least the mercantile classes?"

The man must indeed be eager for news, if he seeks my observations. "Ah, well, the English in general seem far more exercised by the fate of Mr. John Wilkes than they do over any injustice their Parliament has done to the American colonies with its Stamp Act. Not that I can—" I was about to say I couldn't blame them for objecting to Wilkes' treatment, he having been driven abroad merely for expressing in print irreverent opinions of H.M. such as every one of royal George's subjects freely lets fly nightly in the taverns. However, I was interrupted by a lusty call of "Tom Dordrecht!" by a voice I recognized, one of few friends whose inveterate use of my nickname I tolerated.

"Marinus!" I rose and waved, my unsteadiness almost gone. As he bounded, grinning, across the road, his long brown hair, loosely caught behind his nape, bouncing against the back of his smudged, open shirt, I noted an increased girth to his chest and musculature, a solidity that indicated the full arrival of manhood, and wondered—given that Marinus Willett and I are exactly the same age—if others would perceive similar changes in me.

Instantly, he grasped my shoulder and began vigorously shaking my hand. As he crowed, "Where the devil have you been? I haven't seen you in—" I had just enough time to perceive how very rough his hands were … before my friend so abruptly went rigid that my breath was taken from me in surprise. Three seconds passed. "Mr. Kempe!" he said, glaring icily, not offering his hand.

"Willett," Kempe stated, equally bluntly, barely nodding, not offering his hand either.

Was it February? I thought it was a fine, fresh, sunny afternoon in September! Evidently there was no need for me to make introductions. Before I could venture any emollient remark, Kempe said, "Congratulations on your return, Dordrecht. Take good care!" and strode away, quickly lost in city traffic.

Marinus Willett stared after him, mouthing the words, "Rude bastard!" Astounded, I was equally beginning to wonder about *him* … when he shook himself and asked if Kempe had come to greet me.

"No no, my meeting him was just as accidental as my meeting you," I replied, slightly irked by the question. "What on *earth* was all that about?"

The grin reappeared. "*Bah!* Nothing, nothing!" He pointed to the ship. "You just got off this? You were in England?"

"Yes, but I also—"

"That's right, my brother told me that! Hey, I'll be you don't even know that we are both *uncle* to the same healthy little lass!"

Introduced through our friendship, Willett's younger brother Roderick had courted and wed my favorite sister Lisa. "No!" I shouted, delighted. "Finally! When? When?"

"*Uhh* … oh yeah, three weeks back. The fourteenth—the same day the Bostonians had their rampage," he added gleefully, "though we didn't know that at the time."

The *Bostonians* had a *rampage?* "What did they name the child, Marinus?"

"*Uhh* … Katryne! After the godmother, your mother's friend."

A curious choice—but I liked it. "Katryne Willett! Very pretty!"

"And she is, too! Takes after her mother, not my side of the family!"

"Hah!" I elbowed him in the ribs as we chuckled.

One of the ship's black sailors approached us, carrying my portmanteau, and knuckled his forehead. "Mistah Dodrick! Cap'n sent me tell you. Cargo shifted. Won't get yours out this aft'noon. T'morrah, prob'ly."

"None of my goods damaged, I hope?" I said anxiously.

"Cap'n don't think. Shift more aft, next to hatch."

"Aha. I'll check back in the morning, then. You lads be careful with my stuff. I've some real fragile items in there!"

"Aye sir. We careful!"

"Oh … rats!" I grumbled as he loped back up the gangplank. "I suppose it was too much to hope to get it settled today."

"You have cargo aboard?" Marinus asked.

"Aye. Oddments I bought with the last of my savings that I think will be wanted over here. Two pianofortes, a clarinet, some cloths, some carpentry tools. A set of four Chippendale chairs!" I added, recalling that he was in furniture.

"How'd you afford *that?*"

"Each of 'em has something wrong with it, and the *milady* couldn't tolerate them. Got 'em for a song."

"I can fix them, Tom! I can match the wood, match the color, match the finish!"

"I was planning to take them to Mr. Cooper, my cousin Charles' father."

"Let me at them first. They'll be good as new! And they'll sell, too. Rich folk still have money here, even if no one else does!"

4

That was the intuition I'd been counting on, based on the news from America and my correspondence, but it was odd to hear the incorrigibly optimistic Willett express it with such a bitter edge. "Well ... first I have to find myself a place to stay, Marinus."

"What's wrong with your old boardinghouse? Hasn't burned down, that I've noticed."

"*Uh*, Marinus, please don't publish this, but I can't *afford* my old boardinghouse right now. Until I sell off some of the things I've brought in, I have to stretch every last farthing." Maybe even *after* I sell them, I thought grimly.

"*Huh!* Well, what are we standing here for? We'll come up with something if we put our heads together. Look, I'm done with my chores. Let me buy you a glass. We'll raise one to little Katryne!"

It was far too good an offer to pass up.

Just crossing Front Street and walking three doors up to the nearest public house, we were, to my surprise, accosted by two beggars. Times had been bad in New York when I left, but ... Nothing like Europe, of course, but still upsetting. Marinus gave each a small string of wampum; I had nothing that could be spared.

"Beggars?" I asked, once we'd toasted our niece and quaffed the first long, grateful swallows.

"Aye. Rotten state of affairs. Sometimes I think the Parliament means to beggar the lot of us!"

"Mr. Leavering always said that business invariably retrenches after a war, that it's to be expected and will pass, sooner or later."

"Oh? Well, I wager he'll be singing a different tune the next time you see him. It's the taxes, Tom, and their confounded rules. You have read through the Stamp Act, I trust?"

"I only got to it on the crossing. I was in Amsterdam last winter, and traveling all spring."

"Really!" For a second, I thought he might inquire about my travels. Given that I've had no few adventures over the past twenty-eight months, I was disappointed not to be invited to trumpet my experiences.

But my old friend seemed too preoccupied to concern himself. "This is so much worse than anything they've done before. Worse than all their interference with our trade during the war. You've been away—what?—two years? You must have read about the Molasses Act? The—"

"Oh yes, I—"

"The British seem to think we never paid a penny into the war effort!"

"Oh they do think that, very definitely, Marinus. I could never dissuade—"

"Well, you can imagine how very *convenient* an assumption that is for their politicians! The more they can load onto us, the less they have to tax their own!"

"*Uh huh*," I agreed cautiously.

"Then came the Currency Act. And then even after they hit us with the Stamp Act this spring, they've passed a Quartering Act that says we have to pay for all the army's provisions!"

"Yes, I heard about that before I—"

"The infuriating thing about that is, the whole rationale for keeping the army at such strength is supposedly to protect the frontiers, yet some of them are sitting right here in New York City, as if we're in any danger of being scalped in full sunlight!"

"I dimly recall there was some fracas with the Indians?"

"The Hurons, yes—Pontiac, the chief. But that's all been over for nearly a year, and it was way, way out west—it started even beyond the Ohio country. And it wouldn't have happened at all if they'd just left the redskins alone, and not insisted that they venerate Great White Father George instead of Great White Father Louis!"

I was dumbfounded—as much by my friend's vehemence as by the situation he related.

"So the upshot is, instead of *asking* us to contribute to the army's upkeep, as they've always done in the past, they're *telling* us we *must* contribute. And they're assessing us in a manner that will drive all our commerce further into the ground."

"That was my reading, too, Marinus. But you know, the English pay stamp taxes themselves, and it doesn't seem to annoy them half as—"

"The English pay taxes to the English Parliament, which is elected by the English people. We pay taxes aplenty to our own Assembly, which represents us, for better or worse."

"Usually for the worse!"

"*Ha*, I'll grant you that!" he said, finally cracking a smile. "But the point is, in the hundred years since they booted out the Dutch, they've never presumed to *command* us to pay them taxes, and we've always shelled out for them when we've seen they needed it. But if they can get away with one peremptory demand for our money, even one that at first seems negligible, you have to grant that they'll be back for more the following year!"

"In for a penny, in for a pound sterling!"

"And that's what tops it, Tom. Thanks to that Currency Act, all of these stamp taxes are going to have to be remitted in *specie*—and there's next to none to be had on the whole American continent!"

"What happened to all the coin the soldiers and sailors dropped here during the war years?"

"Gone, Tom. Some of the major merchants were shaking their heads over it at the meeting."

"A meeting?"

"An irregular meeting, open to all the freemen of the city. Some want to formalize it, call it the *Sons of Liberty*."

To cover my bemusement over the entire idea, I mumbled, "Oh, after the phrase in Colonel Barré's speech, I suppose?"

"Aye. The notion is, we have to work together to fight this monster down. You must join this!"

Marinus' use of the imperative seemed to suggest that he was deluded that he and I were still, respectively, the lieutenant and sergeant of our provincial regiment. "I *must* join this?" I said archly.

He caught himself. "Well, you *should* join it!"

I hope my rolling eyes conveyed that I considered the restatement only a marginal improvement. But I was barely an hour back in America, and hardly wished to make a fuss.

"I think you'll *want* to be a part of this, Tom," he persisted. "Amazing things are suddenly happening here! Just a week ago Monday, the man who was to be New York's stamp commissioner resigned—after what happened in Boston—and then—"

Before I could ask what *had* happened in Boston, he'd rushed on.

"Then some of us met the *Royal Charlotte* last Saturday, and cornered a man who'd gone over to England to secure a tax-collecting post for his son, and made him foreswear it on the dock!"

"You *made* him foreswear it?"

"It's amazing what ten dozen men can do, if they all scowl at once!"

I had to smile. "No, we didn't touch him, Tom. We just made it clear that nobody was going to do any business with him if he didn't tear the commission up right in front of us."

"And he did?"

"Yes sir, he did indeed."

"*Hmpf!*"

A young fellow I didn't recognize, whose back had been to us, appeared to notice Willett and was trying to get his attention.

Marinus turned as I pointed him out. The fellow was nodding his head in the direction of the door. "*Ah. A member of the committee!*"

The *committee?*

"Something must be afoot. I'll have to go." He chugged down the last of his glass.

"But—"

"Great to see you, Tom! I'll be in my shop tomorrow. Bring those chairs over, and Cooper will never know they had a blemish!"

"I— Well, thank you for the beer, Marinus!"

"Oh hey, friend!" And he was gone, engaging in earnest conversation with the young fellow as they walked out.

Puzzled—and frankly, a trifle hurt—I slowly drained the rest of my glass, wondering what it was that could call a man so compellingly from the side of an old chum without exchanging news of his business, his wife and son, mutual friends—and without explaining the shocking hostility between himself and John Tabor Kempe. Willett seemed as intent on his new project, whatever it was, as he'd been when we were bearing muskets in earnest, thrashing through the woods near Ticonderoga.

But the *war* was over.

On standing up, I suffered a recurrent bout of the sea legs. The whole tavern swirled about me for thirty seconds as I clutched the table and the chair. It lasted just long enough for me to wonder if it was a portent that I had returned to a world gone mad.

But I dismissed the thought as soon as I got outside and inhaled a fresh northeasterly breeze.

I had no time for idle fantasy. My immediate need was to find myself lodging in the two hours of daylight that were left. Marinus had suggested I look in the new area of the West Ward known as the Church farm—so-called because the tract belonged to Trinity Church, which had astutely divided it into parcels small enough that the "middling sort" could afford to build there.

But before heading to the west side of the city, I stopped by the Brooklyn ferry and wrote a quick note to my family in New Utrecht, trusting that some worthy traveler would be found to deliver it.

Had New York City changed during my absence? Of course, it constantly changes. Old structures had gone missing, new ones were in their place. Quite a bit of new construction was in progress, notwithstanding the complaints of my correspondents about the dearth of commerce. Redcoats were back, but though their numbers were fewer than in the war years, I sensed they were less welcome.

At length, asking around, I located the Nugents, a shy bricklayer and his garrulous wife, whose small, brand new home on Reade Street served them, their six children, and another lodger, but who nonetheless had an attic room to spare. It would be hot in summer, cold in winter, but at least, unlike a room in a basement, it would not be prone to flooding when it rains.

Charles Cooper leant back from the table, and smiled slyly. "You've changed, Cousin Thomas," he asserted. "Despite your straitened circumstances, you seem altogether more in command, more self-possessed."

I nodded warily as the waiter removed our dinner plates. One never knows where Charles' mercurial train of thought will be leading.

"Dare we speculate that you are no longer a virgin?"

I'd been just wary enough that I avoided choking on my beer. As he so often does, Charles evoked both amusement and impatience. One wondered why he, of all people, assumed I'd been a virgin when I departed America! But despite his being perhaps my most intimate friend, I had no intention of discussing any dalliances with him—however interesting he might find them. I do trust he lacks malicious intent, but the man's a notorious gossip. And further, a clandestine publisher of political chicanery. "I can hardly dissuade you from *speculation*, dear cousin," I replied, choosing my words carefully but expressing them as blandly as I could manage, "but I regret that *Sejanus* will have to subsist on more mundane grist from my mill. For example—"

"Oh *my!*" pouted the often-feared author of pseudonymous letters to newspapers. "But it's high time!"

Look who's talking! I thought. Charles is eight years older, unwed, and far more adept than myself at withholding his private affairs. "You needn't concern yourself, Charles—though I'm grateful for your solicitude!"

"One could interpret your reticence in many ways, Thomas," he observed cagily.

"I daresay one could, couldn't one!"

Be damned if I need yet another relative interfering in my private affairs! My mother, sisters, aunts—all have been writing in a panic to see me married and encumbered with children. Each has the one *perfect* lass already picked out for me. And now this libertine capon—how I wish he'd at least get a *new* wig!—is equally clamorous to see me *un*-settled.

Charles swirled his Madeira and sighed with an infuriating, all-knowing smirk on his face. "Well, at least tell me this. Did you have yourself any *fun*, while you were in Europe?"

"In two years?" I said, laughing, "I should hope so!" But that was insufficient to satisfy my cousin. "There were points high and low, of course, Charles, but in fine, I very much enjoyed my time abroad."

"Ah."

He means well, I reassured myself, as he finally appeared ready to forego seeking further titillation.

"I've retired *Sejanus*, incidentally, Thomas. Wrong choice in the first place. Nasty piece of work, the historical Sejanus. Now I write as *Leisler's Ghost*—and I'd appreciate equal circumspection about *his* identity!"

He'd stumped me. Oh yes: Jacob Leisler had led a rebellion against New York's powers-that-were at the time of England's Glorious Revolution—and gotten hanged for his pains.

"Thomas?" His arched eyebrows were prompting for a response.

"Oh, of course, Charles, of course!"

"*Dank u*," he said, relaxing and showing off what little Dutch he has. "You were asking what has transpired in Boston, I believe?"

"Yes!" *At last we revert to a less sensitive topic!* Merely the future of the British Empire was now in discussion.

Charles avidly launched into a political explication—an activity in which I've found he excels. "We should look back a bit," he began. "Ever since the treaty was signed—just before you left—Whitehall has been in a frenzy to pay down the spectacular debt it accumulated in seven years of battle all 'round our celestial orb."

"Yes. The national debt was doubled, I'm perfectly aware."

"So the politicians, led by Mr. Grenville, conceived the unprecedented notion of taxing the American colonies directly, obviating any tiresome necessity of asking our several assemblies to decide for themselves how much, or how, or even *whether* to contribute. Thus we had the Sugar Act, the Currency Act, and the Quartering Act in quick succession. Now each of these might be said, through extremely tendentious argument, to be a regulation of trade, rather than an assessment for revenue. Most people here, as you know, concede trade regulation as a legitimate function of Parliament."

He'd said this last with such disdain, I couldn't help challenging him. "You don't?"

"Not any longer, Thomas—but that's for another discussion. So while there were howls of outrage about these enactments from New Hampshire to Georgia, due to the unfair burden they imposed, no one really protested against them as a matter of principle."

"That may actually have encouraged Grenville, d'ye think? After all, no one expects anyone to *like* getting taxed!"

"Could well be, Thomas, although the howls were pretty fierce. But the Stamp Act, now, it can't be disguised as anything other a naked demand for cash, from an entity that has never, ever before presumed to demand it. When we first learned of it, in April, everyone was so shocked, they simply moaned and whimpered. We'd just spent two years petitioning and protesting against the Sugar Act and the Currency Act, to no effect. No one could quite believe that even more was to be foisted on us—even though Grenville had been threatening it for months. Fortunately, a fellow down in Virginia was not fooled, and—"

"Henry Patrick! I did try to catch up, with a newspaper last night."

"Patrick *Henry*, the man's name, Thomas. He induced the Virginia Burgesses to pass a series of resolutions stating that a stamp tax from Britain was simply not acceptable and, one way or another, must not be paid."

"*Huh!* Outright defiance, then. I hadn't realized that."

"Aye, the same as you'd venture toward a highwayman!" He took a sip as I pondered the consequence to New York of defying the British Parliament. A century ago, I'd been told, the Dutch had surrendered the entire province when the city had been threatened by four naval vessels. I'd counted upwards of forty lying idly at anchor as my ship maneuvered out of Portsmouth harbor.

"Well, Virginia's resolutions set the rest of the colonies ablaze. Certainly here, we've been debating how to put a stop to the tax all summer long. But it was Boston that brought matters to a head last month."

"August fourteenth! The day my niece was born … Marinus Willett told me."

"Of course," Charles sighed, rolling his eyes with strained toleration. "The radical faction there put it about that everyone was to gather at noon for a ceremony, and the ceremony was to hang the stamp collector in effigy. They made quite a histrionic production of it. The governor sent the sheriff to disperse the mob, but he took one look at it—some two thousand, Thomas!—and ran off in fear for his hide." I stared, fascinated. "They cut the effigy down and marched it through the city—passing right by the government house, of course, and then they tore down a warehouse the stamp collector had just built."

"Good heavens!"

"Then they carried the effigy up onto a hill and *beheaded* it! And that evening, they quite thoroughly destroyed the man's house—he having prudently removed his family to the military garrison."

"But that's excessive! Surely the merchants of Boston must disapprove?"

"It's reported that a goodly number of Boston's merchants were in the crowd, Thomas. Dressed as workmen."

"But … beheading a scarecrow is one thing, you know, while destroying a warehouse and ransacking a private home is quite another!"

"Well, consider: the man had agreed to be the salaried official who would coerce people into paying this tax. How much sympathy would you muster for a brigand, Thomas?"

That did place matters in a fresh light. On the road from London to Harwich, last fall, my coach had been waylaid by a highwayman. I'd been carrying all the money I had left to me, to fund my trip to the continent and back home. I'd not found much cause for dismay when another passenger had unexpectedly produced a pistol and shot the criminal dead. "What has been the consequence of all this, Charles?"

"Well, the tax collector resigned his commission the next day, to start!"

"He did? *Huh.* Well, that's fine … but surely there's been the devil to pay for the rampage? Arrests? Floggings? Executions?"

"None. The one man arrested was allowed to walk free when it became known the customs house would be pulled down if he wasn't."

"Such things could easily get out of hand, Charles."

"Well, it's arguable that they *did*, Thomas. Just a fortnight ago, the mob got riled again, and laid waste the mansions of three more placemen—being especially thorough on the home of the lieutenant-governor, Hutchinson." When he saw what was undoubtedly an appalled look on my face, he added, "All three had endorsed the Stamp Act, Thomas, and each intended to profit by it." He paused. "The word is, the leading merchants—who were indisputably at one with the mob—have since put a damper on further rioting. There's been no report since that event."

"Has there been anything of the sort here?"

"Nothing to match it. Yet."

"Yet?"

"Well, the man appointed to be New York's commissioner resigned before anyone even asked him to! The New Jersey commissioner followed suit just this Monday."

"Ha!"

Charles smirked sarcastically. "Grenville's oh-so-shrewd idea of appointing Americans to the lucrative tax commissions, rather than his own cronies, has rebounded on him, you see. He intended to mollify us, but if the panjandrums had been British, here only to bleed us for a few years and then abscond back to Albion, we'd never have been able to intimidate them!"

"Hoist by his own petard!"

"Aye. You know there's to be a congress of the continental colonies, here, next month, to coordinate protests against the Stamp Act?" I shook my head. "None of my lot expects much of it. Concerned they'll be too timid about it." Charles leaned forward and whispered, "There are some here who have written that the Stamp Act is sufficient outrage to justify the independency of the American colonies!"

"*What!* Charles, that's ... mad! Simply mad. In England, I sometimes came across people ranting that Americans were aiming for independency, and I took pains to disabuse them, and now you're saying—"

That infuriating smirk again. Charles shrugged. "I only report what I hear and read, cousin. The notion has not gained any great traction, I can tell you."

"Still, just the suggestion—"

"But what has gained acceptance is the conviction that those stamps must never be employed in New York. Did you see the notice in yesterday's *Post-Boy?*"

"The issue I read was a month old."

"On the day the Act is to be effected—"

"November first?"

"Aye. There is to be a solemn funeral procession for Lady North American Liberty—from the common, down Broadway, to the fort. All New Yorkers who revere their rights as Englishmen are anticipated to be present."

"Certainly that is one event I should have no objection to—"

"Ah, but *you* must do more, Thomas! You must join our effort to *direct* the protests against—"

"Stop right there, Charles!" *Another "must!"* "I do not respond well to imperatives, cousin!"

"I beg your pardon," he said smoothly, after a second's hesitation. "I only suggest you may well *desire* to join me and your friend Willett—and even Benjamin Leavering—in thinking through all options available to our suffering populace."

"The *Sons of Liberty*, I presume?"

"Not dignified with a name, just yet—though we could do worse." As if struck by an idea, he leant forward with both elbows on the table. "Your participation might be especially valued, Thomas, given your travels abroad and your former engagement with the shipping interest."

Startled, I was bemused.

"And you may have the time available, given your current lack of employment."

"Given my current lack of employment, I should spend my time *seeking* employment," I protested, "lest I end up applying to the alms house!"

"Or worse, to Harmanus Dordrecht!"

Charles was only teasing, but he occasioned a convulsion of shivers: the prospect of ever having to throw myself on my elder brother's mercy was a horror that didn't bear contemplation. "You know what I wanted to ask you: As I stepped off the boat, yesterday, to my surprise, I came face to face with John Tabor Kempe."

"Kempe! What on earth was he doing at the wharf?"

"Hoping for news, he said."

Charles snorted. "I dare say!"

"We endeavored to make conversation for a few minutes, but then along trots Marinus Willett, who sees me, comes over—and all of a sudden, the temperature drops to a hard freeze! The two men were barely civil to each other! That Kempe might be impolite was no surprise, but I've never known Marinus to—"

"Thomas, be warned, passions are getting very high, here. You realize that Kempe is unquestionably in the Court faction?"

"What, he thinks the Stamp Act is justified, then?"

"Well, no, nobody in America thinks that—saving perhaps the supreme jackass, Governor Colden. He and that Army major who so charmingly vowed to cram the stamps down our throats with the point of his sword!"

"A redcoat actually said that?"

"Yup! The contention, I say, is all over what we should *do* about it. And though Kempe will not be directly administering the Stamp Act, he's one more royal placeman who believes anything Parliament decrees has got to be obeyed, to the letter."

"*Ugh!*"

"And Willett is aware of that. And Kempe, our attorney general, our esteemed public prosecutor, is all too aware that Willett is a partisan on the opposing side."

"Oh."

"And considering the way in which the Crown has been whittling away at our traditional understanding of our legal process, Willett's right to be guarded about the man."

"I just thought it odd that Marinus would—"

"He might also be … chary of the fact that Mr. Kempe, who was penniless when he inherited his high position six years back—along with his father's debts, his widow, and his four homely maiden daughters—is now managing nicely and engaged to marry an heiress."

"Now seriously: Kempe *inherited* the position of attorney general?"

"Well, his father had been appointed to it back in England, and when he died, Governor DeLancey—"

"The late James, Senior?"

"The same. He took pity on the family and raised young John Tabor to eminence beyond that to which his experience and his admitted native application entitled him, bypassing many who were more qualified. *Noblesse oblige*, you know."

"I see. But there's never been a taint of corruption regarding—"

There was no point in continuing. Charles was suddenly not listening. He was eavesdropping on a nearby table. He presently turned back with a shamefaced grin. "Sorry! One can hardly resist any possible morsel of our town's current scandal!"

So much for Mr. Kempe! "What scandal is that, Charles?"

"Thomas, you've been back on these shores thirty hours, and you haven't yet heard?" I shrugged. "And my heavens, it's your former employer's wife"—I looked at him blankly—"who was murdered!"

For a horrified second, I thought he was speaking of Hermione Leavering ... but Charles would never be glib about that dear lady. "*Which* of my former employers, Charles?"

"Oh. Aaron Colegrove, of course. His wife was found dead, horribly beaten and stabbed. Right in their backyard. Broadway, just north of Trinity Church. Middle of last week. High noon!"

"Good grief!"

"The one subject that's taken everyone's mind off the Stamp Act for a blessed moment!"

"I can imagine!" Aaron Colegrove is one of the city's most prominent merchants. He'd been my employer for all of two months, back in the winter of 'fifty-nine. My friend John Glasby had worked for him for four years, but left him shortly after I'd been summarily dismissed. Not because of me, I think; rather, it was because he'd come to doubt Colegrove's probity. "That's appalling, Charles! You know I've no love for the man, he's been associated with some of the worst experiences I've ever had, but I can't recall anyone ever complaining of his *wife*." Charles looked at me quizzically. "I saw her once, though I was not favored with an introduction: a pleasant-looking matron, modestly dressed, a tad on the stout side—"

"Oh!" Charles exclaimed. "You're talking of *Lavinia* Colegrove."

"Of course."

"Oh, but— Not her, Thomas. She died. Of pleurisy, if I recall. When? Two years ago, in the summer?"

"I left in April."

"Ah right, that explains it. Well, not six months after Lavinia passed away, your Mr. Colegrove—"

"Please, Charles! I disown him!"

"Actually, I think it was only five months. He remarried—a sprightly lass of *eighteen* or so, younger than most of his children by his first two wives. That by itself set tongues wagging. The set over at the Royal Exchange were both piously disapproving and, I think, secretly envious, because the third Mrs. Colegrove was quite a feast for the eyes!"

"And it's she who was—"

"Murdered, yes. Artemis, her name."

"There's really no possibility of it being an accident? Or even suicide?"

"Not with that many wounds. Rumor is the lass was stabbed a dozen times."

I had to fight down my gorge, which was rising with revulsion. "But … why would … Have they apprehended the murderer?"

"They have a man in the jail. A sailor who'd been seen imposing himself on Mrs. Colegrove's attentions for several weeks. Insists he's innocent— and his claims have just enough credibility to occasion a constant public debate." Charles looked out the window for a second, and sighed. "And there's another complication: whoever did it—or rather, *somebody*—left a message."

"No! People leave suicide notes, not murder notes!"

"That may be. Usually."

"What did it say?"

"Big letters: 'Liberty, Property, and No Stamps!' " I was baffled. "It's a slogan, Thomas—the slogan of our committee, the opponents of the Stamp Tax."

I whistled. "You don't think …"

"I do *not* think, Thomas, that anyone on the committee had *anything* to do with this crime. It was clearly a crime of passion against the woman! She was—it's only common knowledge—the sort of woman who inspires passions. The tax protesters have roughed up some men, here and there in the colonies, men who were designated placemen—tar and feathers and so forth. But no woman has ever been attacked, and no man anywhere has been permanently injured, much less murdered."

"A clumsy attempt to cast blame aside, then?"

"Precisely. Except, of course, that the committee's opponents have fastened onto it, and won't let it rest."

"They insist on taking it seriously?"

"Exactly."

"*Ugh!* Where was her husband when this happened?"

"Oh he was on the high seas, Thomas. He only got back from England last Saturday. She'd been buried by then." I gaped. "He got quite a reception. One almost felt sorry for him! First we, *uh, confronted* him with a demand that he renounce the commission he'd traveled across the ocean to get, then he was informed that his wife had been murdered."

Callous. I swallowed my disgust. "What commission was that?"

"A place as assistant customs inspector, for his son James. We made him tear it up before he even got off the boat."

"Wait. Willett was telling me … the *Royal Charlotte* … it was Aaron Colegrove who was intimidated?"

"Oh yes. Can't really say I didn't enjoy it! Young James—your age, I think—came out to greet papa—and to collect the royal benefice. He saw what was happening, turned tail on both, and has apparently decided to inspect the family's country estate in Mamaroneck. For a few *months.*"

Now I began to smile too. Normally, I might have managed some sympathy for a man in Colegrove's predicament. However, too many vivid and unsavory recollections of him interfered, especially the fact that he'd been implicated in the gigantic fraud that had been unearthed three years ago by Mr. Daniel Sproul—who had been murdered to ensure his silence. It was John Tabor Kempe, I recalled with annoyance, who'd considered the evidence of Colegrove's chicanery insufficient to merit further investigation. However … "Well, tell me more about what happened to this new Mrs. Colegrove."

Charles seemed embarrassed. "Wish I knew more, Thomas. I didn't pay that much attention to her while she was alive, and I've been really busy with the committee for the last month, so … I fear I may be losing my touch!"

"Surely not?"

"Well … She was quite a parcel, that one! I told you she was fine looking, did I not?"

"Aye." And I confess it added to my interest!

"Well, to put it bluntly, her indisputable charms were more the sort that please us males rather than the ladies. Not exactly the glass of delicacy, the pinnacle of refinement, young Artemis Colegrove!"

"Aha."

"And her deportment matched her appearance, much to the horror of my mother and even my sister."

Aunt Janna, I knew, was quite easy to scandalize, but if Artemis Colegrove had upset my sensible cousin Mary Cooper Fitzweiler, she must indeed have been careless of our province's social norms. "Her family? Where was she from?"

"No one really seems to know!" Charles said gleefully. "She appeared of a sudden, at his side, just before they wed. Family non-existent! And where she came from? I've heard Maryland, I've heard Yorkshire, I've heard the West Indies. Her voice was so corrosive, no one could endure it long enough to guess the locus of her accent!"

"I can't imagine Aaron Colegrove consorting openly with a woman who could not possibly enhance his stature here, much less marrying one. He—"

"He seems to have changed a bit, Thomas. Word is, his successes have completely gone to his head, and he's become quite reckless. So far from being discreet, he invited half the city to the wedding. Trinity has never seen the like!"

"You were *invited* to this wedding?"

"No, but I went anyway! *Sejanus*—that shocking charlatan—had his last field day describing its vulgar prodigality!"

"Did Colegrove write back in protest?"

"He had the good sense—or the loftiness—not to."

"He does sound changed. He was always a calculating swine, before."

"Against all advice, he ran for the Common Council, last election. He spread a lot of money around and still lost spectacularly. Not even the DeLanceys would support him."

"Hey, wasn't Mrs. Colegrove—Lavinia, that is—*related* to the DeLanceys?"

"She *was* a DeLancey, Thomas. Of the cadet branch," he sniffed sarcastically, "but a DeLancey nonetheless. Easy to forget, because she'd been married before Colegrove, to a fellow named Boyce. They'd both been married before. Both their first spouses were lost to the smallpox epidemic of 'thirty-nine."

"So Aaron Colegrove has been married *three* times?"

"Aye. And now he's thrice a widower!"

We each sipped our Madeira. "How many children are there by all these women?"

"Well, there were none by Artemis. But my understanding is, there are at least a dozen still living by the first two. Plus stepchildren. And grandchildren."

"Really! You know, I knew he was married and had a family, but I never realized … they were never in sight, the few times I went to his house."

Charles shrugged. "You know of Catskill Lumber Company? That's run by Lambert Colegrove, the eldest son."

"Owned by Aaron, though?"

"No. Owned by the son. Strained relationship with his father. I've been watching Colegrove's businesses for some time."

I'll wager on it!

"There's another son I've gotten to know: Timothy. Hates the old man, hates his whole family!"

"How do you know him?"

Charles sighed again. "Member of the committee. Haven't seen him since the murder—but perhaps he didn't want to commit the hypocrisy of shamming regret for a woman he detested."

"So you haven't had an opportunity to ask him what he thinks about that message on the body?"

"No."

"I wouldn't imagine a young girl like that would have anything to do with politics. Why would anybody remotely associate her with the protests?"

"Oh, well, she famously lacked inhibition. She made a spectacle of herself during Colegrove's election campaign, making public pronouncements of monumental ignorance and vapidity that she thought might please him. Perhaps we should be grateful to her, as it's occasionally argued that she contributed to his defeat."

"She sounds harmless enough," I said. "Risible, if anything."

"Aye, but she did persist in imposing herself on everyone—particularly after he left on his mission to Whitehall, when a dutiful wife is normally expected to retreat quietly to her hearth."

"Uh oh."

"She constantly repeated her one great, infuriating witticism, no matter how urgently her friends begged her to hold her tongue."

"And what was that?"

"Artemis Colegrove knew Aaron meant to capitalize on the Stamp Act, so she was all in favor of it, and loudly in opposition to its opponents."

"So?"

"She couldn't resist telling everyone, 'The Sons of Liberty should be *stamped out!*'"

CHAPTER 2

THE PRESENTS I'D BROUGHT for my family were at last distributed. They'd not been as opulent as I'd once dreamed—tokens, rather than proof of stellar commercial success—but anything hauled from far-off Europe won unstinting approbation. "There's one more, I've saved for last." A flurry of anticipation, as expected. "It's not from me, actually. It's for Mother, from Uncle Thomas."

As Mother paled and turned her face aside with filling eyes, young Lena exclaimed, "But *you're* Uncle Thomas!"

Her Auntie Geertruid explained, "No, dear, it's your grandmother's brother Thomas, not your father's."

"Your great-uncle, Thomas Pennyman, who lives in London," I added by way of clarification—useless to a five-year-old—as I passed the packet across the table.

Mother's hands trembled slightly as she carefully cut the ribbons around the oilskin. For thirty-seven years she had treasured Uncle Thomas's letters, the sole remembrance of her childhood. "Ooh, *lace!*" Lena breathed as the whole family gasped.

"It's a shawl?" Mother asked, unfolding the fragile triangular form.

"Oh, it's so beautiful!" Anneke said.

Her daughter Berendina, showing the unexpected alertness and helpfulness that has made her my favorite, jumped up and moved behind her grandmother to assist in placing the shawl smoothly and delicately about her shoulders.

"Thomas bought this for me?" Mother asked breathily.

"He commissioned me to acquire it on his behalf, Mother. I bought it in Antwerp. He was very pleased when he saw it back in June."

21

"Must have cost a king's ransom!" Harmanus murmured, shaking his head.

"Oh … a knight's ransom, perhaps," I demurred.

Anneke slapped a filthy hand away in the nick of time. "Don't even dream of touching that shawl before you wash, Willem!" Willem pouted, clearly regarding a wash as too great a sacrifice.

"Do you think I dare wear something so extravagant in *kerk?*" Mother asked, looking anxiously toward my elder brother, a deacon of the church. He and his wife exchanged nervous glances. A half-century back, there had been laws against such display, specifically against lace; now only the prejudice lingered.

"I shall be most upset, Mother," my elder sister Geertruid interjected, staring Harmanus down, "if you do *not* wear it in *kerk!*" To everyone's relief, Harmanus smiled and shrugged, conceding the issue.

"I'll wear it with my dark green gown," Mother said, bringing me a quiet flush of pride, as she'd made that gown from satin I'd given her years back, out of the prize money I'd won in the war. "Oh, if you'll excuse me, I simply must have a look in the glass!" she said, rising. "Berendina, be a dear and fetch another candle!" The two of them left and climbed the stairs, the mirror being located in the hall at the top. In response to agitated squirming, Harmanus dismissed the children, leaving me with himself, Geertruid, and Anneke.

"Did you have a chance to visit the graveyard, Thomas?" Geertruid, who had been last to arrive at the *Arms*, inquired.

"Aye. Mother and I took a walk as soon as I got here, late this afternoon." The year 'sixty-four had been hard on the Dordrecht clan. "I, *um* … I'm so terribly sorry about the lad, Harmanus, Anneke! I mourn Grootmoeder, of course, and Pa, too, but … What happened to little Petrus?"

Anneke sighed. "He was skylarking on the horse when Hendrick wasn't looking, Thomas, and the beast took a fright and he got thrown and—"

Geertruid shuddered. "It brought back Aalbert's loss so terribly!" Our own younger brother had died of colic at the age of eleven. Eleven years ago, I realized with a start. "Poor little scamp!" Seeing general dejection, she hastened on. "Grootmoeder passed away in her sleep, without a whimper."

"The death of the innocent," Anneke said. Grootmoeder had been sweetly daft for years. "Gathered unto Jesus!"

Unlike Pa, no doubt! I had to ask. "And Pa?"

Sighs all around. "It was only a week after we buried Grootmoeder," Harmanus said. "He was wandering around barefoot, and—"

"Drunk?" I asked.

"Afraid so. He stepped on a broken pot but didn't tell anybody, and lockjaw set in four days later. Took him six horrible days to die."

"Awful, just awful!" Anneke said.

This was all far too grim. I inquired of family business. "Did you manage to settle Grootmoeder's estate?"

"Oh yes," Harmanus replied. "That was all arranged long, long ago, when Pa and Grootmoeder were still fully *compos*. Frederik got our dray horse, Betje got a dozen chickens and six bushels of wheat a year, and Janna accepted five pounds in cash."

"And Pa, of course, got the house and the fields."

"That's as always understood, Thomas. Otherwise, we'd have had to sell off the fields."

Someday, when Mother passes, Geertruid, Lisa, Brevoort's widow, and I will be similarly expected to receive a token inheritance, while the house and fields will remain in my elder brother's hands. This realization used to infuriate me; now, I have more important issues with which to concern myself. "So Ma now owns *The Arms of Orange?*" Historical accident had arranged that under the Dutch law that still obtains in our township, the property of an intestate man passes wholly to his widow—quite a contrast to the English insistence on primogeniture in most counties of the province.

"Aye," Harmanus agreed, evidently appreciating the irony of the Dutch law having passed the property to a woman wholly English, while the English law would have conveyed it entirely to Harmanus. "But nothing essential has really changed, Thomas, given how little either Grootmoeder or Pa involved themselves in the workings."

"You miss the horse," Anneke reminded him.

"Oh yes, I do. Still haven't replaced that horse!"

Conversation turned to our wonderful Uncle Pennyman, about whom they expressed great interest—never, of course, having met him. The father of four, grandfather to two, our Uncle Thomas lives in a poor but respectable section of the capital with his wife, his youngest daughter, his widowed daughter-in-law, and her two young girls. He is a maker of musical instruments who had sustained me as a shop and sales assistant for thirteen months before realizing his business, too, was contracting and could no longer support a hireling.

Fortunately their curiosity was sated by the stories I was content to tell. Just hours before, Mother had sworn me not to reveal what I'd learned of our horrible grandfather, or the wretched and pathetic reason for her own emigration to New York. In my turn, I was also withholding the embarrassing fact that I'd become enamored of her niece Anna Pennyman, had actually proposed and been accepted—only to face my uncle's intransigent objection. Though she and I were both adults when we met, the insuperable blood truth remained that we were first cousins. That situation, as much as his business, had precipitated my travel to the continent. Anna had married another suitor this past spring, which Uncle Thomas and I eagerly seized upon to effect a reconciliation before I left Europe for home.

Given my announced plan to visit Lisa, way out in Jamaica, immediately after the morrow's service, I was honored how many people stopped in at the tavern after supper to welcome me home. Not only my cousin Bertie Hampers, but the Nijenhuises, Van Klosts, and Van Voorts paid a special visit. Mother came back downstairs wearing not only the lace shawl—much admired—but the dark green gown. As both my brother and sister-in-law seemed very tired, I volunteered to tend the bar, taking it over as mechanically as if I'd been away two days rather than two years.

Bertie was the only one who appeared to have any interest in my adventures in Europe, but I'd barely conveyed the tale of the near-foundering in the Irish Sea before Lodewyk Nijenhuis, Harmanus, and Vrouw Van Voort joined us, demanding beer and cider as they talked excitedly of the record prices they'd been receiving for their crops. "I've noticed bread is very dear in the city," I said. "What has brought this about?"

"What I've been reading, Thomas," Nijenhuis began, after a pull from his long-handled clay pipe, "is that our grains are being bid way up by the New Englanders, who are anticipating a general boycott to commence later this year."

For a couple seconds, I was mystified. Then it dawned. "This would have something to do with the Stamp Act?"

"Oh yes. Some of the Bostonians are so strongly opposed, they plan to shut down their commerce rather than endorse any contract on stamped paper."

"More power to them, I say!" Bertie asserted—prompting a scowl from his father-in-law, Floris Van Klost.

"And whether they agree or not, the merchants are being pressured by the radicals to comply," Harmanus added with some consternation. "That's why they're buying now—so they'll get through the winter."

All of which will make it harder for the city-dwellers—for *me*—to get through the winter, I thought grimly. "Is there anything that people here in New Utrecht will need to have stamped?" I asked.

"Not unless we're buying or selling land."

Dominie Van Voort joined in for a cider. "I thought I'd have to publish my sermons on stamped paper—but they've exempted all religious works."

"Thank heaven!" Marijke Van Voort murmured.

"Smart!" Bertie jested. "Otherwise, they knew they'd be preached against, every Sunday morning!"

"What about the tavern's license, Harmanus?" Nijenhuis asked.

As always when confronted with a business question, my brother, who truly is a simple, honest farmer, looked alarmed, then confused—and then referred the question to our mother, who had been absorbed in the shawl's intricate patterns with Katryne Nijenhuis.

"It's not due until February, dear," she replied, "but I asked Berend"— Geertruid's husband, who has a brewing concern in Flatbush—"about it, and he urged me to settle it before October's out. And so I shall!"

"What about that quartering requirement, Mother?" I asked. "It specifically mentions taverns, doesn't it? Have you asked whether—"

"What! Soldiers? *Here?*" Anneke cried in alarm.

"Surely they wouldn't—" Harmanus began, his face reddening. The thought had obviously not occurred to him before.

"I really doubt it, Harmanus," Mother said hastily. "It's the taverns in the city and up-river that will have to be concerned. We're outside the military area."

"Unless they send a company out to repair the King's Highway," Dominie Van Voort observed, occasioning another flurry. "And it could certainly use some maintenance!"

I shared the palpable agitation in the room: none of us wanted any redcoat anywhere near young Berendina, much less living in the same house. I was sorry I'd voiced the question.

"Does your mother's bakery require a license, Meneer Hampers?" Vrouw Van Voort inquired, tactfully shifting the subject.

"No, thank heaven," Bertie replied, "but we'd need one if we had a flour mill. Father wanted to start one in Flatlands, but it seems it's illegal, and only the New York City establishments can mill flour in the entire province. So I'll have to take the wheat that's her due from Grootmoeder's estate into the city, and then take the flour back out to Flatlands. Nuisance!"

"Oh, but we have to support the city mills, Hampers," Van Voort said. "Otherwise, they might not be able to make ends meet—and we surely wouldn't want to be without flour mills!"

"Did your father think he could make a going concern of a mill in Flatlands?" his wife asked.

"He thought so, ma'am. After all, it would save everyone on Long Island a day's trip across to the city. It's really an absurd regulation, Dominie!"

"*Hmm.* Well, at least your parents won't have to worry about getting any stamped documents!"

"Tell us about your stay in the Netherlands, Thomas," Van Voort demanded a few minutes later. "Now when I was there fifteen years ago—" His wife silenced him with a black look. The dominie and I were likely the only two "Dutchmen" in Kings County who had ever set foot in old Holland.

"I enjoyed a very worthwhile stay in Amsterdam last winter, sir. I was privileged to visit many of the great counting houses and factories. But I had some difficulty making myself understood!"

"Indeed, so did I, at first—and they kept insisting that I wasn't speaking correctly. The language of New York has grown apart."

Should I mention that the way I surmounted the difficulty was by imitating the inflections of his sermons—which I'd always before thought horribly affected? "*Um*, my host in Amsterdam, Meneer Leendert Tobius, a merchant, asked me to join him on his trip down to Paris, and on the way—Did I write this?—we spent a night in Dordrecht!"

Hendrick was back in the room. "There's a *place* named Dordrecht?"

"Oh yes, young man, of course there is!" the dominie asserted. "It appears you have not been paying sufficient attention in *kerk*, young fellow! How many times have I recounted the details of the famous synod held there in sixteen-nineteen, where the very foundations of our Reformed religion were laid down? The clergy from all the united provinces were gathered, and many from abroad, too, when—"

Perceiving that eyes were glazing over, all about the room, Katryne Nijenhuis deftly shoved the hapless lad toward the dominie, who continued to lecture him, and turned the rest toward me. "Thomas, you're just out from the city! Tell us, has anything new come to light in the Colegrove case?"

Her desperate gambit—I nearly laughed aloud—worked, as everyone's attention instantly shifted. I daresay the dominie might have listened had he not felt it his solemn duty to enlighten Hendrick. "*Um*, well, I only heard of the situation last night, Mevrouw. Cousin Charles Cooper told me of it."

"Well, you can trust Cousin Charles to know all there is to know, *eh*?" Bertie smirked.

"They've collared the swine who did it, haven't they?" Harmanus asserted. "Some low sailor?"

"He was actually a mate on an ocean-going brig, I heard," Nijenhuis said. "Not a common seaman."

"Scum of the earth—all mariners!" Van Klost declared between draws on his pipe. "Seldom seen here, thank the lord!"

"Charles says there's some doubt of the man's guilt," I offered.

"No!" Bertie exclaimed. "I heard they caught him not an hour after they found her, not three blocks away!"

"And wasn't he one of those confounded Liberty Boys?" Van Klost said. "He even had the nerve to paint one of their unnatural slogans on the fence after he'd done the poor woman in!"

"There was a note, I understand—"

"I've heard that that 'poor woman' was something of a brazen hussy, Meneer!" Marijke Van Voort said, blushing furiously.

"Oh, surely not!" Anneke protested. "The wife of a prominent man of affairs? How could that be?"

"Oh my dear!" Vrouw Nijenhuis sighed, rolling her eyes. "Did you know that her husband was no less than forty years older than she was?"

"Oh my!"

"That does happen," Harmanus began nervously, "even among truly Christian folk."

"The most scandalous thing I've heard," Vrouw Nijenhuis continued, "is—"

"Hendrick! Off to bed with you!" Harmanus commanded, abruptly terminating the dominie's history lesson.

"I was shopping in the city on Tuesday, and I chanced upon your aunt, Janna Cooper, who told me there were pagan statues of *undraped ladies* all over their garden! Right in the middle of the town!"

"Oh Mevrouw!" Geertruid objected. "Surely anything quite so outrageous would be far more notorious! It can't be that—"

"All the gardens in that area are fenced in," I observed. "Most have seven-foot brick walls."

"What Janna told me was that there's no more than a hedge facing the alleyway, and that it's possible to peer in through the leaves!"

"I absolutely cannot imagine Aunt Janna doing any such thing!" Geertruid declared.

"No," Bertie piped up, grinning, "but you can imagine who might!"

We all knew exactly who he meant, and I reflected that our common cousin Charles must indeed be losing his touch if he'd neglected to share this tidbit with me.

"These city folk!" the dominie protested. "Shameless heathens, the lot of them! Make you yearn for the likes of Pieter Stuyvesant to lay down godly law!"

He was serious, I do believe. While Floris Van Klost nodded approvingly, the rest of us—even Harmanus—cringed over the dominie's eccentric politics. Conversation shifted again, to the problems of swine— actual swine—until rolling thunder, in an attenuated crescendo, urged our guests home and the family to bed.

I had been apprehensive that Mother, Geertruid, Anneke, and Vrouw Nijenhuis would all fall upon me with demands that I consider various eligible future Mrs. Thomas Dordrechts. However, each of them was gracious enough merely to hint that they did have such an individual in mind. My brother Harmanus, on the other hand, belabored the subject for half an hour before the service on Sunday morning, insisting that the daughter of a deacon of the Reformed congregation in Bushwick, whose father owns three fields comprising some thirty-seven acres, would be my perfect mate, and implying none too subtly that the Almighty Himself was keen for such a union to take place. Only after arduous fishing did I learn that the "lass" is a widow with five children, "perhaps a little" older than Harmanus himself. It took some work to persuade him that it would not be a kindness to insist on a meeting.

But if he was disappointed by my indifference, he'd reconciled himself in time for my departure. "I'm glad we have you back, Thomas," he avowed, shaking my hand and smiling with an unfeigned sincerity that moved me greatly. Perhaps we were both adult enough at last to be loving brothers.

"We were half-afraid we'd never see you more," Anneke asserted.

"Many have been known to establish themselves as factors abroad and not return at all."

"Why *did* you return, Thomas?" Geertruid asked bluntly.

I elected to summarize. "Oh, the state of business in Europe is as slack as here, Geertruid, and I thought it advisable to renew my contacts at home, and to market the goods I'd bought on speculation." Their interest in those goods spared me from having to add that I had simply run out of funds. Or to admit that I was frankly homesick. Or that I had some predisposition toward marriage—but with someone of my *own* choosing, not theirs! "I was very fortunate to be able to use introductions from Mr. Leavering and from Uncle Thomas, to meet substantial men of affairs in Belfast, Bristol, London, and Amsterdam; and through my patron in Amsterdam, Meneer Tobius, factors in Antwerp and Paris. Many were glad to know of my acquaintances in New York and Philadelphia—and in Saint Eustatius. In that respect, the trip has at least been promising."

Perhaps, I thought mordantly as I started off for Jamaica, my tombstone will be engraved, "He had such *promise!*"

"Thomas," Benjamin Leavering began, his tone slightly more hesitant than I'd have expected, "if we may turn to business for a moment, while the ladies have left us?"

We were seated, two evenings later, in the Leaverings' parlor on Hanover Square. It was the first reunion of the odd collection of six friends that had constituted the social high point of my earlier years in the city. We were still awaiting Charles, but Hermione Leavering and Adelie Glasby had repaired to the kitchen to oversee the final preparations for our supper. Thus, I was left with my host and former employer, and with John Glasby, now a full partner in their shipping firm of Castell, Leavering, & Glasby. Two and a half years had wrought some change in all of us—in me, more than any other, I suspected. But the ladies seemed to me as vibrant and youthful as ever, and Mr. Leavering had regained most of the color and decisiveness he'd had before Mr. Sproul's death, without gaining back the excess of weight. The only one to appear more careworn was my first friend in the city, John Glasby, who, at forty-six, looked rather borne down by the responsibilities of owning and managing ships.

I was in high spirits, jubilant to be reunited at last with these dear friends ... and I was also quite ready to have some of the conversation turn to business. "Of course!"

"First of all, we were more than satisfied with your handling of our commissions in Belfast, in London, and in Amsterdam."

"I'm most gratified to hear it, sir!"

"And John has seen the goods you brought back on your own account, and tells me he's impressed with your choices, which should fetch good prices here, despite all."

"I was at the east warehouse yesterday," John explained. By arrangement, I had stowed my goods there on Friday, pending distribution and sale.

"Thomas, we—" Benjamin uncomfortably looked to his partner to carry the discussion.

"We know you must have some hope of rejoining the firm, Thomas," John stated—quite correctly. "And we have considered it ... but we cannot manage it at the present time."

"Ah."

"Our affairs are completely unsettled, Thomas," Benjamin explained.

"There are the wildest propositions being floated regarding the city's commerce," John continued, "and we dare not commit ourselves to any increase in staff."

"I see." Though disappointed, I was not completely surprised, having spent some of the hours since my family visits absorbing the news of recent events. Had I a business to run, I reckon I'd be as cautious.

"Withal that we cannot offer a steady position, Thomas," John resumed, "we are in the anomalous situation of urgently needing competent and reliable help on a more limited basis."

"Sir?"

"If you are available, Thomas, we could surely use you ... until November first."

"We will gladly restore your old rate," Benjamin added.

The proposition did not require any thought on my part. I breathed more easily immediately. "I should be delighted, gentlemen! But ... November first being the date the tax becomes effective?"

"It is not only Boston that is in an uproar over the Stamp Act, Thomas. New York is, too."

"And Philadelphia. And Newport ... Charleston ... Baltimore," John moaned. "There are even publicly-stated fears of civil insurrection erupting. Just since you returned last week, the governor has met with both the provincial council and the city magistrates, arguing that several companies of troops should be returned from the Québec regiments, to maintain the peace."

"Good heavens!"

"Both of them refused to endorse Colden's request," Benjamin continued, "on the reasonable ground that increasing the number of redcoats here would only constitute a provocation."

"I see." Indeed, I could: the only force that could now conceivably be deemed a threat to New York's *peace* was an irate citizenry. Were the army again to be increased beyond the few platoons resident in the fort, it would be a direct affront.

"I have been to many a *pow-wow*, Thomas"—Benjamin smiled as he used the Indian term—John did not—"along with your cousin Charles, where a complete rejection of all commerce in British goods has been proposed, rather than—"

"Madness!" John muttered softly, shaking his head.

"—rather than comply for a minute with the stamp tax. Now, as sensible businessmen, whatever we may think of all this—and I have come to agree that such a response may be our best way forward"—John uncomfortably looked up at the room's elegant crown moldings—"we, along with most of our competitors, are choosing to hasten the departure of our ships before that dire event."

"And to do that," John said, rallying, "we shall need to accomplish four months' work in seven weeks."

"But after the Stamp Act comes into force … we simply don't know what is going to happen!"

"It is a terrible situation," John said. "Whatever the reasoning and whatever the outcome, it cannot bode well for New York's commerce—or its people."

"Indeed." We all sighed. "Well, whatever help I can provide, I shall be more than—"

Charles Cooper rapped the knocker on the front door and presumptuously let himself in, just as Hermione was inviting us to the dining room.

"There's a great deal of experimentation going on," I observed as our supper was drawing to a close, "attempting to increase the efficiency of the Newcomen steam engine." John Glasby had inquired about business developments in Europe. "There is hope that such devices can someday be made to do more than pump water out of mines."

"Really? Such as what?"

"Oh ... if they could be made to work more smoothly, they might haul stone out of quarries, or even pull barges along canals."

"Engines?" Charles said. "As opposed to horses or oxen? Or men?"

"Aye."

"How very peculiar," Hermione Leavering interjected. "Imagine!"

As opposed to my family, and even such chums as Willett, this circle of friends had encouraged me to discourse freely on my experiences abroad, and I was greedily responding. "There is also a rumor in the City that a man in Lancashire has invented a device—some sort of framed apparatus—that allows a single worker to spin eight spools of thread at a time."

"No!" John said, his eyes bulging. "As if he were trundling eight wheels simultaneously? Has anyone seen this prodigy?"

"Very few, I'm told, as the inventor is fiercely jealous of his handiwork—and also wary of those whose earnings might be threatened by the new machine."

"Ah."

"But just think," Benjamin mused, "how great a blessing such a contrivance might prove. Since the loom has been so greatly enhanced by the fly-shuttle, the spinners have never been able to create enough yarn for modern weaving machines to turn into cloth."

"Lord knows we can never get enough finished cloth into America!" John said.

"Half our business!" our host agreed.

Supper being completed, Hermione urged us back to the parlor for a glass of Madeira.

"Now Thomas," Adelie said as we sat down again, "we've had quite enough of newfangled mechanics! Surely you are not going to tell me you never went to the theatre in London?"

"I, *um* ... Only once."

She was indignant. "In fifteen months!"

"Dear madam, I had neither the time nor the money! But I did see Mr. Garrick's '*The Clandestine Marriage*,' at the Drury Lane itself. It was very comical and entertaining!" I was pressed for a detailed evaluation and for commentary whether it was too advanced for our provincial audiences; I could see both Adelie and Charles were instantly engaged in eager speculation.

"As a consequence of my uncle Pennyman's profession," I continued, "I did attend many fine concerts. Mr. John Christian Bach—he's the brother who lives in London—and his partner Mr. Abel have created what they call a *series* of public concerts. They're scheduled, months in advance, and my uncle purchased a subscription to the lot of them!"

"What an extraordinary idea!" Adelie exclaimed.

"Sounds like an invitation to bankruptcy, I fear," Benjamin said.

"It appears to be working, sir."

"Could we ever do anything of the sort in New York?" Charles mused.

"Only if you think New York will ever be as large a town as London!" John scoffed—and we all had a good laugh at that.

"While I was in Amsterdam, a friend procured a seat for me at a memorial concert for Locatelli, and I made time to attend a retrospective for Rameau, at Notre Dame Cathedral in Paris."

"Well, I'm relieved to hear your trip wasn't *all* business, Thomas," Adelie said.

"Oh—and when I got back to London, this June, Uncle Thomas and I attended … it wasn't a serious concert, just a *divertissement*, as the French say, in a public house. Some family from Vienna. The papa played the violin, and his young daughter sang, very prettily, but the chief draw was the lad, not even ten. He was so short, he had to hop up onto the chair to reach the clavichord. They'd play one trio—all very nice—then they'd play another, with the little fellow blindfolded! And then the lad would cross his arms and play the bass notes with his right hand, and the treble with his left!"

"You don't mean it!"

"The father asked for a volunteer from the gathering, to verify the blindfold was genuine, and—"

"So of course *you* stood up!" Charles asserted preemptively, to everyone's amusement.

"And yes, I couldn't see a blessed thing with it on!"

"What was this family's name, Thomas?" Hermione asked.

"Oh … Heavens, I forget! Something … something to do with 'art.'"

Benjamin again topped everyone's glass with the fine sherry.

"Were the ladies dressed as fashionably in London or Amsterdam, Thomas, as in Paris?"

"Oh now you've put me on the spot, dear Mrs. Glasby! Fashionable? *Uhh* ..."

"That's a rather unfair question for a young fellow, Adelie!" John objected.

"Not quite so unfair for a young fellow who hopes to make a career importing dry goods!" Benjamin countered. He'd adjured me long ago to be as observant of our feminine customers as our male patrons. "Surely you took *some* notice of ladies' dress, Thomas?"

"Well ... I'm not certain how *à la mode* they all were, but I can say the ladies were as *opulently* dressed in London as in Paris. The English look to the French to set the course, it seems. I know I saw more English in the shops of Paris than I saw French in London's emporia."

"So that's where all the money goes!" Charles murmured, bringing the conversation to a momentary halt and prompting a warning glance from Adelie.

"I was at the Ranelagh Gardens," I said quickly—and it caught everyone's attention—"and a lady at least explained an innovation in fashion accouterments to me. Someone got the fine idea to hinge the entire set of hoops that support a lady's gown, both in front and in the back, so that the wearer can lift the entire assemblage up to the sides, still preserving her modesty, and thereby pass safely through a doorway facing forward."

"So she doesn't need to turn sideways?" Benjamin queried. I nodded.

"Why didn't anyone think of that years ago?" Hermione demanded. "My next gown shall certainly take advantage of this creation!" she added, a droll smile on her face.

"Fortunately for our family exchequer, Mrs. Leavering *contemplates* buying many more gowns than she actually purchases!" Benjamin said indulgently.

"So you really went to Ranelagh, Thomas?" Adelie said.

"My uncle was playing in the orchestra, and was renting instruments to several other players, so I was allowed in as his assistant—with an injunction to keep a modest presence."

"And did you?" Adelie teased.

"*Umm*, well, no. I snuck away and explored the place."

"I don't suppose you've yet been to the new Ranelagh Gardens and

Vauxhall Gardens *here*, Thomas?" Hermione said. "It would be most curious to compare them!"

"I walked around the Ranelagh perimeter just yesterday, ma'am," I said. "It would take two hours to do that in London."

"Well, you must *go in!*"

"I'd love to, sometime!" But given my pecuniary restrictions, I reckon it will snow in Hades first.

"I venture London's Ranelagh is altogether more grand?"

"Indeed, it's very beautiful ... and yet rather intimidating."

"You've never been easily intimidated, Thomas," Adelie observed.

"Not usually, but I was wearing my humble finest, and all the blades there were dressed in embroidered silks and overflowing with laces and freshly-powdered wigs—"

"Oh, I see," she said, nodding sympathetically.

"I felt out of place, quite uncomfortable. That happened more than once as I traveled in Europe."

The room rustled as everyone adjusted to a shift in the conversation. "How so?" Charles inquired.

"The wealthy are richer, there, and the poor are far more constrained, but I didn't feel at ease with either class. It's so strange! Even my uncle, a fine gentleman, a quite reasonably successful tradesman, feels a need to scrape and bow before his silk-stocking customers in a manner I found excruciating."

"Tradesmen in general get little respect there, I have always gathered," Benjamin said with some asperity.

"Surely there's a way to perform one's duty to one's customers without needing to abase oneself!"

Adelie, who had been born and raised in England like my mother, but who, again like her, seldom spoke of her childhood, seemed agitated. "I had forgotten how distressing it can be," she said.

"I didn't find the extraordinary wealth of the upper classes so offensive"—I noticed Charles frowning at that observation—"but their superciliousness was unendurable. And what was worse ... We've seen hard times, here in America, and—"

"We'll see them again this winter, I can tell you!" John asserted.

"But I've never seen anyone in America, even in the slave quarter at home, literally on the verge of starvation. Yet in many a hamlet ... in

France, particularly, but also in Ireland, England, you see people positively emaciated, barely able to lift their hands to beg, as your coach clatters blindly through. I found it quite upsetting!"

"You must join Charles and me when our committee has its next meeting, Thomas," Benjamin said.

"See! I told you!" Charles gloated.

The last person from whom I expected another *must* was Benjamin Leavering. My brother-in-law Roderick Willett had piled on his admonition during my Sunday visit.

"Now Benjamin," John protested, "Thomas hasn't even been home a week! Give him some time to find his bearings again before you involve him in politics!" His tone was mild, but I sensed he was irked by his senior partner.

"Our time is running out, John!" Charles said. Adelie hissed in dismay.

"Nonetheless, I feel sure Mr. Dordrecht can make up his own mind whether he desires to join anyone's committee!"

"Thank you, John," I agreed quickly, "I do have plenty to occupy me as it is."

Hermione poked her husband in his midriff. "Well …" he said.

"Did you hear," she said brightly, "that Aaron Colegrove has asked to re-inter his wife in the Trinity churchyard?"

Everyone looked startled. I certainly appreciated Hermione's deliberate switch of the subject, but … Oh, can we *never* get away from this tawdry gossip item?

"She was buried on the family estate in Mamaroneck, I heard," Adelie said, looking relieved.

"With rather unseemly haste, I understand," John agreed.

"They had her planted by the cabbage patch up there within forty-eight hours!" Charles asserted. I had to wonder how much he'd had to drink.

"Charles! It's hardly necessary to be vulgar, my dear!"

"Sorry, Adelie. But she was, after all, a vulgar young woman!"

"She was a … a *silly* woman, Charles. And perhaps that made her seem—"

"Our pew is just four rows behind the Colegroves'," Hermione said, "and I confess I found her interminable fidgeting during the sermons most irritating. I've seen ten-year-old children better behaved!"

"But I thought she was barely twenty herself," I said, bemused by the continuing enthusiasm for the subject.

"You weren't twenty when we first met, Thomas," she replied, "but you had basic manners, for heaven's sake!"

"She was just a foolish child who was in society well over her depth," Adelie said. "And whose undeniable prettiness constituted a positive misfortune!" She reddened slightly as the others looked askance.

"I'm relieved to hear someone defending the lass," I opined piously. "After all, no one deserves such a terrible fate!"

Oh no!, they all agreed. But then they all returned directly to recounting the deceased's foibles.

"You know my friend, Mrs. Pannikin," Hermione said, "from the St. Alexius Guild?"

Adelie nodded. The Leaverings and the Glasbys all attend Trinity Church, as does Charles—on occasion.

"She ran into Mrs. Colegrove on Broadway—this was early last month—and Mrs. Colegrove abruptly began berating Mrs. Pannikin's twelve-year-old slave girl. She was dressed improperly, she was not showing respect for her mistress, she wasn't carrying her purchases carefully enough! And on! The girl began crying and Mrs. Pannikin finally simply pulled the little wench away and continued about her business. But did you ever? Bad enough for people to be horrible to their own servants, but—"

"She *was* horrible to her own, our friend who lived next door to her told us," John offered. The Glasbys, I recalled, reside just a block or so north of the Colegrove home on Broadway.

"I heard she whipped the poor old things on a regular basis," Charles said. "And the horses, too!" Amid general wagging of heads, he added, "The grand jury was to consider that sailor's indictment today. I don't know what's become of it."

This was unprecedented. Three years back, he'd have already wormed details out of half the jurors. "What on earth were you *doing* today, Charles?" Adelie asked.

"Oh … writing letters to members of the committee. We must meet soon to discuss our strategy."

The Leaverings and the Glasbys appeared as mystified by this uncharacteristic disinterest in scandal as I was.

"Does no one know anything of the poor girl's family, or where she came from?" I asked.

They all shook their heads. I'd assumed somebody would know *something* about her. "A few months after Lavinia Colegrove died, she was suddenly a fixture on the widower's arm," Hermione said. "That's all anyone knew."

"And the next thing we knew," John said, "she had slapped one of the British officers in the face, at the regimental gala. He claimed he'd no idea she was Colegrove's guest, and that she was being as coquettish as any maid he'd ever met!"

Adelie continued. "And it was just two days after that—Wasn't it?—that the banns were read, and we all got invitations to the wedding."

"*I* didn't get an invitation!" Charles said.

"And you were the only one who *went*! Half the town had already found her so unbearable, and the whole situation so distasteful, they stayed away."

"I fear you overestimate the proportion that worked up the good taste to resist," he rejoined. "Nothing like a scandalous liaison combined with free refreshments to entice a crowd!"

"Did any of you ever have a conversation with the girl?"

"Beyond 'How do you do?' No," Hermione said.

But Adelie Glasby sighed. "A year ago, Thomas, I decided to offer elocution lessons on my days off, and—"

I must have registered sufficient confusion at her reference to *days off* that John interjected, "Both Adelie and Hermione are working for the firm, Thomas—on a part-time basis."

"Oh!" I was somewhat taken aback, though it was hardly unprecedented for New York's wives to participate in their husbands' commercial endeavors. I've even met widows who *ran* them. "I'm sorry ... you were saying?"

"Mrs. Colegrove was one of my first pupils. She came to me in tears, as a matter of fact, distressed that her husband's sister had even suggested lessons might be desirable. She engaged my sympathy at first, but—*oh my!*—she was an awful student. She never practiced, and she never improved."

"She didn't *listen*, you said," John observed.

"She was deaf to any nuance, blind to every gesture ... and when she simply ceased to arrive after four sessions, I made no effort to encourage her."

"What was it she told you, about him?" John prompted, smiling.

Adelie chuckled. "Oh yes—that she was expecting Aaron Colegrove would be knighted in the near future, and that she would become Lady Colegrove!" Everyone's jaws dropped. "I think she was serious. I never told anyone—there were quite enough embarrassing stories going around!"

"Goodness, what foolishness!" Hermione exclaimed. "How many American-born have ever been knighted?"

"Can't think of any," Charles ventured.

"Sir William Johnson, the king's ambassador to the Indians, comes to mind," Benjamin said, "but he was born in Ireland. Far more prominent than Colegrove, at any rate."

"What did I hear …" I began. "Charles, mother's friend Katryne said *your* mother had told her there was immodest pagan statuary in the Colegroves' yard!"

He looked stunned. "Seriously?"

"Charles!" Adelie exclaimed. "You didn't know?"

Was he shamming? No! Charles Cooper *is* losing his touch!

"Everyone knows the tradesmen won't permit their apprentices to bring goods into the house anymore." Hermione said. "The slaves have to go out into the alley to collect things, in all weathers."

"Well, who did tell Aunt Janna then?"

"It's common knowledge, Thomas," Adelie said. "Might have been me!"

"Is it truly so very shocking?"

"*Ohh,*" she said, her voice a mix of tolerance and exasperation.

"Katryne said there were glabrous nymphs gamboling all about!"

"Oh no! No no. There is *a* statuette, a bronze of Diana the Huntress, about two feet high—"

"*En déshabille?*" I said, feigning the horrors.

"As always in mythology, my dear, save for the flimsiest of shifts and a quiver of arrows strapped to her back. And it's set in the middle of a granite bird-bath. And the whole business is covered by a preposterous Greek temple roof, probably ten by sixteen feet, supported by four wooden *faux* Corinthian columns about seven feet tall. We might ask to borrow it," she said, looking at Charles, "should we ever be so mad as to essay a production of *Julius Caesar*!"

"Adelie!" John said. "How is it you know all this?"

"Well, I *looked,* of course, John! I walk through that alley all the time, and I simply peered through the hedge." Everyone laughed as her husband openly gaped for a second, then shut his mouth.

"It sounds completely absurd," Charles said. "Must take up half the yard."

"Near about!"

"Something of the sort was pointed out to me as we passed one of the great houses in Berkshire," I said. "It was called a *folly*. It seems such extravagant constructions are in vogue among the landed gentry."

"That appears to be the idea of the thing," Adelie said. "The proportions are all wrong for a tiny city backyard, but—"

"An eyesore, I'll wager!" Benjamin said.

"Well … I think the statuette itself is really quite lovely! I presume it's a scaled-down copy of some ancient masterpiece—maybe something they found when they unearthed Pompeii twenty years ago."

"Why Diana, do you suppose?" John mused. "You'd think a paragon of commerce would set up a statue of Mercury!"

"Or Venus," Charles said, "if he has a predilection for naked ladies?"

"Or Minerva," I ventured, "if he has pretentions to a knighthood?"

"Oh, now you've all had far too much of this splendid Madeira!" Adelie teased. "Come on: Diana is the Roman name of which Greek goddess?"

The whole party groaned and slapped their foreheads in unison. It didn't have to be said aloud.

Artemis.

CHAPTER 3

As the supper party broke up, the two business partners had a brief *tête-à-tête*, and called me aside to suggest that I start the day after next, as they realized both had demanding Wednesday appointments outside the office. Though eager to begin, I had to admit a day's delay would give me needed time to rearrange my affairs.

We were reunited at the door. "I understand the case against the sailor is extraordinarily weak," Charles was saying.

"But if he didn't do it … who on earth did?" Hermione asked.

"It is indeed a puzzle, ma'am!" he replied.

"Well, thank heaven none of us has to sort it out!" Adelie said.

Charles, the Glasbys, and I walked uptown together in some haste to avoid an impending thunderstorm. After we parted company at Maiden Lane, yours truly was inundated while dashing the last half-mile to my humble billet.

I was all the more surprised to find my landlady, Mrs. Nugent—who'd not paid me the slightest notice since I moved in—waiting up for me, all atwitter. "Mr. Dordrecht!" she burbled excitedly, "a Negro in a fancy uniform came by to deliver a letter for you! Everyone on the block was staring at him!"

Liveried servants were not common in our furthest reach of town. "Indeed?" I said, shaking the rain off my coat. "Well?"

"Oh!" she exclaimed—and ran to fetch it. "You must have an admirer, Mr. Dordrecht!" she said with a disagreeably lewd visage. "It's perfumed!"

I sighed, wondering if I'd be able to return to my old boarding house, given my anticipated wages from the firm. My prospects were better than I'd anticipated as I'd stepped off the boat, but … *no, no, not prudent.*

The small missive was floridly addressed to "Mr. Thomas Dordrecht, Esquire," and closed with red wax. Given the "Esquire," I had to wonder if Charles or even Bertie was playing a practical joke. As there were two candles lighted at the table, I sat to open it there.

"What does it *say?*" Mrs. Nugent demanded. Nettled—and sensing she was illiterate—I simply spread it out in front of her. "You'll have to read it to me," she whined.

Well, I decided I'd read it myself first, then.

> Sir,
>
> A lady desires to retain your services. Please meet me tomorrow at noon behind the pavilion in Ranelagh Gardens. I shall be wearing a Lancastrian rose. Please identify yourself with a Yorkist.

A clap of thunder shook me from seconds of total disbelief. "Oh for crying aloud!" I said.

"What does it *say?*" the woman wailed again. I recited it to her and sarcastically inquired if she could recall which faction of the Wars of the Roses wore red totems and which white.

"Huh?" was my expected response.

Barely resisting the temptation to throw the missive into the fire, I decided I really needed to go to sleep.

Just as I lay down, it occurred to me that someone might have purchased one of the pianofortes I'd consigned to my friend Mr. Fischl—and must be assuming I know how to play the thing well enough to teach her.

"So," Mrs. Nugent said in the morning, "will you go?" She seemed ready to withhold my bowl of oatmeal to provoke an answer. Her family and the other lodger looked on dolefully.

But I'd made no decision. My chief object for the day was to sell or consign the tools. Time spent with some ninny who wanted to play like the Austrian lad after three lessons would be time wasted.

However, I managed to dispose of the tools at the second retailer on whom I called, thereby acquiring a wallet-full of tawdry New York paper money that I calculated, even at the current exchange rate, afforded me a small profit on the sale. The relief of it did not prevent me, however, from resenting the penny I spent on a rose—only red were available—or the sixpence I sacrificed for admission to the Gardens.

The park seemed sparsely occupied, perhaps because the skies were overcast. I had to lecture myself, as I walked toward the pavilion, that it's never good to appear cross when anyone, no matter how oddly, offers to "retain" one's services.

"You would be Mr. Dordrecht, then?" a woman demanded, coming up behind me before I'd begun to look around.

At first glance, I took her to have passed the half-century mark. There were gray streaks in her dark brown hair, and tight lines of bitterness could be seen in her plain, round face despite her veil. It was only with later peeks that I realized she was probably not even thirty-five. Relatively tall for a woman, her figure had no appealing softness, even though she was slightly rotund. The fact that she was dressed in heavy black mourning garb did nothing to enhance her looks.

Nor did the fact that she was scowling. "That's not a Yorkist rose!" she said severely.

"I beg your pardon, ma'am. It was the only rose the flower-seller had on offer."

"Hmph! Mr. Dordrecht, I'm told you can be relied upon for discretion in matters of great private and public sensitivity!"

Not having the faintest idea of how to respond to the remark, I simply gawped. I hope I didn't look too foolish.

"You're very young!" she observed, with clear distaste.

Shall we try humor? "The hour of my birth was not subject to my control, ma'am."

No reaction. "Discretion is not a normal attribute of youth, and it is surely called for in this instance!"

It surely occurred to me to wonder how indiscreet, or how impolitic, it would be, simply to turn and walk out of the park. *But then the admission charge would be forfeit!* "Indeed?"

"I had hoped to find a fellow of greater matur—"

"Shall we sit down, ma'am?" I interrupted, my post-adolescent impatience clearly surfacing. "Or take a stroll?"

After two vexed seconds of staring at me, she turned, walked to a nearby bench, and sat; I followed. "The matter for which I require your service is already the subject of excessive public comment."

That bad, eh? "Madam, I must disabuse you of any assumption that, merely because I have imported pianofortes, that I am at all competent to teach the instrument."

"*Pianofortes?*" she exclaimed, a look of stunned surprise on her face. "Pianofortes, indeed! Mr. Dordrecht, I need you to discover who it was who so foully murdered Mrs. Artemis Colegrove!"

"*Uhh …*"

"It is a matter of great importance and great urgency, and I require someone who will give it his full attention!"

Well—thank heaven—that lets me out! "Ma'am, I—"

"Let me finish, sir! It is critical to proceed immediately, as that wretched man Tenkus has been freed and could sail within the week!"

I was speechless. *Tenkus?*

"The *authorities*," she said, in a tone of bitter sarcasm, "are evidently too busy defending His Majesty's modest request for funds to concern themselves with his subjects' need for basic justice, and—"

"Madam, will you please tell me to whom I have the honor of speaking?"

She halted, made a face, raised the veil for two seconds, and announced, "I am Miss Theodora Colegrove, of course."

And of course I know my own name well, too—but I don't expect people I've not met to conjure it out of the invisible phlogiston! "You are then related to the victim, I take it?"

"No!" she exclaimed vehemently, her fists suddenly clenched. "That is, I … Mrs. Colegrove was"—she turned away with an expression of disgust—"my father's wife. His *third* wife."

"Your father, then, is …?"

"Aaron Colegrove, the merchant. I *trust* you've heard of him if, as I'm informed, you have some awareness of the city's commerce. It is very important that this unpleasantness be cleared up directly, as it … affects his ability to respond to the outrages perpetrated against him by the radicals, and I happen to know"—again she turned away—"that he is also greatly distressed by the loss of his spouse!"

I couldn't care a fig for Aaron Colegrove's distress—and I was having difficulty mustering any for this damsel's. "Miss Colegrove, I—"

"You shall be properly remunerated, Mr. Dordrecht. I understand that you are low in funds."

I flushed, hot with indignation that this perfect stranger should be somehow acquainted with my pecuniary difficulties. It took an effort to suppress an outburst of temper. "It is neither here nor there, madam, as I am entirely engaged to my former employers for the next seven weeks."

"Oh!" she exclaimed. "That is most inconvenient. I was told you had no immediate prospects, and so I—"

"I'm sorry: told *by whom*, Miss Colegrove?"

"By Mr. Kempe. He assured me—"

"I beg your pardon? By *John Tabor* Kempe? The attorney general?"

"Of course. He's a family friend of long standing. He is also"—she twisted her handkerchief in irritation—"the *authority* who cannot manage to spare a moment, or even the moments of his underlings, to investigate horrific murder in the bosom of his province!"

My mind was aswim. "I, *uhh* …"

"He said you had no occupation, but he assured me that you could be relied upon to pursue such an investigation to its necessary completion."

"Ma'am, I'm at a loss. I suppose Mr. Kempe is thinking of the efforts I made three years ago that led to the arrest of a man who was later executed for murder, but … that was entirely a personal quest, a matter of seeing justice done for a gentleman who was my benefactor and a friend to all who knew him. I am in shipping, ma'am, hardly making any career out of pursuing criminals!" I would have laughed aloud if she hadn't looked so upset.

"I am very disappointed, Mr. Dordrecht. The more I think of it, the more I am persuaded you are the man for the job, despite your relative immaturity."

"Miss Colegrove, I beg you to understand that it is simply not possible. I am committed to Castell, Leavering & Glasby, full-time, until the first of November. I daresay I shall be working seventy or eighty hours a week." *And the last of my unscheduled moments are right now being frittered away!*

"Is that all? Well, that should leave you ample time to make a start! I admit I was hoping the villain could be caught within a fortnight, but … if you can assure me that you can give me your full attention in November, I—"

"Miss Colegrove, I'd have no idea *how* to make a start. This is not my business! I would have no authority, for example, to demand anyone's assistance, or even impose on them to respond to plain questions."

"Mr. Kempe said all this obtained three years ago, but you nonetheless discovered the guilty party."

Curse the man! "Ma'am, I'm sorry for your predicament, but I have my own, and I don't see how I can possibly help. Perhaps Mr. Kempe can suggest an alternative to you."

"I am ready and willing to remunerate you, as I said, Mr. Dordrecht!" I shook my head in exasperation, thinking that, despite her father's fortunes, she herself hardly appeared wealthy. She wore no jewelry, and the gown had likely seen a dozen periods of bereavement over as many years. I was resentful, too, of my apprehension that it would be beneath my dignity to request compensation of the seven pence this absurd interview had already cost me.

"I have no idea," she continued, "what a proper compensation for such an endeavor would be—"

Nor have I, madam, but it's no—

"But I thought I would offer you ten pounds, sterling, on retainer, and twenty pounds more upon the conviction of the guilty party."

My breath left me. Suddenly she had my entire attention—*aside from a conscious effort to avoid twitching!* "I, um, uh … I still don't see how I could be of service, Miss Colegrove. I'd not know where to begin."

"You must *begin* by tracking down the sailor, Mr. Dordrecht. If it is truly conclusive that he could not have done it, then it must have been one of his vile confederates!"

"I … I suppose I could make some progress on Sunday afternoons …"

"Sunday afternoons! Good heavens, that would be quite blasphemous, Mr. Dordrecht. I certainly can't allow that!"

Then what would you suggest? I wondered.

"Besides, it's quite against the law, sir!"

Would the impressive sum under discussion truly be compensation for having to deal with this woman? "Surely you've noticed that particular law is more honored in the breach, Miss Colegrove?"

"It is quite shocking how standards have fallen, Mr. Dordrecht, but—"

"Miss Colegrove, between now and November, I shall have to get *some* sleep, and I cannot imagine any other block of waking hours to advance the project." She was fuming, I could tell. "Perhaps you would like to reconsider your offer, ma'am?" It would be better to have this out, now—though the more I thought on it, the more her project intrigued me, irrespective of the welcome prospect of cash. I stood. "Shall we take a stroll, ma'am? I've not been here before, and … it may help clear our thoughts." Automatically, I offered my arm. With an annoyed hiss, she started off without availing herself of it.

"I'm told that Tenkus is a familiar of an establishment on Water Street that caters to mariners. It's known as the *Hearts of Oakum*," she added, her nose crinkling.

Oh right: Tenkus is the accused but exonerated sailor. "Indeed. And how did you come to hear that, ma'am?"

"It was my father's servant, Caesar, who made the observation, I understand."

"Aha. I shall want to speak to him of it, of course."

"To Caesar? Whatever for? Go to the *Hearts of Oakum* and see what you can find out!"

"I shall need to interview all residents of the house, including the slaves."

"What! Mr. Dordrecht, I'm sure I can tell you all you need to know of them."

No, I thought. "Excellent!" I said aloud. "But I shall also need to see for myself, ma'am. I shall certainly need to examine the scene of the murder, and—"

"Sir, I told you that a modicum of discretion is required, did I not? It would be very disruptive to have you … *poking about* my father's residence!"

"Miss Colegrove, I see no possibility of discovering the true criminal without examining the crime, the victim, the surroundings. I shall certainly need to speak to Mr. Colegrove and everyone living there at the earliest opportunity."

"I absolutely forbid you to speak to my father, sir!" she exclaimed, so loudly that a trio of black gardeners looked askance, chuckling with speculation why yours truly might be desiring an interview with *her father*.

We turned a corner of the property and walked on in silence for a minute. "Perhaps it would be best were I to withdraw from your commission, ma'am. Among other things, I have had some dealings—not altogether pleasant—with your father, since I began working in the city. For a very brief spell, I was employed by him to manage his warehouse on Front Street. His endorsement of your project, I would consider essential to its success."

"I don't wish my father to know of it at all, Mr. Dordrecht. He has quite enough to worry about at the moment. I wish to have the fiend discovered and prosecuted without bringing him any new distress. Surely your limited time would best be spent by hieing directly to that low tavern and—"

"Miss Colegrove, if you truly desire me to pursue this for you, you are going to have to allow me to direct the investigation in my own way!" I paused briefly, to afford her another opportunity to change her mind; she turned her face away with an expression of great displeasure, but did not contradict me. "Now, I first need to have a summation of the facts surrounding the murder itself. Please bear in mind that I arrived back in New York over a week after it happened, and so all I know of it has been gleaned from snatches of simple gossip. First of all, it was Wednesday, the twenty-eighth, last, correct?"

She sighed heavily. "That is so, Mr. Dordrecht."

"At what time of day did it occur?"

"Mid-day."

"Surely something more specific was noted, ma'am? The churches chime every quarter-hour, after all."

"It was established that she must have been killed between eleven forty-five and twelve-thirty."

"How?"

"The slave woman received an ordinary delivery around eleven forty-five, and the body was discovered at twelve-thirty."

"No one, I take it, actually witnessed the event?"

"It appears not. However, that sailor was imposing himself on Mrs. Colegrove the very evening before! The slaves swore to that!"

"Who was the last person to see Mrs. Colegrove alive?"

"My Aunt Eudoxia—unless it was one of the slaves."

"And at what time was that?"

"Nine-thirty, she said." She seemed suddenly struck by the same factor that struck me.

"No one saw Mrs. Colegrove in the intervening three hours? How many people are residing in that house at present, Miss Colegrove?"

"There are, *um*— My father and, *uh*, her. My father was, of course, still at sea. And my aunt and Mrs. DeLancey. Mrs. Jacqueline DeLancey is the widowed mother of the *second* Mrs. Colegrove, and thus grandmother to the eight children of that marriage."

"*Eight?*"

"Seven survive, but only the three youngest—a boy and two girls—still live there with him. So that's seven, counting my father and ... her."

"There were no children by the deceased?"

"No." It was clearly taking all her self-control to avoid adding, *Thank heaven!*

"There's a slave?"

"Oh yes. Caesar and his woman live in the basement."

I added up. "None of these seven residents can attest to Mrs. Colegrove's activities that morning?"

"Well, as I understand it, Mrs.—"

"I'm sorry: you yourself were not present at the time?"

"No. I was told Mrs. DeLancey was ill. She had been ailing a few days, and was lying abed. Dr. Boyce—one of father's stepsons—came to bleed her, as usual, but she kept her drapes drawn against the sun."

"There are stepchildren?"

"Yes. Four. Father adopted them when he married Lavinia DeLancey Boyce after my mother died."

"Ah. And how many—"

"I'm one of six, four of whom survive."

I'll need to contract a genealogist! "I'm sorry, I interrupted you. How were the other residents of the house engaged that morning?"

"My aunt visits with a friend—Governor Colden's wife—every Wednesday morning. I believe she saw Mrs. Colegrove as she was departing. The two girls were at their schools and the lad, Oliver, was"— she grimaced with apparent distaste for Oliver—"probably at his club, the Macaroni Club." She shook her head, frowning.

"The slaves?"

"Ah. Caesar spends most mornings doing the marketing, and Calpurnia was attending Mrs. DeLancey and Dr. Boyce."

Calpurnia? Another idiotically pretentious name inflicted on the slaves! "Right. Well, so no one saw her after Miss Eudoxia Colegrove left the house?" She nodded. "Who discovered Mrs. Colegrove's body?"

She sighed with vexation. "It was young Oliver, who was returning to the house for dinner and came in through the alley. He, *uh*, made quite a— She had been stabbed, and he was deeply shocked at the sight."

"Word has it the sight was indeed terrible, ma'am. I presume the coroner saw the corpse?"

"So I understand. He reported on it at the inquest."

"What was the result of the autopsy?"

"Autopsy? There was no autopsy."

"Surely that's ... very irregular in such a circumstance?"

"Not at all. It's most offensive to religion, and ... Mr. Dordrecht, it was perfectly obvious how Mrs. Colegrove had been killed!"

Hmph ... that's that, then! "Ma'am, I have to ask: did you yourself see Mrs. Colegrove's body?"

"I did not. By the time my sister-in-law and I heard of it and came to pay our respects to my aunt ... matters had been taken care of."

"By whom, ma'am?"

"By my aunt, and my half-brother Peter, and Dr. Boyce."

"I see. About what hour was it that you arrived at the house?"

"Mr. Dordrecht! Surely time is wasting that you could be spending in pursuit of that sailor and his cronies!"

No, time's wasting thanks to your objections, ma'am! We scowled at each other for ten seconds. "Can you pinpoint the hour at which you arrived at the house, please?"

After another furious hiss, she said, "It was after four, probably four-fifteen. I could've been there sooner, but my sister-in-law dawdled over her attire, and— Everyone was moving slowly. It was, you'll recall, probably the very hottest day of the summer."

"It was? That's important to know, Miss Colegrove. *You'll* recall that I was a thousand miles away on August twenty-eighth!"

"Oh yes," she said unapologetically.

"When was your last previous visit to the house—and when did you last see Mrs. Colegrove alive?"

Mutual scowls forestalled another outburst of objections. "I usually visit my aunt on Sunday afternoons, Mr. Dordrecht, but the weather had been so horrid, I had not done so for a fortnight. I would occasionally see Mrs. Colegrove in church on Sundays—but, come to think of it, she had been absent from the most recent services. It would have been the second Sunday in August that I last saw her."

I had a thousand questions, but I couldn't decide which were most important. "There was a piece of paper, ma'am, I was told? Inscribed with a radical political slogan?"

"Indeed—the puerile rallying cry of the Liberty Boys."

"Did you see it when you arrived?"

"No. Oliver had ripped it up, and my aunt had consigned the remains to the privy."

She seemed startled by the look of horrified disbelief that I undoubtedly presented. "They destroyed—"

"Mr. Kempe was upset too! However, my aunt had read it first, so it's not only Oliver's word for what was written on it."

I shook my head, with bafflement as much as irritation. We were back at the pavilion. I had many unrelated chores to manage, and she was right that I needed to catch the sailor before he could be called away. "Miss Colegrove, I … I have to say that I … don't anticipate any easy success with this enterprise. Are you quite certain you wish to undertake this? It's a great deal of money, and—"

"I am quite sure, Mr. Dordrecht!"

"Are you sure you want *me* to undertake it?" She hesitated. "Despite my callow immaturity?"

She fidgeted uncertainly. "*Will* you pursue the man Tenkus?"

"I agree that he must be attended to directly, ma'am. I'll venture there before the day's out." She sat again on the bench, and concentrated on a small flock of geese, honking loudly on their journey south. "And the next thing I would plan upon, ma'am, is a visit to the house. I insist on Mr. Colegrove's acceptance of the project, and I shall want to look over the premises and talk to … everyone. I shall be needing *your* help on a regular basis, Miss Colegrove!" Still she twisted her handkerchief. "We could meet there this coming Sunday, say at one-thirty?"

"I … didn't want to disrupt …"

"Miss Colegrove, it's *murder* we're talking about! It's a foul business, and no one should be surprised that a certain *disruption* ensues!"

She sighed heavily, then set her face grimly and rummaged through her reticule. She extracted a small cloth purse and practically threw it at me. "Here!"

I opened the bag and, while knowing what I was supposed to find, still gasped to perceive gold coins. But I pulled the string taut again and placed the purse gently back in her lap. "Ma'am, if I am to undertake this for you, I require your assurance that you will support me and not interfere. But I will promise in return that, within the time constraints that I have indicated, I shall do my utmost to see this through."

Her pleading eyes assured me that, whatever her reasons, she truly did want to find the murderer of Artemis Colegrove. She passed the purse back. "I don't think it necessary to write a formal contract, Mr. Dordrecht. Please be about the business."

"Shall we plan on Sunday afternoon?"

Another sigh. "Very well."

I slipped the purse into my pocket and stood. "May I see you home?"

"Thank you, no. I shall stay here a mite longer. It would also … not be seemly."

As if anyone would notice in New York City! "Very well." A sudden thought amused me. "It's a good thing we can make do without a written contract, Miss Colegrove."

"How so?" she said, looking displeased in advance.

"Well, if it were already November, we'd have to pay a tax to get one of the king's stamps on it!"

She was stony-faced. "That's not funny, Mr. Dordrecht!"

And so we parted.

CHAPTER 4

⤳⫷⫸⤳

THE STOUT, LONG-SUFFERING BARMAN pointed out a huge, powerfully built young sailor, thoroughly unkempt and disreputable in appearance. One glance was enough to explain why so many had rushed to name Henry Tenkus a murderer. A scar ran vertically for three inches on the left cheek of his square face, which conveyed bewilderment, resentment, and pugnaciousness in equal measure. I judged him two inches taller, thirty pounds heavier, and five years older than myself. A lad it would be reckless to challenge in a brawl! I'd dealt with his ilk on many a ship over the past four years, but I might still have felt intimidated had he not obviously been close to passing out from drink. He was standing—leaning heavily—at the bar, alone, morosely draining the last of a tankard.

"Mr. Tenkus?"

Suspicious gray eyes turned on me. "Who wants to know?"

"My name is Thomas Dordrecht," I said, offering my hand.

It was disdained. "Preacher?"

My clothing did set me apart from the clientele. "No, I'm in shipping."

His brows lifted a bit. "You got work?"

Oh. "Afraid not." He glared at me for a few seconds. "You want another of those?" Disbelief. "Barman, two beers, please." I had to pay and put a fresh glass in his hand before he relaxed at all. "Join me at that table?"

Fortunately, it was still early enough that the place was relatively quiet. In another couple hours, I knew, one would need to shout into one's neighbor's ears to be heard. Tenkus shambled uncertainly across ten feet of sawdust to join me. I feared the stool might collapse as he sat; it didn't. "What?" he demanded.

No small talk. "I know it's proven that you didn't murder her, Mr. Tenkus, but—"

"Damn straight!"

"But I've been commissioned to—"

"I don't want to talk about it."

"I've been commissioned to determine who did murder her, and I need your help to do that."

Tenkus drank half the glass, clunked it down, and belched. "Can't help you. Don't know who did it. No idea."

"You could still help by—"

"If I knew, I'd have killed him by now."

Is it true, *In vino veritas*? Whatever the case, I detected no dissembling about Tenkus. Nor did I have trouble believing him capable of killing the first other man *suspected* of Mrs. Colegrove's murder. "You must have some theory."

Tenkus looked as if he'd never heard the word *theory* before. "One of them agitators, I reckon. What everybody says. But ..."

I waited.

"But I don't know. I went to one of their meetings a month ago, before, *uh*, it. I can't figure any of those mollies lifting a finger against anyone. Blowhards, the lot of 'em, yapping 'Liberty, Liberty!' all day long. Damn fools! Out at sea, you think there's any difference between a free man and a slave? Only free man's the captain!"

Though I thought it more than a technicality, I'd long since quit arguing with drunks. "Did anyone see you at the meeting?"

"See *me*? Half the city!" He finished the glass. "Can I have another one of those?"

I signaled the barman. "How far back did you know Mrs. Colegrove?"

"Mrs.? Is *he* the one paying you? I don't trust him for nothing!"

"No—and nor do I. But you have to know that he couldn't have killed her?"

"Yeah," he said reluctantly. "So who is—"

"Someone who wants to know the truth." *At least I hope she does.* "When and where did you first meet ... the victim?"

"Hattie? Three—"

"I'm sorry, it's Aaron Colegrove's wife we're talking about—Mrs. Artemis Colegrove."

Tenkus grimaced sardonically and downed another gulp. "Yeah, she said that was what they called her. *Arty-miss.* Christ!"

"Her name wasn't really Artemis?" *Why be surprised?*

"Hell no. Hattie. Hattie Mercer. Ask her damn sister!"

"Sister?"

"Yeah. Reade Street. Peggy, her name."

"Peggy Mercer?"

Tenkus just looked confused. "It was this time of year, three years ago, I met her. Prettiest, prettiest little lass! She— Bought her a ribbon, a red and white ribbon, and she kissed me on the cheek!" He tapped the scar. "Most girls— Wasn't like most— She—"

The big brute— *No, that's unjust!* The big mariner was close to tears. I became impatient with myself for being impatient with him. "You courted her?"

Tenkus wiped his nose on his sleeve. "Yeah. Well, off and on, 'cause I shipped out. Went to Bristol, then Kitts, then back here. I had a couple months ashore then, saw her a lot, and got her to promise to marry me after my whaling trip. Had to take that cruise, it was the first time I'd been a mate—second mate on the *Wellsworth*, out of Sag Harbor, Captain Foley. Took the Horn to Valparaiso and back." After indifferently tickling his gold earring, he came to a halt, staring at a dusty block-and-tackle hanging above the bar.

"A long trip! When did you see her next?"

It was another minute, and a repetition of the question, before he responded. "In the spring. Early April. Good voyage, and I'd been paid off handsome, and I was all ready to—" He finished the second glass. "Peggy told me she'd married some rich bastard, and I should forget her. I tried! Right here I tried, for near a fortnight. Then I went back and pulled it out of her where Hattie was, and damned if the rich bastard hadn't gone off and left her alone. Well, alone in a fancy big house with a passel of kids and old ladies and slaves."

When I coughed to get his attention back, he shoved the empty glass toward me. Amazingly, he seemed more alert after two beers than before. "You did get to see her?"

"Yeah. Prettier than ever—but all tricked out like a princess …"

"She didn't put you off?"

"No. Lonely. But we couldn't meet there, not with all those people in and out. Met her at a tavern up by the jail, Mondays and Fridays. Only times she could get away, she said. Wednesdays, she said she had to see some girlfriend. I told her, if she went off with me, she could go out when she damn well pleased!"

"You wanted to run off with her?"

"Damn straight I did! Thought we could settle far away—in Barbados, maybe."

"And she ...?"

"She liked the idea. At least, at first. Then ..."

"Then what?"

"Well, I got myself some work here on the shore. I ... stayed clear of the rum and called on her as often as she'd let me. I thought we— I thought she—"

"She changed her mind?"

"Middle August, she got wind that Colegrove would be back by September, and she began worrying this and that. She ..."

"You think she was afraid of him?"

"Don't know. I wanted to get her out before he got back."

I'll bet you did!

"Tried over and over. Finally bribed the slave woman to let me into the house, the day before, *um*, and ... and she told me she wasn't going."

"Did she give a reason?"

"She ... just kept saying she simply couldn't. She was crying, but no matter what I argued ... she couldn't." He was slurring words.

"I reckon you must've been put out by this? I mean, after four, five months, and she balked when—"

"I may have raised my voice some. That old black flunky came in with the fire poker. But I never touched her. Never. I could've done for both of them right then and there, if I'd meant to!"

That boast was perfectly credible. "What did you do?"

"I couldn't believe she really meant it. I just waited for the longest time. Finally, she says, 'Henry, just go,' and I just did, and I came here, and that was ..." He finished the third glass I'd bought for him.

"So you were here when—" His eyes were glassy. He lurched to the side, tried to grip the smooth top of the table, slid, and capsized onto the floor. With a deep groan, he rolled onto his back, shut his eyes, and was snoring in seconds.

The barman finished drying a glass and came over. "*Aw*, not again!"

He bent down and grabbed one of Tenkus' armpits. "Well, come on, you got him drunk, you can at least help me move him!" The situation was familiar from my own family's tavern, so I grabbed under the other arm, and we hauled the big man off to the back corner, where there was room under a large table to stow him. The barman sat on the floor, leant back on his elbows, and shoved him toward the wall, briefly disrupting the slumber of a basset hound. "Right! Nobody'll trip over him there. I thought one of those beers was for you!"

"Sorry. He seemed as if he could hold his liquor."

"He'd already had a few. What were you asking him? That man needs to get back to sea!"

"Asking about the woman who was murdered."

"Yeah? Thought he was out of that!" He slapped the sawdust off his breeches. "Damn, I hope he don't mess himself! If that fool constable had listened to me, they'd never have hauled him in!"

"He *was* here, that morning?"

"Right where we just put him, mister. Wife and I found him there—him and the dog—when we opened at seven, and he was still right there at two in the afternoon, when they came for him. Judge didn't have trouble believing me, I don't know why the constable couldn't! Cost the town his room and board for ten days, all for nothing!"

"You've seen him a lot? He ever talk about her?" I placed a sixpence on the bar.

"Oh, I listen with half an ear to all of 'em, y'know. Sailors are as dumb ashore as landsmen are at sea. This one— He was a loon for that gal! No matter how often I said, 'But she's already married, Tenkus!' he just raved on and on. Fool passed up a mate's berth on the *Alice Denby* six weeks ago. Now he's down to his last pennies and he'll be lucky to sling a hammock before the mast!"

"Did he have any special pals that you saw? Any of the Liberty Boys?"

"Nah, nah. He'd tell his woes to anyone who'd listen. Not many did for long!"

"Any chance he'll find work, you think?"

"Well … all the shippers trying to clear before November … possible. It's when the ships come *back* that worries me. Then we're all in trouble!"

Another customer claimed his attention. I drank up and took my leave.

That evening, I asked my landlady, who claimed to know everyone on Reade Street, where Peggy Mercer lived. Having never heard of her, she was positive there was no such person. But … Reade Street is three blocks long, it's densely populated, and Mrs. Nugent does seem rather prone to overstatement. However, none of the local tradespeople I queried recognized the name either.

When I arrived at the familiar office of Castell, Leavering & Glasby on Peck Slip, Thursday morning, the two partners were closeted with a customer. At Mrs. Leavering's suggestion, I made myself useful straightening a cache of manifests into chronological order. I had wanted to inform them immediately of my decision to assist Miss Colegrove's investigation, but John Glasby greeted me, with "Oh! I've been so distracted, I'd forgotten you were coming. But thank heaven you're here! We've got a problem—it's good news, really. The gent who just left consigned sixty barrels of cider to us, which have to go into the *Dorothy C.*, which is to sail on this evening's tide for Jamaica. That's in addition to the kegs of peas and the pine boards which are already waiting by the quay."

"I didn't see her outside, sir."

"Couldn't dock her here at the slip. She's three blocks down. Have to run back and forth."

By seven-fifteen, when the *Dorothy C.* was warped out into the East River, I had been off and on the ship, back and forth to the office, two dozen times, and—notwithstanding that we were old friends—I'd endured plenty of grumbling from Captain Trent and the mates. I'd not had a further word with either Leavering or Glasby, and I was aching in every muscle. I nearly by-passed supper in my eagerness to get to bed.

And so it went for the ensuing three days.

At our appointed hour, Miss Colegrove, still in mourning but without the veil, rapped the polished brass lion's-head knocker on the door of her father's impressive brick mansion. An elderly slavewoman answered. I watched as she recognized the caller with raised, pitying eyebrows, and suspiciously examined myself. "Could you tell him we've come to call, please, Calpurnia?" Miss Colegrove said.

The slave shrugged and stolidly walked back toward the room I recalled was the study, while we waited at the threshold. "Miss Theodora Colegrove and a gentleman to see you, sir," we heard faintly, followed by a desultory grunt and the scrape of a chair over the floor.

Seconds later, he emerged, a tall, vigorous-looking man of six decades, only slightly grayer than I recall him last. A black crepe armband was tied about his right arm. "Theodora, my dear, how wonderful to see you," he exclaimed, oozing the insincerity of a father who'd been returned a fortnight without having initiated any effort to see his daughter. He allowed her to give him a dutiful filial kiss. "And you are … ? I do believe I recognize you?"

"This is Mr. Thomas Dordrecht, Father, who worked for you briefly some six years back. He—"

"Oh yes?" he said blankly, not offering his hand.

"I have retained his services, Father, for—"

We were still standing in the doorway. Colegrove's face registered perplexed alarm. Notwithstanding our past conversations, I was unsure whether he did recognize me—much less whether he recalled the fact that I'd produced evidence in the Sproul case that had implicated his name along with DeLancey's and the Aldridge Brothers firm. "Oh, well, come in, come in, of course."

We followed him back into the study and, at his gesture, sat in the elegant green rococo chairs. The room looked less cluttered than I recollected, but I'd forgotten there was a window to the garden somewhat obscured by an armoire. Colegrove looked back and forth at us for an instant, clearly mystified. "Tea?" he suggested, shaking his head.

"Thank you, Father, but it's not necessary," his daughter replied. "We shall not need to take much of your valuable time."

After another brief pause, he eschewed further chitchat. "You have *retained* his *services*, Theodora?"

"Father, it has distressed me deeply to think of the double indignity you have suffered since your return—not only having to face a mob at the wharf, but having to live with the unsolved murder of your wife."

"Ah! Well, thank you, my dear, it has been, *um*, hard."

"I know that many loyal souls are striving to bring our populace to their senses with regard to the king's excises, but I thought I might be able to assist with the latter."

"With …?" He was unable to follow her.

"I have asked Mr. Dordrecht to investigate Mrs. Colegrove's murder, Father, and I hope—"

Colegrove's consternation was plainly visible. "Oh, well … that's hardly necessary, Theodora, hardly necessary at all. I'm sure the proper authorities will do all in their power to, *uh*—"

"I took the liberty of raising the issue directly with Mr. Kempe, Father." He seemed startled, as if it had never occurred to him that his daughter, whom he seemed to regard practically as a stranger, would ever do such a thing. "On two occasions. He insisted that, given the ongoing public turmoil, he could spare no one to look into the outrage that you have suffered as a husband. When I pressed him on the injustice of this parsimony, he recommended that I engage Mr. Dordrecht for the purpose."

"*Kempe* suggested this?"

"Yes."

"Why on earth … You know my son Peter is betrothed to his sister Catharine?"

"Of course," she replied, coloring perhaps with hurt and indignation over his callous manner of referring to her half-brother.

He again shook his head, then turned, frowning, to me. "Do you boast any qualifications for such a task, Mr. Dordrecht?"

"Sir, I boast no such qualifications. I have made extensive inquiries into criminal matters in the past, but they were entirely prompted by personal connections. I should never have put my name forward in this instance, and was quite bewildered to learn that Mr. Kempe had done so. That said, barring my prior commitment through next month to Castell, Leavering & Glasby, I should—"

"You're Glasby's man. That's where I've seen you!"

"Yes sir. *Um*, but I should be pleased to assist with Miss Colegrove's project to the full extent of my capability. That is, if—"

"If *what?*" he demanded, his voice rising.

"If we may be assured of your cooperation in the effort—your blessing, as it were."

He looked about the room, his lips tightly compressed. "I still don't understand why Kempe let that damned sailor go! Surely—"

"At least two witnesses observed the man constantly during the hours in question, sir. He was asleep in a tavern the whole morning, dead drunk, right until the constable came to arrest him. Tenkus could not possibly have murdered Mrs. Colegrove."

He still glowered. "The witnesses?" his daughter demanded.

"The judge determined that they had nothing to gain by lying, ma'am." She too looked skeptical and unsatisfied. "So the question is still hanging, sir: if he didn't murder Mrs. Colegrove, who did?"

"One of those damned radical agitators, of course!" Colegrove thundered. "They even left their filthy slogan, for god's sake! They murdered poor Artemis to get at *me!*"

I was about to assert that that hardly corresponded with the impassioned viciousness of the crime when Miss Colegrove interjected, "That's why we need Mr. Dordrecht to pursue the matter, Father—to find the one who must be brought to justice and—"

"Hang the lot of them, I say!"

Not what you said *in public*, Mr. Colegrove! I reflected, repulsed as in the past by the man's phenomenal hypocrisy.

After a few seconds his daughter persisted, "Well, but that not being possible, Father, wouldn't it be advisable to—"

"Mr. Dordrecht, could you take a seat in the entryway for a moment? I wish to speak privately to my daughter."

I nodded, stood, and opened and closed the door for myself. I remained standing outside the door, however, and was not disappointed when Colegrove made no effort to speak quietly. Happily, too, the Sunday street traffic was light, reducing the ambient racket that would obtain on most afternoons.

"Don't you realize he could be one of them?" Colegrove was saying. "You never know, these days. Even a lad who has worked as a commercial factor for some years can end up making common cause with riffraff foremast hands!"

"He used to be your employee, Father!"

"Well, that's no guarantee at all! There are plenty such, and I let him go, didn't I? Do you know what these people have done, Theodora? Up in Boston, they've completely destroyed the homes of more than one man of social standing! Who's to say they won't try the same thing here?"

"I have every confidence—"

"I have your aunt and Mrs. DeLancey to worry about, not to mention Élise and little Agnes!"

"Father, it was Mr. Kempe who suggested him. Surely you wouldn't imagine that—"

Three or four seconds passed. "Well, that's true. And I suppose we can trust Kempe to keep a watch on the Liberty Boys. Shouldn't be surprised if he doesn't keep a watch on everyone in the city!"

"Well, then...."

"Oh, all right, all right! Call him back in, if you must." I arranged myself primly on the bench, just before she opened the door.

"So what is it you want of me?" Colegrove demanded.

"I shall need to talk to your servants, sir, and the family members, to see if anyone observed anything that might lead to the culprit. And also to examine the house itself and—"

"The house!" he exclaimed, raising his eyebrows toward my client in alarm. "She was murdered out in the yard! Why do you need to disrupt my household, for heaven's sake?"

A disconcerting anomaly, that the investigation of a murder might be deemed more disruptive than the murder itself! "It will be needful to understand how the villain could feel assured that he wasn't observed, sir."

He sighed heavily. "You really want to do this?" he asked Miss Colegrove.

"I do, Father—for your sake, not only for justice to—"

"Oh very well then. You can tell Eudoxia that I want everyone to cooperate with this young fellow's explorations, for whatever they're worth." He turned to me impatiently. "But I surely hope you'll keep the intrusions to a minimum, sir!"

"I'll do my best, Mr. Colegrove."

The hall clock struck two. "Oh," he moaned, "don't go upstairs now, it's the hour for their naps. I'll let your aunt know."

"I wish to concentrate on the backyard, and to interview the servants, this afternoon, anyway, sir."

His scowl would have curdled milk. "Indeed! Well, get on with it, then!"

Coldly, barely avoiding overt rudeness, he shortly dismissed us from his presence. Did Miss Colegrove observe, as I did, that so far from offering to defray any of her costs, he hadn't offered a word of gratitude for her concern?

Come to that, I hadn't seen much of the distress she'd ascribed to him over his wife's death.

Miss Colegrove and I stood in the entry hall. She appeared rather at a loss. I wondered again what she hoped to gain by this quest.

Seeing a new-looking, full-length portrait of a portly young military figure, his straight arm pointing imperatively and inexplicably off to the side, I inclined my head toward it. "My brother, Captain William

Colegrove," she whispered. "Heroically martyred five years ago at the Battle of Sainte-Foy."

The slave woman reappeared. "Would you be wanting anything, miss?"

"No. Thank you—"

I cleared my throat aggressively.

"Oh. Calpurnia, this is Mr. Thomas Dordrecht. I— We— *I* have retained him to make a private investigation into Mrs. Colegrove's death." The slave woman shuddered violently, which briefly shook my client's resolve. "We have my father's blessing for this, and he'll shortly have Aunt Eudoxia inform you that you are to give Mr. Dordrecht whatever cooperation he needs."

The slave regarded us both in mute resignation. Miss Colegrove was again irresolute. After ten seconds' wait, I spoke up. "Would you show us the other rooms on this floor, please, Calpurnia—and then I wish to see the yard."

She seemed appalled that any interloper should be making such demands and waited for Miss Colegrove's nod—which was a brief interval arriving.

Six years back, I had spent a few hours in this house, but I'd only seen the study and the library. The layout of the building was an elongated rectangle, like many private New York homes, with the narrow side fronting the street. This house, wider than most, boasted commodious rooms on either side of the central hallway leading back to the stairs.

Standing next to the library door, Calpurnia shrugged and opened it. As Miss Colegrove hesitated to precede me, I finally walked in ahead of her. Once again, I was impressed by the beautiful room's hundreds of books, pink pastel walls, brass sconces, and handsome moldings. "This is much as I recall it." Curious that there did not appear to be any *new* books. Incongruously, a few were left out on the table, precisely arranged in a pyramid squarely in the center. "Whose are these?" I asked the slave.

Miss Colegrove spoke up. "They are probably there for my brother Peter. He is currently the most regular user of the library. He is reading the law under Mr. Kempe, who will soon be his brother-in-law."

"I see." The library was the middle room on the north side of the house. "And this is the parlor, in the front?"

"Yes, sir," Calpurnia said, opening its door. It had a window facing Broadway and handsomely appointed furniture and draperies.

We moved across the hall, into an enormous ballroom—perhaps sixty by fifteen feet, with pier mirrors and a huge fireplace. As large as the commercial establishment where I used to take dancing instruction! It even reminded me of the *soirée* I'd been privileged to attend in Paris—though I couldn't help wondering how often it was used here in New York.

"A most impressive room, Miss Colegrove. I'm surprised I have no recollection of even noticing it."

"The ballroom was only created four years ago, when Father moved the business into offices on Broad Street. It was originally conceived as a ballroom, but for years its use was pre-empted for the firm." At the end farthest from the street was a round mahogany table with chairs. "The family takes their meals here," Miss Colegrove said. "You've just cleared Sunday dinner away?" she asked the slave.

"Yes, ma'am."

"All right. Now the kitchen, please."

As we re-entered the hall, we heard a hiss from the kitchen, and the slave looked into it with alarm. "Boiling! Excuse?"

"Yes," Miss Colegrove said as she rushed away.

We were standing in front of the stairs. "I don't see any immediate need to go up to the second story, Miss Colegrove, but can you quickly describe the rooms for me?"

She looked very startled. "I ... would if I could, Mr. Dordrecht, but ... I've never been upstairs. I've never lived in this house, you see."

"But your father has lived here nearly twenty years!"

"That is so but, as I say, I've never been up there." I'm afraid I stared. She added rather tightly, "Hulda and Timothy and I were born in the old house, and then we were raised mostly by my uncle Edward, in Mamaroneck."

"I see." I didn't, actually, but the slave called out that her problem was under control, and we walked into a kitchen that was functional but unremarkable. It was larger than my mother's in New Utrecht, but looked as though it got one-tenth the use. There was a tiny window facing out and an interior door immediately next to the exit to the garden. "Is this a pantry?"

"No sir. Here. That to the basement," the slave explained.

"Surely there's no need to go down there!" Miss Colegrove exclaimed.

"I see no call for it—at present—ma'am," I replied tartly. "Let's go outside, shall we?"

It was a single door, unlike the split Dutch doors of my family's home. Notwithstanding all I'd heard, when Calpurnia opened it, I was taken aback to find myself staring directly at the statuette of the near-naked goddess—*whose arrow was drawn and aimed directly at me.* "Quite remarkable!" I said lamely. Miss Colegrove's face turned fiery red.

I stepped out onto flagstones that led to the small, whitewashed privy, just off to the right. It took an effort to turn my gaze from *Diana* to observe the surrounding details. The yard extended the outside edges of the house by another forty feet, with seven-foot brick walls running out to a tall hedge at the end of the property. I moved out toward the privy to get a better view of the folly. It was built on a low stone platform, which leveled the slightly sloping ground and provided a base for the wooden "temple." The more I looked at the thing, the more I really was tempted to laugh. Just as Adelie had described it, it did indeed take up half the entire yard. The birdbath, with the statuette on top, was situated in the middle, but the roof—cedar shingles, not red clay tiles—could at least provide shade if one carried a chair out to sit in the fresh air on either side of it.

We moved around it toward the back gate. The grass was neatly trimmed, but rather faded as one might expect so late in the summer. Miss Colegrove saw me looking at the floral borders that lined the walls. They needed weeding. "Mrs. Lavinia Colegrove planted them," she observed neutrally, "but I'm afraid they haven't been well maintained in the last few years."

The hedge was as high as the walls and nearly as opaque. One would have to be quite determined to see through it. I knew plenty of lads, however, who could muster the requisite determination—I myself might have been one, not that many years back. The gate was a solid wooden door, designed to secure the privacy of the household.

With a nod to Miss Colegrove, I unlatched it and walked out into the alley. Just wide enough for two carts to pass each other, the alley neatly divided the block so that the five houses on either the Broadway or the Nassau Street side could be serviced without disrupting the main entrances or necessitating passageways between the houses. Most of the regular traffic was passing on the paved side streets to the north and south, but one tea water vendor was industriously pushing his cart, burdened by a full hogshead from the Minetta Brook, through this short-cut, which one would surely tend to avoid on rainy days. I walked back into the garden and stood next to the folly, about ten feet from the gate, and looked up and around. Because all the houses had walls, fences, or hedges obscuring the alleyway, and their buildings were set back some distance by their gardens,

I couldn't see anything from this vantage of the houses that fronted Nassau Street. And in fact, the roof of the folly completely blocked the sight of Colegrove's upper stories and almost all the back windows of the houses that fronted on Broadway. Aside from the chance that a rude passer-by might peer through the hedge, the folly was an oasis of privacy in the bustling city.

"Where, exactly, was Mrs. Colegrove's body found?" I asked the slave.

The trembling woman seemed struck dumb with fright. "It's all right, Calpurnia," Miss Colegrove said with unexpected gentleness, "you can please just answer Mr. Dordrecht's questions." Slaves seem nervous at the best of times, especially when being examined by a stranger. But this woman's teeth were chattering. "What's the matter with you?" Miss Theodora demanded. "Stop that!" With obvious effort, the slave stifled her racket, but continued shaking like a leaf. Finally she simply pointed to the floor of the folly, on the alley side of the birdbath—precisely where I had just guessed the crime would logically have taken place.

"Which direction was the head—" I stopped and turned to Miss Colegrove. "She wasn't the one to discover the body?" A nod. "It was Mr. Oliver Colegrove who found her, you said?" I turned back to the slave. "How soon after Mr. Oliver raised the alarm did you come outside? You did see the body yourself?"

"It's all *right*, Calpurnia!"

"Yes, I see."

"And how soon was it, after Mr. Oliver called out, that you came out to the garden?"

She shrugged. "Few minutes. I in the back. I hear, but I thought he stung by bee."

"What made you go outside?"

"Miss Eudoxia, she go to see."

"Did she call for you?"

"No. Caesar. He back from market. He scared, he yell."

"He would have returned through the alley gate?"

"Yes."

"Did you see anything that—" I was going to say, *anything that struck you as unusual*, but the context made that absurd. "Anything that you think we should know?"

Miss Colegrove was looking impatient, as people often do when one asks serious questions of a slave.

The black woman's face contracted with horror. "Blood! There be blood everywhere! All over her, all over floor, all over him!"

"There was blood all over Mr. Oliver?"

"He crying. He hugging her." She sighed. "Ruin new suit!"

That was disconcerting—to Miss Colegrove as well. "I trust someone made a search for the murder weapon?"

"I recall the coroner, at the inquest, saying that no knife had been found at the scene."

"Did anyone examine Oliver Colegrove's person with that in mind?"

"Oliver! *Oliver!* Oh, for goodness sake, Mr. Dordrecht!"

"He was covered with blood, she said."

"You must stop right there! He's only a boy—and a very high-strung, foolish lad at that. Don't be—"

"Miss Colegrove, we need to—"

"Caesar say no," the slave asserted. "Miss Eudoxia say Mr. Oliver must change and Caesar help. Caesar look. Throw out new green suit. No knife."

Miss Colegrove looked as if she was equally perturbed that a slave had had the presumption to look for a knife, and gratified that he hadn't discovered one.

"When was that, Calpurnia?" I asked. "Right away?"

"No. Later. Half-hour? Caesar sent to fetch Dr. Boyce. I sent to get Mr. Peter."

A great deal, I thought, could obviously have happened during this interval. What about the brother who was the intended recipient of the Stamp Act sinecure? "Did no one call for Mr. James Colegrove?"

The slave shook her head.

"I think he was away," Miss Colegrove said tentatively.

"When the coroner came, what did he do?"

"He say she stabbed."

"At the inquest, he stated that the cause of death was multiple stab wounds."

This struck me as problematic. "If she was stabbed many times, she must have been fighting back. She must surely have screamed for help. Did no one hear her scream?"

Both looked startled, as if this had never occurred to them before. "With all the windows open on a hot day ... And surely a passer-by could have heard shrieks, even from the corner!"

"I ... just can't say, Mr. Dordrecht. I—"

"Nor can I, Miss Colegrove. It's a myst—"

"Theodora!"

It was a woman's—a girl's—voice that called. I looked up to behold a smiling, extremely comely lass of some seventeen summers, attired in Sunday best. I gulped. Her blonde hair was a charming waterfall of loose curls. She was a perfect epitome of all the world would call *marriageable.*

"How lovely to see you," she burbled, "it's been— Oh! I didn't realize you had company!"

The perfection of the vision was slightly tarnished by this entirely disingenuous statement: the girl had been looking me over from head to toe, and paying no attention whatever to my client ... who, I noticed, was scowling even more deeply than usual, and clearly summoning her deepest reserves of forbearance. "Lovely to see you, too, my dear," she said tightly. They clumsily kissed each other's cheeks. "Allow me to present Mr. Thomas Dordrecht, who is—"

"Charmed, I'm sure!" the vision exclaimed.

"Mr. Dordrecht, this is my ... *sister*, Miss Élise Colegrove."

The young lady offered her dainty hand and I noticed the tiniest of black ribbon bows pinned to the right arm of her dress—minimal mourning! Still rather bedazzled, however, I collected enough of my dancing school manners to take her hand gently, bend from the waist, and brush my lips against it. "*Enchanté, mam'selle*," I ejaculated—and immediately felt like a pompous fool. The young lady, however, seemed rather pleased. She fluttered her hand to her breast and, apparently as tongue-tied as I, grinned at me as idiotically as I felt myself grinning at her.

Not pleased at all, however, was Theodora Colegrove, whose forthright pique now extended to myself as well as the vision. "Mr. Dordrecht is here to investigate the murder of our stepmother, Élise," she announced emphatically, with somewhat ghoulish relish. The lass jumped in alarm. "His time is severely limited in this quest, so I'm sure you'll excuse him if—"

"I beg your pardon, Miss Colegrove," I interrupted, "but, as long as Miss Élise is here, I may as well pose some queries to her."

The elder Miss Colegrove's teeth gnashed while the younger—whose coquettishness had evaporated—looked bewildered. "If you must," the former said, echoing her father.

Though I really wanted to inquire whether she had any musical interests or might fancy a stroll along the Battery, I pushed those thoughts away and asked, "Where were you, Miss Élise, when you learned that Mrs. Colegrove had been killed?"

After a second's discomfiture, and an impatient stare from my client, Miss Élise seemed to rally. "I had just returned to the house for dinner. I was in my room when *Grandmère* called to me to open her drapes and tell her what was going on down in the garden."

"I see. Which is your grandmother's room, please?"

A flicker of impatience clouded the vision's face, but she pointed to the third of the four windows on the second floor.

"Whose rooms are behind the other windows, please?"

"The two on the left are my father's room ... and *hers*, of course. Aunt Eudoxia's room is on the right."

"Your own room?"

"I share with Agnes, on the front side of the house. If Oliver ever moves out," she added cheerfully, "I'll get my own room!"

"And the third floor?"

"Just storage now. Older brothers had their rooms there."

"So what did you see when you opened your grandmother's drapes?"

"Not very much. I saw my aunt, wringing her hands. And I could see Oliver's feet sticking out from under the roof of the temple. He was moaning loudly, so I thought something had happened to *him*. I called to Aunt Eudoxia, but she ignored me."

"What did your grandmother do?"

"She was too weak to get up, but she still yelled at me to go down and find out what was wrong."

"So—"

"So I went downstairs, and came out here. I was nearing the folly when my aunt saw me and told me to stop. 'Not for you, child!' she said, trying to point me back into the house. But by then I'd seen that ... *she* was lying there on the floor and Oliver was lying on top of her. Aunt Eudoxia grabbed my shoulders, turned me around, and *pushed me* toward the kitchen! I nearly tripped, she pushed so hard! But as I started back, I noticed a piece of paper, caught there on the statue's arrow, and I said, 'What's this?' And Auntie came over and tore it off the arrow. 'Oh my god!' she said. Then she stuck it under Oliver's nose, asking if he'd seen it. And he quit wailing and lifted himself up to look at it, and that's when I saw all the blood and realized Artemis was dead. I screamed, and my aunt again spun me about and yelled, 'Get inside!'"

"It must have been very difficult for you," I said sympathetically.

There was just a hint of histrionics—heavy sighs—as she replied, "Oh yes."

"Were you able to read what was on the paper, Miss Élise?"

"Yes, though it didn't make any sense to me. It was 'Liberty, Property, and No Stamps!' just as my aunt says."

"But you saw it yourself?"

"Oh yes. I *can* read, of course!" she added indignantly.

"Of course. *Um*, what did the handwriting look like?"

"The *handwriting?* Oh. Well, it wasn't careful penmanship, for certain. Looked like it was scrawled as fast as could be done. Couple drips of ink. Probably broke the quill!"

"Élise *has* received commendations for her elegant hand, I've been told," Miss Theodora asserted. Her half-sister frowned at this faint praise.

"What did you do next, Miss Élise?" I asked.

"Well, I had to go back up to *Grandmère*, of course." She smiled impishly. "As I went into the kitchen, I heard Aunt Eudoxia ordering Oliver to 'quit sniveling, for god's sake,' so she could think!"

"Aunt Eudoxia!" Miss Theodora exclaimed.

"That's what she said, Theodora," Miss Élise replied.

"What was your grandmother's—Mrs. DeLancey's—reaction?"

"It took a couple minutes to explain to her! Then she posted me at the window for the longest time."

"*Uh huh*. And what did you see?"

The girl now looked completely disenchanted and impatient with myself. Had Miss Theodora not been present, I daresay she would have simply ignored me and bolted. "People came and went, Mr. Dordrecht."

"Can you recall who, and in what order? Just your brother Oliver and your aunt were in the garden with the corpse when you left, right?"

After another irritated sigh, she tackled it. "Yes. Aunt Eudoxia was sitting on the floor of the temple, in the shade. I could see her knees and feet. And Oliver was still"—she shuddered—"where he was." She pointed to the easterly half of the folly's floor, where Miss Theodora was standing. "All of a sudden, he screamed, he got up, wandered about a few steps, tore the paper into pieces, and then fell back down on the grass, wailing. Auntie groaned and picked all the paper up and took it over to the privy. Then Caesar and Dr. Boyce came in from the kitchen. Dr.

Boyce—Gideon—took one look at Oliver and *her*, and ran to the flower bed at the wall and threw up!"

Miss Theodora looked stunned.

"Dr. Boyce is your half-brother?" I asked her.

"Gideon is Élise's half-brother, my father's stepson. No blood relation to me at all. And I barely know the man."

I surely need a chart! "But he is a doctor? How old?"

"Oh he's not yet thirty. Returned last spring from two years' study in Edinburgh."

"Caesar fetched him a glass of water from inside," Miss Élise resumed, "and then he was sent away again. I think Gideon ordered Oliver to get up and stand out of the way, but he still stayed under the roof. Gideon collected himself and knelt down where Oliver had been before, and I assume he was examining *her*. Couldn't hear anything or see anything but his legs for minutes."

"They were all trying to keep out of the sun, I'd imagine," Miss Theodora asserted reasonably.

"Yes, I think so. Then Peter came in through the gate. I believe Calpurnia had fetched him." The slave nodded. "Aunt Eudoxia seemed very relieved to see him. He and Gideon and Aunt Eudoxia talked about what to do for a couple minutes, and then Caesar came back with a constable and the coroner."

"Did you get their names?" I asked Miss Theodora.

"No. I heard them at the inquest, but … I'm afraid neither made a very favorable impression."

"When the coroner asked Gideon to stand aside to let *him* examine her, Peter began insisting to the constable that he should start searching for the sailor who'd come to the house the day before. The constable said he didn't know how to find him, and Caesar spoke up and told them to look in some sailor's grog shop on Water Street. The coroner said it sounded like a good idea, so the constable left. And soon after that, the coroner stood up and pronounced that she'd been stabbed to death. Gideon and my brother looked very impatient with him, but Auntie caught both their arms and thanked the man earnestly. He asked if he might be offered a tot of brandy for the road, and—"

"He *asked* for brandy?" Miss Theodora interrupted.

Miss Élise shrugged off the man's impropriety. "*Uh huh.* Calpurnia fetched one for him, he downed it in one gulp, and left. Aunt Eudoxia had Peter lock the garden gate and they all went inside for dinner."

"Dinner?" Miss Theodora exclaimed. "After all that, they had *dinner?*"

"Yes. I was hungry too! Gideon didn't stay. He said he'd arrange for an undertaker as he returned to his office, but the rest of us sat down. It was just cold meat, because it was such a hot day."

Miss Theodora and I simply gaped for a second. "Was your sister Agnes at school during all this commotion, may I ask?"

"Agnes? Oh no, she was in our room the whole time. She was reading, as she always does. Hadn't heard a thing. Hadn't even noticed that dinner was late!"

"Who was present for dinner?"

"Well … Oliver, Agnes, Auntie, and me, as usual. *Grandmère* had Calpurnia take hers upstairs. Peter stayed. And, obviously, *she* wasn't there."

I had the uncomfortable sense that the lovely Miss Élise was beginning to enjoy this macabre interview. "What did anyone manage to talk about at dinner?"

"Well, I tried to talk about my friend Amy's new pony, but Auntie gave me a look that made me hold my tongue. Oliver started whimpering again, until she told him if he didn't stop, she'd have Peter smack him."

"My goodness!" said Miss Theodora.

Miss Eudoxia and Peter, Élise continued, had debated where and when to inter Mrs. Colegrove, and decided to bury her without delay in the old family plot in Mamaroneck. Objections offered by her siblings had been met with sharp rebukes from their aunt, causing not only Agnes, but Oliver, to flee the table in tears.

"Oliver … is your *younger* brother?" I asked, confused.

"No, he's two years older than me, he's nineteen, he's just, *um*—"

"Sensitive and temperamental," Miss Theodora finished for her.

"How does he manage his militia duty?" I wondered aloud.

"Oh, Father bought him out of that!" Miss Élise said cheerfully—as if it were the most normal thing in the world.

I shrugged. "Was anything else discussed?"

"*Um*, yes, they had to decide *when*. Peter suggested we bury her as soon as possible. Auntie suggested Saturday, but Peter said we should get it over with on Friday. And it was just then that that smarmy undertaker knocked. He was so disappointed when they told him all they wanted was a casket and a hearse up to Mamaroneck! His face fell so hard, I laughed, and Auntie ordered me upstairs to change into my mourning dress."

Though I might have profitably employed more time at the Colegrove home, I had promised I would report for work by three o'clock. My employers had taken the unprecedented step of begging their staff to work on the Sabbath afternoon. They were now frantic to get the *Pretty Phyllis* to sea—so that the *Zephyr*, waiting at anchor in the Upper Bay, might claim her berth in Peck Slip. Mr. Glasby's distress had been palpable when I informed him I had a previous engagement.

Though the *Phyllis* was only thirty paces from the office door, she'd been damaged on her last cruise, and I accompanied her petty officers several times over the next days to a shipyard a mile up-river, to acquire new stores of rope, tar, turpentine, brushes, tools, and sailcloth to refresh her holds. The upshot was that by Wednesday afternoon, when we finally did see *Pretty Phyllis* off and *Zephyr* safely in her place, we were all exhausted. Mr. Leavering treated the staff to an early round of spirits in one of the finer local taverns. Mr. Glasby and I, however, manned the empty office until closing time, fortified by the promise of an especially hearty supper at Hanover Square.

At length, Benjamin returned, and we three made our way to his home, where Hermione and Adelie had enthusiastically resumed the standard wifely duty of organizing repasts. I had been curious to observe them at the office, where they seemed comfortably at ease and intent upon their tasks. Hermione was attending to the bookkeeping; she caught an error of mine where I had inadvertently underpaid one of our suppliers, and insisted I make immediate restitution. Adelie Glasby was working with Mr. Leavering to deal directly with the customers; when one of the consigners had been irate, Monday, that the *Phyllis* had not already set sail, she had escorted him aboard, and had coaxed the captain into explaining the difficulty in layman's terms. Though the other members of our staff seemed awkward about them—some shy, some resentful—I was struck by how sensible it appeared to employ females for such undertakings.

"Charles is here," Hermione said brightly as we arrived. "I thought you'd like to see him too!"

"Wonderful!" exclaimed her ever-hospitable husband. But I noticed that John looked less than overjoyed.

Good food and drink raised all our spirits, however, and Charles nodded complacently as the common business problems of the firm were the predominant topic of conversation. For my own part, I was anxiously watching for an opportunity to make a confession of my other project, which I was determined to have out this evening. It finally arrived as a platter of cheese was passed around the table as dessert, and Benjamin concluded, "With any luck, then, we'll have the *Zephyr* laden by the end of the month, and the *Hermione L.* will be back from Charleston in time to claim her spot."

I nervously cleared my throat. "There's something I have to tell you all," I announced. "Last Wednesday, the day after your last gracious supper and the day before I started again at the office, I had one of the oddest encounters of my life. I received a perfumed missive from 'a lady,' requesting a meeting at mid-day in Ranelagh Gardens!"

That got their attention!

"And you … *went?*" Adelie asked, barely able to contain her glee.

"Yes. It was Miss Theodora Colegrove, and what she desired was to pay me an exorbitant sum of money to investigate the murder of her stepmother."

For some seconds, they were all so stunned, no one spoke. John Glasby finally spluttered, "But Thomas, you've made a commitment to—"

"I stated as much immediately, John. I had trouble taking her seriously, and so I hastened to explain that I expected to be working twelve or more hours a day, six days a week, through October, but to my surprise, she presently seemed satisfied that I might devote my remaining conscious moments to her inquiry."

"*That's* why you were engaged, on Sunday?" John instantly deduced.

"Aye, sir."

"You've accepted this, Thomas?" Hermione demanded, looking a trifle cross.

"I have, ma'am. As I say, she is content that I cannot devote full time to her before November, and she offered a great sum of—"

"*How* much?" Charles demanded, ever willing to ignore decorum.

"She retained me with ten pounds, and has promised twenty more if my efforts lead to a conviction."

"Oh!" all five gasped in unison.

"Sterling," I added smugly. The discount of New York pounds is now over forty percent.

John whistled as eyes rolled and incredulous laughter broke out.

"But Thomas," Adelie said, "how on earth did this come about?"

Relieved that I had apparently surmounted the main hurdle, I more easily related the reasons Miss Colegrove had cited for her decision.

"Which one is Theodora?" John asked. "I can't recall ever meeting a Theodora!"

"She's the very dour one, John," Hermione said. "Sits two rows behind her father in church, never has much to say to anyone. Early thirties, I'd guess. Daughter of the first wife."

"Spinster?"

"Yes. I reckon her looks and her personality have overwhelmed any attractions a possible inheritance might present."

"I don't think I even realized she was part of that family."

The discussion suddenly presented an idea to me. "Oh! You know what I need, urgently, is a concordance of the entire Colegrove clan. During the months I worked for him, I never realized how many children Aaron Colegrove had."

"Quite a few, I recall," John said. He'd worked with Colegrove for four years.

"*Fourteen* children, Miss Theodora said, by two wives! Plus stepchildren, grandchildren, a sister, a brother, the DeLancey mother-in-law, a manor in Westchester County—"

"I stopped by there once, ten years ago, but I've heard he's doubled its size since then."

I looked eagerly at Hermione and Adelie. "Maybe if you have some available time, it would really help to—"

"Oh no, Thomas," John objected. "That's really an imposition, even among friends!"

"Well … I could remunerate you! Yes! With all the lucre being thrown at me, I could pay for some private research of my own." The Glasbys and Leaverings looked mollified but bemused. Charles seemed unusually abstracted. "You could probably help, too," I said. "You always seem to know everything about everybody in New York City."

"*I* have other priorities at the moment, Thomas!" Charles said, with a self-righteous edge to his voice that was very unlike him. "Perhaps you were too occupied with the *Pretty Phyllis* to read the letter in this week's *Mercury*, which explained exactly how the Stamp Act is a Trojan Horse that will serve as an entering wedge to future impositions and oppressions. It will—"

"I did see it, but—"

"You really *believe* that, Charles?" John demanded.

"I do indeed, sir! The British ministry is evidencing a clear pattern of disdain for all American liberty! We must protest with all our might!"

Hermione gently broke the seconds of silence that followed this peroration. "Well now, Charles, what Thomas is seeking assistance with, is an investigation of a murder. And wouldn't you say that a murder is about as serious an imposition on an individual's liberty as one could imagine?"

Charles reddened slightly and smiled. "You do have me there, ma'am!"

"I would like to be whatever assistance I can, Thomas," Hermione said.

"But—" John began.

"And me, too!" Adelie said. "Even now, we're not needed at the office from dawn to dusk."

"It would be really helpful if someone could straighten out the Colegroves for me. There's two dozen of them, plus the Boyce stepchildren, and they're all somehow related to the DeLancey family. I really need to know their relationships, their businesses, their histories … their enemies! If you could assemble that, I'd gladly offer a … a crown to each of you!"

"*Hmm!*" Hermione said, coquettishly pushing her gray hair back under her mob cap. "I was rather thinking such an effort would be worth at least *ten* shillings! Wouldn't you say so, Adelie?"

"Oh, most definitely!"

The commercial acumen of the husbands had rubbed off on their ladies. "Well, perhaps it would!" I agreed.

We all looked at Charles. "You're not going to tell me the notion doesn't intrigue you?" Adelie challenged him.

It obviously had. He had a glint in his eye. "I'll make you a deal, Thomas. I'll add my efforts to those of the ladies, for the same emolument … if you'll at least attend the Sons of Liberty meeting on Friday Noon."

"Oh but Charles, I can't—"

"*I* shall be in attendance," Benjamin asserted, to John's dismay, "and I see no reason why Thomas should not take the time also. Usually less than an hour," he added quietly to his nettled junior partner. "I really think you should come as well, John!"

"*Somebody* has to mind the store!" John protested—with an uncharacteristically self-righteous tone in *his* voice.

"In that case, you've a bargain, Charles," I said quickly. There was no need to add that, while I was indeed eager to observe the Sons directly, it was plainly the unanimous opinion of the Colegrove family that one of that faction had been responsible for Mrs. Colegrove's murder, and that posed another reason for my attendance. "Perhaps your cronies at City Hall might have some observations?"

"I was thinking we could examine the church records," Hermione said, more to Adelie than me.

"Except that he wasn't always Anglican, Hermione. When he first came to the city, he was … What?"

"Presbyterian," Charles asserted. "Used to attend my brother Henry's church. I could get the records that are there."

"I thought you weren't on speaking terms with Reverend Cooper," Hermione said.

"I'm on great terms with the sexton!" Charles replied, grinning.

"When do you need this, Thomas?" Adelie asked.

"*Um*, as soon as— How about, a week from Sunday, in the evening, after supper? That way, I can try to corner a Colegrove or two during the afternoon when it's not too alarming to have callers."

"Should be feasible."

"Oh, and— Miss Colegrove is very eager to avoid all public notice, so the more discretion and indirection you can muster, the better!"

"*Ah!*"

"She'd be very distressed to learn that I've confided so much to this evening's party."

"Depend upon us, Mr. Dordrecht!"

"While we're at it, *Mister* Dordrecht," Charles added, "*you* would be well advised to avoid publishing the fact of your employment by anyone with the name of Colegrove. Aaron has sworn up-river and down that he deeply regrets ever having sought a place in the revenue service for his son James, but no New Yorker with sense trusts the man or anyone associated with him. The rogue is flirting dangerously with tar and feathers!"

Thinking of Colegrove's cold-blooded reaction to his wife's case, I could only agree. "Point taken, Cousin!"

"You've been to the house, have you?" Adelie asked. "Have you formed any conclusions about it yet?"

I shook my head vigorously. "Not the remotest, ma'am, not the remotest!"

CHAPTER 5

"HAVE YOU ATTENDED ANY of these gatherings before?" I asked Cyrus Mapes, making conversation as we walked together through a light drizzle, from the firm's office to the public house where the Sons of Liberty were to meet.

"*Uh*, twice," he replied. "Back in August and then, again, early this month, after the firm had recalled me—just before you got back. Mr. Glasby was not pleased, but Mr. Leavering insisted that I go."

I realized I'd not had a single personal exchange with Mapes in the week that we'd again been working together. The firm had let us both go in March of 'sixty-three. "They only called you back this month? What have you been doing these two years, may I ask?"

"While you were gallivanting about Europe?" he smirked. But his envy was less pointed than I remembered. "Oh … odd jobs, Dordrecht. A lot of carpentry, some construction. I'm very glad to have the pay they've offered, even if it's only for two months."

"Where are you living?"

"We rent a floor of a house up in Greenwich village," he said unenthusiastically. "Wife takes in sewing, but we can barely keep food on the table."

"Ah."

"And the only thing we've accumulated is children. I've got five, now."

"Congratulations!"

"*Hmm*."

Catching a good look at him as we crossed Gold Street, I realized he was appearing pretty drawn out for a man not even thirty—his form very thin, and his red hair already fading to gray. His reticence discouraged further prying. "Do the Sons ever do anything besides talking?"

"Oh indeed," Mapes said, evidently appreciating my change of subject. "They urged us all to get to the wharf when the *Royal Charlotte* arrived, end of August. They were eager to have a crowd meeting the fellow who sought a preferment for his son: Aaron Colegrove. You remember him?"

Oh yes, I nodded.

"He got quite a reception: a hundred men shouting 'No stamps, no stamps!' Women beating their pots and kettles! Didn't take him too long to renounce the whole project and tear up his son's commission."

"*Huh.* Was the son there? The one who was to get the job?"

"James Colegrove? Aye. Couldn't miss him. Wearing a fancy striped coat—maroon and silver. But he scampered before his pa got off the boat."

"Discretion the better part of valor?"

"I expect."

We negotiated our way through a thicket of delivery wagons with agitated horses. "This is the man whose wife got murdered?" I asked ingenuously. "When did anyone tell him?"

"I saw Mr. Lawson—his son-in-law who works with him—breaking the news, after he reached the quay."

"Must have been a shock!"

"He fainted. I jest not, he fainted! Lawson got knocked to the ground trying to catch him when his knees gave way."

We arrived at the tavern just as noon was chimed. There were two dozen ahead of us trying to get inside. The press of men was terrific, as the establishment was already jammed to the walls. Somehow, we—and another score who followed us—managed to get standing room at the back. The frustrated publican had given up service in the already smoke-filled room, as there was no possibility of movement at all. Many were sitting on the bar—I waved to Marinus Willett, among them. I finally saw Mr. Leavering, seated against the back wall next to old Mr. Helden, a major client of the firm. On a dais near them, two men were standing, and another was seated at a tiny table, paper, quill, and inkstand at the ready.

"Your famous cousin, Cooper," Mapes indicated, his eyes rolling. "Good for something, it appears!"

Mapes had always found Charles objectionable, I recalled. "Who are the two men standing?"

"*Ah*. The older one is Isaac Sears. Merchant, ran a privateer during the war."

"Neither of 'em are graybeards!" Sears looked no older than Harmanus.

"Aye. Other one's John Lamb—once an optician, now a wine merchant. They say his pa was *transported* here from England, as punishment for burglary." I raised my eyebrows. "But he seems square enough."

I looked back at the door, and saw a fellow signaling to the dais. Sears tapped a goblet with a spoon, and the room fell quiet. "Good afternoon, gentlemen—and ladies!" Sears began, a confident grin on his face.

But of course everyone strained to verify the fact that there *were* a few women present, seated toward the front. While some shook their heads in disapproval, others ... straightened their neckerchiefs.

"The happy news of the moment is that we are at last in possession of copies of the first issue of the *Constitutional Courant*, which proclaims itself "Concerning matters Interesting to Liberty, and in no wise Repugnant to Loyalty!"

The immediate round of approbation was cut short when Sears raised his hand. "Its publisher, Mr. *Andrew Marvell*"—

"Thought he was dead!" a clerk in his late teens blurted out.

"Century ago!" an older man responded. "It's a pseudonym, dolt!"

"Mr. Andrew Marvell, I'm informed, accumulated two important letters he deemed worthy of public note, but he applied in vain to every printer in this city to publish them. In devotion to the public cause, he ultimately turned to a firm over in New Jersey to run them off." He paused to let some indignation rise and fall. "He also took care to avoid the authorities' notice as the copies were returned."

"How'd he get away with that?" the incontinent clerk whispered to Mapes during another wave of dismay.

"Sears used to smuggle shiploads of lumber and sugar," Mapes whispered back. "You think a crate of newsprint will stop him?"

"Our purpose today is to recruit as many as possible to distribute these valuable essays, which propound a purer devotion to American liberty than any yet seen!"

Huzzahs were heard about the room.

"Mr. Lamb and I propose to read these essays to you, to show why they must be presented with dispatch to all the town's men of consequence. They were authored, one by 'Philo Patriae,' the other by"—he squinted at his sheet—" 'Philoeutherus.'"

"Philo-*who?*" the same clerk squawked. He clamped his hand over his mouth as Mapes elbowed him. But the whole crowd was momentarily stumped.

"God of sunshine," an ancient softly asserted. "Father of Helios."

Everyone had to repeat this. "How did *sunshine* father the *sun?*" Marinus suddenly challenged, grinning.

"Have to ask Hesiod!" the old scholar gamely replied.

"All Greek to me!" Sears quipped loudly, garnering a chuckle and retrieving the focus. "With your permission, I shall now read to you the letter of Philoeutherus, after which Mr. Lamb will favor us with a recital of the missive of Philo Patriae."

Do you suppose they're the actual authors? I wondered. Our modern correspondence is rife with the tedious trope of pseudonyms. *Why can no one avow his opinions openly?* Notwithstanding the crowded circumstances of the usually rowdy tavern, his audience seemed ready to give Sears the respectful attention to which Dominie Van Voort is accustomed in our quiet country *kerk*.

Philoeutherus—whoever he is—began with the observation, which I'd have found tendentious just a fortnight ago, that "everyone who has the least spark of love to his country must feel the deepest anxiety about our approaching fate." He then itemized the objections to the Stamp Act more cogently than I'd yet heard: "that no Englishman can be taxed, agreeable to the known principles of our constitution, but by his own consent, given either by himself or his representatives; that these colonies are not in any sense at all represented in the British parliament; that the first adventurers into these uncultivated deserts were, in every colony, either by royal charters, or royal concessions, in the most express terms possible, assured that all their rights and privileges as British subjects should be preserved to them unimpaired; that these original concessions have been repeatedly allowed by the crown, and have never been controverted 'til this memorable period." In short, he inferred the Stamp Tax will be an unprecedented and completely unjust imposition, "that reduces nine-tenths of us to instant beggary."

Having thus recapitulated his premises—with which most were already in agreement—Philoeutherus came to the point: "What then is to be done?" Should we trust in "one of the best of kings" who "glories in being King of freemen?"

Hmm. Having just spent two years in greater proximity to George of

Hanover than Philo-sunshine probably ever knew, I've absorbed a modicum of disloyal skepticism directly from H.M.'s English subjects that would probably shock most of our countrymen. But I noticed that these fulsome stock phrases did not elicit the habitual cheers that they might have when supplied for George the Second just six or eight years back.

Should we, he continued, "besiege the throne with petitions and humble remonstrances"—trusting in the wisdom of Whitehall to sort this out properly? And he answered, "If we throw in petitions against them, they need only say, *'tis against the known rules of this house to admit petitions against money bills,'* and so forever deny us the liberty of being heard!" Given the disdainful reception of all of America's recent petitions, the assembly applauded loudly when Sears raised his voice to declaim, "Poor America! The bootless privilege of complaining, always allowed to the vilest criminals on the rack, is denied thee!"

"Let none censure these free thoughts as treasonable," Philoeutherus continued. "I know they *will* be called so, by those who would gladly transform these flourishing colonies into howling seats of thralldom and wretchedness, but we cherish the most unfeigned loyalty to our rightful sovereign ..." Philo even professed a high veneration for the British *parliament* before stating the obvious: "the wisest of kings may be misled," he said, and parliaments sometimes "fall into capital errors," which "would soon unhinge the whole constitution!" The "true sons of liberty," he proclaimed, "offend none but a set of villains, and these we must always offend! With them, liberty is always treason, and an advocate for the people's rights, a sower of sedition. Let it be our honor"—the speaker's voice rose again—"let it be our *boast*, to be odious to these foes to human kind; let us show them that we consider them only as beasts of prey...." *Et cetera.* I detected that a few—not many, actually—were beginning to squirm uncomfortably, but Sir Philo was just warming up. Praising the "noble spirit" prevailing in the New England colonies, he blasted those who would profit as placemen for the Stamp tax as "blots and stains of America! Vipers of human kind! Parricides!"

And having lauded the Bostonian rioters, Philoeutherus addressed those functionaries who "would bear a part in freedom's extinction" with a naked threat: "Can you expect to escape the unseen hand of resentment, awakened by injuries like these? Assure yourselves the spirit of Brutus and Cassius is yet alive: there are those who dare strike a blow to avenge their insulted country!"

Sears sat down amid thunderous cheering and applause. Some stomped their feet, some jumped up and down in their enthusiasm. For my own part, I … was troubled more by what I foresaw as possible consequences of these admonitions, rather than any disagreement. Clearly, we are in uncharted territory!

After a minute, John Lamb rose and gestured for silence. His vocal style was a contrast to the measured presentation of Sears. It had more in common with the soaring rhetoric of the preachers of the New Light, whom I'd heard once in a revival tent—located, oddly enough, in the country town of Clapham, south of London.

He began with a dutiful head-shaking regarding "the late violences" committed in Boston, warning that the "terrible effects of those popular tumults" would startle those who "delight in peace and order." Then he promptly charged the guilt of same not to the rioters, but to "the authors and abettors of the Stamp Act," and piously avowed, "I would wish my countrymen to avoid such violent proceedings, if possible."

Was I the only one wondering whether the ambiguous *"if possible"* might not be construed as an incitement?

He outlined the familiar reasons the Stamp Tax should be regarded as the imposition of "Turkish despotism" on America, but added the inroads on the right of trial by jury that would be faced by everyone accused of violating it. Imagining myself dragged off to Nova Scotia to face a military judge, I howled as loudly as anyone in the room at that.

He posed an ironical objection to the notion of "virtual representation" that Sunshine had missed: the British constitution requires members of the parliament to possess landed property, as each will therefore be "affected in his own fortune by the laws he is making for the public." Yet—the second Philo demanded—do any of them have property *in America*? "Will they each feel part of the burdens they lay upon *us*? No! But their own burdens will be lightened by laying them upon our shoulders!"

Quite right, I thought. That's an outrage, if anything is!

Drawing on his predecessor's assertion of the Whig principle that the rights of liberty and property are "necessarily connected together," Philo Patriae argued convincingly that, if the English parliament could tax Americans without their consent, "they can also, if they please, take our whole property from us, and order us to be sold for slaves, or put to death!"

And that brought great growls of concurrence—though some seemed to dismiss it as rhetorical excess.

Perhaps to mollify the latter, Philo now avowed further professions of undying affection for the Mother Country … before his most outrageously provocative statement: "But if she would strip us of all the advantages of the English constitution, *why should we desire to continue our connection?* We might as well belong to France, or any other power! None could offer a greater injury!"

Several men, hearing only the shocking words *"as well belong to France,"* made for the exit, grumbling. Mr. Helden looked appalled, and even Mr. Leavering seemed dismayed. But the younger Sons cheered as loudly as ever—one fellow my age was repeatedly thrusting his fist into the air and shouting, "Curse them! Curse them all!"

Philo Patriae confidently assured us that the Stamp Act will "doubtless" be repealed. *Glad he's got no doubts!* I thought. "But meanwhile," he admonished in the sternest tones, "let us never, for one moment, acknowledge that it is binding upon us, nor pay one farthing in obedience to it!"

Defiance! Defiance was the watchword. Defiance of the whole British empire! All rose to shout their approval as Lamb sat down—yours truly joining in. Mr. Leavering stood to applaud … though Mr. Helden remained seated … yet he was clapping.

It continued for two minutes, until Sears halted it. He reiterated the adjurations of both Philos that our protests must be "orderly," asked everyone to be alert to future calls of the Sons of Liberty, and wished us all a good day. It was only then that it occurred to me how odd, even offensive, my brother Harmanus would have found it, that there was neither a prayer at the commencement of the meeting, nor a benediction at the end. But Harmanus, of course, lived in New Utrecht, not New York City. I shrugged the quirky thought away.

Subduing an impetus to escape the stifling tavern, I pushed forward after the adjournment to pay my respects to my cousin, who introduced me to Lamb and Sears, then pulled me aside and whispered in my ear. "Another you'll want to know: by the bar, no coat, loose hair, gesticulating to Willett…."

I turned carefully and observed a tall, gaunt, impassioned fellow, the one who'd called curses down on the placemen. He seemed to be trying Willett's patience. "Who's he?"

"Timothy Colegrove. He—"

"Oh!"

"Not many know him. New to the city, I think. Can't quite bring myself to trust him. Holier than thou, you know!" We both took another peek. Willett was all but turning his back on Colegrove, talking to another fellow. Though still young, Colegrove's hair oddly had a gray streak. "He's been to almost all the meetings. Shouts *Huzza!* with enthusiasm. Sears thinks I'm too suspicious."

"You do have a tendency—"

"Granted, granted."

"How does Timothy justify his participation to his family, do you suppose?"

"Exactly! Just what I want to know. He *says* he hates his father, has no commerce with any of them."

"*Whew!* Married?"

"Don't think so. Anything you find out about him, Thomas, you can tell *me, eh?*"

"What, you imagine he's some sort of spy for John Tabor Kempe or something?" Charles shrugged elaborately, suggesting that he did not completely dismiss the idea. And the even grimmer supposition that hung unstated in the fetid air was that, if it *had* been a radical who'd murdered Artemis Colegrove …

The room was fast clearing out. Mapes and Mr. Leavering were already gone—as was Timothy Colegrove. "Have to get back to the office, Cousin. Good day, now!"

"Take some copies of the paper, Thomas!"

Should I? "Will do!" I went a couple hundred yards out of my way as I returned, to pass by the Brooklyn ferry, where I forwarded one copy of the *Constitutional Courant* to *The Arms of Orange* in New Utrecht.

Through dubious arrangements of my cousin, about which I am reluctant to inquire, a shiftless guard admitted me on Sunday morning into the empty City Hall at Wall and Broad Streets, where the records of the inquest into the death of Mrs. Artemis Colegrove and the grand jury proceeding brought against Henry Tenkus, mariner, had been mysteriously left out on a table conveniently near a south window.

The inquest had taken place at eight a.m., the morning after the murder. The judge's name was unfamiliar to me, but Charles had said he was a DeLancey appointee of staunch royalist temperament. The coroner and the constable were present, as were Miss Eudoxia Colegrove, Mr. Peter Colegrove, Miss Theodora Colegrove, and Mrs. Irene Colegrove. Mrs. Jacqueline DeLancey, Mr. Lambert Colegrove, and Mr. Timothy Colegrove had declined to attend. The married daughters of Aaron Colegrove were not summoned, nor were his minor children or his slaves. Oliver Colegrove had been called, but the court accepted his aunt's assertion that he was still too "overwrought" to appear. Dr. Gideon Boyce's absence occasioned neither remark nor explanation. The deceased's husband, then still at sea, had of course not been expected.

The coroner—apparently well sobered from the afternoon before—had described the corpse as he had found it, and concluded from the multiple wounds and the effusion of blood that Artemis Colegrove had been stabbed to death in a savage frenzy. An autopsy, he claimed, was unnecessary. The constable supported that analysis, and no one present offered any reason to contradict it.

Miss Eudoxia Colegrove then testified, answering the judge's questions regarding the time-line of events; her responses closely agreed with the recitals that Miss Theodora, Miss Élise, and the slave woman Calpurnia had given me. Mr. Peter Colegrove, who had arrived late on the scene, concurred entirely with his aunt's statements. It was he, however, who volunteered the fact that a note had been found and destroyed by his brother Oliver, which set off a long and furious tirade from the judge about the sanctity of evidence ... particularly evidence that might implicate His Majesty's enemies.

After extorting an abased *mea culpa* from the entire family, the judge concluded with the coroner that Mrs. Colegrove had been murdered by a person or persons unknown, in the back garden of her home, between eleven forty-five and twelve-thirty of the afternoon of Wednesday, August twenty-eighth ... and set Henry Tenkus's grand jury hearing for twelve days later.

The folder recording the grand jury proceeding was thinner still. It was conducted by John Tabor Kempe on Tuesday, the tenth of the instant month, before a different judge, with the same officials and family members, plus the bereaved husband, in attendance. Tenkus, still incarcerated, was not present. Although Kempe's statements were entirely neutral, it was clear to me that he knew perfectly well that there was no case against the mariner, and wanted only to conclude the session with all haste. Miss

Eudoxia Colegrove was again the chief witness. She vividly described Henry Tenkus's visit to the house on the night prior to the murder, the "violent" argument that had ensued, and Mrs. Colegrove's "terrified" state after the sailor's departure. Tenkus had only left, she claimed, when she and the family slave had threatened him with bodily harm. She avowed that the incident proved that Tenkus was the culprit, and she trusted—seconded by the entire family—that he would therefore soon receive his just deserts at the gallows.

Odd. Tenkus had made no mention to me of Miss Eudoxia's presence during that encounter, and I couldn't imagine him so easily frightened away.

I read on. Kempe calmly called the constable, who admitted he'd had to wake the sailor up in order to drag him off to jail. Kempe thought to ask a good question: Was any blood seen on Tenkus' person? The answer—one could only wonder how long it was in coming: No. Then he called the publican and the publican's wife, both of whom testified that Henry Tenkus had lain insensate on the floor of their tavern, snoring, during all the hours in question. Perhaps having anticipated that these testimonies might be considered tainted by virtue of insufficient social class, Kempe also called a counting-house clerk and a junior clergyman of the German Reformed church, both of whom had stopped in for a tipple that noon, recognized Tenkus from previous encounters, and forthrightly confirmed the publican's testimony. Over vociferous protest of the family members, who evidently believed all five individuals had to be part of a radical conspiracy, the judge ordered Henry Tenkus released, declared the murder unsolved, and adjourned.

Hearing the presence of other people in the building as church bells chimed one o'clock, I replaced the records exactly as I'd found them and quietly let myself out.

Thinking I could fortify myself with a quick repast at the *Hearts of Oakum*—I had to smile every time I thought of the irreverent twist on the navy's sacred *Hearts of Oak*—as well as at any other dive, I walked there in search of Tenkus. I found my porridge and ale, but learned that the sailor had had a dubiously lucky break. He had shipped out—before the mast—on a slaver to west Africa. "Filthy work!" the publican commented. "And near as dangerous as getting pressed into the navy!"

A few minutes later, I presented myself again at the Colegrove mansion. Calpurnia let me in, told me to wait in the vestibule, and walked up the stairs without asking who I'd come to see. I sat on the bench, fuming. Aaron Colegrove appeared from the kitchen, carrying a glass of cider. I stood up and wished him a good afternoon. He declined to return the wish, grunted, and proceeded directly into his study.

I sat back down, striving to suppress my indignation—*Does the swine think he's already Sir Aaron?*—and concentrated on wondering *why* I was thus mistreated. A minute later, the slave came back down the stairs, said "She be soon!" and turned into the kitchen. Three minutes after that, a woman of advanced years but strong posture, dressed in mourning, came downstairs and walked forward, scowling.

"Good afternoon, ma'am, I'm—"

"I know. What do you want?"

Again affronted, I had to remind myself that Miss Theodora had never suggested the family would be cooperative. "Am I correct in assuming that you are Miss Eudoxia Colegrove, ma'am?"

"Yes."

When I realized she was not going to volunteer another syllable, I decided to be blunt. "I have recently read the transcripts of the inquest into Mrs. Colegrove's death and the proceedings against Mr. Tenkus. Do I presume correctly that you would confirm the statements you made on those occasions?"

"You *are* presumptuous, Mr. Dordrecht! I was under oath in the King's court. Of course I affirm my statements!"

I paused to draw a full breath. "Do you have anything to add to your testimony, ma'am?"

"No."

"Do you still consider that it was Henry Tenkus who murdered Mrs. Colegrove?"

At last she appeared at a loss. "I continue to doubt the individuals who managed to exonerate him. But if it was not he, then it was surely one of his Jacobite accomplices!"

Jacobite! Good lord. My first impression of Miss Colegrove's acuity crashed. In addition to being twenty years dead, the cause of the Stuart pretender had absolutely nothing to do with the present opposition to the Stamp Act. "*Umm* ... Well, I may need to seek more details from you in the future, Miss Colegrove, but today I should like to speak with Mr. Oliver Colegrove."

"He's not here."

In vain I waited for further elaboration. "Could you possibly tell me where he *is*, Miss Colegrove?"

Again she was clearly debating whether to comply. "I believe he likes to take the air in the Ranelagh Gardens with his friends on Sabbath afternoons."

"Thank you. I'll try him there. I also wish to speak with Dr. Gideon Boyce. Can you—"

"Lectures at the college. I don't know where he lives."

"I see." Hadn't she sent the slave to fetch Boyce? "Well then … Good day to you!"

Like her brother, she disdained returning the wish. I saw myself out, and with difficulty resisted the urge to slam the door.

Curses! It'll cost me another sixpence!

The ticket booth clerk looked askance when I inquired after Mr. Oliver Colegrove. "Yeah, he's here … somewhere," he replied, rolling his eyes. Having only a vague notion of my quarry, I walked three-quarters of the perimeter before I spotted a short, slight, extravagantly dressed lad who appeared to be shy of twenty. Watching his flaccid, ineffectual gestures, I had the instant impression that he'd have trouble spreading butter with a knife, much less wielding one in anger. He was sitting in animated conversation with an equally extravagant lass who couldn't have been more than fourteen. It was hard to discern their ages, as both were wearing white wigs and had their faces painted. Their expansive gestures abruptly halted as I approached.

"I beg your pardon. Would you be Mr. Oliver Colegrove?"

The pair seemed to think this hugely funny. "Oh, Gin-Gin," the lad said, "he thinks that *I'm* Ollie! Can you believe that!"

"Oh my *goodness!*" quoth she.

Despairing of a single-syllable response, I said, "I take it you at least know Mr. Oliver Colegrove?"

"Oh we *know* Ollie, yes, by gad, we do!"

"*Ooh!*" she squealed, as both giggled behind her fluttering lace fan.

"Can you tell me where—"

"My lord Edward," a high-pitched, but stronger voice interrupted, "*who* is *this?*"

Garbed entirely in crimson sateen trimmed with purple, was another powdered and bewigged youth, gesturing with his walking stick as he came toward us. But he was physically the opposite of my expectation, over middle height, solid and healthy of build. I offered my hand. "Mr. Colegrove, I'm—"

"He has not yet favored us with an introduction, your grace," interrupted the other boy, "but he has come here expressly looking for *you!*"

All three raised their eyebrows and giggled. I resolved upon expedition. "Mr. Colegrove, my name is Thomas Dordrecht, and you may have heard that your sister has asked me—"

"My *sister!* Prudence? No! And *surely* not Mrs. Pugh!" This was another source of mirth.

"I'm sorry: your half-sister, Miss Theodora Colegrove, has asked me—"

"Oh! Theodora!"

"*Ohh! Theodora!*" echoed his companions satirically.

"I've been charged to investigate the murder of your stepmother, Mr. Colegrove," I said brusquely, trying to contain my irritation.

"*Ah!*" he wailed, clutching his chest and collapsing onto the bench between the other two.

"I would appreciate a few moments of your time. Perhaps over there?" I nodded toward the next bench. The park was much busier than on my previous visit, and most seats were occupied—save those within earshot of this trio.

Colegrove seemed to be affecting a readiness to swoon, and his friends were affecting deep concern. The play-acting was horrendous. "I beg your pardon, Mr., *uh*, Dordrick—"

"Dordrecht, if you please, sir."

"Yes. It is—*Ah me!*—still so soon, since that *awful* day!"

"His grace and Lady Colegrove were deeply, *deeply* fond of each other," the other boy asserted.

"He has drawn *beautiful* sketches of her," the girl added wistfully, "three of them, with angels and cherubim, since—*Ah!*" She covered her face with her fan as she looked away.

Good Christ! But the question was, Was *anything* about them genuine? While it would be difficult to imagine the slight lad, for example, physically capable of striking a healthy young woman down, unless he made a lucky first surprise hit, there was no doubt that Oliver Colegrove had the native strength.

"Mr. Colegrove, could we please sit apart and continue this privately?"

"These are my *dearest* friends, sir! I have no secrets from Lord Edward and Lady Virginia!" The three hugged each other all the more tightly.

Rot! Getting him apart might reduce the theatrics. But it was not to be: he adamantly shook his head. In order to observe his reactions, I had to remain standing in front of them. "Oh very well, then! When was the last time you saw Mrs. Colegrove alive?"

The three of them quailed at the bluntness of this direct question. They would have tried Job's patience. I repeated the question.

"I saw her the evening before, at supper. She seemed ... *happy* then." His voice caught and he bit his knuckle in apparent anguish.

"Did she say why?"

"No. *Alas!*"

"And you had no further communication?"

He whimpered briefly before answering. "Sometime after supper, I was planning my wardrobe for the morrow, when I heard *him* stomping out, slamming the door."

"Henry Tenkus?"

"Yes. The great *beast!*"

"Wait. How did you know it was he?"

"I walked out into the hall after I heard Artemis running up the stairs to her room, and saw our slave man. He told me it was the monster. I went to her door, and knocked and asked if she needed me—We were the closest of friends!—but she told me to go away and leave her alone."

"Had you seen Tenkus before?"

"Twice. Earlier in the summer. A heathen savage, no better than a Mohawk!" he exclaimed floridly. His companions dutifully shuddered—to young Colegrove's evident satisfaction. "He—"

"Did you see her at all the following morning?"

I had the impression my question disrupted a planned portrayal of the mariner in loincloth, feathers, and face paint. "No," he admitted disconsolately, "she was gone when I arose."

"I see. And what was your activity that morning?"

"Why, we three had planned a perambulation of the Battery—as we do every Wednesday. We meet with Squire William and Bishop Teddy."

"You were late, as usual!" the other fellow carped. "It was near eleven when you caught up with us in Bowling Green."

"Edward, how *dare* you! I had to go back and get my parasol against the sun!"

"It was *so* hot!" the girl moaned.

"Billy and Teddy never came," Edward whined. "The louts! Of course, if we'd had any sense, we'd have stayed in too!"

Common sense was obviously scarce among their circle. "So what did you do?"

"Good heavens, this was *ever* so long ago!" Colegrove exclaimed. "How can you expect—"

"It was shy of a month ago, Mr. Colegrove, and a day that most in your position would vividly remember."

"Oh, well, indeed!" He was flustered. "Gin-Gin, do you recollect what—"

"We stopped by Otterby's, your grace, to examine the enameled snuff boxes they'd just received from Italy."

"Oh yes, and they were exquisite, were they not, my dear?"

Otterby's Beaver Street emporium caters to the town's wealthiest. Only after two promptings from Mr. Leavering had I once dared venture inside it—fearing that I might be charged for sneezing.

"Lapis lazuli, chased with gold!" the other lad enthused. "They also had—"

"And what did you do after leaving Otterby's shop?" I demanded.

"We were there some time," Edward breezed. "Mrs. Otterby also wished to show us—"

"I'm sorry: *after* you left the shop?"

I looked at Oliver Colegrove, who stared blankly back. "*Uhh …*"

Both lads looked to the young girl, their improbable companion. "We went home, didn't we? We were all getting peckish, and the bells chimed a quarter past noon, so we decided to go home for dinner. But it was *so* hot, it took us *forever* to climb back up the hill!"

This brought me up short. I had been scrutinizing Colegrove as a prime suspect—wondering if he were completely mad, half-hoping I might resolve the mystery in a trice—but this one simple observation exonerated him as surely as Tenkus had been. It was inconceivable that the three had concocted a false time-line. It was not that he or his ludicrous companions were incapable of acting, they were merely incapable of *good* acting. Their exaggerations and fantasies were completely transparent.

I sighed. "Where and when did you part?"

"We parted when we came to my block on Nassau Street, and they went on— This is the Viscount Edward Ramsay, you know, the laird of John Street, and his sister, Lady Virginia."

Mad, definitely, but not a murderer.

"And you are?" Ramsay prompted artlessly.

I repeated my name for the third time, then ascertained that the siblings had proceeded directly to their home and only learned of the murder much later that afternoon.

"Now, Mr. Colegrove, I have to ask you about your discovery of your stepmother. I take it you proceeded by the alley and came in through the back—"

"*I* know where I've seen you before!" Ramsay whooped with astonishing rudeness. "You were with *Adelie Glasby*, just recently! I spotted her one evening on Nassau Street. There were two other men—"

"You *know* Mrs. Glasby!" Colegrove breathed.

"She is *so* beautiful!" the girl swooned.

"She was *magnificent* in *The Recruiting Officer*! Didn't you think so?"

Bereft of speech, I bleated, "I missed it. I was in London."

"London! *He* was in *London!*"

"Oh, I say!"

"Mr. Colegrove—"

"You may call me Ollie, Sir Thomas!"

No. "Mr. Colegrove—" He had taken my hand in both of his. Suppressing an urge to yank it away, I gently removed it. "Will you tell me what you saw when you entered your back garden?"

"Oh that is *very* painful, Sir Thomas!"

"No doubt, sir. But in justice, we owe it to your stepmother to—"

"Oh very well!" He affected a few more sighs, was soothed by his friends, and then made an effort to concentrate. "When I first came in through the gate, I had urgently to answer a call of nature, so I went directly to the privy, not noticing anything."

All of them dutifully mimed embarrassment at this. "And then?"

"Well, as I came out, I was surprised to see a piece of paper stuck on the statue's arrow, so I moved toward it ... and then I noticed a woman's feet sticking out onto the grass from the floor of the folly. My first fear was that my aunt might have fainted or suffered a stroke from the heat, but I moved closer and saw ... the *blood*! And that it was Arte— It was my stepmother, my dear, *dear* friend!"

I sensed that *some* of the gasping and shaking represented genuine emotion. "What did you do then? Did you understand immediately that she was dead?"

"I shrieked and fell onto my knees, and then embraced her, hoping— I kissed her, wishing that I might breathe life back into her. Or that I could transubstantiate my unworthy soul, to reanimate her body!" He fell to weeping. Not too loudly, thank heaven. The Ramsays pouted at me as they offered him their handkerchiefs.

Madness! I shifted my weight, hoping his spasm would pass. "What happened next?" I finally demanded.

"My aunt—" He stopped to blow his nose. "My aunt came out into the garden, and for once *she* was taken aback! But she presently demanded I rise off the body of my sweet lady, and ..."

"Yes?"

"Well, but then Caesar came in, from the alley, and he saw what was going on, and he howled and dropped his groceries, and Auntie had to go and quiet *him* down."

"It was undoubtedly a shock for everyone. Did you get up then?"

"Calpurnia came out, and my aunt sent Caesar to fetch Gideon, and then she sent Calpurnia to fetch Peter. I wept and wept! Then Élise was out there—being nosy, as usual—and suddenly the piece of paper from the arrow was in front of me. I read it, and it was then that I knew—*knew!*— that it was that horrid sailor who'd killed her! The *beast!* Had he been there, I'd have torn him *limb* from *limb!*"

No, he'd have knocked you flat on your arse. "What made you so sure it was Tenkus?"

"Well, it was obvious, Sir Thomas! It was the radicals' slogan, and everyone knows all the mariners are part of the radicals' mob!" I was about to raise a skeptical objection when he added, "And of course, as Auntie said, he'd been pestering her for months, ever since Father went away."

"Bounder!" Ramsay exclaimed. "Let it be a lesson to you, Sister, never to trust—"

"Mr. Colegrove, I'm sure this will seem an odd question, given the circumstances, but did you notice anything else that seemed out of the ordinary? That seemed wrong, or out of place?"

"Wrong?" he wailed. "Wrong, when the whole *world* has been turned upside down?"

"Yes," I persisted. "Any odd detail."

They looked at me as if I were the crazed one. But finally a thought struck him. "I couldn't imagine why she was wearing such pedestrian attire. She had much finer summer dresses. It was not like her to venture out looking so … common!"

"What was she wearing?"

"A plain blue linen smock, and a farmer's straw hat. I can't imagine where she bought the horrid things! At least the dress was ruined!"

I had no idea what to make of this—other than to *make note* of it. "Anything else?"

"No. Alas, no!"

"You said you were surprised that she was wearing her hair down," Ramsay prompted. "Not at all fashionable!"

Ladies' hairstyles? *You asked the question,* I accused myself.

"Well, it wasn't meant to be down, Eddie, it had come loose. In her struggle, I suppose. All over the place!"

"But that was when you found the combs, didn't you say?" Miss Ramsay said. "Next to her in a tidy pile? The ones you gave to me?"

"Oh," Colegrove sighed, "I guess it was. I was in rather a state!"

People had been strolling past us—and rapidly deciding to keep their distance—but now I espied, with dismay, a group of a dozen or so slowly wending our way, mostly women crowding around a pale young man in black, who was declaiming on some scriptural detail that he had negligently glossed over in his sermon, hours before. He was very loud—even louder than Oliver Colegrove. "*Egad!*" the latter exclaimed, in a volume sufficient for the Sunday orator to overhear, "It's a dissenting minister, railing against the follies of youth! Let us flee to calmer climes!"

And with that, the three nobles of Broadway and John Street picked themselves up and walked smartly away—without a word of farewell.

What an extraordinarily rude family!

Ranelagh Gardens is assuredly a splendid addition to the city's amenities, but I was disgruntled and sour, and had had my fill of it. The racket and foul smells of the city streets pointedly revived me and persuaded me, given the afternoon's progression, to hasten to seek out Dr. Gideon Boyce at the college.

Walking south from the park, the imposing five-story structure was constantly in view. I'd never noticed that the cupola in its center was surmounted with a crown. The building might have intimidated me if I didn't recall the furious controversy King's had occasioned just a decade ago. The fact that the Anglican institution is still partly supported by public funds appears to have become too familiar to generate on-going rancor, particularly now that we have the Stamp Act to distress us.

At Murray Street, I crossed the quadrangle green two hundred feet to the center entrance, passing youths and men in black academic caps and gowns. Up the stairs, inside, a white-haired gent greeted me very civilly, but when I inquired for Dr. Boyce, he informed me that he was not on the premises. He volunteered that Boyce resides around the corner, on Church Street—and also that he was today visiting a colleague at the College of New Jersey, and not expected back until late. "He lectures on the fourth floor every day," he added. "Are you interested? 'The History of Medical Thought.' Someday we might even offer training in *medicine*," he added sardonically, "but for now, this will have to do!"

"Thanks, but it's a matter of private business, sir. Can you tell me at what hour he lectures?"

"Oh surely. From eleven o'clock until twelve-thirty. I'll gladly pass on a message." He smiled. "Happily, we can still afford note paper, as it does not yet need a government stamp!"

Laughing, I borrowed his knife to sharpen my pencil, and wrote that Thomas Dordrecht, on an errand of Miss Theodora Colegrove, hoped to speak to him in the near future, and inscribed my addresses both on Reade Street and at the firm. "There!"

"I have to warn you, young sir," the man said. "Dr. Boyce is a fine, honorable man, perhaps even a brilliant one, but he is … not the most organized individual. He's … forgetful."

"Ah, I see. Thank you very much. And a good day to you!"

It was back to work again the next morning. I was enjoying the work, but the pace was frenetic and relentless, and there was absolutely no time left over for any other concern save calls of nature.

Mapes told me he'd heard that Governor Colden, infuriated by the *Constitutional Courant*, had sent constables to every printer in the city, disrupting all business, vainly hoping to learn who had been responsible.

On Thursday afternoon, an unexpected delay provided an unexpected opportunity. I had arrived near Corlear's Hook, where our coastal schooner *Maia* was undergoing emergency repairs, when the mate informed me all the officers were momentarily preoccupied with stepping the new mizzenmast. Could I return in an hour?

An hour. It'd be pointless to walk back to the office, only to turn straight around. It occurred to me that Willett's workshop on Rutgers Street was closer, and I could at least learn how he was progressing with the chairs.

"Well, Tom!" Willett whooped, after I'd spent a full minute hammering on the door. "Come in, come in! Sorry for the delay—I've got a project going in the backyard."

"That's all—"

"The chairs are done! Put the last coat of varnish on them yesterday. Here you are! Your uncle, William Cooper, came by two days ago—I have an order from him, too—and said he thought they'd sell handsomely. Ask me, I'd bet Chippendale himself couldn't tell they'd been repaired!"

My friend was not known for false modesty—but the repairs were so expertly done, one really had to look hard to find their trace. Which I did, never fear. "Excellent, Marinus! Will you take them over to Cooper's for me?"

"Aye. And you owe me eighteen shillings!"

I feigned shock. But it was good work.

"When he sells them."

"Oh, all right then!"

"Great. Say, you have a minute? Come see what we're working on, outside." Curious, and not that pressed for time, I followed him out the rear door. The strapping free black man who'd helped when I'd delivered the chairs grinned and jumped up as we came out. A sullen white fellow remained slumped against the fence. "It's for the funeral of Miss American Liberty parade," Willett explained, ignoring both men. It was a heavy wood platform that took up most of the yard. "It's upside down, right now. We've just completed the axle fittings."

"It's to be a float on November first?"

"The *gallows!*" he bellowed cheerfully.

"You're not planning to—"

"Effigies, Tom, of course. As in Boston."

"Should be the real men!" mumbled the peevish bloke. Did I recognize him? Yes: a young face with gray in the hair!

A scowl briefly crossed Willett's face. "Tom, you know Tim Colegrove? He's volunteered to help us all week. Tim, this is an old mate of mine, Tom Dordrecht."

Colegrove looked up sharply—from which I gathered he certainly recognized my name—but made no attempt to rise. So we nodded at each other.

Willett touched my arm. "Oh! Just got a great idea! If you can spare just a couple minutes, Tom, I can fetch the neighbor, and the five of us can flip this baby over, so I can start on the superstructure." Without waiting for my assent, he asked the black assistant to mind the shop, and dashed out.

Uneasily, I sat on one of the axle-posts.

"You're the great sleuth Theodora has taken it upon herself to enlist," Timothy Colegrove asserted dolefully, eschewing preliminaries. "A fool's errand, man!"

"How so, Mr. Colegrove?"

"Call me Tim, Tom."

"Only my best friends call me Tom, Mr. Colegrove."

He smirked. "She said that *Kempe* had recommended you."

"Aye."

"*Hmph!* One way to keep watch on the Sons, *eh?*"

Oh dandy! While Charles suspects *him* of being Kempe's informer, this scion of the Colegroves presumes to suspect the same of *me*. Confident that both Willett and Cooper would scoff at the charge, I ignored it. "Why do you call her intent to discover Mrs. Colegrove's murderer a fool's errand, sir?"

"Because it's obviously the work of some DeLancey henchman, Dordrecht! They wanted to stir trouble against the Sons, and since nobody cared a hoot for the stupid woman anyway, they did her in and tried to throw the blame on us!"

Another theory! "One or two blows with a knife would have been sufficient for that, Mr. Colegrove. A dozen strikes suggest a deeply passionate crime."

He snorted. "Maybe, maybe not. But—"

"Where were you at that particular moment, Mr. Colegrove?"

"*Me?*" he practically shrieked. Then he collected himself. "What was *I* doing? We had a Sons of Liberty meeting at the very hour it happened! That's what's so ludicrously obvious about that paper slogan!"

"You don't think it was the sailor?"

"Tenkus? Hell no. All too convenient. Lucky for him he'd publicly drunk himself into a coma, or he'd've been strung up by now!"

"You're the only member of your family who doesn't think him guilty. Even Miss Theodora isn't disabused of the notion."

"Theodora … still suffers the delusion that our parent has redeeming qualities!"

Oof! Well, he was far from alone in thinking his sire a swine. But was his apparent candor affected? "Do you have any specific idea who might have murdered your stepmother, Mr. Colegrove?"

"My *stepmother!*" he spat. "Don't be obscene, Dordrecht! My real stepmother, Lavinia Boyce, was not particularly objectionable. It wasn't her idea to banish my sisters and me to Westchester. That tart Aaron married after she died was seven years my junior!"

"Do you have any specific—"

"No. Not worth thinking about! Who the hell cares who did the fool slut in? World's better off without her!"

Reeling from the vehemence of the statement, I had to acknowledge that the man's emotional violence seemed genuine. But would a murderer so forthrightly spew his hatred in front of a man charged with his discovery? Timothy Colegrove didn't appear to be stupid. "Why would the DeLancey faction—"

Willett bounded back into the yard, followed by the assistant and a burly workman. "Right!" he breezed. "Now, Tom, you and Abner take that corner. I'll take this one with Heinrich." To my friend's evident annoyance, Colegrove wasn't budging. "Tim, could you *possibly* bear a hand, here?" Colegrove sluggishly shifted himself to respond. "Just stand in the middle, there, and put your foot on the edge as we raise it upright. Keep it from slipping, that's all we ask. Ready, gents? Go!"

Though the float platform was heavy, it was nowhere near the size or weight of the side of a barn. Following Willett's instructions, the four of us raised it, carried it vertically to the other side of the yard, lifted it well off the ground, and lowered it down flat onto the axle fittings. Colegrove seemed to be trying to help with the last, most awkward move, but managed to be underneath as the platform's weight was falling, and was predictably knocked to the ground.

Willett and I both scrambled underneath to his aid. Colegrove looked dazed, but insisted he was all right. We scanned for bleeding, but didn't see any, and crawled out. "The man wants to help, but he doesn't know what he's doing!" Willett whispered to the others as Colegrove, grunting with effort, hauled himself toward the sunlight. Wiping the dust off my breeches, I had to wonder if Marinus was perhaps being overly generous.

"Man *is* bleeding," said Abner. He and Marinus took Colegrove by the arms and pulled him upright.

Colegrove swayed for a second, then felt the side of his head, and perceived a little red wetness on his fingertips—which seemed to amuse him. "Well, well! Now no one can say I've never shed blood for the cause, *eh?*"

Marinus managed a chuckle. "Abner, you know where the bandages are, right? Take him inside and patch him up, will you?"

Colegrove allowed the black worker to escort him into the shop.

"Doesn't look too serious," Marinus said, shaking his head. "Could have been a lot worse."

"Anything else, Marinus?" Heinrich asked. I was surprised that he had no accent. I realized that I'd seen him before, standing somewhere behind me at the Sons' meeting. "I have to get downtown. I'm getting my freemanship today."

"Are you now! Wonderful! We need all the— Tom, are you a city freeman yet?"

"Never saw any reason to bother with it, Marinus."

"The Sons are encouraging everyone to do it, Tom. Why not? Only eight shillings, and you can vote and start a business and—"

"They say we've the most liberal franchise in all America," Heinrich asserted.

"All very well," I protested, "but if I do that, they'll be after me to rejoin the militia, and I'd rather put that off as long as I—"

"Sons are encouraging everyone to do that, too, Tom!"

"The Sons are? Whatever for?"

"Well … to keep public order, of course," Marinus said rather evasively. "And—"

Colegrove and Abner rejoined us. Having caught the gist of the conversation, Colegrove said, "In case it comes to blows, Dordrecht! In case—"

"Well, the militia's at the beck and call of the governor," I objected, "and we all know where he stands, so why are the Sons of Liberty—"

"Because they know full well the patriotic men of New York would never obey wretched old Colden in this instance."

"You won't find a soul in the militias who supports the stamps," Heinrich said confidently.

"But I still don't— What are you imagining, that the New York militia is going to face down the British army?"

"It wouldn't be the whole British army, Tom," Marinus said. "There's only one company there in Fort George."

"And New Jersey's militia would be here with us the next day, and Connecticut the day after that!" Heinrich added.

"You really must do that, Dordrecht! It's your patriotic duty to—"

"Excuse me, Mr. Colegrove," I said hotly, "but I think *I'm* competent to decide where my patriotic duty lies!"

In the sudden stillness, we could all hear the clatter of work in the nearby rope walk. Colegrove snorted dismissively, and again ensconced himself on the ground against the fence.

"I really have to be going, Marinus," Heinrich said, turning to leave. "Thanks so much for your help, friend!"

Church bells recalled me to my duty to the *firm*. "I have to get back to work, too, Marinus."

"I'll see you out." As soon as we were in the shop, he said, "I'm really sorry—"

"How do you put up with him, Marinus? I was ready to slug him!"

"He thinks he has to be more assertive than everyone else, Tom. To balance the fact that his name is Colegrove."

"Oh *phoo!* He's just an arrogant—"

"You might want to think about it, though, Tom. You're living on Reade Street? We've a good man heading the West Ward militia. I know he'd be glad to have another veteran of the regiment. A sergeant to boot!"

"I'd be just as happy never to go back to that, Marinus."

"Oh, to be sure, Tom, but—"

"I've got to go."

"Think about it. Thanks for helping with the lift!"

What I thought about, as I tried to cool my temper while rushing back up the East River shoreline to the *Maia*, was Timothy Colegrove. Willett was not a naïve man. Could he be right, that the infuriating fellow actually meant well?

And would anyone who'd just stabbed a young woman to death ever think to call attention to the first blood he'd "shed for the cause?"

CHAPTER 6

EVERY EVENING NOW, as I hauled my exhausted self back to my garret on Reade Street, it seemed I could look forward to a perfumed missive from Miss Theodora Colegrove. They were no longer delivered by the liveried Negro, but by a shoeless street urchin—for a farthing that was appended to my rent. The letters were full of useless suggestions for investigating sailors' haunts, imprecations against the radicals, and demands for reports of my progress. I had only responded twice, and the sole worthwhile result was that she had, following my urgent request, arranged for me to meet with her half-brother, Peter Colegrove, who had been summoned to the scene shortly after the murder.

On the last Sunday afternoon in September, I made my way to Colegrove's residence. Having come to expect incivility in that household, it was a relief to be greeted with common respect. In contrast to the rest of his family, young Mr. Peter Colegrove affords a fine first impression: a tall, trim, elegantly dressed man with genteel manners. One might even call him dignified—surely a rare accolade for a fellow even younger than myself. He stood as Calpurnia ushered me into the library. "It's a pleasure to meet you, Mr. Dordrecht!" he exclaimed effusively. "My sister speaks very highly of you, and my mentor and future brother-in-law, Mr. Kempe, also commended you. I think it showed estimable initiative for Theodora to retain your services—to pursue justice for the deceased on our father's behalf." He indicated one of the chairs by the library table. "Please tell me how I may be of assistance!"

I was decidedly gratified, but elected to merit all this esteem by getting to the point. "Thank you. Mr. Colegrove. I'd like you to tell me everything you saw and did on the twenty-eighth of August."

"Ah. From the moment I first came upon the body?"

"The whole day, if you please."

"*Uh huh.* Well ... I rose and breakfasted as usual. I'm living alone over near the docks—in Fletcher Street—while I search for a proper abode for my bride. Do you really want all this?"

"Please go on."

"Well, it has been my practice, the first thing every morning, to avail myself of father's library, to pursue my studies. So I came here, as usual, around seven o'clock that day."

"Did you notice anything out of the ordinary?"

"Nothing at all—except, of course, for the weather. It was fiercely hot."

"Did you see anyone?"

"No, actually. I let myself in, and I tend to immerse myself in my reading. My family are good enough to leave me alone while I'm at it. I heard the girls leaving for school, and Aunt Eudoxia giving Calpurnia orders as she departed for her tea, but I didn't see them."

"Mrs. Colegrove?"

He frowned. "I didn't see her at all that day—alive, that is."

"You left the house at some point, I understand?"

"Yes. About ten-fifteen. Four days a week, I clerk for Mr. Kempe, but not Wednesdays. On normal Wednesdays, I'd have stayed here all day, but the heat was so overwhelming that morning, I returned to my billet, attended to some domestic chores, and simply took a nap. I had also been planning to pay a call on my intended, later—when circumstances disrupted all plans."

"I see. And when—"

"Oh. I happened to see Dr. Boyce—my half-brother Gideon—who arrived as I was leaving. He was attending to *Grandmère*, who'd been feeling poorly for several days."

"*Uh huh.* When did you learn—"

"*Um*, after twelve-thirty. I suddenly heard Calpurnia hammering on the door and blubbering frantically to a passing workman—my landlord lives on the other side of town—and so I came out. Poor old wench was barely coherent, thanks to the shock."

"And when—"

"The three-quarter chimes were struck as we crossed Nassau Street. It was a good thing Calpurnia had warned me what to expect—the sight was truly horrifying!"

"What did you see?"

"We came in through the alley, to save time. They were all under the roof of the folly. Oliver was prostrate, Gideon was kneeling over the body, and my aunt was standing by the statue. It took me a minute to get my bearings, as you can well imagine."

"Indeed."

"Particularly when Oliver shifted around, and I saw the blood all over his front."

"Did you suspect that your brother may have—"

"*Ollie!* Oh good heavens, no! I mean ..." He squirmed slightly in his chair. "Mr. Dordrecht, I hate to say this, but my brother Oliver is ... a silly and ineffectual lad. He's ... prone to emotional ... *fits*. But he certainly couldn't have lifted a knife against Artemis. I mean, I suppose he's strong enough, it's just ... just preposterous!"

Well, no matter. I had already eliminated him. "I presume Dr. Boyce was examining Mrs. Colegrove's corpse. What did he say?"

"Gideon is extremely deliberate in his judgments, and does not rush to assert his findings. In this particular case, anyway, we were interrupted before he'd said a word."

"How was that?"

"Caesar—our black—arrived, very shortly after I did, with the coroner and a constable. The coroner demanded to examine the corpse, and Gideon stood aside to allow him to do so. If Gideon had any thoughts or observations, I never heard them—which was a shame. I felt rather cheated!"

"Did he confer with the coroner?"

"Not that I saw. He appeared to accept the man's findings." He leant backward, noticed that a book had been placed upside down on the shelf, and automatically righted it.

"I met your sister Élise here a fortnight ago. She intimated that the coroner appeared intoxicated ..."

Colegrove looked dismayed. "I'm afraid that was my impression also. He nearly tripped over the baskets of groceries that had been left out in the sun. They shouldn't have been there, of course, but still ... A shame that the Council cannot manage to retain more professional service for us! At any rate, my aunt was exclaiming that she felt certain the crime was the work of a sailor who'd been repeatedly foisting himself on the household, including the very evening before, so I urged the constable immediately to arrest him. Fortunately, Caesar knew not only his name but his most likely whereabouts."

"Had Mrs. Colegrove ever expressed any feelings about Henry Tenkus?"

"Not to me, Mr. Dordrecht. She and I were cordial, of course, as was my duty, but far from intimate friends. My aunt asserted that she'd been deeply upset the previous evening, however."

"Did you see the message that had been stuck onto the statue's arrow?"

"No, Oliver had already torn it up, and Aunt Eudoxia had disposed of it. Inexcusable, even under such a stressful situation—but there you are."

"I see. And what happened next?"

"Well, the coroner announced his finding, and told us he would ask a judge to schedule an inquest, and then he departed. Dr. Boyce volunteered to contact an undertaker on his return to the college. And when my aunt and Oliver and I were finally alone, we were suddenly overcome by the accumulated horror of it all, the outrage that this excellent young woman had been so foully attacked in our own home, and that my poor father would be faced with the appalling prospect of being a widower for the third time, robbed of his helpmate."

No, I thought for the first time, there is something *not* quite right about Peter Colegrove. We all have a disdain for those who speak ill of the dead, but given what I'd already learned of Mrs. Colegrove's social reputation, this level of familial piety did not ring true. However, I merely nodded, to encourage him to continue.

"So, anticipating the arrival of an undertaker at any moment, we placed a sheet over the body, and went inside for dinner. I had, first, to go upstairs to inform my grandmother; but she had already been told by Élise. Then I had to tell our youngest sister, Agnes, who had been in her room the whole time, reading."

"I should like to speak with her, at some point."

"Really? Can't imagine what she'd have to add—but if you must, please go gently! She's a shy lass, very bookish, and only twelve."

"Was she very upset?"

Colegrove seemed startled by his recollection. "She ... accepted the fact with commendable stoicism, but was very distressed by the manner in which Mrs. Colegrove was murdered."

"Did you learn any new details while at dinner?"

"Not really. No one knew where Mrs. Colegrove had been that

morning, though the slavewoman was certain she'd not been at home. I learned of the sailor's previous visits, and how offensive they'd been to her. We speculated about his connections to the radical faction, given that he'd chosen to flaunt their slogan so openly."

Disappointing. Uncritical people can believe things in defiance of all evidence, but Peter Colegrove was a budding lawyer, and he had attended the grand jury hearing that proved the sailor had slept straight through the morning, yet he nonetheless appeared to feel sure the posted slogan was Tenkus' handiwork. "You do recall, sir, that Mr. Tenkus could not have been in the yard at all that day?"

"Oh! Oh right. Well—that's what we were thinking at the time."

"Was anything else discussed?"

"Well, of course we had to discuss what to do next. The family, our friends and colleagues—all had to be informed, and the obsequies planned. I was ill at ease, because these decisions properly belonged to my elder brother."

"To Lambert Colegrove?"

He twitched, rather sharply. "No no, I ... uh ... Lambert Colegrove is ... somewhat estranged from the rest of us, Mr. Dordrecht. He's been careful never to break openly with our father, but ... he seems entirely wrapped up in his own business and his own family. I was referring to my full brother James, of course."

"I see. Where was Mr. James Colegrove?"

"Well, none of us knew, off-hand. But we assumed he was at father's office, working with Mr. Lawson, and so as soon as we'd sat down, we sent Caesar off to collect him. But it was ninety minutes later before Caesar returned, having been to the office, to James's club, to his home, and finally to his wife's sister's home, which is where he learned—to our great surprise—that James had informed his wife the afternoon before that he was going up to the family estate in Mamaroneck."

"This was not a regular trip, on his part?"

"No. It was quite unusual. I never have learned why he went there. Oliver and the girls had spent much of the summer there with Uncle Edward, and we usually have reunions there at Easter and Christmas, but ... At any rate, it was serendipitous, because Aunt Eudoxia and I had just decided that the funeral and interment should be at the estate, which we thought would be father's wish. So we arranged with the undertaker to have a hearse move Mrs. Colegrove's body to the estate, and hired a courier to dash up there to convey our plans to Edward and James for a ceremony on Friday."

"And ...James Colegrove was in fact in Mamaroneck?"

"Of course." He suddenly must have surmised why I'd asked. "*Of course!* Well ... the courier returned with a response in his handwriting, just before we departed the next afternoon."

He seemed a trifle nettled—and more so when I changed the subject. "I recently met your brother—I'm sorry, your half-brother, Timothy Colegrove." He grimaced. "He has a theory—" My host sighed impatiently. "He has a theory that the city's mercantile faction conspired to murder Mrs. Colegrove and focus the blame on the radical Liberty Boys."

"Oh for heaven's sake, Mr. Dordrecht! Surely you don't— Mr. Kempe said that, whatever your political stance might be, you could be trusted to let the chips fall ... Timothy Colegrove is our family's black sheep, Mr. Dordrecht. Even Aunt Eudoxia barely speaks to him. He lived with Uncle Edward in Mamaroneck until fairly recently; I don't even know where he's staying here in the city or how he supports himself. He is supposed to be possessed of extreme, conspiratorial New Light enthusiasms in both religion and politics ..." He shook his head vigorously.

"I take it you don't agree. Do you have a theory as to who might have murdered Mrs. Colegrove?"

He raised his eyebrow. "I ... have to concede that the knife could not have been wielded by Henry Tenkus, Mr. Dordrecht. But he might still have been behind it. Given that my father has his enemies among the mariners, Tenkus could well have persuaded one of his cronies to attack his wife."

Now who's engaging in conspiratorial fancy?

"He may even have paid someone to do it!"

"I happen to know that Tenkus had run through his earnings and was almost penniless, Mr. Colegrove."

He seemed to be upset. "Well, then perhaps it *was* one of your—one of the Sons of Liberty! Unless you've got a better idea?"

"I have not formed any idea, as yet."

"Of course," he said, regaining composure. "The villain has done a fine job of covering his tracks!" We held each other's glance for a few seconds as I realized I had no more to ask. "Let me know if I can be of any further assistance, Mr. Dordrecht!"

My next thought was to canvass the neighbors, in the hope that they might have noted some crucial detail. I rapped on the front doors of the houses on either side of Colegrove's, but got no answer. Even though they were nearly as commodious and impressive as number one forty-four, it was hardly surprising that no one was at home on a Sunday afternoon. Deciding that it would still prove the best use of the remaining afternoon hours, I repaired to Sweet's, a public house on the west side of Broadway, where I nursed a beer and assiduously watched the traffic on the east side. Over an hour passed—I was berating myself for a foolish waste of time—when two stout ladies, arm in arm, halted in front of number one forty-two, immediately to the right of the Colegrove place.

Then they stood and talked for another twenty minutes. I got the impression that the younger one was frequently preparing to bid her elderly friend adieu, but the latter kept discovering new topics. Finally they parted, and the more talkative lady entered the house. I screwed up my courage, finished the beer, crossed the street, and again made bold to knock. After a trying moment—during which I again considered, and again rejected, the possibility of presenting myself in an entirely fictitious manner—a short, very young, black servant girl opened the door by a crack, and meekly requested my business. I gave her my name, and explained that I was on an errand of Miss Theodora Colegrove, the daughter of their next-door neighbor, and wished to speak with her master or mistress.

"Mr. Pannikin is gone, sir, he died last winter. I'll see the missus."

Before I could ask to enter, the door was shut, and I heard her throwing the bolt. Just as temptation was arising to rap again, the lock was pulled back, and the door reopened as before. Both the elderly lady and the girl stared at me through the aperture. I restated my mission, adding the adjective *urgent*, and observed a lively curiosity overwhelming the lady's natural hesitation to admit a male stranger into the home. When I suggested I might need several minutes of her time, she led me into her parlor, but did not dismiss the servant.

"Ma'am, Miss Theodora Colegrove—daughter of Mr. Aaron Colegrove by his first marriage—has commissioned me to make enquiries that she hopes will lead to the discovery of the murderer of her father's wife, Mrs. Artemis Colegrove."

"Oh!" she exclaimed. "Such a horrible, horrible thing, Mr.—"

"Dordrecht."

"Mr. Dordrecht. I can't tell you how upset it has made me! I've not spent a minute in my own garden ever since it happened."

"Truly? How awful! Perhaps you can tell me—"

"I never used to lock my door, Mr. Dordrecht. But with such an appalling crime right beside me and with mobs running wild in the streets every night— Cordelia and I were just talking about that poor Mr. Ingersoll, up in Connecticut, who was surrounded by a thousand men and forced to resign his post for fear of being *lynched!* Whatever is the world coming to? It's only me and this little girl Leah here, sir; my husband's dead and my children have all left—"

"Perhaps it would relieve your mind, Mrs. Pannikin, if it were possible to determine the true villain who killed your neighbor, and to bring him to justice."

"Oh! Yes, I see. But I saw Jacqueline DeLancey just two days ago, and she is convinced it was that horrid mariner, whom the government let go due to some nonsensical technicality."

How very irresponsible of Mrs. DeLancey to repeat the fable! "Mrs. Pannikin, I happen to have read the court's transcripts, and I can assure you the judge did not free the mariner for frivolous reasons, and he emphatically stated that the case was unsolved."

"Oh heavens, how terrible!"

"… which is why Miss Theodora Colegrove has asked me to—"

"Oh, Theodora! I tried to befriend her in church. But she's so very distant! Such an unhappy young woman, it's very sad."

"Ah. Well, she cares very—"

"I fear it's because she realizes she's not as pretty as any of Lavinia's daughters. If she kept herself up better, she'd be perfectly marriageable, but— I do rather miss Lavinia Colegrove. She at least was civil! It's very irksome when one's immediate neighbors are testy and peculiar, don't you know! Not like the Van Brunts in number one-forty—the *nicest* folk! The only one I enjoy– Well, young Peter has decent manners, I suppose, but I've become quite fond of little Agnes. She comes over regularly to borrow books from me, and always returns them promptly."

"Did you know Mrs. Artemis Colegrove, ma'am?"

Mrs. Pannikin sighed. "Well, of course, I knew who she *was*, but— My late husband and I felt duty bound to attend their wedding, and to pay our respects when she moved in, but … it was hardly possible to consider her a friend, Mr. Dordrecht. Particularly after they put *that statue* in the backyard! That disgraceful object was in the open for three weeks, for all to see, before they built the roof over it. My husband complained to Mr. Colegrove that we could not avoid looking at it from our second story window, but he was rebuffed in the most callous and peremptory terms!"

"Dear me!" I mumbled, with somewhat overstated sympathy.

"Aaron Colegrove was simply infatuated with that ridiculous girl, sir. It was most unbecoming in a man of his age and stature in the community. One surely hopes that, if he seeks a fourth wife—and who'd put it past him at this point?—he'll have more sense!"

"Oh my!" My interlocutor was clearly in full flow … and I was not about to discourage her.

"My husband's business acquaintances were all agreed that he had let his success go so far to his head, that he even thought he could snub his nose at his DeLancey connections!" She barely paused while I *uh-huh*-ed. "I almost felt sorry for his sister. And for Lavinia's mother! Imagine your family being a prime subject for all the town's gossip! And most of his children were older than she was! He has a *grandson* who's older, I'm told."

"Good heavens!"

"None of them could stand her, of course. I've never seen a family so rent apart! The two older girls—twins, you know—rushed into marriage right after their father—possibly just to escape her—and the older sons decided it was high time to find their own domiciles. Perhaps Marguerite was—"

"Goodness! How do you suppose Mrs. Colegrove managed at all?"

"Well, Mr. Colegrove was very attentive and—"

"But he'd gone off and left her for five months!"

"Quite shocking. He should have taken her with him, if you ask me! It's not as if she was needed to watch out for his children or to manage the house. The two older ladies attend to that, and did so even before Lavinia Colegrove died."

"Really!"

"*How* they manage it, I'll never know, as the two of them perpetually seem to be barely on speaking terms. It's quite disagreeable to be in their company together, I must say—and I'm not the only one!" I … shook my head. "Perhaps James, the eldest—Lavinia and Aaron's eldest—offered some support to the girl in his father's absence. They always expected James would take over the business, you know, always put him forward. Surely you've heard of his debacle with the Stamp Tax preferment? But I've always thought James to be an indolent and selfish young fellow. I always found his brother Peter more commendable, but the parents doted exclusively on their first-born. He married last year, James did—I think Miss Eudoxia or Mrs. DeLancey arranged it—but the word is, it's not a happy marriage, and the young man did spend an inordinate amount of time here with his stepmother while his father was away."

"Very awkward, I should think!"

"Indeed so!" she affirmed. "But for the epitome of awkwardness, one can only look with horror at how that family tolerates and coddles young Oliver! They stand aside and allow that preening, out of control adolescent to make a public nuisance of himself. His father should have put him in the army, Mr. Pannikin said, like that excellent, much-lamented son of the first marriage, Captain William, to straighten him out!"

I shrugged noncommittally, and did not voice my apprehension that the late Mr. Pannikin had had an overly glamorized view of the effects of military life.

"But Oliver! He was *inseparable* from his stepmother! They matched each other in their dreadful immaturity! Always fussing with each other's hair and clothes. Shameful, really!"

"Oh my, oh my!"

"Leah!" she said brightly, turning to the slave. "Fetch Mr. Dordrecht some of our lemon water! You must be parched, sir, after all this talking!" The girl curtsied and left—escaped—the room.

"If I may, Mrs. Pannikin: Did you—"

"While she's away, Mr. Dordrecht, I have to confess to you that my last encounter with Mrs. Colegrove was most unfortunate. We had been out shopping one morning—early last month, it was—and passed the woman out front, and she arbitrarily began reproaching my girl for all sorts of infractions that were entirely her own inventions!"

Oh yes: the story Hermione Leavering related.

"Chastising *my* servant in public! It upsets the child to this day! Imagine the gall—" The slave girl walked back in with the refreshments. "You were saying, Mr. Dordrecht?"

"Were you here at home on August twenty-eighth, Mrs. Pannikin, the day Mrs. Colegrove was murdered?"

"Indeed I was, sir. Many of my friends have asked! But I'm sorry to have to tell you, I did not see or hear anything at all."

"It was extremely hot, I understand. Were your windows not open?"

"Oh they were open! I had kept the drapes closed against the morning sun, but as soon as the sun was overhead, I had Leah open wide for whatever zephyr might relieve us."

"I keep wondering why Mrs. Colegrove would not have screamed for help. Were you perhaps back here, in the front parlor, or—"

"I was actually upstairs in my bedroom at mid-day, sir, doing some embroidery on a blouse for my granddaughter. The light's better. Yet I was never once moved to look out until I heard Oliver carrying on in the most unseemly, unmanly fashion."

"Did you grasp what had happened, at that point, ma'am?"

"Oh no. I assumed the lad was throwing another of his fits of pique, so I sat back down and concentrated on my work for several more minutes until I heard Miss Eudoxia raising her voice at Oliver and Élise. Then I got back up and realized there was a woman prone under the temple roof. For a second, I feared it might be Agnes, but the figure was too old to be Agnes—and too young to be Mrs. DeLancey—and presently I realized the intensity of the hysterics indicated that something was really amiss. But it was not until Dr. Boyce arrived—A true gentleman, he, if rather diffident!—and Oliver rolled over to allow him to proceed, and I saw the blood all over creation, that I knew! I knew it wasn't any sort of accident. This poor child saw it, too, and she ran away, crying! Didn't you, Leah?"

"Yes, ma'am," the girl agreed meekly.

"Then the slaves were running about, and Peter arrived, and the coroner and the constable. I have to admit, I was riveted to the window! Then after another fifteen minutes or so, they all left or went inside, and Calpurnia came out and threw a sheet over the body. And there was no further activity until the undertaker came two hours later and took her away. I was beginning to feel quite ill, myself, but whether it was repugnance or simply the heat … I can't honestly say."

"Had you by any chance noticed anything unusual earlier in the day?"

"No, I don't— Leah, didn't you say you saw Mrs. Colegrove leave through the alley?"

The girl started.

"Now don't be scared, Leah, just answer my question."

"Yes, ma'am. She left right after Mister Caesar left."

"She calls their slave 'Mister Caesar.' Isn't that dear?"

"*Hmm.*"

"Go on, child."

"Lady not supposed to go out the alley!"

"About what time would this have been, Leah?" I asked.

"Oh she can't tell time, Mr. Dordrecht! But— What were you doing when you saw this, Leah?"

"Making bed, ma'am."

"Ah well, that puts it around nine-thirty in the morning, you see. I've become quite a creature of routine since Mr. Pannikin left me, and I always send her up to make the bed right after I finish breakfast."

I was intrigued. "Did you notice which direction Mrs. Colegrove took, Leah? Uptown or downtown?" As we were virtually in the center of town, this would hardly pinpoint her destination, but ... The girl pointed, her arm trembling slightly. "Uptown, then?" She nodded. "And it was truly unusual for her to use the alley?"

"Oh, Lavinia Colegrove would never in a thousand years have set foot in that alley! No proper lady—or gentleman, for that matter—would neglect to use the front door!"

I nearly gagged, covering my bemusement at being ruled down a social notch. The slave girl stared impassively. "*Um*, was there anything else out of ordinary, that morning?"

"She dress plain," the girl asserted. "Always dress fancy, usual."

Mrs. Pannikin seemed surprised. "Really? Well, she's quite right about her habit, Mr. Dordrecht. Artemis Colegrove invariably selected the most ridiculous of all our modern fashions. The hats just got bigger and bigger!"

"She wear straw hat that day."

Mrs. Pannikin shrugged. "Very odd. Not like her."

"I don't suppose you ever observed her with the sailor, Henry Tenkus, ma'am?"

"*Oof!*" she exclaimed. "I did! Twice—yes, twice—back in the spring, but after Aaron Colegrove had left for England, of course. Really! Entertaining a man so brazenly in the garden! And a frightening big ogre he was, too—not that *she* seemed scared of him. I wondered if he was her brother, but ... Leah found out from Calpurnia that he was no relation at all. I had no difficulty thinking *he* could have stabbed anyone!"

"It's proven beyond question that he was elsewhere that morning, ma'am!" I reiterated stubbornly.

"Well ..."

"Did you ever see Mrs. Colegrove with anyone else you didn't know? Any of the radical faction, perhaps?"

"Oh good heavens, even she had more sense than that! No. Perhaps she entertained in her parlor, but I never saw ... Well, there was that boy."

"A boy?"

"A little older than Oliver. Bright red hair! Middle of the summer. She took a turn around the garden with him once. And I thought I saw him again, not long before—you know—leaving the house, out front on Broadway."

"You've no idea—"

"Who the boy is? No."

For once, Mrs. Pannikin seemed as bereft of topics as I was. The girl lit a candle in the room, as it was getting dark early now. I stood up. "Mrs. Pannikin, I should be taking my leave. I thank you, you've been extremely helpful."

"Oh my goodness, sir! Nothing at all!"

I had another thought. "Oh. You know many of your neighbors, I take it. Do you know who owns number one-forty-six?"

"Oh, one-forty-six is empty, Mr. Dordrecht. Since last spring. The man who owns it was a merchant, but his business was ruined, he said, by the effects of the Sugar Act, and he has given up altogether and moved his family back to their farm out in Suffolk County. A particular friend of my husband's! His decision jarred everyone down at the Royal Exchange, I was told. Not having much luck selling the house, either, I'm afraid. Perhaps he's asking too much!"

But I could tell she was perfectly aware: no one was dreaming of buying a house in New York City as long as the Stamp Act controversy was coming to a head.

"There you are!" Adelie Glasby exclaimed, welcoming me into the Leaverings' house, two hours later. "Thanks to you, we three now know much, much more than we ever wanted to know about the tribe of Aaron Colegrove!"

She, Hermione Leavering, and Charles Cooper had clearly been enjoying themselves famously, collating on my behalf all the gossip ever breathed about one of New York's richest families. Benjamin Leavering had retired to his study, and John Glasby was at home in his, properly attending, as good businessmen should on Sunday evenings, to their devotions—or their ledgers.

The trio was quite merry from the effects of Madeira wine, which they immediately pressed upon me. Having just fastidiously partaken of a cold and chaste repast in my room, I readily agreed.

"Look at this, Thomas!" Adelie said, plunking down a sheet of paper after I'd taken my first sip. "We've mapped them out for you!"

"*Adelie* mapped them out for you!" Hermione and Charles insisted. "She's so clever!"

It took a moment even to begin to absorb the diagram, filled with two dozen Colegroves, five Boyces, and four DeLanceys. But it was well-organized to clarify the family relationships, and I would need to immerse myself in every detail. "Excellent! Really! Well ... what do we know about any of these folks?"

"Start at the beginning," Charles said. "We don't know anything of Aaron's parents, save that they were Baptists and had a small farm in Mamaroneck."

"Which Aaron expanded greatly, using Lavinia's money!" Adelie exclaimed.

"You're jumping the gun, Mrs. Glasby!" Charles declared with mock censoriousness. "Aaron has two surviving siblings—his elder sister Eudoxia, who lives with him, and a younger brother, Edward, who maintains the Mamaroneck property, which Aaron and Eudoxia now own entirely, because Edward gambled his share away many years ago. Edward, by the way, has a common-law wife and three grown children. His siblings disapproved of the wife because she has Indian blood.

"Aaron's first wife, Ruth," Charles continued, "was a Presbyterian, so Aaron converted for the first time. And shortly, they moved into the city and joined the congregation where my esteemed elder brother now presides with a heavy hand."

"Charles, do be serious!" Adelie teased.

"Right! The first-born, Lambert Colegrove, owns the Coxsackie Lumber Company, which is apparently completely independent of his father's enterprises. A stubborn fellow: when Aaron married Lavinia, he converted a second time, became Anglican—quite scandalous—but Lambert, then only sixteen, refused to go along, and still attends Henry's dreary sermons."

"He's a frequent client of *the firm*, Thomas!" Hermione observed significantly, "though Benjamin tells me he spreads his business among all the town's shippers."

"Including his father?"

"It appears there's no formal break between them," Charles said. "But no great love, either. He has his own family, and also gives some support to his sister—Miss Theodora—and his late brother's wife and children. Lives not far from here on Beaver Street."

"You know, I don't even know where Miss Theodora lives!"

"She lives with her sister-in-law, Irene Colegrove, the late army captain's widow. North Ward. She's the governess of their three younger children."

"Right. Do we know anything of the noble Captain William? I saw a most imposing portrait in his father's house."

The three of them smiled mischievously. "I got a story about him from a very soused veteran several years ago," Charles said. "This bloke had served under William Colegrove in Canada, and considered him the most monumental jackass he'd ever met. Colegrove had dueled with a fellow officer and actually killed the man, then feigned remorse with crocodile tears. On the eve of his last battle, outside Québec, he was blind drunk, walked out onto a redoubt to relieve himself, and caught a bullet in his extremely ample backside—as a result of which he was completely debilitated during the battle, and expired a hero's death from infection two days later."

"He died of a bullet to the arse?"

"A *great* tragedy, Thomas! It was the year George the Second died, and the veteran speculated that the king had succumbed to laughter … but the event was months too early for that."

We *had* to keep going. "Theodora's older sister?"

"Hulda MacGregor. Married, several children, lives up in White Plains, only sees the family on holidays."

"*Uh huh.* "Did Willett tell you I had an extremely odd encounter with Timothy Colegrove at his workshop? Just last Thursday."

"No."

"Willett is constructing some enormous wagon to be a float in the November first parade"—a knowing smile flashed between Charles and Adelie—"and Timothy Colegrove was there, supposedly helping him, but he was actually more of a hindrance."

"I *do not* trust that fellow!"

"Tried to badger me into joining the militia. I was ready to clobber him!"

Charles was abashed. "Well ... we—the Sons—*are* encouraging—"

"Well, once *you* join up, Charles, maybe then—"

"I have joined up, Thomas."

I was brought up short, trying to imagine my willowy cousin fumbling with a musket. "*Uhh* ... Oh! He nearly jumped when I asked him where he'd been when Artemis Colegrove was murdered. He said the Sons of Liberty were having a meeting at that exact hour?"

Charles suddenly glowered dangerously. "That's true, Thomas. But did Timothy Colegrove imply that he'd been present?"

"That was the impression."

Charles stared at me for a second. "Then he's *lying*, Thomas. He was not there that day!"

He seemed excessively certain—and there were serious implications. "Charles, with all due ... There were a lot of people at the meeting I attended, and couldn't you be—"

"There were barely a score at *that* meeting, Thomas, and I've been making it my business to keep track. That meeting was called on the fly—the news of Boston's second riot had just galloped in that morning."

The fact that Timothy Colegrove had prevaricated about his whereabouts at the critical time sobered us all. "I shall have to press him on this matter," I said grimly. We all nodded. "He voiced a theory—now I'm finding it even more dubious—that the murder may have been the work of the DeLancey faction, with the slogan posted in order to discredit the Sons of Liberty."

The ladies' jaws dropped as Charles shook his head. "You know I'm no great lover of the DeLanceys, Thomas. A pretty ruthless bunch, ready to stretch the law whenever it suits them! But murder? That's really preposterous." He pointed to Adelie's genealogical chart. "Half of these Colegroves *are* DeLanceys!"

"But," Adelie began almost reluctantly, "like everyone else in the city, the DeLanceys were infuriated by Aaron's marriage to Artemis. And perhaps ... humiliated?"

We all thought for a second. "No," Charles asserted. "Still too far-fetched!"

"*Um* ... let's go on. Why did you include this poor infant that died?"

"Oh, because it was a controversy at the time, Thomas," Charles continued. "She didn't die of smallpox like her mother, she survived until the middle of the winter. People at Henry's church contended—this really is no more than gossip—that Aaron and Lavinia had criminally neglected the babe. Just … thought you should know of it."

"Very well. So the smallpox epidemic of 'thirty-nine carried off Ruth Colegrove, and a year later Aaron married the recently-widowed Lavinia DeLancey Boyce. This is the DeLancey connection? Who was Bernard DeLancey? I don't think I've ever heard of him."

Charles chuckled. "There's a reason for that! But back up. The patriarch of the New York DeLanceys was Stephen, who fled France after the revocation of Protestant toleration, came here, married a Van Cortlandt, did quite well for himself, and sired an impressive brood. His father, meanwhile, who never left Europe, remarried after Stephen departed, and produced another son."

"Bernard?"

"The same. Bernard was a seafarer who also found Europe insupportable, and arrived here around seventeen-ought-eight, with a wife in tow, and knocked on his half-brother's door. Stephen took to him, and set him up as a privateer during Queen Anne's War. They both prospered, and soon Lavinia came into the world. Unfortunately, once peace broke out, Bernard—like his colleagues Kidd and Blackbeard—found it irresistible to continue plundering. He had successfully deposited the tainted winnings of two such endeavors with Stephen, when he was indicted for piracy. He absconded to avoid the noose, or perhaps in search of more booty … and went down in a hurricane. Stephen dutifully nurtured Lavinia's inheritance, and she was a very wealthy catch when she married Elisha Boyce."

"Those were the days!" Hermione sighed, surprising the rest of us. *Was she being ironic?*

Adelie explained that John Glasby had gotten their information on the Boyce family from a colleague in Albany. Elisha Boyce was a respected fur trader there, who kept his wife's inheritance intact for their children's sake. Visiting the city when the plague struck, he succumbed after a short illness, leaving Lavinia—and her mother, who never remarried—with four young children. So they returned here and again put themselves under DeLancey protection. "Then the widower Colegrove—who was doing well but not fabulously on his own—saw the glimmer of wealth and social connections through the widow Boyce, and pursued her relentlessly … until her half-uncle Stephen gave in, not long before he died in 'forty-one."

"How'd you learn all that?"

"Some of it we had directly from Lavinia, Thomas," Hermione explained. "Adelie and I knew her from church, of course, though neither of us knew her well. She was … not haughty, exactly, more … distant and self-absorbed."

"You couldn't hate the woman," Adelie said frankly, "but she wasn't easy to love, either."

"Now, I learned from a property broker's wife," Hermione continued, "that there was some wrangling about the living arrangements. Aaron had a small house on Dock Street, and Lavinia balked at moving in—until Aaron dispatched his four youngest children to Mamaroneck, to the care of their uncle and his woman. He promised to build a new house, but it took him five years to do it, and he didn't recall his older children once he'd finished it."

"He sent his own children away, in order to accommodate hers?"

"Yes. And by the time the new house was ready—this was in the middle of King George's War, and he was running privateers and supplying armies and raking in money—he and Lavinia by then had had four children together."

"So he never brought Hulda, Theodora, and Timothy back?"

"No. They grew to adulthood on the estate. He did expand the estate— but whether that was to enhance his children's comfort or to create an impression of being a land baron, people differ."

"*Ugh!*"

"Well, we've always known the man for a callous wretch," Charles said.

"I'm sure he has a raft of rationalizations. Men always do!" Adelie added, to Charles' and my discomfort.

"All right. The Boyce children?"

"All four are grown and married," Hermione said. "Theresa lives in Hackensack, Nathaniel is a sea captain—away most times—who keeps his family in Brooklyn, and Martha lives just up-river in Greenwich. Gideon Boyce is recently returned from his medical studies, and is living near the college."

"I've been trying to meet him. He was in the house both before and after Mrs. Colegrove was murdered."

"His wife is very sweet," Adelie observed. "But she says she has her hands full keeping him organized."

"And she's expecting!" Hermione added.

"*Hmph!* Now: the Aaron-Lavinia brood?"

"Golden boy James is still cowering in shame up in Westchester," Charles almost snarled. "Hasn't got the mettle to come back and make his public renunciation like all the others!"

"*Should* he be concerned?" Adelie asked.

"The only blokes who get tarred and feathered are the ones that insist that they can't abjure their sacred royal commissions, Adelie. 'Oh dear, how could I do that without His Gracious Majesty's express permission?' And yet his father did it for him before he put his foot down on New York soil, so I rather wonder if Mr. James Colegrove hasn't got other reasons to keep himself away from the city!"

"Are you suspicious of him, Thomas?" Hermione asked.

"Do you discount the idea that it might have been a sailor? Or a radical?" Adelie added. Charles snorted derisively, but she ignored him. "You seem to be concentrating on the Colegroves themselves!"

"I still have absolutely no opinion formed, as yet, Adelie. I'm just trying to absorb all the information I can, and … Let's go on. I understand 'sixty-three was a banner year for Colegrove marriages, notwithstanding Lavinia's death?"

"Oh yes," Hermione said. "It's all right there in the parish ledger. James was married in January, with great fanfare, though it was obvious to everyone that he was being pushed into it. Though the lass was rich as could be, she was eight years his senior."

"She has not seen fit to join her husband in his Mamaroneck exile," Charles observed archly. "Perhaps separation suits her well!"

"Lavinia Colegrove died in May, but her daughter Marguerite's wedding date had already been set, and they went through with it in July. They live in"—she checked her notes—"Pelham, Westchester County. Aaron, as you know, remarried in October, to everyone's scandalization. And the other twin, Prudence, married his new business partner, Caleb Lawson, in December."

"He has a partner? Since when?"

"Lawson's new to the city, Thomas," Charles said. "From Philadelphia. Former employee of Aldridge Brothers, which—surely you knew?—went bankrupt two years ago, after a certain scurrilous, defamatory poem appeared in Philadelphia newspapers alleging that Aldridge had a hand in Mr. Sproul's murder?" I had heard, and I knew that I was looking at the poem's author.

"And did you know that Samuel Low Aldridge is in debtor's prison?" Adelie asked, grinning.

"Justice—or Nemesis—has her way at last!" Hermione added with grim satisfaction. Evidently, she was now also a party to Charles' former secret pseudonym.

Though I didn't want to divert our conversation from the Colegroves, I had to admit I felt gratified that Aldridge and his firm had been punished; my own efforts to get John Tabor Kempe to investigate them had been in vain. "So … Lawson …?"

"Caleb Lawson was not implicated in the failure, but he quickly left Pennsylvania anyway, and Aaron Colegrove not only took him in as a partner, he gave him one of his daughters."

"And that was almost as scandalous as his own marriage," Adelie averred, "because Lawson is almost as old as Aaron, and Prudence is almost as young as Artemis!"

"And nearly as daft," Hermione added, "though it's said that she has the sense to be satisfied with her marriage from a mercenary point of view."

"They live near here—William Street," Charles observed. "Just had their first child."

"And what of Artemis herself?" I asked. "I did learn from Henry Tenkus that she has a sister named Peggy Mercer on Reade Street, but I haven't been able to locate her."

"Really!" Adelie exclaimed. "That's more than anyone else knows about her background, Thomas. She appeared *ex nihilo* on Aaron's arm in the summer, two years ago. I'm afraid that's all we could find."

"Her real name was Hattie, he said."

Their jaws dropped. "Aaron likes to impose new names on people," Charles said. "Look at the slaves."

Adelie suddenly grabbed up her chart and studied it. "My word! I didn't— Aaron and Lavinia's sons. Do their given names ring a bell?" Charles seemed to grasp what she was driving at; I didn't. "They're the same as those of the DeLancey men. His four sons were *named* to flatter the DeLanceys!"

We all shook our heads in wry amusement. A church sounded nine o'clock. I passed when offered another tot of Madeira. "I must leave you, dear Mrs. Leavering," I said. "Your husband will not forgive me if I oversleep tomorrow!"

"Oh now!"

"But this has been extraordinarily helpful, and I thank you enormously!" They looked at me expectantly. *"And* I have carefully made change." I distributed the money they had certainly earned.

"We're rich! We're rich!" Adelie joked.

"Shall I have the servants call milady's carriage?" Charles persisted.

"No, but you may walk me home."

"Can we do anything more for you, Thomas?" Hermione asked as we all stood up to leave.

"If you learn anything more— But please continue to maintain discretion. The Colegroves are a suspicious lot, and I'm having trouble enough talking to them as it is!"

"Do you feel any closer to—"

"A solution?" I shrugged. "It seems we're just beginning!"

We managed to complete the *Zephyr*'s cargo by October second, sending her off to Bristol almost on schedule. After we berthed the *Hermione L.* at Peck Slip in her stead, I had just a few moments to introduce myself to her crew and appreciate the newest of the firm's ships before Mr. Glasby cleared his throat and reminded us all that both *Hermione L.* and the *Maia* had to be off-loaded, re-loaded, documented, and dispatched in the next four weeks.

But time was allowed—by Mr. Leavering, again to John Glasby's dismay—for another gathering of the Sons of Liberty, at noon on Friday the fourth. I walked out of my way to refresh my memory of the three short blocks of Fletcher Street. Peter Colegrove's residence was the only remaining house, a tiny, old wooden domicile in a faceless warehousing area—just enough for a thrifty bachelor, I thought grimly. The barman at the smelly corner dive said he had no idea who lived there, and was rather surprised to think that anyone resided in this busy neighborhood of transient seamen and stevedores.

I gave up hope of confirming his schedule and hurried off to the radical conclave. The tavern was even more tightly packed with people than the preceding meeting had been. Once I had squeezed myself inside, it was barely possible to turn around, much less carry on a conversation. I waved to Marinus, but couldn't even find Mapes or my cousin Charles.

The Sons were adopting a watch and wait stance with regard to the congress that was to commence the following week. The delegates from far-off South Carolina had already arrived and been feted by some of our wealthier adherents. No great hope was held out for the congress by Mr. Sears; he asserted that even our own province's delegates were known to be lamentably cautious men. In mitigation, he argued that the mere fact that nine colonies had united to send delegates was at least a sign of the seriousness with which all America was confronting the Stamp Act.

Mr. Lamb took the floor to urge all men who could afford it to acquire the franchise for themselves, in order to boost the vote of the liberty faction in all future elections. And no sooner was he done with this irritating admonition than he commenced berating those of us who had evaded the militia to do our supposed duty and join it.

Sears announced that it was known that English ships bearing stamped paper were presently *en route* to the seaports of America, and debate was afoot everywhere regarding what to do with the stamps once they arrived. "The governor's plan," he said, "is to store the stamps within the fort, and to—"

"Torch the ships!" a man shouted. "Torch them the instant they drop anchor!"

"*Before* they drop anchor!" another called. Was that— Yes, it was Timothy Colegrove's voice.

A full minute of roaring and screaming ensued before Sears regained control of the meeting. "My friends," he said, "we strongly recommend against any insult to His Majesty's navy or any private shipping, which would be counter-productive in the extreme. Rather, we hope to organize a watch along the shore to prevent the stamps from being landed. We want them sent back to Whitehall—and distributed among the poor for use as the coming winter's firewood!"

That merited some laughter and applause.

"Navy will load their guns with grapeshot!" one man bellowed.

"They wouldn't dare fire on British subjects!" another rejoined.

"What makes you think they wouldn't?" others challenged.

It was another moment before Sears recaptured his audience. I got the impression he was assessing the mood of his listeners, deliberately allowing the chaotic screaming to play itself out. "We are taking all methods of protest under advisement," he said, finally, "and hope that we can unite with one voice to demand that the tax will not be implemented and the Act will be repealed. Until then, we beg all citizens to prepare themselves for whatever eventualities may come to pass."

With a few more announcements, the meeting was adjourned. The tide of humanity exiting the tavern was irresistible, and I soon found myself standing in the middle of Broadway, where all traffic was obviously going to remain at a standstill until the crowd cleared. I heard, and then saw, Timothy Colegrove arguing and gesticulating on the far curb. I crossed toward him, thinking no time would be better than the present.

The portly man he was haranguing was wide-eyed, open-mouthed, and speechless.

I interrupted the firebrand to request a private word.

"No! Can't you see I'm—" But his victim had absconded. "What the devil do you want, Dordrecht?"

I looked him in the eye and waited a few seconds for his breathing to calm. "Why did you lie to me, Colegrove?"

He flushed angrily. "Who the hell do you think you are? I *didn't* lie to—"

"You said you were in a meeting of the Sons of Liberty at the moment your father's wife was murdered. Now I happen to know—"

"I never said that! I never said that!"

"You most clearly and definitely implied it, Mr. Colegrove! And I have it on good authority that—"

"I never said it. You're making this up!"

"Well, then let's return to the original question. Where *were* you during the hour that Mrs. Colegrove met her end?"

"Are you suggesting— Don't be absurd, Dordrecht! I had no reason to attack the fool woman. Just because she infuriated the whole city by telling anyone who'd listen that the Sons of Liberty should be stamped out ... You've got some nerve—"

"Your sister has asked me—"

"And Theodora's a fool too!"

"*Where were you* at that hour, Mr. Colegrove?"

"I wasn't killing the bitch, Dordrecht!" he nearly shouted, drawing stares. "But where I *was* is none of your goddamn business!"

And with that, he turned his back and stomped away, leaving me both dazed and furious.

"What'd he have to say?"

I whirled about. Charles Cooper had come up behind me. "He insisted he'd never said he was at the meeting in so many words, he avowed he didn't murder her, and he nevertheless refused to tell me where he had been."

"*Whew!*"

"A murder inquiry is not important enough, I suppose!"

"I don't like it, Thomas." He kicked an apple core into the curb, where the sweepers might more easily get it. "I'll find out. He's angling for a position on the operations committee …"

"You don't want that?"

"Correct. I don't."

The churches chimed one o'clock as we held each other's gaze. I made my excuses, and hustled back to Peck Slip to join the afternoon's exertions despite an empty stomach.

CHAPTER 7

IMMEDIATELY AFTER SUNDAY DINNER, I presented myself at the college—only to learn that Dr. Gideon Boyce was again unavailable, despite having promised the appointment. His hastily scrawled note explained that he'd been called to set a roofer's broken leg across the East River in the town of Brooklyn, and I had to concede that such an emergency would trump my request. He added that he didn't really see what help he could be, but if I still desired to meet him, we could try again the following week.

However unavoidable, the frustration was immense. I would have to shift myself somehow for two fruitless hours awaiting the meeting Theodora Colegrove had arranged for me with her aunt Eudoxia and with Colegrove's slaves, who I was determined to interview in greater depth, no matter how unpleasant it might prove. My client was maddeningly insistent the slaves could only be queried in Miss Eudoxia's presence, and the appointment could not be arranged earlier than the completion of that lady's regular afternoon nap.

Without much internal debate, I set off on a walk along the Hudson shoreline, of which I'd seen little since my return, my business being largely on the East River. It brightened my mood a trifle to see that gold and russet leaves had begun to appear in profusion on the trees in New Jersey. I faced up to the personal quandaries I'd been avoiding: should I apply for a freemanship; and more importantly, should I rejoin the militia? I had no great desire to do either, given my distaste for political life and for regimentation, but I knew I couldn't postpone the militia service indefinitely. It seemed obvious that the Sons of Liberty would be looking to the militia to ignore Governor Colden and to stand fast on the shore to prevent the stamps from ever being landed. And I had to agree that the best thing would be for the stamps to be refused and sent straight back whence they came. But then, the militia would practice at interminable length, and would perpetually be called out to quell our town's ceaseless rioting. Every last bone of public contention—from Romanists to Methodists, from paper currency to idle soldiers taking longshoremen's work, from free blacks to loose women—all occasioned raucous public tumults that dragged the militiamen out at all hours.

But could any of this really be avoided? Not unless I cared to live as a vagrant! *So get on with it, Thomas, and stop puling!*

While on personal quandaries, what of even larger issues? How was I to get a start in my chosen career, when the government seemed determined to crush all American enterprise? How could I even think of marriage and a family when my prospects were so shaky?

I had to admit that Élise Colegrove had turned my eye, for a while— for quite a while. But even apart from her unbearable father, who would surely forbid the likes of me from courting her anyway, I sensed a sad vapidity in the lass that would be hard to endure.

Barring a fluke encounter with the perfect bride, marriage and a family would simply have to wait.

Distant church bells and the realization that I was well past the foundry and nearing Greenwich Village prompted me to reverse my heading. And when a sudden gust of wind swirled fallen leaves about me, I turned my thoughts back to the Colegrove case.

Adelie Glasby was right that I appeared to be concentrating suspicion on the Colegrove family members. The inescapable fact was that the crime could not have been safely committed without detailed knowledge of the house and intimate awareness of its inhabitants' schedules.

Except …that it could have been a true crime of passion, in which case the murderer would have been careless of the consequences. Perhaps he escaped immediate apprehension only through extraordinary luck?

But the mere fact that a slogan had been posted argued against that, against any impulsive crime, in favor of pre-meditation. And it was surely apparent that those who possessed familiarity with the house also possessed violent emotions regarding Artemis Colegrove.

If the murderer had any political motivation—whether partisan to the radical or the DeLancey faction—he also had to know the household.

He could not have been a total stranger if he hoped to escape punishment.

He? Could a female not have wielded the knife? Horrible to contemplate—yet why any more horrible than a man so engaged?

But the ultimate imponderable always nagged: if she was being attacked with a knife, why didn't she scream?

———◇———

"You're late!" Miss Eudoxia Colegrove accused venomously. I held her gaze, disdaining to apologize, given that the bells had rung not five minutes before. "Since you were tardy, I dismissed the servants to return to their duties."

"Ma'am—"

"We cannot afford to have them lolling about in idleness, Mr. Dordrecht, and any questions you may have for them, I'm sure I can answer!"

Standing in the doorway, she also seemed determined even to prevent my entry into the house; after two more seconds of silent scowling, she finally moved aside to allow me to pass. "Miss Colegrove, I'm afraid that will not serve at all. Please ask them to join us at their earliest opportunity."

"They are busy with important projects, and—"

"Meanwhile, I should like to speak with Mrs. Jacqueline DeLancey."

"Mrs. DeLancey saw nothing of the event. She was bed-ridden that day."

"Nonetheless ..."

She exhaled with an emphatic shake of the head, which I ignored. "In that case, we must repair to the upstairs sitting room. She is not at the moment disposed to come down."

"Very well. And please remind your servants!"

She went back to the kitchen door, where I cynically guessed she was telling the slaves to delay their appearance as long as possible. While waiting, I had to suppress a smile as I again contemplated the bombastic portrait of the late Captain William.

"If you'll follow me!" she ordered, stepping up without looking back. "Mrs. DeLancey!" she called, nearing the second floor. "This fellow of Theodora's, to whom my brother has immoderately given the run of the house, insists on speaking with you."

"Indeed!" was the soft response, which was tinged with a French accent.

I gained the floor, turned, and beheld an attractive, open area with two windows facing Broadway, where sunshine was still pouring through. Two settees were placed against the opposite walls, and on the one to my right was a woman just a few years older than Eudoxia Colegrove, but otherwise quite a contrast to her. Where Theodora's aunt was large, loud, and hardy, Mrs. DeLancey was petite, soft, and slight. Miss Eudoxia was austerely dressed in black; Mrs. DeLancey was swaddled in pink satin. It occurred to me that she might once have been pretty—unlike Miss Eudoxia—but there was a disconcertingly predatory aspect to her visage that reminded me that it was a pirate's loot that had sustained her through half a century of indolent widowhood.

I walked over and bowed, to present myself. "Thomas Dordrecht, your servant, Mrs. DeLancey."

The brown and white canine in her lap—a King Charles spaniel—growled softly. "Ah yes. Please don't mind Augusta, Mr. Dordrecht, she doesn't take kindly to any disruption of her routine, silly thing!"

I somehow wondered if the little beast's snarls were the point, particularly when Miss Eudoxia sat on the other couch, and the white cat sleeping there awoke, saw me, arched its back and hissed.

"Stop that, Regina!" Miss Eudoxia said—while indulgently scratching its ears. She then picked up a knitting project and resumed work upon it.

With four pairs of eyes regarding me malevolently, I searched out a chair and sat without asking permission. "Mrs. DeLancey," I began directly, "it has been established that Mrs. Colegrove left the house for at least two hours on the morning she was murdered. Would you have any idea what her mission was?"

"None at all, sir. Mrs. Colegrove and I were never on intimate terms."

"She replaced Mrs. DeLancey's daughter, you see, after she died two and a half years ago," the other asserted, unasked.

"*Thank you*, Miss Colegrove," the older woman said acidly. "But I'm sure the gentleman is already aware of this!"

Eudoxia Colegrove shrugged indifferently and attended to her knitting. The two animals glared at me.

"When was the last time you saw Mrs. Colegrove, ma'am?"

"It had been some time, sir. I had been ill near a week, and had not left my bedroom."

"Mrs. Colegrove had not visited, to ensure your needs were attended to?"

"*Hah!*" both women exclaimed derisively. Then they scowled at each other.

The two slaves—Calpurnia and a short, slight old fellow dressed fantastically in dark blue velvet finery with a white wig—Caesar, I inferred—appeared and stood nervously at the top of the stairs. The women ignored them.

"My grandchildren saw to my wants, Mr. Dordrecht."

With some occasional assistance from the slaves, I'll venture!

"I did, however, catch a glimpse of her, the evening before. She was running about hysterically, after that sailor left, and I saw her here in the hall."

"What appeared to have upset her?"

The front door slammed, below. "I'm home!" trilled a loud, falsetto male voice. "Oh heavens, where *is* everybody?" Oliver Colegrove's grandmother and aunt both rolled their eyes and sighed.

"The girl was terrified of him, obviously!"

"How long did she remain in distress?"

"*Eh?* It seemed like hours! I finally—"

There was a piercing shriek from the kitchen area, below. Alarmed, I stood up.

"Don't concern yourself, Mr. Dordrecht," Eudoxia Colegrove said. The screaming continued. "My brother will take care of it."

"I finally—"

The screams continued, preventing all conversation. We heard a chair rumbling across a floor, a door being thrown open, and Aaron Colegrove bellowing, "Oliver, what the hell is the matter with you?"

More screams. We all stood immobile.

"Will you shut it? What ..." Two seconds passed in silence. "Oh, Christ!" Two more seconds. "Oh, Jesus Christ! Where's Calpurnia?" he roared.

The two slaves began shaking violently and backed up against the wall.

"She's up here, Aaron," Eudoxia called.

He thundered up the stairs, followed by the blubbering Oliver. "What the devil is *this?*" he demanded, seeing the slaves. He thrust forward an object in his right hand.

A voodoo doll. A blonde female voodoo doll in a white satin dress, with a dozen straight pins protruding from it. I wondered if it weren't also a pin cushion. Calpurnia shrieked and collapsed, wailing, onto the floor. Caesar knelt protectively over her.

"*She* did it?" Miss Eudoxia breathed, seemingly confounded.

"What in blazes is this, Calpurnia? Did you kill her? Did you murder my—" He noticed me. "*You're* here! Well, goody goody! Fine help you've been! We've got the culprit right here, no thanks to you!"

"Lord Jesus, have mercy on this sinner," Calpurnia was moaning repeatedly.

"Oliver! Pull yourself together and go fetch the constable!"

"But Father, really, I—"

"Do as I say, damn it!"

With an excess of fuss, Oliver backed down the stairs and left the house.

"You'll swing for this, wench!"

"Lord Jesus, have mercy!"

"She don't do that, Massa!" Caesar whimpered. "She can't do that. She can't!"

"Shut your trap, you old fool!" Colegrove gave him a shove that sent him sprawling. "God damn you, bitch!" he yelled at her, raising his hand.

"Maybe ..." I began, moving closer in the hope of discouraging him. "Maybe we can talk through the happenings of that hour, and see if it's plausible that she could have done it." I didn't have much hope for that, but ... anything to stall him.

"Lord Jesus, have mercy!"

Colegrove had the doll in his right hand and the slave woman's wrist in his left. "What d'you mean?" he demanded. He twisted her arm again, prompting a shriek.

"There was a delivery. She took a delivery of something Caesar had purchased at the market, at eleven forty-five."

"So?"

"Who made the delivery? Let her talk, let her talk!"

"It be from Martin's," Caesar said.

"Martin's, on Stone Street?" I asked. Old Mr. Martin was a personal friend, though I was currently shopping nearer to my boarding. "Who made the delivery? Was it the boy, Willie?"

"Boy," she whispered, seconds later. She was frightened half out of her wits.

"Martin's great-nephew," I explained. "I'll query him."

"Why?" Colegrove groused.

"What had you been doing when the boy hammered the back gate, Calpurnia?" She howled as Colegrove twisted the arm harder. "She can't think straight when you do that, Mr. Colegrove!"

Somehow, Colegrove saw my reasoning—probably because he realized he was in the process of wrecking his chattel property. Eudoxia shoved the chair I'd used behind him and ordered him to sit.

"Calpurnia! What had you been doing? Everybody remembers the details of a day of such upheaval. What were you doing?"

"I washing window."

"Which window?"

"Parlor. Ballroom."

I looked to the two ladies for confirmation. "That … does make sense," Eudoxia Colegrove said. "I'd instructed her to do them as I left for tea with Mrs. Colden. Plus the pier mirrors."

"How long does this chore usually take?"

"Well … she's not the speediest. An hour and a half? I … saw her on the ladder in the ballroom when I returned."

"Around ten minutes past noon, according to your testimony?" She nodded, looking startled at my recollection. "And … had the windows and mirrors been cleaned?"

"Yes. Well, not to my perfect satisfaction, of course, but as well as she ever manages."

"But she'd have had all morning to do it, Dordrecht!" Aaron Colegrove objected.

"I was told she was waiting on Dr. Boyce while he was attending to Mrs. DeLancey, sir."

"Yes," said the latter. "He wanted her standing by in case he needed anything. There was no one else in the house at the time. Except Oliver, but, *um* …"

"So she was with you, the whole time Dr. Boyce was here?"

"No. He had her fetch water and a towel, but she came right back. Then she took the blood away. I can't bear to look at it!"

"Did she again return?"

"Oh yes. And stayed until after he left. He had to be at the college in time for his lecture."

"At eleven o'clock? So he would have left the house by about ten to?"

Mrs. DeLancey nodded. "Did anyone else see you at work that morning, Calpurnia?"

At first she shook her head. Then: "Leah!"

"Who the hell's Leah?" Colegrove demanded.

"The slave girl next door," I replied—startling them all.

"Oh well ... a slave girl."

"Miss Agnes!" Calpurnia exclaimed. "She wave."

"When would—"

"Agnes usually gets back for dinner before Élise does. Right around noon," Mrs. DeLancey said.

"I see. I don't calculate much time unaccounted for."

Mrs. DeLancey looked especially disconsolate at that. "Well, but the windows weren't *finished!*"

"They had it all cleared away before we sat down for dinner," Miss Colegrove asserted. "And come to think of it, she helped me change for dinner as soon as I got in."

Colegrove angrily shook his head—and the doll. "Well, but what the devil is *this?*"

Mrs. DeLancey quivered with repugnance. "She made it happen even if she didn't do it herself! She wished it! She conjured it! *Elle est une sorcière!*"

"Lord Jesus, forgive!"

"Sois maudite, damnée!"

The dainty old lady was surely working herself into a state. At that moment, as Colegrove was trying to calm her, Oliver returned and he and the constable noisily tromped up the stairs.

"This the one?" the constable, a hulking, ill-groomed oaf, immediately demanded, grabbing the still quivering slave woman roughly by the back of the neck.

"No!" Caesar cried. But the constable shoved him aside, again knocking him down.

"Come along, you!"

"Wait! *Wait!*" I cried—and somehow, they all actually froze. "Mr. Colegrove, this is just too ... She couldn't possibly have done the deed herself, and ... and nobody will convict even a slave of witchcraft in our enlightened age. It's—"

"Lock her up, and we'll think about it!" Colegrove decreed.

Oh wisdom of Solomon! crossed my mind.

"Lord Jesus, have mercy!" she wailed as the constable forced her down the stairs. Caesar picked himself up slowly and stumbled miserably after them, without asking leave—but without objection.

"*Damnée!*" Mrs. DeLancey breathed, clutching the spaniel tightly.

"Perhaps if I looked around in their quarters, Mr. Colegrove, I might—"

"You want to go down into the *basement?*" he cried in disbelief.

"I might be able to find evidence to … support or refute the contention."

He stared dumbly for a second. "Do what you please!"

I pulled Oliver Colegrove after me as I walked down. We heard his aunt blandly saying, "You really do need to get a more competent one anyway, Aaron!"

"Oh this is so, so terrible!" Oliver Colegrove whined. "Witchcraft in our own—"

"Had you ever seen that doll before, Mr. Colegrove?"

He dried up. "No, never. Never! Evil thing! And she was always a sweet slave, so devoted to us, Mr.— Sir Thomas."

"'Mr. Dordrecht' will be quite sufficient, thank you. Can you show me where you discovered it just now?"

"Oh I can't bear to look, to think of that hideous object!"

"The doll is still upstairs, Mr. Colegrove." He stood irresolute in the hallway. "Where did you go after you entered the house?"

"Oh, very well! I went back here, to the kitchen, in search of a snack." He led me there, opened the pantry door, and pointed to a stoneware canister. Among the aromas of the pantry was a pleasant whiff of recently baked molasses cookies.

I noticed a lid on the floor. "Is that the top?"

"Oh! Yes. I dropped it, in my distress. I—" He bent over to retrieve the lid—a dutiful action I'd bet was not characteristic of him.

"Are you partial to the cookies, Mr. Colegrove?"

"Oh yes. Calpurnia is an excellent baker. She …" He trailed off, working up a spasm of tears.

"She knows, I daresay, that you are wont to avail yourself of the supply in the larder?"

"She is so forward as to affect being cross with me. Saucy wench! Do you think they'll whip her?"

"If she's convicted of murder, she'll be *hanged*, Mr. Colegrove!"

He wailed and collapsed into a chair.

"When did you last investigate the jar, Mr. Colegrove?"

He shook himself from a brief reverie. "Oh … well, just before I went out, after dinner. Lord Ramsay and I perambulated—"

"Just three or four hours ago?" He nodded. "And of course, there was no doll there then?"

"No!" He appeared thunderstruck.

"Who in the house—besides the slave woman—is aware of your partiality for cookies, Mr. Colegrove?"

"Oh everyone, Sir … *uh*, sir. *Grandmère* upbraided me just the other day. She thinks it's uncouth."

"I see." Obviously, no one with any sense would imagine that the cookie jar was a good place to hide *anything* from the most unstable and demonstrative member of the household. Yet someone had. "Will you show me about the basement, please?"

"Oh no! Surely you don't want— I never go down there, Mr. Dordrecht!"

Caesar had been hovering morosely at the kitchen door, looking like a man in shock. Oliver Colegrove imperiously ordered him to show me the way, carefully inspected the cookie jar, claimed another one, and started back upstairs without another word.

The distraught slave obeyed without any indication that he even understood who I was. Reaching the cement floor, I could see that the basement was a large single room divided only by the posts supporting the house's main beams. Caesar was short enough that the beams didn't trouble him, but I could only stand upright in between them. A dim, late afternoon light was coming from the front window, roughly at the sidewalk level. The floor was cluttered—much like my family's cellar—with disorderly piles of cordwood, coal, sacks of potatoes and provisions, old furniture, and so forth. I cautiously moved toward the street end, where the slaves had carved out a section for themselves.

The bed, which sagged terribly in the middle, was neatly made. A few hooks supported their alternate garments. A rough set of shelves held tools and grooming implements. A poor abode, but probably better protected from the elements than those of most in the slave quarter of New Utrecht. "Do the family ever come down here?" I asked. He shrugged. With the beam in my way, I was unsure whether he shook his head.

On the top shelf, I noticed a box with some cloth remnants spilling out of it. Caesar winced when I pulled it out. It contained several scraps of cloth, a scissors, a few threads, needles, straight pins, a thimble … but no pin cushion. "Calpurnia sews for the family?" Again, just a nod. I rummaged in it a bit more and, to my surprise, uncovered a book. Caesar now looked even more dismayed. I took it next to the window. It was *Robinson Crusoe.* The bookplate inside proclaimed it belonged to the library of Herbert Pannikin.

The normal reckoning—my own first assumption, instantly—would be that the book had been stolen, in the hope of gain from its resale. But … even an illiterate slave would understand that the bookplate would betray a theft. Could it have been purloined as some sort of revenge? To cover some unrelated error? By accident? "Can you account for this, Caesar?" I asked.

"No. No. No." He was moaning incoherently. "All wrong, all wrong."

I recollected that Mrs. Pannikin lent books to Agnes Colegrove, the youngest of Aaron's offspring. "Is Miss Agnes present in the house this afternoon?"

It seemed to rally him. "Room. Upstairs," he managed.

Remarkable that the child had stayed put in her bedroom through all the recent commotion!

Taking the book, I turned to leave, but recalled another query. "What other errands did you have on that morning, Caesar?"

He rallied a bit more, while clearly wishing me gone. "Horses. I walk horses."

"Mr. Colegrove keeps horses in town? Where? At Central Stables?" The best-regarded stables were just east of the house, at the bottom of the slope.

He grunted affirmatively.

"How many? Two?" Another nod. "I reckon they weren't getting much exercise, with Mr. Colegrove away?" A nod. "How often do you walk them? Daily?"

Caesar shook his head. "Four."

"Four mornings a week? Where do you take them?"

"Out of town." He rummaged through some tools and produced an official paper that constituted a pass, verifying his authorization to walk two horses on Monday, Wednesday, Friday, and Saturday mornings. "Sometime far as Bowery."

The Stuyvesant property—about two miles away. "How long—"

"That day, too hot for horses. Cut short. Back by eleven."

I wondered if the stables kept records of such matters. "Did you return to the house at that point?"

"No. Store."

"Martin's?" A nod. "How often do you shop there?"

"Much."

Right. It all makes sense, and he seems as ingenuous as any slave I've ever met, but … *to be verified.* "Thank you, then, Caesar." I turned and began walking back toward the stairs. I heard him sink onto the bed, groan, and begin weeping.

I turned back. His face was in his hands. I cleared my throat, and he gasped, looking up. "I … don't think they'll harm her, Caesar," I said, truthfully. But as soon as I said it, I realized I meant I didn't think they'd *hang* her. He stared blankly past me. After another two hapless seconds, I retreated.

As I arrived back on the second floor, four pairs of eyes again regarded me venomously. "Ladies, I desire now to converse with Miss Agnes Colegrove, who I understand is—"

"Agnes is only a child, Mr. Dordrecht!" Eudoxia Colegrove immediately objected. "It is quite preposterous for you to—"

"She can perhaps confirm or deny the slave's assertion that she was occupied in the front of the house at noon."

Mrs. DeLancey shrugged dismissively. Miss Eudoxia seemed mightily irritated—but not so irritated as to rise and disrupt the cat, now settled in her lap. "Ohh … the second door on the left … if you must."

Now I was flummoxed, not expecting to interview a young girl in the absence of a chaperone. But time was wasting and heaven knew her father, brother, and formidable aunt were all within call. I walked around to the girl's door and knocked.

After waiting ten seconds I knocked again. Presently, I heard something being kicked away from the bottom of the door, which then opened to reveal a lanky, toothy, freckle-faced young girl who shyly regarded me with widened eyes. She perhaps resembled Miss Theodora more than Miss Élise, but she seemed strangely more self-possessed than either. "Yes?" she squeaked.

I was befuddled by the closeness of the room—the window was shut tight and a blanket had been pushed to the side of the door. "Miss Agnes?"

"Yes. I'm sorry I didn't respond at first, sir. I get caught up in my reading."

A child after my own heart! "I quite understand."

"When my brother starts carrying on, I barricade myself in so I can concentrate."

She hadn't heard any of the tumult in the sitting area! I quickly resolved at least to delay telling her. Trying to appear more at ease than I felt, I introduced myself and stated my overall errand. She had heard of Theodora's commission, fortunately, and indicated that I might sit on one of the two beds that occupied the narrow room; she sat on the other, opposite me. I left the door cracked open a good six inches—to circulate some air as much as to preserve respectability. I was bemused again when I noticed the book she'd placed open, face-down, on her side table: *Fatal Friendship*, by Catharine Trotter. Not one I'd read, but I knew it dealt with a subject matter usually deemed wholly inappropriate for twelve-year-olds.

"I don't want to take much of your time, Miss," I said awkwardly, recalling that I'd wanted to direct the same questions to her that I'd posed to the others—but the plight of the slaves was preoccupying me. I produced the copy of *Robinson Crusoe*. "Do you have any idea how this book came to be among the slaves' things?"

The lass was neither surprised nor alarmed. "Oh yes! But … you're not thinking … She didn't steal it, sir. I … lent it to her." I'm sure my confusion now had to be plain on my face. "Mrs. Pannikin lent it to me. I read it and lent it to Calpurnia."

"Really? Then Calpurnia is able to read?"

She brightened considerably. "Oh yes. I taught her!" I was stupefied, and she blushed, realizing she'd said too much. "She didn't want anyone else to know, but she loved it so terribly, I couldn't deny her! I borrow books from our dear neighbor, I read them quickly, pass them to Calpurnia, and we always get them returned in good time!"

"I … see." Briefly speechless, I put *Robinson Crusoe* on her table. "I'll leave this here then."

"Thank you."

"Miss," I whispered, "I'd not be so forward as to say I disapprove—I don't—but it's only right to warn you that many do disapprove. When I was about your age, my mother got embroiled in a great controversy in my home town for teaching slaves to read. You'll want to be very careful!"

"You won't tell my aunt or my father, sir? Or *Grandmère*?"

"No, no. *Um*, where was I? Oh: did you teach her any writing?"

"No. We only got started this past spring, after Father went to England."

I was thinking of the handwritten slogan. "Does Caesar know how to read or write?"

"Not that I'm aware, sir."

Unless his woman taught him? In the few weeks since she'd learned to read? *No, no—preposterous.* "You remember, specifically, about the day that Mrs. Colegrove was murdered, Miss?"

"Oh yes."

"Had you seen her that morning?"

"No, sir. Élise and I were off to school, before—" Faintly, we heard a knock on the front door, below. Someone was admitted. "Before she was up and about. We very seldom saw her in the mornings."

"Calpurnia asserted that you waved to her that day, while she was working, as you returned home for dinner. Is that so?"

Her intelligent eyes registered confusion regarding the relevance of the question, but a readiness to humor me. "Oh yes. I remember seeing her through the ballroom window, high up on the ladder. I was afraid she might fall."

"About what time of day was that, Miss? I'm trying to pinpoint the sequence of events very precisely."

"Oh, I see! Well, it would have been just after noon, as usual."

Feminine voices were suddenly raised in the sitting area. "And you *let* him?" one howled.

"I remember being startled when I saw Calpurnia, because I'd just waved at my brother, who was walking up Broadway, but he didn't see me, and—"

Theodora Colegrove burst into the room, her face scarlet. "Mr. Dordrecht, this is outrageous! How can you even *think* of sitting alone in a room with a young lass?" She rushed to Miss Agnes' side and embraced her protectively. "Are you all right, child?"

"I'm fine, Theodora!" the girl said, plainly shaken by her sister's alarm. "Fine."

My client glowered at me. "It's getting dark, and you have the *nerve* to—" She embraced the girl again—rather too fiercely for the latter's taste, I thought. "Wait for me downstairs in the parlor, Mr. Dordrecht! It's time we caught up. If this is all you've accomplished, I really don't know!"

Obviously, my interview was finished. "Thank you for your time, Miss Agnes!" I pulled the door closed as I left.

The two elderly ladies pointedly ignored me as I passed to the staircase, but the dog and the cat glared vindictively.

I saw Caesar at the bottom of the stairs, leaving the office with a lit taper, and asked him to light the candles in the parlor. Staring out at the late afternoon traffic on Broadway, I had a moment to reflect on how remote the various family members seemed from each other: despite all Miss Theodora's rumpus, Oliver had stayed unperturbed in his room, and Aaron Colegrove had not budged from his study.

No sooner had I sat down, than the front door opened, and Miss Élise and another young lass walked in. I came to the hall and bowed, grinning—no doubt idiotically.

"Oh, it's you," she said with perfect indifference. She took her friend's arm and the two hastened up the stairs in a great rustle of silk. The portrait of the so-heroic Captain William seemed to be pointing at me derisively. Much deflated, I resumed my wait.

Three minutes later, Miss Theodora stormed into the parlor and slammed the door behind her. "A fine thing, this, Mr. Dordrecht! Molesting an innocent maiden in her bedroom! For shame, sir! If you are impervious to religion, surely common decency would—"

Whether she was retaining me or not, this was entirely too much, and I struck blindly back. "Madam, I *trust* you noticed the door was ajar, I *trust* you perceived the lass was in no distress, I *trust* you understand that her aunt and grandmother were within call and had given me permission, and that her male relatives were within easy shouting—"

"It *will not do*, Mr. Dordrecht! I asked you specifically to avoid disrupting the household, and yet you—"

"Your primary goal, as I understood it, Miss Colegrove, was to determine who murdered your stepmother, and every action I have taken has been directed to that end, including those taken today. Now if you wish to cancel our arrangement, I am prepared to return half of the money you have given me, and—"

That seemed to shake her resolve to berate me. "Oh. Oh … no," she said irritably, "but I do wish that you would refrain— Why could you not have interviewed Agnes in front of her aunt and grandmother?"

"I had frankly expected that they would insist on it, Miss Colegrove. When they did not, I was rather glad, because the lass would never have spoken so freely in their presence."

"Agnes is too young to be speaking *freely* at all!"

"And how, then, are we to learn whatever facts she alone may be able to point out? Have you been acquainted with what happened here but an hour ago?" She was not, so I related the incident of the slavewoman's voodoo doll.

She seemed deeply rattled. "Calpurnia? Do you think—"

"I find it very doubtful that she could have murdered Mrs. Colegrove, ma'am, though I need some corroboration to be sure. I … hope to interview another person this afternoon, as a matter—"

"Not here, I hope!"

My welcome was unquestionably worn out for the day. "No." She sat down, finally, and I followed. "If you're concerned for the child's welfare, Miss Colegrove, you may want to tell her gently about the slave's arrest. I have reason to think the news will distress her."

"About Calpurnia?"

"Yes." She appeared to be considering it. "And if you're willing, Miss Colegrove, you might also be able to check one item regarding the case for me. That would spare my Sunday time next week!"

She was intrigued. "What's that?"

"Your father has two horses at the Central Stables. Caesar asserts that he walked them that morning, following a regular pattern, but that he returned them earlier than usual, at eleven o'clock, at which time he went directly to Martin's Grocery on Stone Street. I plan to visit the grocery, but the stables are surely already closed."

"I see. And you want—"

"Simple verification, without prejudice, in as much detail as possible."

"I see. Very well." She paused. "But I'm upset that you have not been responding to my letters, sir!"

"Ma'am, I'm sorry, but I simply do not have the hours in a day to conduct an epistolary correspondence!" She smirked at my big word. "I'm afraid there's one other matter, regarding which I'd appreciate your assistance. Your brother Timothy—"

"Oh no!"

"I have encountered him twice in the past fortnight, and—"

"More than I have!"

"And I've queried him regarding his whereabouts at the hour of Mrs. Colegrove's murder."

She froze. "Yes?"

"On the first occasion, he clearly insinuated that he'd been present at a meeting of the Sons of Liberty, which I've since learned was simply untrue." She moaned. "More recently, I confronted him with this lie, and he starkly refused to explain himself. Perhaps you might—"

"I don't even know where he's living, Mr. Dordrecht," she sighed bitterly. "Should I see him, I'll of course learn what I can."

"Excellent." I paused, hoping we were finished. "Now, if you'll excuse me ..."

"Have we made any progress at all, Mr. Dordrecht? I had hoped—"

"Miss Colegrove, we have made progress, it's just ... not visible." An analogy occurred to me. "When you cross the ocean, ma'am, the sea looks much the same whether you're fifty miles from America or fifty miles from Ireland. Only your navigator's daily calculations tell you you're making progress, but finally you discover yourself on another continent."

She shuddered. "It must be very ... hard."

"It is." Particularly on days when the navigator determines that you've gone *backward*. "But we persevere!"

"Yes." We shook hands and parted.

As I walked down Broadway toward Martin's grocery, smarting from Miss Theodora's disapproval and Miss Élise's snub, I briefly wondered who Miss Agnes had seen as she'd arrived that day. Oliver was the last of the brothers to leave the house that morning, but—

None of it made any sense!

CHAPTER 8

"WILLIE!"

"Mr. Dordrecht! I'm sorry, sir, I'm just locking up. Be open again first thing—"

"No no, Willie, I'm, *uh*, not shopping. Actually, I came here to talk to you."

"To *me!*"

"Aye. Glad I caught you. Can I buy you a drink?"

The lad was completely baffled—but not one to look a gift horse in the mouth. "I'd never say nay, Mr. Dordrecht!"

"Good!" In our town, you never have to go far to locate a public house, so we were comfortably settled, potables in hand, three minutes later. Willie had asked for a whiskey and, since I knew he was all of thirteen, I figured he was old enough.

"Who d'you think will take the Hempstead race next week, Mr. Dordrecht?" the boy asked enthusiastically. "I was going to put money on Mr. Livingston's Arabian, but I hear there's a new two-year-old filly there—Atalanta—what's even faster!"

I was briefly confounded: while most of my acquaintances were agog with the agitation against the Stamp Act—the great Congress was to open on the morrow—this ingenuous lad was obliviously preoccupied by a horse race. "Afraid I don't follow the sport, Willie. Can't help you!"

"My uncle don't approve of my betting, anyways, but I only—"

"I was hoping you could give *me* some information, Willie! You see, I'm very curious about the murder of Mrs. Colegrove, and—"

"Oh! I know *all* about that!" the boy exclaimed joyfully. "I made a delivery to the Colegrove house that very morning, Mr. Dordrecht!"

"Really!" I said, feigning surprise. "About when was that?"

"Oh, let's see. Caesar—he's their black—he come in a little early that day. He usually gets in around noon, after he walks the master's horses, but he cut their walk short on account of it was so hot. But he had a lot of shopping to do, so I had a full wheelbarrow before he was even finished."

"Oh yes?"

"They has an account with Uncle—with Mr. Martin—so I didn't need to wait for him to pay up, so I started off—"

"About when was that, Willie? You remember?"

"Well, I got there, bells rang eleven forty-five. Everybody's asking me, y'see, once they knowed she was killed that day."

"Aha! Did you see anything out of order at the house?"

"Nothin', nothin' at all. Happened right there, in that backyard temple thing, I been told, but— The slave woman, she come out to the back gate— Mr. Martin don't let me go inside no more—and I rolled the barrels up to it, so she could pull them inside."

"You couldn't take them into the house for her?"

"It's 'cause of that statue. Uncle says I ain't to look at it—but, hell, I always do! Right pretty lady, that statue! Course I wouldn't want her shooting no arrows at me! Less they're *love* arrows!"

"It's Cupid who shoots love arrows, not Diana!"

"Yeah? Well, hell, can a pretty little girl like her even shoot a real arrow anyway?"

"I'm not volunteering to find out, Willie!"

"Yeah, I guess … me neither."

"Did the slave woman seem, *uh*, normal?"

"Yeah. She's always nice. Bringed me an apple. We griped about the heat. Usual. Said she was glad to get off a ladder. I'd've stayed longer, but she said she has to get back on the ladder, or Miss Eudoxia will have her hide. She's the old battle-axe what runs the place, y'know—it weren't the young missus what got killed."

"*Uh huh.*"

"Don't never want to get on *her* bad side!"

Tell me! "Did you happen to come across Caesar again that day?"

"Oh yeah, he was still in the store when I got back—and I'd had another delivery in the same block, to Mrs. Van Brunt. But he'd only bought a lot of small stuff and he carried it away hisself."

Willie and I finished our drinks in amicable if ungrammatical conversation, but I learned nothing more of import to the case.

Fully aware that all New York City wanted to eavesdrop on their deliberations, the first act of the Stamp Act Congress was to close their doors and impose secrecy on the delegates—much to the annoyance of every Son of Liberty I came across. Deprived of this item of gossip, some actually did ruminate publicly about the Hempstead horse race. Not Marinus, however, who was in a tetchy mood when I ran into him on Tuesday. He fretted how "indecent" it was that the Macaroni Club toffs had ostentatiously put up a purse of a hundred fifty quid on a horse race, when ninety-nine out of every hundred citizens were desperately worried about getting through the winter. Then he capped his outburst by nagging me again to join the militia.

Miss Theodora's Tuesday night letter informed me that Central Stables keeps a strict log of horses in and out, and that Caesar had taken Colegrove's pair out at eight-fifteen that morning, and returned them at eleven-ten.

I replied with an itemized time schedule for both slaves, which showed how far-fetched it was to think that either of them might have murdered Mrs. Colegrove. I still had questions about the woman's voodoo doll—which at least seemed to be hers—but the notion that she could have flitted in an hour from attending a sickbed to washing windows to receiving groceries to murdering her mistress was beyond absurdity.

Miss Theodora's next letter, received the following evening, announced that Colegrove's slavewoman had been returned to the house, with charges dropped, presumably only slightly the worse for wear.

Bowing to the inevitable, I posted a request to my mother, to send me the musket I'd carried during the war; and I paid the fees and took the oath that secured my franchise to vote. On Saturday afternoon—my employers were only surprised that I'd circumvented service for so long—I made my way to the common for militia drill. While the lads appeared to regard the drill more seriously than I recalled from my New Utrecht days under the preposterous leadership of Floris Van Klost, I still found it tiresome exercise. The captain seemed a reasonable fellow, but the sergeant-at-arms belligerently informed me that, though he'd heard I'd been rated a sergeant in the provincial regiment, *he* was in charge here and I mustn't forget it. I assured him that was fine with me, and that his orders would be received as gospel—that is, I didn't add, until I considered them idiotic, which I was positive would be soon.

Being new to the West Ward, I knew none of the men in the unit, but of course I met a few as I tagged along for the traditional post-drill tipple. A couple of lads sought me out—regulars among the Sons of Liberty prompted by either Charles or Marinus. While a great deal of chatter about the horse race was heard that afternoon, there was also a palpable undercurrent of nervous speculation about the looming arrival of the stamps.

When I presented myself at the college the following day, I was directed to an office on the third floor where, I was relieved to hear, Dr. Gideon Boyce was expecting me. My pleased first impression—a grave, slender, fair-haired fellow of medium height, whose formal academic garb suggested more authority than one might expect in a man still young—was somewhat dispelled by his apparent inability to look one in the eye. He was also so reluctant to put aside the book he was studying that he wouldn't remove his finger from his place in its Latin text. He was not grotesquely rude like so many of his family, but he was not as well-mannered as his punctilious half-sibling Peter, either. He immediately struck me as intelligent, but his disposition was maddeningly bland and diffuse. I first tried to establish a rapport—the Hempstead horse race, travels in the British Isles, the Stamp Act controversy—but in each instance, he appeared either indifferent or utterly ignorant. Gideon Boyce truly seems to be more conversant with Hippocrates and Galen and Avicenna—engravings of whose busts were framed on the wall—than with anyone in our eighteenth century. Disconcerting in a fellow New York native barely older than myself!

Disappointed in this attempt to establish collegiality—and the ever-present hope that I might have discovered a new friend—I lurched into the matter at hand. He did recollect the murder of Artemis Colegrove, at the least, but he had to be reminded that Theodora Colegrove was his stepfather's daughter by his first marriage. "So … she has you conducting an investigation because she doesn't believe the sailor was the malefactor?" he asked carelessly.

"The innocence of the sailor, Henry Tenkus, has been conclusively demonstrated, Dr. Boyce," I insisted. "He may well have provoked or menaced Mrs. Colegrove, but he could not possibly have committed the murder."

Boyce shrugged.

"You must have met Mrs. Colegrove while she was alive, I presume?"

"Only once, Mr. Dordrecht," he replied. "My mother was still living when I left for Scotland, and my stepfather had just departed for London when my bride and I returned in April. *Grandmère* arranged a reunion at the house. It was the only time I saw any of them until she got ill in August."

Obviously a doting, attentive family! "Were you able to form any impression of Mrs. Colegrove at all?"

His face fell. "*Uhh* … perhaps the less said, the better, Mr. Dordrecht?"

"I see. Well, I wonder if you'd be good enough to describe your observations of the day of the murder—starting with your first visit to the house, please."

As opposed to Mrs. Pannikin and young Willie, Dr. Boyce had *not* repeatedly rehearsed his activities of that critical day, and had to struggle to organize his recollections. "Oh dear! Well, *um* … yes, I … *Grandmère* had been sick, you see, for several days by then, and I'd been coming over every morning to bleed her, which is prescribed for stomach ailments, and—"

"About what time did you arrive that morning, sir?"

"The bleeding takes less than half an hour with the new scarificator I brought back from Edinburgh—it's much preferable to leeches or cupping, really—so I had by then a habit of arriving about ten-fifteen. That way, I could examine her, let the blood, and still have a couple minutes to walk over to the college for my eleven o'clock lecture."

"Did you see anyone else at the house that morning?"

"Anyone else? Oh. Well … Miss Eudoxia Colegrove? No, that morning she was out. House was empty! Except for young Oliver, who barged in at one point, to show off his new green suit."

"No one else? The slaves?"

"Oh, well, the woman was there, yes. In case I needed anything. The man I didn't see until later."

"Was the woman there with you the whole time?"

"She fetched water and a towel directly after I arrived. And she took the bowl away, once the bleeding was finished."

"Did she come right back after that?"

"The slave? Yes. I instructed her to watch over *Grandmère* another ten minutes before resuming her chores. I showed myself out. Oh, that was the morning I tripped over a ladder the fool had left in the hallway—I remember being very irked!"

"All right. So, aside from the house being virtually empty, everything seemed normal at that point?" He nodded. "Your lecture, I presume, occurred without incident?"

"Aside from one of the students fainting from the heat, yes."

"What happened then?"

"*Um,* I walked down to the refectory, where I was refreshing myself with some lemon water, when Mr. Colegrove's slave man appeared, in a state of ferocious agitation. I feared my grandmother had suffered a relapse, so I immediately rushed back to the house with him, removing and passing him my academic robes as we went. I had actually put my foot on the stairs to the second floor, when he said 'No!' and tugged me out into the back yard."

"*Uh huh.* And what did you see there?"

"Nothing I had remotely expected, I assure you!" His eyes met mine for once, then scanned about the room, as one might if fighting queasiness. "It was, *um,* so very shocking, I fear I lost my self-control for a minute."

I wouldn't suggest a career in the military, Dr. Boyce! "I'm afraid I have to ask you for details. What did you see?"

He sighed heavily. "Mrs. … Colegrove was stretched out on her back, under the porch roof, and there were several cuts in her dress … and there was blood everywhere—all over the floor of the folly, and … all over Oliver's suit. I had a disquieting thought—"

"That he had killed her?"

"It crossed my mind. Absurd! The lad's temperamental and high-strung, but I've never known him to be violent."

"Were you immediately certain the woman was dead?"

"Oh yes—though I felt for a pulse, as a matter of form."

"Could you estimate how long she'd been dead?"

"Not long. The body was still supple. Not long at all. And they were positive she'd not been there an hour before."

"How many times had she been stabbed, Dr. Boyce?"

"*Eh?* Oh, I counted eight wounds, in two strangely neat rows, but, *uh*—"

"Sir?"

"Well, that wasn't what killed her, you understand. She—"

"I beg your pardon?"

"Surely the coroner explained—"

"The coroner declared that she'd been stabbed to death, Dr. Boyce."

"Oh no. Oh no no, that's wrong. Surely he—"

"Miss Eudoxia Colegrove had the impression the coroner was inebriated. Would you concur with that?"

"Well, I couldn't disagree, but I wouldn't want to—"

"Wait. Why do you think she— What—"

"My conclusion was that she'd been strangled, Mr. Dordrecht. The stabs were inflicted after she was dead."

"*After?* But—all the blood?"

"Not hers. Not even associated with the wounds, just dribbled over her front."

"But how could— Would you describe what you saw, please?"

Boyce finally seemed engaged with the problem at hand. "Well, as I say, it was very odd to find eight evenly spaced strikes. They were in two parallel rows on the sides of the torso. Four hit the rib cage. Only two would have been fatal, eventually, if they *had* been struck before she was dead."

"It sounds"—I had to swallow hard—"somewhat *ritualistic*. Would you say?"

"No, I don't think so," he sighed. "Rather ... *formalistic*. Not the strikes of a trained killer, but of someone ignorant of anatomy who urgently wanted to *suggest* mayhem."

"And there were no wounds to the neck or the throat?" I asked, greatly confused.

"Yes, that's right."

"But ... the blood? I still don't understand. You say it wasn't hers?"

"Dead people don't bleed in any profusion, Mr. Dordrecht. Dying people do, dead ones don't. The killer must have wanted us to think she'd been stabbed to death, so he stabbed her. When she didn't bleed noticeably, he located some blood and carefully poured it in a straight line from her neck down, then spilled some about the folly."

It *still* makes no sense! "How could you possibly tell that after Oliver had prostrated himself onto the corpse? He must have smeared the gore over her as well as himself?"

"Ah. Well, some of it had already dried before he discovered her, I think. It was clear where it had been poured in the first place."

"But if it wasn't her blood, where—"

He shrugged. "A butcher's shop? Simple enough."

Not simple at all! Not in such a constricted place and time! "Wait. You had just bled Mrs. DeLancey!"

He was startled. "Oh, but … but that was over an hour before, sir. And I trust the servant had long since disposed of it."

We both paused, thinking. "You believe she was strangled? How?"

He drew a deep breath. "With the bare hands, I think. There was no narrow line, such as a garotte or a scarf would have left."

"How could the coroner possibly miss such a detail?"

"I don't … Her hair happened to flow over the faint marks on her neck. Perhaps he—"

"You didn't point the marks out to him?" *Oliver said she normally wore her hair dressed up.*

"Oh, it would have been insulting, Mr. Dordrecht! It was *completely* obvious!"

Obvious to any sober person who *looked*, that is! Boyce seemed nettled that I found his degree of professional deference excessive—or perhaps his conscience was troubling him. "You might have challenged him at the— Oh. But you were *not present* at the inquest. Why was that?"

He started, and finally lost his place in the book. "When was the inquest? I was never called to an inquest! I was expecting a summons to an autopsy as well as an inquest, but none ever came!" My transparent skepticism—I was finding him hard to believe—upset him. "Mr. Dordrecht, I swear to you, I never received a call to an inquest!"

"Well, why did you not inquire about it, sir? It's hardly credible that a judge would not have wanted to hear the opinion of a medical professional who was the first on the scene!"

He shrugged and gestured helplessly. "I fear I had my own preoccupations at the time, sir. I just— I suppose I am remiss in this. In retrospect, it looks very terrible!"

Though his eyes still would not meet mine, I could not ascribe the tic to dissembling. But I could offer no reassurance. I was also beginning to wonder how the oversight might have come about, when Boyce rocked me by adding, "Surely the coroner at least reported that the woman was with child?"

I simply gaped.

"You're not telling me the man didn't see that?"

"Nobody ... *nobody* suggested, in the record, or to me personally, sir, that Mrs. Colegrove might have been pregnant!"

"Oh dear. Well ... but she was. She was at least five months gone. Another fortnight and it would have been blatant to everyone."

It crossed my mind to wonder whether Dr. Boyce was a fabulist. "Sir ... are you quite sure of this? I mean ... barring an autopsy, how does one *know?*"

"Well, it regularly escapes us males, Mr. Dordrecht. And it was very little part of my medical education, frankly. But I happen to know thanks to very personal observations. My own wife, you see—she looks nothing like Mrs. Colegrove did, save that she's only a couple years older, and has the same height and build. And we are anticipating a blessed event after the turn of the year. So—"

"My felicitations!" I mumbled automatically.

"Thank you. So it happens that my wife's gravidity was coeval with that of the deceased. And like Mrs. Colegrove, my wife was very late in presenting outward appearances."

"I ... see."

"If one is closely watching a woman in the same condition, however, one can certainly observe the signs."

"*Uh huh.*"

"The similarity was perhaps one of the reasons I was so completely undone on beholding the corpse, you ken."

"Yes. Of course." I was suddenly preoccupied in counting months backward. If Boyce's timing was correct, the father ... could of course have been the husband. But my recollection was that Henry Tenkus had reappeared in the victim's life very shortly after Aaron Colegrove had sailed for England ...

"Well," Boyce began after seeing me distracted, "I think it might not be considerate to make this public at this point, Mr. Dordrecht. It would only pain Mr. Colegrove, the deprived father, and it would surely sully the coroner's reputation, so—"

"Dr. Boyce, that man thoroughly deserves to be impeached from any position of public trust! I do hope you'll be ready to testify to the truth of the situation?"

He was taken aback. "Well, yes, if we must. But ... what does it matter, at this point?"

His naivety was almost risible, but I was beyond laughing. "Sir, it could bear very heavily on the question of the murderer's *motive*."

"Oh! Yes, well …"

"It matters a great deal!"

"I see, I suppose it does."

Staggered by the entire conversation, I presently completed the interview. But when I was halfway down to the first landing, I rushed back to him.

"Dr. Boyce, you note that we males seldom realize that a woman is in the early stages of pregnancy, but—"

He intuited the question. "Women normally perceive it long before we do, Mr. Dordrecht, yes. Perhaps not maidens like Agnes or Élise, but … women always know when another is with child."

Then why didn't any of them mention it? I wondered. Why did no one raise the issue at the inquest?

I left the college building feeling overwhelmed and agitated. I had hoped that Dr. Boyce's observations might point me clearly toward a resolution. Instead, he had thrown all my assumptions into a cauldron.

A chilly autumnal thunderstorm was in violent progress. I ducked into a public house, hoping to straighten my thoughts while it passed. The storm lessened after half an hour, but my confusion remained.

I decided that examining Boyce's revelations with my client would likely be the most productive activity at this impasse. Bundling myself against the continuing nasty drizzle, I made my soggy way across the common to the modest clapboard house on Frankfort Street where Miss Theodora lives with her sister-in-law. She was less than delighted to see me, but fortunately Mrs. Irene Colegrove and her children were out of the house paying Sunday social calls.

Once we were settled—she did offer me tea, which I gratefully accepted—I relayed Dr. Boyce's astounding new assertions, which stunned her as much as they'd stunned me. "Why did you not tell me Mrs. Colegrove was with child, ma'am?" I demanded—with perhaps more asperity than a contracted menial should permit himself.

"I did not realize it, sir!" she retorted. "Dr. Boyce doubtless attributes keener perspicacity to my sex than is entirely warranted. I did not know!"

"Did your sister-in-law not remark it?"

"Irene hasn't been in that house since Father left, Mr. Dordrecht. She has her hands full right here."

"Did you both not see the woman at Trinity Church?"

"We *avoided* her at church services!"

"Surely your aunt and Mrs. DeLancey must have realized—"

"I couldn't say, Mr. Dordrecht. Neither ever remarked on it to me. Nearly two years had passed since Father married the girl, so it would have been the last thing anyone would be anticipating." She paused, frowning. "I'm not sure I see how it makes a difference anyway, because—"

She's as naïve as Boyce! "Miss Colegrove, the mere fact of being in an interesting condition is regularly known to inspire passions in people, and—"

I stopped, struck by a new thought. "It was *not* a crime of passion, though, was it?"

"Mr. Dordrecht?"

"From the first, I've assumed that whoever murdered Mrs. Colegrove did so by striking her with a knife in a mad frenzy. A dozen times, I'd heard, though Boyce said it was only eight. But if that's *not* how she was killed … then the knife strokes were a shadow-play deliberately designed to disguise the nature of the crime, an act of calculated pre-meditation!"

Miss Colegrove's face was drained of color.

"And assuming he's right, that she was throttled … it finally explains why she did not scream."

"It's … very terrible, Mr. Dordrecht," Miss Colegrove managed after a minute.

"Just so, ma'am."

"But … but this pre-meditation could indicate that her condition was *not* relevant, and that the murder may well have been an attempt to persecute my father."

She had a point.

"And combining that thought with the discovery of a posted political slogan—"

"Yes … but considering the awareness of the surroundings and the daily habits of the household, Miss Colegrove, I—"

"Could it not be a matter of *political* passion, Mr. Dordrecht? Willingness to take an extraordinary risk of discovery to assert a hideous contention?"

My friends would scoff, I was sure, but … was it *entirely* inconceivable? I swallowed the last of my tea without arriving at any resolution. "Another matter, ma'am: Dr. Boyce insists that he never received notice of the inquest that was conducted the next morning. Can you— How did you learn of the arrangements?"

"A servant of the court came to the house shortly after Irene and I arrived, later that afternoon, Mr. Dordrecht. He told us that we should ensure that all interested parties would be present."

"And Dr. Boyce was not in the house at that moment?"

"Oh no. My aunt said she'd attend to it. She … manages everything."

"Yet the inquest record explicitly notes his absence!"

She shrugged. "I … can't say."

I sighed, and then recalled another issue. "Have you been able to locate your brother Timothy, Miss Colegrove?"

She gulped and turned her head for a second. "I had planned to mention that, sir. On Thursday, I troubled my aunt for his address, and accosted him at his domicile."

"Which is?"

She grimaced. "A low sailor's lodging—Brown's—on Cliff Street."

"Ah, I know it! I lived there myself, briefly, years ago. I'm surprised it hasn't tumbled *over* the cliff!" Should I mention that her father owns it? *Perhaps not.*

She smiled wanly.

"You saw him, then?"

"Yes." She was a portrait of anxiety and misery. "He told me his whereabouts at the moment of Mrs. Colegrove's death were none of my business either!"

"I see."

"I … nonetheless can't believe Timothy … could have had … anything to do with—"

"I shall have to pursue the matter, ma'am."

"Yes."

"Does your father have a will?" I was suddenly inspired to ask.

"A will? Father? I can't imagine that he doesn't, Mr. Dordrecht."

"But to your certain knowledge?"

"Well, I don't— My father is a highly responsible businessman, Mr. Dordrecht!" she asserted—recalling to me Timothy Colegrove's cynicism regarding her grasp of their father's character.

"He knew he'd be crossing the Atlantic in the hurricane season, ma'am!" The riskiness of that choice had been impressed on me several times. My estate's not a hundredth part of Colegrove's, but *I've* written a will.

"What could this matter, sir? It was Mrs. Colegrove who was murdered, not Father!"

Again, she had a point. I could not really say what prompted my curiosity regarding the man's testamentary arrangements.

"What will you do next?" she asked, after observing me stumped.

I equivocated. It was pouring again. "I should go back to the house. I need to talk to your aunt and Mrs. DeLancey again ... and the slaves."

"You may find Calpurnia somewhat obdurate. I fear she was ... not properly treated by the authorities. Father is very annoyed about it."

Annoyed at *himself*, I should hope ... but I doubt. "Then that offers me an excuse to wait until next Sunday—with your permission, Miss Colegrove."

For once—looking out the window—she was sympathetic. "Very well. I do understand that all the shippers are frantic to send their boats out legally by the end of the month. Will that affect—"

"I shall try not to let it delay our project, ma'am, but you recall I have a primary commitment to my firm, and there is no question but they are under extraordinary pressures at the moment."

"Thank you."

Shortly thereafter, I took my leave—but I was headed for supper and home.

John Glasby and I had a rare few minutes together two days later, as we shared a ride up to the boatyard at Corlear's Hook. "I've been meaning to tell you, Thomas," he began. "This may be nothing, but I overheard a bit of gossip at the Exchange last week. About your Colegrove case. One hears less and less of it, but some still care. Anyway, a couple rich young sprogs were discussing their friend James Colegrove, and—"

"James the Missing!"

"The same. And one said that he'd been surprised when James had asked to borrow a large sum of money, all of a sudden, just two days before the murder, the same week his father returned. Wouldn't state a reason."

"The fellow declined, I expect?"

"Indeed he did. He found it very odd."

"*Hmph!* Well … so do I. But I hardly know what to make of it." We both pondered the anomaly for a second. "But I thank you for telling me!"

The newspapers were continually running doggerel and would-be epic poems excoriating the Stamp Act and its excessively clever Parliamentary creators. Most I barely scanned and instantly shrugged away. But the week's issue of the *Post-Boy*, on Thursday, ran a brief verse that bitterly affected me, recalling those heroes I had myself seen bleeding at the hands of the Gaul.

> Ah! My dear country, curs't in peace,
> Why did you wish the war to cease—
> The war in which you strew'd the plain
> With thousands of your heroes slain.
> When Britain to your bleeding shore
> Impetuous pour'd her squadrons o'er,
> And snatch'd you from the Gallic Brood—
> To drink *herself* your vital blood!

Much as I despise the cowardly argument of emotion, I could not banish this artless, anonymous instance of poesy, which I had involuntarily memorized before the day was out. Did my mates Eakin, Ferris, Lloyd, and Hannamore really die to spare us the negligible threat of domination by the French—only that we should then succumb to the palpable exploitation of the English?

At the militia exercise on Saturday, I detected that I was not the only one with a more sober attitude, with greater readiness to devote grim concentration upon *casting about* and *ramming home*.

What will we do when those stamps get here?

God help us all!

With great difficulty, early the next Sunday afternoon, Caesar coaxed Calpurnia up into the kitchen. I wanted to speak to both the slave pair and the elderly ladies, but the latter were napping as usual, so I simply presented myself at the door and presumed upon my original mandate to demand the former's attention. The woman moved with painful slowness, avoiding all contact. She had a bandage tied about her head and a few unmended tears in her dress. I had offered to talk in the basement, but Caesar had emphatically shaken his head. "Don't ask about doll!" he had begged. I don't know what she had suffered in the past week, but …

Caesar himself looked exhausted. Because he was doing the work of two, I supposed. Seeing all this, I resolved to make our interview as short as possible. "Calpurnia, on the morning Mrs. Colegrove was murdered, Dr. Boyce was here to bleed Mrs. DeLancey, as he had done for several days before. When they were done, you were given the bowl, to dispose of the blood. What did you do with it?"

"Blood?" Caesar asked.

I moved my stool so that I was facing her from the far side of the kitchen. She resolutely turned her head to the side.

"You wash?" Caesar asked.

Calpurnia shook her head and whispered, "They call back."

"Tub?" She nodded. "She put in wash tub," Caesar said, pointing at the latter, which was on a counter behind me, full of water and soiled dishes.

"You put it directly in the water?" I asked.

She shook her head. Caesar explained that she set it in the tub, which would have been empty at that moment—breakfast clean-up having been completed—and that the usual procedure was to pour most of the blood into the privy before washing the bowl.

"*Uh huh.* And you did this, after Dr. Boyce had left?"

Calpurnia's torpor lightened slightly. It appeared to me that she was both uncertain and curious. "No," she said, slightly more loudly. "Windows."

"I see." Mindful of "the battle-axe," she had attended directly to the front windows. "Well, when did you wash the bowl?"

She looked to Caesar. "I don't— You?"

They both looked like they were struggling to recollect the day. "Yes. I wash—before dinner." He thought some more. "But bowl empty. You dump?"

"No. Windows."

"You didn't take it with you when Willie called you to collect the groceries?"

She shook her head. I looked back to Caesar.

He shrugged. "Bowl empty."

"None of the family would have—"

They shook their heads. Someone in *my* family might have volunteered to expedite a nasty chore, but never a Colegrove!

I sat back and took a deep breath. The murderer had coolly gone into the kitchen, taken the bowl, poured it over the corpse, and replaced it in the tub! Had he seen it there beforehand? Did he know it would be there? Was it planned, or an instant's inspiration?

I had another question. "Dr. Boyce … believes that Mrs. Colegrove had been in a family way—with child."

Calpurnia grunted affirmatively. Caesar expressed no surprise.

"Did she confide in you? Did anyone else remark it?" Negatives.

"Dr. Boyce thinks she was five months gone, yet—"

"She five months," Calpurnia asserted, somewhat more confidently. "She puking, back April."

"When did you first see the sailor?"

"April," Caesar said, guessing my drift. "Masta's child."

All right, I thought. But … would everyone have come to the same conclusion?

Another issue. "I'm sorry, I have to ask. Why did you make that pin cushion doll?"

Calpurnia turned further away, squirming and moaning in anguish.

Caesar put his hand on her shoulder. "She hear Missus' plan. She to give Calpurnia to Mista Peter wife for wedding!"

"Mrs. Colegrove planned to give *Calpurnia* to the bride? As a wedding present?" He nodded miserably. "Just Calpurnia, not the both of you together?"

"That right." He was trembling as much as she was. "But she no put doll in—" He gestured toward the pantry. "Never expect they see … and she no kill Missus, she washing windows!"

Right. "I think that's fairly well established, now, at last," I said uncomfortably. "*Um*, how did— How did you learn of Mrs. Colegrove's intention to give Calpurnia away? Did she tell you so directly?"

Calpurnia still faced the wall. Caesar answered for her. "She overhear her say. She in library one eve, hear Missus tell Mista James in parlor."

"You can hear between the rooms?"

"Sometime."

"Why were you in the library?"

Caesar looked blank. He squeezed her shoulder. "Bring Mista Peter tea," she said. "He listening hard. Shush me. They argue money. I about go when she ... she ..." The slavewoman fought back tears.

When she obliviously fired that mortar into the other room. I wanted to ask what the money argument had been about, but stopped myself when I realized the slave would have been too distraught to hear it. "Can you think— Can you remember when this occurred? How long was it before Mrs. Colegrove was murdered?"

"Ohh ... not long."

"It be a Sunday," Calpurnia managed.

"Sunday, before the murder? Or a week before that?"

"That week," Caesar declared. "Just before killed."

James was quarreling with his young stepmother. About money. Less than three days before ...

"I'm sorry to detain you, but ... can you remember who was in and out of the house in those last days? Who had been visiting all summer?"

"Not many, sir. Men go to office, now. Ladies sent away, summer. 'Cept widow neighbor. ... Mista Oliver friends, Miss Élise friends?"

"All right. But the adults—in the last three days?"

"Sailor."

"I've heard about his visit."

"Mista Timothy here, day before."

My blood ran cold. "Mister Timothy! Did he visit often?"

"Most never. He see Miss Eudoxia in afternoon."

He who professed himself completely estranged from his family. I had to shake myself.

"Boy!" Calpurnia prompted weakly.

"*Eh.* Captain William boy. He here many times, see Missus."

What? "That would be ... *Vincent* Colegrove?"

"Him. He here just before sailor. Night before she killed."

Another one! "What about the eldest son, Lambert Colegrove? Any of the sons-in-law? The other stepson, Nathaniel Boyce?"

"No. Him at sea. All go Masta's office, now, not ever house."

"So, in the last three days," I thought aloud, "James was here on Sunday evening, and Timothy, and Vincent, and Henry Tenkus were here on Tuesday. Plus Dr. Boyce. And Peter of—"

Calpurnia was suddenly gasping, reeling on the stool. "She not well, Mista! I take downstair."

"Of course!" He helped her up, and they moved toward the basement steps. "If you can, Caesar, I'd—" The door banged shut after them.

The house was very quiet; I had long since realized the master had to be out. Feeling awkward and alone, I stared idly through the little window at the ridiculous backyard temple, particularly forlorn in the gray autumnal mist. After a moment, I rallied, sat down, and occupied myself making notes of dates and times and people. Much to be straightened out!

Near fifteen minutes later, just after I'd heard a bell ringing in the sitting room above, Caesar clomped back upstairs. "They want tea," he said. Moving by rote, he filled a kettle with water, set it over the hearth, and stoked the fire.

"She better?"

"She rest."

As he searched out the tea canister, a realization came to me: Calpurnia *believed* in the voodoo. She believed that by sticking those pins into a pin cushion she had caused the woman's death. Would she carry that self-reproach to her own grave?

After another minute, another thought struck me. "You *still* don't know whether they intend to separate you when Peter marries!" Caesar was facing away, measuring tea leaves. His hands clenched tightly. "I'm sorry! Not my business."

And nothing I could do about it, either.

Caesar finished preparing the tea, and lifted the tray. "Would you tell them I'm here, please, and wish to speak with them?"

He nodded and left.

They took their sweet time. Twenty minutes later, I was angrily debating whether simply to make my own way upstairs when Caesar finally returned with empty teacups. "They see you now," he said.

"So it's you again!" Miss Eudoxia hissed by way of welcome. The two pets glowered. Mrs. DeLancey sniffed indifferently.

"Yes ma'am," I replied—struggling for an even tone.

"After all this time, one would think—"

"I have a few more questions, ladies, which have been prompted by my researches elsewhere."

"Oh do get on with it, then!"

"Thank you. Dr. Boyce—who I finally met last Sunday—asserted that Mrs. Colegrove had been pregnant when she was murdered." They both bristled indignantly at the bluntness of my announcement. "Did neither of you notice this? And why did you not point it out at the inquest?"

"It is hardly relevant, Mr. Dordrecht," Mrs. DeLancey opined.

"I don't quite trust Dr. Boyce anyway," Miss Colegrove said. "He—"

"My grandson is an excellent physician!"

"I mean his judgment, Mrs. DeLancey. He is so indefinite about everything! He seems—"

"Gideon has had the best education in Europe! The college here immediately accepted him to teach! How can you—"

"Ladies! Had you *noticed* Mrs. Colegrove was five months gone with child?"

A flicker of eye contact passed between the two, but they instantly focused back on their pets. Had my vehemence startled them?

"Of course," Miss Eudoxia said coldly. "But what does it matter now? It is but another crime that has robbed my brother of a blessed addition!" Mrs. DeLancey looked ready to spit. "Another crime that the radical faction here has perpetrated—"

"Why did you not point this out at the inquest, Miss Colegrove?"

"Did I not? It must have slipped my mind. We were eager to conclude the formalities, as we had to travel that day to Mamaroneck for the funeral, and—"

"I was of course not present at the inquest, being still indisposed," Mrs. DeLancey interjected.

"I assumed the coroner deemed it not relevant, and so—"

"Miss Colegrove, I have persuaded Dr. Boyce to register a complaint against the coroner—this was not the man's only mistake!—and I trust you will endorse his effort? Miss Élise told me you had found him inebriated at one in the afternoon!"

"This is very tiresome!" Mrs. DeLancey exclaimed.

"All the more reason the government must be granted more reliable funding, Mr. Dordrecht!" Miss Colegrove argued.

They were adamantly avoiding the issue. "Another matter! Dr. Boyce says that he was never informed of the scheduled inquest, and that that is the reason he was not present and able to contribute his observations. Miss Theodora tells me—"

"Oh, Theodora! She really must learn to take better care with her dress!" Mrs. DeLancey exclaimed.

"There's nothing wrong with her dress, Mrs. DeLancey!" Miss Eudoxia rejoined. "She's very conservative, and—"

I raised my voice. "Miss Theodora tells me that the court's messenger asked you to ensure all relevant parties were promptly informed. And yet—"

"Good heavens, Miss Colegrove! A *terrible* oversight!"

"We were quite frantically busy that afternoon, if you'll recall, Mrs. DeLancey!"

"Why—"

"As Mrs. DeLancey says, it was indeed a terrible oversight, sir. But—"

"It would have been easy enough to send one of the slaves," I observed. "It's barely three blocks away."

"Mr. Dordrecht, if our niece, in her wisdom, has—"

"*Your* niece!" Mrs. DeLancey asserted smugly.

"If Theodora has commissioned you to discover Mrs. Colegrove's murderer, why are you here annoying *us?*"

"Oh, an excellent question, Miss Colegrove!"

"*Thank* you, Mrs. DeLancey!"

And one to which I had no intention of responding! "*Another* matter, ladies!" They both scowled furiously, and fidgeted on their couches, disturbing the pets. "Your servants have informed me that Henry Tenkus was not the only visitor to this house on the day before Mrs. Colegrove was murdered. For one, I understand Mr. Timothy Colegrove was here to see you, Miss Colegrove?"

"*Timothy!*" Mrs. DeLancey exclaimed indignantly. "I thought he was forbidden the house! You allowed *Timothy* to—"

"I had private family business to discuss with my nephew, Mr. Dordrecht," Miss Colegrove stated, ignoring her companion, "and I assure you it's of no relevance to what happened the following day."

"You were of course aware that Timothy Colegrove has become a passionate adherent of the Sons of Liberty, ma'am?"

"Timothy's wretched political affiliations were no part of our discussion, sir! As I say, it was purely a family matter, and—"

"Yet the late Mrs. Artemis Colegrove was also part of your family, was she not?"

Both women managed to convey disdain and disgust simultaneously. I had a brief fantasy that the dog and the cat felt the same way.

"My discussion with Timothy was *my* business, Mr. Dordrecht, and so it shall remain. If you persist in hectoring us, I shall certainly complain to my niece of your impertinence!"

"Oh! Very well said, Miss Colegrove!"

"*Thank* you, Mrs. DeLancey!"

Resolving to pursue the issue by other means, I swallowed my indignation and forged onward. "I understand Mr. Vincent Colegrove paid Mrs. Colegrove a visit shortly before the sailor arrived, and that he had been a frequent visitor throughout the summer. How did this ... friendship ... come to be?"

They both spoke at once. "Mr. Vincent is a dutiful lad—" Miss Colegrove began—while Mrs. DeLancey was sneering that he was an absurd young fellow. "He thinks himself a poet!" she cackled.

"He will doubtless settle in time, Mrs. DeLancey!"

"*Phoo!*"

"Have you any idea what the substance of their meeting was? They had met on many occasions? Did no one think this inadvisable?"

"Artemis was a grown and married woman, Mr. Dordrecht," Miss Colegrove huffed. "She had servants at her beck and call. She had no need of a chaperone, and neither of us saw fit to intrude on her private conversations."

I felt certain it was not for lack of trying. "Can you at least confirm that he *was* present, late that afternoon?"

"Oh he was here, all right!" Mrs. DeLancey said. "He was here over and over, and—"

"Vincent was frequently here in the early evenings, Mr. Dordrecht, perhaps twice a week. He—"

"Loitering in the hope of being invited to supper! His penurious uncle doesn't pay him enough, it seems!"

"I'm sure Lambert pays him every farthing his work deserves, Mrs. DeLancey!"

"*Hmph!*"

"It's most Christian of Lambert, really, to offer Vincent a start in business! You do know that he is the orphaned son of the heroic Captain William, whose portrait hangs downstairs?"

He who got shot in the—

"An excessively flattering portrait, really! The captain was—"

"What *are* you insinuating, Mrs. DeLancey? The captain was—"

I could bear it no longer. "Ladies, thank you so much for your time! I may have to visit you again, of course, but we'll adjourn for the moment. Please don't trouble yourselves to ring for the servant—I'm sure I can find my own way out!"

I was breathing fresh, cold air thirty seconds later.

Were they being deliberately obstructive—*or was that merely the way they always were?*

CHAPTER 9

A SWIFT COASTAL PACKET out of Perth Amboy brought the long-dreaded news on Tuesday afternoon, October the twenty-second. The *Edward*, a London merchant brig reported to have been consigned the first batch of the province's stamped paper, had dropped anchor at Sandy Hook, and was awaiting a pilot into the harbor.

Within an hour, every single human being in New York City knew it.

Even at our firm, where we were still frantically striving to beat the November first deadline, it was very difficult to concentrate on the jobs at hand.

But the Sons of Liberty had already made their minds up what the response should be—and so, for that matter, had Thomas Dordrecht.

The *Edward* did not arrive in the River until the next day. Our ancient ninny of a governor had scared its captain into believing that the populace might attack the *ship*, and he therefore waited for the escort of a pair of warships. As they anchored opposite the Battery and Fort George, their crews could not have missed the fact that all the merchantmen in the harbor had hauled their flags down to half-staff—to signify, as the newspaper said, "*Mourning, Lamentation, and Woe!*"

They faced two thousand armed New York citizens grimly determined that the stamps should never land.

I was not surprised to find Marinus Willett, Charles Cooper, or Cyrus Mapes beside me among that throng. I was surprised to see my elderly patron Benjamin Leavering and his often-reluctant partner John Glasby, both bearing muskets that probably had not been fired in twenty years.

We stood for hours and hours, cursing the chilly wind but grateful it wasn't raining, while negotiators—representing the governor, the council, the military, the Sons—were rowed back and forth to the ships. Hundreds of women milled around behind, pushing carts with hot cider and roasted nuts, bringing their menfolk extra scarves and hats. We stood until the night was pitch black, and were then urged to return at dawn.

But at dawn we were dismayed to learn that the navy had roused all its hands during the wee hours, and quietly rowed the crates ashore in the dark. Despite all our efforts, the stamps were now inside the fort! And the gates of the fort, normally open, were barred shut.

Old Governor Colden, universally despised even before the Stamp Act became an issue, was universally excoriated for this underhanded surrender of New York. But the option of remanding the stamps to Whitehall was no longer available.

There was a week yet before the tax was to go into effect, however, and the increased likelihood that work would come to a total halt on that date spurred us forward that morning. Until mid-afternoon, that is, when the broadsides were suddenly in evidence.

Pro Patria
The first Man that either distributes or makes use of Stampt Paper—
Let him take Care of his House, Person and Effects
Vox Populi
We Dare

All productive effort ceased once again, as the populace debated the authorship, the backing, the printing, the distribution, and occasionally even the import of the postings. "Did your cousin write this?" my enraged friend John Glasby demanded.

"I don't think so, John, it's not like—"

"This is outrageous, Thomas! This is a blatant threat to life and property! I don't want the stamps, I'm distressed they've been landed, and I'm indignant that our governor has tolerated it, but the Bostonian solution will get us nowhere! The whole city has gone mad as Massachusetts!"

Could I argue? Although I thought the stamps themselves were the chief offenders against property and persons, the prospect of overt violence was appalling. Though we'd carried arms the day before, we'd been confident that no use of them would be needed. It was, after all, *our* British navy, manned by our *compatriots*, keeping watch out there on the decks of the warships.

But how else was the imposition to be faced down, save that everyone refused the stamps?

Fortunately, the kegs and barrels of cut Virginia pipe tobacco still to be loaded aboard the *Maia* had to be precisely counted at the east warehouse.

The Stamp Act Congress—which had been virtually forgotten during this affray—adjourned itself the following day, and finally announced the product of its three weeks of deliberations: a modest "Declaration of Rights" with which few would have quarreled, even in Westminster. Almost all the delegates fled the city before night had fallen.

"Better than nothing!" Mapes judged.

"It at least shows that the other colonies are concerned," Mr. Leavering said. "Perhaps the farm communities don't feel it as much as the port cities, but … they are behind us in spirit."

For my own part, despite the continuing unease everywhere, I concentrated on my work for the firm and my researches for the obliviously insistent Miss Theodora.

Nothing would bar the interruption of militia practice, however. Saturday's session was full of nervous bonhomie—a crowd of twitchy men trading stories and asking each other where they'd stood in the line on Wednesday. But the drill itself garnered more earnest attention than ever before.

On Sunday morning I went to the firm's warehouse, to attend to the third floor inventory, long overdue, which was much easier to accomplish when no one else was around. I managed to complete it in good time to make my second appointment with Peter Colegrove, the remarkably well-mannered second son of Aaron and Lavinia, arranged by my client for one-thirty.

Again we met in his father's library. He appeared as cordial and precise as before. I thanked him for meeting with me, and he apologized that he hoped I could keep it short, as he was wanted by Mr. Kempe—"Sabbath or no Sabbath!"

The crisis, I gathered, was keeping adherents of the province's court faction as busy as their opponents.

"I shall try to oblige, Mr. Colegrove, but since our meeting a month ago I have learned many new facts that I wish to discuss. *Um*, for example, Dr. Boyce asserts that Mrs. Colegrove was five months' gone with child, and—"

"*What!*"

Another baffled male, it seems! "I take it, you did not know that?"

"No, indeed! I— Why didn't Gideon say so? Oh, perhaps he was aiming to spare my poor father the extra distress?"

"I think he rather expected the coroner to bring the fact to light at the inquest. But he says he never received notice of the inquest. Can you—"

"Oh, well, my aunt was surely very busy and preoccupied that day. Perhaps it slipped her mind. Our plan was to leave for the funeral immediately after the inquest."

"Yes, but— You said before, that you elected to bury Mrs. Colegrove in Mamaroneck in deference to your father's supposed preference, yet I've heard somewhere that he has gone so far as to request that she be reinterred in Trinity Churchyard!"

"Ah, he's abandoned that idea, sir. He may perhaps have preferred an effusive, traditional memorial, but ... such normal expressions of grief and family loyalty are contrary to the temper of the times, regarded by some fanatics as unseemly display. And of course we were right to be nervous about the public reaction. Mrs. Colegrove had unfortunately made herself notorious among the radical faction—and I trust you've been told how my father was greeted on his return just days later?"

"Yes."

"My brother James is still shy of coming back into town for the same reason."

"I see, but—"

"And that's also why," he added with an irritated expression, "my own wedding has to take place up there, when it would be far more convenient to marry here in the city!"

The Colegrove clan sometimes appears to suffer from excess caution!

"Surely you know," he railed on, "that honest citizens have been brutally tarred and feathered simply for performing their contracted duty to the sovereign? That man in Connecticut was nearly lynched! You must ask yourself if you care to be a partisan of mob rule, Mr. Dordrecht!"

A political argument would hardly shorten this interview. "Why do you suppose your aunt and grandmother did not inform you of Mrs. Colegrove's pregnancy? They *were* aware of it."

He quickly reclaimed his poise. "Can't begin to guess. Not casual conversation! And what does it matter, at this point?"

"It matters only because of another observation of Dr. Boyce's."

"What's that?"

"Mrs. Colegrove, he contends, did not die of stab wounds, but of strangulation. The stabs were inflicted after she was dead."

His expression of shock oddly struck me as rather forced—rather theatrical. But such impressions are frequently misleading. "Good god! That's ... sickening!"

"Such a murder implies pre-meditation, it implies that it was not a spur-of-the-moment decision swayed by passion, that it—"

"Then," he said thoughtfully, "if it wasn't the sailor—"

"That was established weeks ago, sir!"

"If it wasn't the sailor," he continued heedlessly, "it must have been one of— Mr. Dordrecht, I trust you will honor your commitment to my sister ... even if your discoveries should prove embarrassing to the city's radical faction?"

"Indeed I would, Mr. Colegrove, but I fear my discoveries are tending ... closer to home."

"*Ah!* But I thought ... I thought the charges against the slave woman were dropped! Have you found something new?"

Mr. Peter Colegrove's reasonability has its limits, I surmised: he too cannot remotely conceive that his blood relations might be involved. "Naught that would implicate Calpurnia or Caesar, sir," I replied.

"Oh, well, that's a—" He stopped himself, and fussed with two candlesticks on the table, resetting the candles perfectly upright.

"I did learn—from them—that you happened to overhear Mrs. Colegrove and Mr. James Colegrove quarreling two nights before she was murdered. Can you—"

He turned quite red, and emphatically shook his head. "James can't possibly be involved in this! James wasn't even in the city, he was up at the estate! It's absurd to—"

"Can you please just tell me what the substance of the disagreement was? It may lead to—"

"Calpurnia told you this? She shouldn't have been listening! We shall—"

"She had inadvertently overheard a statement that could hardly fail to make an impression on her, Mr. Colegrove."

"Oh, about the wedding present? Well ... what does she care whose slave she is?"

I've heard people make such blithe remarks before, but they never fail to amaze me.

"I thought it rather unexpectedly sweet of Artemis to think of my intended, actually," he breezed on. "We won't be able to afford servants for some time, you see."

I couldn't help asking: "Is that still the plan?"

"Oh, I don't know. Father's decision. I don't even know if she ever wrote to him about it. Perhaps my aunt or *Grandmère* might have!" he added hopefully.

"But ... the substance of the disagreement?"

"Oh, my guess is that James was reprimanding her for some minor extravagance, Mr. Dordrecht. Nothing serious. Perhaps even the idea of giving the slave away as a present. James felt it his duty, I believe, to safeguard Father's interests in his absence."

"Regarding just that, Mr. Colegrove, your father's interests: do you know whether he has ever written a will?"

Colegrove looked extremely startled by the question. His face flushed again, and he struggled to make the pile of papers on the table even more neatly arranged than it already was. "I know for a fact that he has *not*, Mr. Dordrecht. I have been trying to impress on him how improvident this is. Especially now, when faithful servants of the king can be threatened by mobs merely for executing their lawful duties!"

"Were your father—I speak in theory only—to suffer an apoplexy and expire intestate, his fortune would go to ... James?"

"It would go to the first-born, sir, Theodora's elder brother, Lambert. Law of primogeniture. But how could this possibly matter?"

"I'm not sure that it does, Mr. Colegrove. It's just ... good to know."

"*Hmph!*"

"Have you any idea why your father's grandson, Vincent Colegrove, was a frequent visitor to this house this past summer?"

"*Vincent?* He was *here?*"

Again there was a slightly histrionic emphasis. Why should Vincent's presence be such a surprise? "So I've been told, Mr. Colegrove."

He shrugged. "Well, I never saw him here. Paying duty calls to his great-aunt? Not likely—not him. And I trust he understands he's too close in blood to court Élise!" He shook his head. "No idea!"

"Did you know that your half-brother Timothy called at the house to see your aunt, the day before the murder?" His face was impassive. "Have you any idea why they would meet? It wasn't a customary, familial visit, I understand?"

"I did know that he'd been here, Mr. Dordrecht. Aunt Eudoxia told me. But I inquired no further, because I know she is extremely jealous of the privacy of her affairs. I forebear to meddle, sir—and so, perhaps, should you!"

"I, however, am investigating a murder, Mr. Colegrove, and—"

There was a knock on the library's door. "Enter!"

Caesar came in, the lace jabot of his uniform freshly laundered and starched. "Beg pardon, sir, but Miss Eudoxia and Mrs. DeLancey say they would like to see Mr. Dordrecht before he leaves."

"*They* want to see *me?*" I couldn't help exclaiming as the slave closed the door behind him. "There's a switch!"

Colegrove suavely overcame his confusion at the announcement. "Well, there's your chance, then, Mr. Dordrecht." After a second, he said, "Are we done for today? I do need to get on to Mr. Kempe's office!"

Having no further immediate questions, I agreed. Colegrove rang for Caesar, who instantly returned to escort me upstairs and announce me to the ladies.

"Mr. Dordrecht! How grand to see you, sir!" Miss Eudoxia burbled cheerily, the instant my head was visible above the floor. Mrs. DeLancey was beaming from her settee. The two pets were asleep on the floor.

I was about to stammer a response when I saw a change to the room that made my jaw drop.

The Chippendale chairs! All four of them. One on each corner of each sofa.

"Oh, do you approve our new acquisition, Mr. Dordrecht?" Mrs. DeLancey cooed. "We just purchased them this week from William Cooper's emporium. I think they work handsomely with this room. Don't you?"

With any room, I thought—silently, happily noting that I'd at last get paid for them. "They're very fine, ma'am—fine, indeed! Did you happen to learn from Mr. Cooper that it was I who imported them from London last summer?"

"No, really?" Mrs. DeLancey exclaimed incredulously. "*You* imported them? My goodness!"

"We had no idea!" Miss Colegrove said. "How very clever of you, sir!"

The ladies were not convincing actresses. *What was afoot?*

"We asked you to join us, Mr. Dordrecht," she continued, "because we desire your judgment on another matter. You see, my niece is trying on the new gown she's to wear to Peter's wedding, and we wanted a *masculine* opinion of it!"

"*Other* than Oli—"

"From outside the family, you see!"

My bemusement was total.

"Élise!" Mrs. DeLancey called out. "Why don't you and *Madame* come out and show your progress on the gown to Mr. Dordrecht? Have a seat, dear sir!" she added.

Élise Colegrove floated out into the sitting room, looking more delectable than ever in a sky blue gown with white flounces—most of which were attached by pins. Deigning to bestow a warm smile on me, she carefully sat on one of the new chairs. The harried seamstress fluttered around, pushing this, pulling that.

"Let him get a good look at the girl!" Mrs. DeLancey snapped at her, in French. The seamstress moved two feet away.

"Isn't she lovely!" Miss Eudoxia sighed warmly.

As Miss Élise smiled at me with becoming shyness, I had to admit that she was. But … it was all too contrary to her previous behavior. They were united to seduce me!

As for the gown … oh heck, it seemed fine. Though I couldn't quite imagine my sister Lisa clad in such a folderol, even if she had the fortune it must have cost.

"Mr. Dordrecht?"

"Oh, it looks very nice, very handsome indeed!"

Mrs. DeLancey and the seamstress commenced a heated discussion in French; I kept my face blank, even though I understood the seamstress to be complaining that the *décolletage* was excessive beyond even the permissive contemporary standards of Paris. Then Miss Colegrove and Mrs. DeLancey, in rare accord, instructed her on the changes to be made. Élise had no say in the matter, but seemed undisturbed.

Presently, the girl and the seamstress were both dismissed—the lass did not neglect to look back at me demurely—and I had to swallow to control my face.

"With a few revisions, I think that gown may serve for her own wedding," Miss Colegrove said off-handedly to Mrs. DeLancey.

"Which should not be too far off," the latter added, looking significantly at me. "As anyone can see, she will *soon* be spoken for!"

It was high time to throw some cold water on myself and this *charade*. "Ladies, as long as I'm here, perhaps you can explain this to me. Mr. Peter Colegrove admitted just now that, on the Sunday before she was killed, he overheard Mrs. Colegrove quarreling with Mr. James Colegrove. Mr. Peter was in the library, and their voices were raised in the parlor. Do you have any notion what the substance of this quarrel might have been?"

That certainly did alter the temper of the room! All smiles vanished, but I couldn't tell who was the greatest object of their irritation: myself, Peter, James, or the late Mrs. Colegrove. Mrs. DeLancey squirmed furiously on her divan while Miss Eudoxia's whole person turned to stone.

"He shouldn't have—" Mrs. DeLancey began.

"Neither of us would have any idea, Mr.—"

"She was such a fool, she—"

"I'm sure it was nothing, and—"

"No more sense than a—"

"Every family has its—"

"So extravagant, and completely devoid of breeding!"

Miss Eudoxia raised her voice to reassert control. "Mr. Dordrecht! As I say, *neither* of us"—she glared icily at her still-fuming companion—"could have any idea what this alleged disagreement might have concerned."

"No," Mrs. DeLancey managed to concur. "Of course not!" She forced a sickly, transparently false, smile in my direction.

"Had James and Mrs. Colegrove ever quarreled before?"

"If James would pay more attention to his own wife, he—"

"Certainly not that we ever noticed, Mr. Dordrecht!" Miss Eudoxia insisted, fixing her eyes on Mrs. DeLancey until the latter recovered herself. "Perhaps you shall have to inquire of James directly ... if you think this trifling squabble so desperately important. Though why you should, I can't fathom."

"Nor can I!" Mrs. DeLancey vehemently agreed, closing ranks.

"I shall endeavor to do just that, ladies, as soon as the occasion permits." They did not look pleased. Obviously no more could be expected from them this afternoon. "But I do thank you for your time, and I wish you a good day!"

I do believe I've made them nervous. *Good!*

But about what?

---◇---

"Oh, Thomas, you're here! Excellent!" John Glasby said on Monday morning, the instant I shut the office door against the cold rain outside. "I need you to go right back out again!"

Though I normally try to avoid whining, I really wanted to warm up and dry off. But, seeing the dark circles under my friend's eyes, attributable to the overwork of weeks, I drew up my chest and awaited instructions.

"I was going to send Adelie, as some selling is involved. But the client is particularly straight-laced—horrified by the very idea of women in business—and—"

"Oh my!" I sneered.

"Don't be—"

Pompous. Right. "Sorry!"

"And I also thought you especially might find it of interest!"

"Yes? Why so?"

"The client is Coxsackie Lumber. Lambert Colegrove's company."

"Oh!"

"Word has it, he's got a customer in New Castle, Delaware, building a granary, that wants eight or ten cartloads of cedar shingles, and—"

"Oh, but the *Hermione* is nearly full, John! There's just the two small holds on the cable deck, and—"

He raised his hand. "*Janie's* back, Thomas. If we send *Hermione L.* out this afternoon, we—"

"But she's not *completely* full!"

"I know, I know! We'd have just enough leeway to get all the shingles into *Janie* before Thursday high tide. Which will be at three-thirty. Which is fortunate, as Benjamin is adamant that I must join him at the merchants' meeting at four that day."

"They'll want you to commit to never using stamps."

"I expect so," he said miserably. "Benjamin's all for it, and— Oh, first things first, Thomas! We have to get the commission. If we get it, we'll send *Hermione L.* on her way today, full or not, pull *Janie* into the slip, and stuff shingles into her until the very last minute. Work into the nights, if we have to."

"Right! Where's he located?"

"Just up on Cherry Street, near Catherine Slip. We've dealt with this man before, Thomas. He's a hard bargainer. The dourest Presbyterian you'll ever meet! Spin him no yarns! His father is positively charming, in comparison."

"Good lord!"

"But there's one major difference between them ..."

"*Eh?*"

"Don't repeat this, all right? As opposed to his father, Lambert Colegrove is honest."

"Yes?"

I shook the rain off my hat, just inside the door, and addressed the tall, spare, balding, black-suited man I took to be a clerk. "Good morning. May I speak with Mr. Colegrove, please?"

"Yes."

It dawned: this was he. Perhaps there was a faint resemblance to Timothy or Theodora, but I saw none to Aaron. The others present studiously ignored me. *Glasby wasn't jesting!*

Still standing in my sodden coat, I launched into my pitch. "Good morning, sir! My name is Thomas Dordrecht, I'm with Castell, Leavering & Glasby, and—"

"Don't I know that name—Dordrecht?"

"Perhaps so, sir. I am also retained by your sister, Miss Theodora Colegrove, to look into—"

"Oh *that!* I've no time for that. Good day to you, sir!"

"Sir, begging your pardon, my present mission is to represent Mr. John Glasby, who wishes to apprise you that we have a coastal sloop available until Thursday that—"

"Which one?"

"The *Janie*, sir. Captain Ford. Twenty-seven tons burden."

"I know Ford, I don't know the boat." A few seconds passed. "I have a large consignment of shingles for Delaware. An emergency. You'd think my fool customer would've noticed what's going on in our colonies before last Tuesday!"

"Most ships not already asea are nearly full-laden, sir."

"How much?"

I stated a per-ton figure twenty percent higher than the *Janie's* usual rate—ten percent for the rush, ten percent for bargaining room.

"Need to see the boat!" Assuming my willingness, he rose, yelled to a clerk to mind the shop, and donned his coat.

"She's anchored off Peck Slip, sir, but we could have her brought in this afternoon."

"*Hmm!*" He opened the door and preceded me out into the rain. The weather was sufficiently dismal that any attempt to chat was pointless. As we strode along, I rehearsed my commercial arguments and calculated that the most plausible moment to raise Miss Theodora's quest would be on our return—presuming the success of the former.

I feared our rower's heart might give out as he strained to pull against the current toward the *Janie*. No one was on deck to pass a line—the crew having the sense to stay out of the rain. But the rower surprised me with a mighty whistle, which raised a mate just as I thought his strength *was* about to fail.

Captain Ford rushed up to greet us, showed us about the *Janie*, and placidly answered Colegrove's queries about his ship, his crew, Delaware Bay, and New Castle harbor, all before I could convey the slightest notion of what business was in discussion.

Colegrove grunted and nodded, and set off back to the deck. I clutched Ford's arm, whispered thanks, and hurried after him. There was the slightest hint of satisfaction on Colegrove's face, as we clambered back down to the dinghy. The rower, now soaked through, ceased bailing, and heaved with all his might to get us back to shore. I paid and tipped him, and dashed after Colegrove, already thirty paces ahead.

"Do you have a consignment form on your person, Dordrecht?" he asked as I caught up.

"I do, sir."

"Can we get a dozen cartloads into her in three days?"

"Aye." I knew better than to say, *We'll try.*

"And you can get the customs officer on Thursday?"

"Aye."

"*Hmph!* Might be the last legal bill of lading we sign for some time, *eh?*"

Was he relaxing, ever so slightly? "That it might be, sir!"

He then informed me he would pay us twenty percent less than I'd asked. With great difficulty, I worked him back up to twelve percent over standard. Glasby would settle for that, as we needed the work.

We arrived back at his shop, and I was distressed by the presence of his staff, as the questions I hoped to pose were undeniably familial. But he walked to a room I'd not seen earlier, opened the door, and scowled to find a glum fellow with bright red hair, a few years my junior, reading a book. "Vincent! Out!"

"Yes, Uncle—sir!" Before he closed the door after himself, I took a quick glance at Aaron Colegrove's eldest grandchild. Though tall and somewhat stoutly built, Vincent's undemonstrative face and abstracted air suggested to me a rather dreary personality.

Lambert Colegrove immediately delved into the details of our agreement. Within fifteen minutes, we had it all on paper. Though we obviously both needed to set work in motion directly, I took advantage of the first hint of a smile....

"Mr. Colegrove, I know we're both under some duress, but ... could I please beg your indulgence for one moment, for your sister's sake?"

He groaned. "Mr. Dordrecht, I have offered my sister a great deal of support over the years. If I'd known she was saving it only to squander it on such a quixotic project, I might have ... endowed the church instead!"

Did I perceive a hint of curiosity, however? "Yes, but—"

"Oh, get on with it, man!"

"Thank you! I ... do understand that you are ... not in constant contact with your father's household"—his face conveyed cold impatience—"but you are a man of business, and I have learned from the servants that on the Sunday before Mrs. Colegrove was murdered, she quarreled with your, *um*, half-brother, James. Have you—"

Now his look suggested not so much hatred, as intense dislike. "Sir, I cannot imagine why this may or may not have occurred."

"I was told the quarrel was about money."

"Really?" He seemed suddenly intrigued. "Well ... that makes a certain— The last time I saw James—and it was the first time in months— was the following afternoon. He came here, and had the effrontery to beg a loan of eighty pounds!" His face worked with indignation. "Refused to say what it was for, but insisted he would repay it as soon as our parent returned with his promised commission."

"As a tax officer?"

"Yes," Colegrove said heavily. "I don't know where you stand on this, Dordrecht, but I was deeply appalled that any man who shared my surname should be counting on the exploitation of his fellow citizens!"

"I quite understand, sir!"

"So I sent the whelp packing. I was especially irritated because I was traveling up-river that very afternoon, to inspect my mills in Saugerties. Nearly missed the tide! I didn't even learn of the murder until—When?—the Sunday following." He shrugged. "Is that all? We really must—"

"One thing more, sir. Do you happen to know if your father has written a will?"

"A *will?* Do I know? No. But I can't imagine that he hasn't. If he has not, his entire estate would go to *me!*" He snorted derisively. "And as things stand between us, I can't imagine that he would encounter that." He thought for a second. "I've always understood that I shall inherit the Mamaroneck property, but that's now a minor part of his fortune. And I've always assumed that old man DeLancey would have insisted on some sort of understanding before allowing him to marry his niece, the widow Boyce."

"You refer to our late governor, James DeLancey, Senior?"

"No no. His father, old Stephen—sire of the lot. He was still alive when my father and Lavinia Boyce were wed. Now we really must—"

"Yes sir," I agreed, rising. "Thank you for—"

"I have my doubts about the practicality of Theodora's enterprise, Mr. Dordrecht," he said, looking me straight in the eye. "But I do wish you success. I may not have liked or much respected Mrs. Colegrove, but I can't sanction murder."

"Of course not, sir!"

"Right. Vincent!" he bellowed, opening his office door.

Vincent quickly appeared—a full-grown young man with a smooth, child-like face. "Sir?"

"The shingles for Delaware: I've contracted with Castell, Leavering & Glasby that they're to go into the *Janie* sloop, with the utmost dispatch. You follow Mr. Dordrecht, here, and make the arrangements." Vincent Colegrove was struck immobile. "*Now!*"

Once his nephew shook a leg to put his coat on, Colegrove bade me a curt good day, snapped his fingers at another clerk, and retired to his office.

What extraordinary serendipity, the chance to query two Colegroves in the simple course of business! The owner of Coxsackie Lumber did not seem to have picked his nephew to accompany me out of any desire to assist his sister's project—rather, he was probably the first staff man visible as he opened the door. Or perhaps the most expendable?

The rain had slowed to a drizzle, and our hats at least kept it out of our faces as we walked. I deduced that Vincent must be the red-haired lad who Mrs. Pannikin had seen with Mrs. Colegrove.

"Mr. Colegrove, has your aunt Theodora acquainted you with the fact that she has retained me to investigate the murder of Mrs. Artemis Colegrove?"

He had been shuffling along, paying attention neither to his pathway nor to me, but he suddenly halted, turned pale, and grabbed a porch railing for support.

"I ... I did not know my aunt had any such project, Mr.—*uh*—"

"Thomas Dordrecht."

"Sir. And she has asked ... *you* to *investigate* it?"

"That is so. And as business has fortuitously brought us together, might I ask your indulgence for the moments we walk to the office?"

"I ... I—"

The fellow seemed positively wracked by emotion. "The servants at your grandfather's home tell me you were a frequent visitor this past summer. I am curious what prompted you to make so many calls. You had a duty to your great-aunt, no doubt?"

"Yes! No! That is, I—" He swallowed hard and took a deep breath. "It was Arte— Mrs.— my step-grandmother that I went to see. She and I became very ... very devoted to one another. She was, you see, one of the noblest ladies you could ever hope to know!" He was looking directly at me, his lower lip trembling. "She was truly a ... a great soul!"

"*Umm*—"

"She had a deep love of poetry, of beauty, of God!" He was transported. "She was all that is perfection in feminine nature. A goddess so far removed beyond that tawdry pagan statue. She was an inspiration, a muse!" In preposterous conjunction, the clouds cleared and the sun made its first pale appearance of the day. "She was a light to the heathen philistines of all the world!"

I was very tempted to laugh—but managed to stifle it.

"And she was so extraordinarily generous! So kind! She would listen to my poems—puny and unworthy of her though they were, Mr. Dordrecht— and pronounce them charming or uplifting. It was she herself who belonged on that pedestal, sir, mark my words!"

My head was spinning. The deluded fellow was besotted by his grandfather's wife—who was, after all, a year or so younger than he was. And the old fox had been far, far away, allowing this disreputable liaison full scope to flower—in the mind of our would-be poet, at least. Did he know she was with child? Did he know she was simultaneously entertaining her old paramour, Henry Tenkus?

"So you met with her … and you read her your poetry?"

"Yes! And many times, she deigned to pay me a compliment. I had never before essayed the sonnet form, Mr. Dordrecht, but she—"

"I beg pardon, Mr. Colegrove, but, *um*, did you ever encounter the sailor, Henry Tenkus?"

He flushed crimson. "No sir! I never met the murdering fiend! I never even knew he existed and was harassing her before she died. If I had, I would surely have thrashed him, by god!"

No, he'd have thrashed you. Tenkus' guilt appeared to be an idea imperviously fixed into every Colegrove brain.

"It would have been the least I could do for the noble Lady Artemis!"

Right. "You visited the house last on the day before she was murdered, I understand. Had you just then inscribed a sonnet, or …"

Now his color and expression suggested mortification, rather than anger. We had ceased walking and moved beside the stoop of a house, away from the foot traffic. He scanned the cityscape evasively for half a minute. "Mr. Dordrecht, I … We knew my grandfather was expected within the fortnight, and … and I knew that she loved him not, and … I confessed to her that I loved her and wished her to fly with me, to defy all our petty precepts of marriage and fidelity in the name of the purest love that man and woman can have for each other!"

Mad! "May I ask, and what was her reaction?"

He sighed so profoundly I detected a hint of overt self-dramatization at last. "She refused, Mr. Dordrecht—on the highly moral ground of fidelity to her husband, my grandfather, whom I was so shamefully ready to betray. It … I fell to my knees and begged her to reconsider, but she would not hear of it. Finally, she said, 'Vincent, you're being impossible, and silly, and this mustn't go on!' And so, devastated, I left. And that was the last I ever saw of her!"

Could this bathetic soul have murdered the woman? Could his mawkish infatuation have led him to violence? "Mr. Colegrove, how were you occupied the following noon, pray tell me."

"What, you suspect that I, that *I* could have harmed that precious jewel, that shining beacon of virtue, that—"

"I simply desire an answer, if you please."

"It's …not a pretty tale, Mr. Dordrecht."

What? "Nonetheless …"

"Ah very well. They say confession is … I was in despair, sir, completely in despair! I considered that I had offended not only the damsel I worshiped, but my grandfather, and the uncle who employed me, and even the good name of my martyred sire!"

Martyred sire? Oh right, the warrior who got shot in the—

"I had gone to my uncle's office that morning, in an effort to make habit overwhelm emotion, but … but it was no use. When we adjourned at noon, I fled to the far side of the island, thinking to end my sorrows, like Leander despairing of Hero's love, in the pure waters of Hudson's stream!"

"You were—"

"I made my way to a cove just north of the town, where I ran, fully dressed, into the waters and made for the far shore, hoping to end it all when my strength gave out!"

"—intending to commit … What happened?"

"I am a fair swimmer, sir. I had proceeded a good fifty yards off the shore when I realized I was not at all in pure waters."

Oh my god.

"I was swimming amid the vile effluent of the foundry, Mr. Dordrecht. Ash, oils, chunks of burnt wood, weeds, dead fish! I realized that should my corpse be retrieved from the harbor, it would be covered in filth. I thought that her last sight of me might be painted with soot, and reek of industrial scum, and so I …turned back."

"And your family?"

"I managed to elude them. I went directly to our laundress, who knows me well, and begged her indulgence and confidence. She had been cleaning my other suit, and I exchanged my garments behind a screen. Then I wandered about the orchards north of town until supper time, which is when Mother and Aunt Theodora gave me the impossible news that she … she had been murdered." He bolted into a passage between two nearby houses, buried his face in his hands, and sobbed loudly.

This lasted but a few seconds, as the mistress of one of the houses came out from the back and was obviously blocked by his presence. He mastered himself and rejoined me, still weeping. I guided him by the elbow, and we hurried onward to the firm's office. There, he managed to order himself while I conveyed the happy news of our last pre-tax consignment.

Over the rest of the day, and the next, I made many trips back and forth to Coxsackie Lumber Company, and on each occasion I managed to elicit some small detail that added to my overall knowledge of events surrounding the murder. Vincent Colegrove told me the address of his laundry. One clerk explained that he had traveled to and from Saugerties *with* his employer, on the same boat, on the dates Lambert Colegrove had specified. Another—a lad I recognized from the West Ward militia—said the staff never broke for the mid-day meal before twelve, and he recalled Vincent's inexplicable absence later that afternoon. He had been moved to wonder about him, once Mrs. Colegrove's murder became public, but couldn't believe the boss's feckless nephew might have had anything to do with it.

Nevertheless, I detoured my return on Tuesday morning to visit the laundry. The simple, comely young laundress there of course recalled Vincent's anomalous appearance in soaked and disgusting raiment. "The poor boy didn't want his mother to know he'd gotten drunk and fallen into the river!" she said. "And I certainly didn't want *my* mother to find out I'd let him undress himself, just over there!" In response to my query regarding the timing, she was able to tell me he'd arrived well before one o'clock; she knew because he had interrupted her own mid-day repast. She didn't know all her customers by name, and therefore had made no connection between his strange visit and the notorious murder she'd heard about the next day.

So, I pondered, rushing back to Peck Slip, *is it conceivable* that young Vincent, in crazed jealousy of his grandfather—or something—could have murdered Artemis Colegrove? To do so, he'd have had to dash from Cherry Street in the Out Ward down to 144 Broadway, strangle and then stab his conveniently available victim, then decorate her corpse with blood, then proceed a mile and a half to the Hudson shore, jump in the river to deliberately befoul his clothes, and arrive at his laundry before one o'clock.

He'd need to be as fast as Pheidippides and as fortunate as Fortunatus—and neither was plausible.

Even less was it conceivable, I noted, that his uncle Lambert Colegrove might have struck the blow.

Might either—or any other—have *commissioned* an unknown and unrelated miscreant to act in his stead? Such a criminal would have had to be desperate to take the risk of committing murderous aggression in broad daylight in the center of town. And would still have needed to know the surroundings and the schedule of the household. And would have had to surprise her so completely that she was throttled before she could cry out.

My own desperation was leading *me* into irrational suppositions!
Back to work!

That evening, dead tired from hours of dealing with bundles of cedar shingles—doing a goodly share of the lifting myself—I arrived back at my humble domicile to find the family already abed. One candle, however, had been left to burn down, which illuminated two envelopes addressed to me. One was from Theodora Colegrove, as usual. The other lacked any return address, and the handwriting was unfamiliar. I lit a fresh candle and took both up to my room.

Dutifully, I opened Miss Theodora's first, and read yet another exhortation to investigate sailors' haunts. This time, however, she also enumerated a dozen of her father's business rivals, including, I noted with complete exasperation, John Glasby. The woman is crazed—or perhaps just as prone to foolish supposition as I am myself.

The other was not actually an envelope; rather, a plain sheet of paper, twice folded and sealed with candle drips. In its hand-scrawled entirety, it read:

Pro Silencia
The Man that makes use of unhallowed Knowledge—
Let him take Care of his House, Person and Effects
Vox Privaci
I Dare

After staring for two minutes in sheer disbelief, my lip began to curl.
Oh you swine! I thought. *You all-too-clever bastard!* You have the gall to think you can intimidate me? With Latin that even I can tell is fake?

I had no doubt the missive was to be construed as a threat. But from whom?

I fell asleep angrily turning over the likely candidates. But I could settle on only one facet of my would-be tormentor's identity.

The surname.

CHAPTER 10

In response to my urgent summons, Charles joined me the following noon, while I was gobbling a meat pasty at dockside. He looked as harried and cross as anyone. "What is it?" he demanded testily.

I showed him the note.

"Oh dear god!" he breathed. "It's that Timothy, I'll lay odds! God damn the man!"

Though I too suspected Timothy Colegrove, I wasn't at all so positive. "Did you—"

Charles shook his head, grimacing in annoyance. "Oh, I'm chastened to admit I haven't checked into him, Thomas. We elected someone else onto the operations committee, and I ... forgot. But *this!*" He stroked his chin breathlessly. "What worries us most about our protest, Thomas, is—" He broke off, noticing the many people near us. He pulled me away, next to a rubbish tip, and spoke in a whisper. "What worries us is the thought that Governor Colden might be insinuating false agents among the Sons, men who would present themselves as patriots, but who would deliberately incite the violence we truly want to avoid."

"And you think Timothy Colegrove— Did I tell you he rebuffed his sister's inquiries, just as brusquely as he rebuffed mine?"

"No. He fits the pattern, Thomas. I'll ... talk with Willett and get right on him. Thanks for showing me this!" He was impatient to be going.

"It could be somebody else altogether, Charles!"

"Aye. Yes, I know. But maybe not." He turned back, with another thought. "Look out for *yourself*, Thomas! However *precious* this memorandum may be, I'd not doubt the challenge implied."

"Thanks, I'll keep watch!"

"We'll speak again—perhaps this evening, Thomas. We need to know more before tomorrow. It would be …" He walked off, shaking his head.

Another cart, piled high with cedar shingles, clattered across Front Street and parked by the *Janie*. Still chewing my pasty, I urged the driver a few feet forward to accommodate the crane.

I pushed our hands and myself hard, straight through the afternoon and well past dark, until Captain Ford shouted to me from the deck. "We can't do any more tonight, Mr. Dordrecht! Wind's come up. Sparks from those torches could blow on board the ship, and we're a blessed tinderbox!"

It was eight-thirty, and I had to concede. The men were exhausted, and tired men make mistakes that could cost us everything. "First light tomorrow, gentlemen?"

Weary nods were sufficient. There was one more cartload to come, besides the stack waiting on the hard. I doused the torch directly upwind of the *Janie* … and found Marinus Willett standing beside the other one.

"My mate Heinrich found him and tailed him," he said without preliminaries.

"Timothy Colegrove?"

"Aye. You'll never guess—"

"Oh come on!"

"We had learned that Timothy has aspirations in the legal field. But since he's disowned, he's of course got no money to pay for proper training, so it appears he's performing mundane clerical work. Now in a city teeming with lawyers, most of whom oppose the Stamp Act, and a few of whom are actually honest, who would you guess is employing Timothy Colegrove?"

I hadn't the strength to shrug my shoulders.

"Darius Gerrison, the lowest, the most mercenary, most royalist of the lot!"

"Gerrison's his father's lawyer!" I recalled.

"Is he? Well, who knows if the old man's even aware of it. Heinrich somehow learned Timothy has been working for him for months."

"*Huh!*"

"Look, Friday, Thomas: I want you to shadow Timothy Colegrove, and—"

"The militia captain said I was to form up at Vesey Street."

"We'll get you off that. If Colegrove starts throwing curses, or stones, or bricks, or punches … he has to be stopped. Did you notice that Governor Colden has moved some of the fort's cannons away from the harbor, and over into the bastion facing Bowling Green? The man's a lunatic and it wouldn't take too many wild rowdies on our side to set him off. Charles and I have our own assignments, as do all the others on the committee. Can you watch Timothy Colegrove for us? You would, of course, be watching out for yourself!"

"If he's the one who sent the threat!"

"True. But—"

"Of course, Marinus!"

"Friday will be big, Thomas! There's to be more than one event, and we're anxious to keep things in focus, to make our point. While most people will be rallying on the Common after supper, I'm to start another parade earlier, downtown behind Old Slip Market, at half past five. Timothy's supposed to be with my lot, but still, finding him will be your first problem. God help us if he decides to disguise himself!"

"I'll do it."

Did I sleep that night? I must have, but all I can remember is lying down and then immediately getting back up.

The last day. I concentrated on loading the *Janie* and managed not to think about it, until we took a dinner break, and the other lads begged me to read them the news in the latest *Weekly Post-Boy*, which we snagged just before noon. The most prominent item was "A Funeral Lamentation on the Death of Liberty," which concluded:

> Who finally expires this
> Thirty-first of October,
> In the Year of our Lord
> **MDCCLXV**
> And of our Slavery
> *I*

Among the roustabouts we had hired for the week were two hard-bitten youngsters with new beards. "Do you think them damn English bastards really mean to enslave us all, Mr. Dordrecht?" one of them asked.

A black crewman snorted, spat, and walked away—without their taking any notice.

"They wouldn't call it that, of course, lads," I replied, "but if they're demanding that you work for them without your consent, then it's something very like slavery, is it not?"

"I want to be the first one to scale the fort's wall!" asserted the taller one who, flush with the coin we'd paid him yesterday, had ordered a pint of grog with his pasty.

"Nah, I'm gonna beat you, you're too heavy!" the other challenged.

"Like hell you will, shrimp! You'll never—"

This was just what Marinus had been worried about. "Lads!" I snapped. "If you want to do any good, you've got to keep order, and listen to the marshals among the Sons of Liberty, all right?"

"Aw hell, but—"

I swallowed the last of my pasty and tucked the newspaper away. "Meanwhile, we have a job to finish here!"

"I'll be the first, you just watch!"

"Let's *go*, lads!"

The last of the nine hundred eighty-two bundles of cedar shingles were stuffed into the *Janie* just after two o'clock, the hour at which John Glasby had arranged for the customs officer to inspect and sign her clearance papers. The officer not appearing, Captain Ford frantically begged me to locate him, mentioning that he knew the man had cleared the *Munificent*, three blocks south of us, two hours earlier. Following leads I discovered there, I tracked him down a mile away, in a public house next to the fort, where I found him barely able to stand. *"Janie?* Janie who?" he said—and roared with laughter. "I've already cleared four ships today, that's enough!"

"Sir, you arranged—you *promised* to clear us out at two p.m.!"

"I did? Oh hell! Well ... you don't happen to have the papers on you, do you, boy?"

Luckily, I did. He was supposed to inspect the ship, but ...

"You buy me just one more tot of rum, and I'll say your honest face makes you trustworthy enough to sign the papers!"

I did, he signed, and the *Janie* was one of a large flotilla that departed at high water on the day before the stamp tax became effective.

"Our last shipment!" Glasby sighed, when I reported to him in his office shortly thereafter. "For how long?" He was straightening his cravat, using the window glass as a mirror.

"There are many who are suggesting that we can't wait for repeal, and we shall have to start dispatching our ships without legal papers," I ventured hesitantly.

"So there are," he asserted noncommittally. "I'm … off to the merchants' meeting, Thomas. You'll be relieved, I imagine, that Benjamin has persuaded me that the Sons' resolutions must be adopted."

"Ah!"

"I'm not a bit happy to be agreeing with him, you know. I think we're heading for absolute ruin either way. But I suppose we must at least put up a fight about it!"

"I concur with that, John."

"*Uh huh*. So … what are you going to do with the rest of your afternoon? Your *free time*?"

"The shopkeepers and artisans are meeting to consider the equivalent resolutions. I thought I'd attend, even though I'm now not employed at all. I doubt my odd commission from Miss Colegrove qualifies me as an artisan!"

He managed a brief chuckle. "We're *all* likely to be not employed before this is over, Thomas! Look, I have to run, but do come by tomorrow morning, and we'll settle what we owe you then, all right?"

"That's fine, John, thank you."

He hurried away. I loitered in the main room, nostalgically looking about and chatting with the two clerks still present. Mapes, whom I'd not noticed, suddenly sprang into view. "So! We're gentlemen of leisure once again, Dordrecht!" he said bitterly. "Me, I'm—"

"Hardly, Mapes!"

"I don't know what the devil I'm going to do! This money has been a godsend, but prices are through the roof, and my family's going to have to scrimp on every last thing to get through the winter. I don't expect to taste meat again before the damned tax is repealed—if it ever is!"

Mapes was obviously exhausted and somewhat panicky. He had probably just settled with Glasby and realized that his situation, like that of most in the city, was dire. "I'm going on to the shopkeepers' meeting, by the Common. Join me?"

It rallied him. "I'll walk with you, but I'm headed for home. Walking— as always."

For the ten minutes it took us to reach the tavern where the shopkeepers were gathered, I did naught but listen to the travails of the Mapes family. It seemed to help. He shook my hand warmly as we parted, and called me his "true friend."

There was a crowd of about a hundred milling around outside the tavern. I chanced to look down Broadway before pushing my way inside, and saw an even larger group outside the establishment where the merchants' meeting was in progress.

My fantasies of getting myself a beer were instantly dispelled. The company was pressed in so tightly I feared the walls might burst. The meeting was under way, and a resolution had just been passed to delay voting—but not debate—until word was heard of the upshot of the principal merchants' decisions. John Lamb was presiding, but I recognized few others present save, to my pleasured surprise, my aunt's husband, William Cooper, and of all people, their eldest son, the Reverend Henry. Surely a terrible family crisis will ensue when the two quarrelsome brothers realize they *agree!*

Marinus Willett appeared out of a cloud of pipe smoke to read the substantive resolution as proposed. It was a "nonimportation" agreement. Lamb interrupted to boast that it would be the first such pact organized anywhere in the colonies. Should the merchants commit not to import, the resolution read, the retailers would likewise promise that no British goods would be bought or sold in the city—until Parliament not only repealed the Stamp Act, but removed objectionable aspects of the Revenue and Currency acts as well.

While Willett was talking, the tumult of a distant cheering crowd was heard—immediately followed by the deafening roar of the crowd outside the tavern door. Half a minute passed, but it did not abate. "I take it," Lamb shouted to the gathering, "that our town's principal merchants have passed the resolutions proposed by the Sons of Liberty!"

Cheering erupted inside the tavern. After a minute more, Willett sat down, and a dignified ancient fellow stood up and gestured for silence. He was wearing a leather apron, and everyone knew him as a maker and retailer of wagons, sleds, and harnesses. He was given the honor of moving that our meeting pass its resolves by acclamation.

If there was any dissent, it was inaudible to me. The cheers inside the tavern were followed by huzzahs outside it and joyful noise further down the avenue. After reminders regarding public decorum on the morrow, and an interminable three-minute benediction from Cousin Henry, the gathering burst out onto the street with great relief.

I moved to the park side of Broadway, gulping in the chilly but welcome autumnal air. The face of my musical friend, whom I hadn't seen inside, suddenly materialized beside me in the dark. "Mr. Fischl! How fare you, sir?"

"I do well, Mr. Dordrecht, I thank you! I trust we have just done the right thing, although I confess I can't make much sense of any of it!"

Having immigrated but ten years before, it was impressive that he'd made *any* sense of it. "The government have put us in a horrendous bind, Mr. Fischl, and I do believe that we must protest with all our might."

"*Ah*. Well … It is a fortunate thing that I have run into you, sir. I've wanted to ask your advice on a most troubling problem. You see—"

Guessing that Fischl's problem would likely have nothing to do with stamp taxes or high tides or cedar shingles, my mood lifted instantly. "Supper, Mr. Fischl? I am utterly famished."

Fischl agreed, and I led him around the corner to a cheap but wholesome tavern I'd been frequenting. When settled comfortably—beer at last in hand—I invited him to explain his problem.

"A very wealthy young man I've never seen before came into the shop the other day, and told me that his family is giving a ball or something at their country estate, and wishes to have musical entertainment."

"Well … how very spruce!"

"And it seems that expense is no object!"

"Oh, it gets better!"

"I had thought I could play the violin and assemble three others into a quartet. That would be easy enough—but, oh no! The fellow said he had heard that pianofortes were the latest thing, and that I had them, and he wanted to know if—"

Ooh, money! "He wants to buy one?" I live in hope that Fischl will sell those instruments!

"Well, no, he wants to *rent* one, and have it be part of the entertainment."

"Oh, well," I said, disappointed. "Surely you pointed out that that will cost him dearly?"

"I did, but as I say, he's of the silk-stocking, Macaroni Club class, and such concerns are not as critical as they would be to you and me."

"*La di da!*"

"What I wanted to ask you is whether you know anyone ready to play the instrument, and also if you have any idea how we should move it back and forth."

"Why don't you play it, Mr. Fischl, and get someone else for the violin?"

"I'd rather not. I was actually hoping *you* might be interested!"

"Me! Oh my friend, my uncle Pennyman gave me a few lessons while I was still in London, but I'm hardly competent to perform with it."

"*Ah*. Know of anyone else?"

"There must be someone in this city!"

"Haven't come across any," Fischl sighed. "Even those who are regulars on the harpsichord are intimidated by it."

I reluctantly shrugged my shoulders.

"Well, can you at least suggest how to move the thing? I kept the packing crates, of course."

"If it's one of the palaces up by Kip's Bay, the roads are good enough. It'd have to be re-tuned, but you could simply put it in a cart, and—"

"No, this is in the *country*—way up north in Westchester County somewhere. Maybe twenty miles away."

"Oh dear!" I had a thought. "Is it in the center of the county, or—"

"He said it was practically right on the Long Island Sound. Could we transport it by boat?"

"It'd be safer, surely, than rattling it across every ditch in between. Even though you'd have to navigate the Hell Gate. But … all the boats are out, Mr. Fischl, they're delivering their last cargoes."

"Well, this is still two weeks away, Mr. Dordrecht."

"Oh? There might be some back by then. I'll keep a watch out—but you realize I'm no longer employed in the business? My stint is over, as of today."

"Ah. Sorry!"

We changed to more agreeable topics: who might play the other strings, what pieces might be appropriate. Fischl's an intelligent and kindly man, and I always enjoy talking to him.

I walked a few blocks down Broadway with him, before we parted.

"Hey mister, where's the parade?" a boy asked me a minute later.

"There's a parade?"

"Ain't there always? You don't know? *Sheesh!*"

Probably the victorious crowds had elected to march through town, shouting "Liberty!"—the slogan of the moment—to celebrate the merchants' and the shopkeepers' resolutions. I, however, was eager to lie flat, and—

There was a noisy group three blocks down in an angrier mood. Throwing stones at windows and the street lamps. *What does that prove?* Pushing back my exhaustion, I strode toward them.

"Death to tyrants!" I heard. "Time for tar and feathers!" "No compromising with the stamps!" "What's good for Boston is good for New York!" I noticed glass on the street, and that a lot of windows and lamps were broken. I heard arguments among the mob, as some were advising restraint and others pushing them aside. They at least seemed to be selective about which houses were attacked: as I caught up with them, the mob was moving southward, and the darkened Colegrove house had suffered three shattered panes. A fellow was taking aim at number one-forty-two, when I caught his arm.

"Hey!" He was drunk.

"Stop! This house has no part of the stamp faction."

"They's *all* against us, in this row, mate! Let go!"

"No! I happen to know who lives here. An old widow woman. You think you're advancing the cause by attacking old women?"

"Aw, bugger off!" he snarled. But he desisted and buggered himself off. I stayed put until the mob had passed to the next block. They were still throwing stones, and no militia were about to stop them, but I headed back to Reade Street, completely knackered.

What a luxury, to sleep as late as you please!

A luxury that might soon bring penury, but I relished it this once. I must have been out over ten hours. Had to chuckle, thinking how deeply my brother Harmanus—nay, the entire town of New Utrecht—would have been scandalized.

Yet I did have matters to be attended. I noticed a difference directly I began walking across town toward Peck Slip. It was a Friday morning, yet the streets were quieter than on a Sunday. Though the weather was fine, crowds were not bustling, hawkers were not calling out, traffic was not congested. I turned down Broadway, to assess the damage in daylight. Someone would doubtless complain that "thousands" of windows and lamps were broken, but I'll have to concede that *dozens* of them had indeed fallen to mob passion … and I hated that, because I have an obstinate revulsion against wanton destruction, no matter what the cause or how deserving the victim.

At the corner of Maiden Lane I paused to verify that the Glasbys' home had at least not been attacked. When I turned back around, an enclosed coach I had noted earlier, harnessed to two very handsome dapple grays, was quietly making its way north … with Caesar, Colegrove's man, driving, many trunks on top, and four females—two very young and two very old—sitting glumly inside.

The rich man's womenfolk were being evacuated!

John Glasby and Benjamin Leavering both seemed pleased to see me at the firm's office, as did the two clerks still working there. Twenty-four hours earlier, the office had been crawling with carters, salesmen, sailors. "Anyone at all makes things seem more normal!" Glasby said.

"I didn't see any broken glass in front of your house," I observed to Glasby.

"They knocked out two panes of mine," Mr. Leavering sighed.

"The swine!" Glasby snarled.

"The way of the world, John," the elder replied with remarkable equanimity. "They know that many rich men support the stamp tax, and if they're drunk enough, they take their frustrations out on all rich men."

"What the devil are they doing, attacking the street lights?" one of the clerks demanded.

"Street lights are only in the wealthier sections of town, so far, so ..."

"No excuse!" I protested.

"None at all!" Glasby seconded.

Mr. Leavering shrugged.

Glasby pulled me into his office and paid me my last wages—in New York paper, of course. "It's still worth something, thank heaven. Guard it well, Thomas! And thank you for your assistance these two months. I doubt we'd ever have sent six boats out by today without your help!"

"*Pas de quoi, mon ami!*"

"Perhaps, when good times return, Thomas ..."

"We'll look forward to that!"

"Are you attending the Liberty funeral tonight?"

"The Sons have a special project for me. I'll surely be out and about."

"Perhaps we'll see you there!"

I made a hasty departure, wondering why it all felt so final. It wasn't as if we were unlikely to run into each other!

But an idea of how productively to spend my "free time" until five-thirty had suddenly occurred to me, and I made my way through the quiet streets to City Hall.

The pattern of activity was abnormal there, too. Although virtually no one was going in or out of the building, the sentries detained me until one of the town's aldermen had required me to state my business. On learning that it was merely to visit the records office, he peevishly waved me inside.

"What ho, a customer!" cackled the ancient, scrawny gentleman I recognized as the city's perpetual Town Clerk, who'd been appointed during the reign of the first George. "You're the only one, today! I was contemplating closing shop early. What can I do for you, young sir?"

"I am hoping to see a will, sir."

"Indeed? Well then, who is the decedent, and when did he or she expire?"

"Oh! The individual still lives, sir."

He snorted and shook his head, smiling, and I realized the request was ignorant and out of order. "Oh we can't do that, my lad. Wills are made public only after the demise, after they have been probated. Until then, they are stored here in confidence."

"Oh yes. I see. Of course."

He seemed reluctant to bid me be gone. "Whose will were you, *um*, concerned about?"

"I'm not even sure the man has written a will, sir."

"Well, that much I can tell you."

"It's Aaron Colegrove, sir, the proprietor of—"

"I do know Mr. Colegrove, of course, lad." He eyed me up and down, hesitating. "I'm curious: this is the third request I've had this year, but the others were from his sons. *You're* not a Colegrove, surely?"

"No, sir, no relation. Thomas Dordrecht, at your service!"

"*Hmm.* Well, I can inform you that Aaron Colegrove, despite the size and complexity of his fortune, has never seen fit to write a proper will."

"Aha! Well … thank you for your time, sir!"

"Not at all, Mr. Dordrecht!"

I started back toward the stairs, then halted and caught his eye again. "I beg your pardon, sir. You said he has never written a *proper* will?"

He chuckled. "*Ha*, you noticed that, did you? Smart lad! Are you studying the law?"

"No sir. I am— I have been employed in shipping, and hope to resume my career as soon as … things return to normal."

"Yes. You and the entire population, Mr. Dordrecht! Well …" He looked about the room, to verify that we were still the only two persons inside it. "There *is* an extremely odd document associated with Mr. Colegrove, that I pull out on occasion for legal students, to show them exactly how *not* to write an agreement, much less a contract, much less a testament."

I was transfixed. "Is that so, sir?"

"It's a sort of memorandum of understanding, you see, but so sloppily written, it's a legal horror, a perfect invitation to a spate of lawsuits."

"My word! Could I possibly—"

"Oh … why not? It's *not* a will!"

He bade me be seated while he hunted it out. I mused on my good fortune in having decided to pose this request on a day in which he was bored to distraction. I wondered how long it would take him to locate it, but was surprised when he returned in less than five minutes. "Here it is!" He sat down, and contemplated it, making a face. "It's not a proper will, you see, but it *can* be construed as a statement of intention. That's the problem with it. I begged them at the time to re-do it. I couldn't even notarize it, because they'd already signed it before they brought it in to me. Terribly stupid behavior, by men who should have known better!"

"*Um*, may I see it, sir?"

"Oh yes!" He passed it to me. "I refused to notarize it, but old DeLancey insisted I sign it."

I scanned it quickly. It was dated April 5, 1741, and signed by Aaron Colegrove, Stephen DeLancey, Oliver DeLancey, and— "This is your signature, here, sir?"

"That's right. Since Stephen and Oliver Senior are no longer with us, I am the only one who can vouch that it was presented as a *bona fide* statement of intention—but I've got quite a few years on Aaron Colegrove!"

He chuckled at that, shaking his head, and allowed me to read the page.

> In the name of God, Amen. I, Aaron Colegrove, desire my family estate in Mamaroneck, New York, to go to my eldest son, Lambert, with instruction to look after the welfare of my siblings and his own. To the four children of the late Elisha Boyce and Lavinia DeLancey Boyce Colegrove, I commend £150 each. All my remaining goods and chattels are to go to my wife and the future issue of my wife.
>
> Aaron Colegrove, April 5, 1741
> *Witness*:
> Stephen DeLancey
> Oliver DeLancey
> Lionel Tolbert

"At the time, it was clear to me that old Mr. DeLancey had had difficulty browbeating Colegrove into signing *anything*. Mr. Colegrove has never struck me as a fellow with either any awareness or any care for his mortality, and I think DeLancey was concerned that the Boyce children—his great-nieces and -nephews—would end up disinherited of the money that his half-brother Bernard had accumulated and that Elisha Boyce had carefully husbanded. I think six hundred pounds was pretty much the extent of it back then. Lord only knows what Colegrove is worth today! DeLancey told me he'd cornered Colegrove at the family's Easter celebrations, but you realize that April was right at the beginning of the Great Negro Conspiracy, and the whole city was then in as frantic a delirium as it is today!"

"Yes! I daresay that would figure. *Um*, I made a will before I ventured abroad, Mr. Tolbert, and … this doesn't seem to follow the form I was given at all."

"Of course not! Oliver DeLancey was the only one trained in law, and if I can see through it, I don't know why he couldn't! My guess is, his father wanted something immediately set down on paper, and Stephen DeLancey was, of course, as persuasive and demanding an old cuss as ever lived!"

A sentry came down the stairs and said that Mr. Tolbert was wanted in the mayor's office.

"I'll have to go. He needs all the help he can get today!" He rose. "Leave that paper—"

"Sir, did you show this memorandum to Mr. Colegrove's sons?"

"Just the younger one. The other one—I told him of it, but I was too busy at the time to search it out. Leave it on my desk, please, lad. Face down."

"Thank you so much for your time, Mr. Tolbert!"

He rushed off. Alone in the room, I carefully copied the document, word for word, into my notebook, before leaving it on his desk.

Once outside, I kicked myself for not asking *which* two sons had requested the document, and when they had requested it. Puzzled by Tolbert's vehement accusation of sloppiness, I studied it again, and finally discerned the basic flaw. The reference, "my wife and the future issue of my wife," obviously intended to protect the DeLancey heiress and her children, could just as easily be construed to *dis*-inherit them, if applied to a third wife and *her* children!

But it was time to get some food into myself before the evening's festivities began.

When I arrived outside the Old Slip Market, the sun had just set and men were already lighting torches, to illuminate whatever was to be the focus of the downtown parade. One was thrust into my hands, and I thought it as good an occupation as any. As bells tolled half-past five, a warehouse door was opened, and two men—Marinus Willett and Timothy Colegrove, by heaven!—walked out into the street carrying a twelve-foot rail on their shoulders. On the rail was perched a life-sized effigy of our esteemed acting Lieutenant-Governor Colden, with an expression of disdain, perplexity, and abject misery painted on its wooden face that I—and everyone else— found wonderfully comic.

"Like it?" Marinus asked, halting as the marshal—a big, heavy-set butcher—organized the precedence of drummers, banners, and flags. I nodded. "There's more to come later this evening!" he bellowed gleefully over the din. I cocked my head significantly at Colegrove. "Oh, well, where better for you to find him, *eh*? But keep watch on him, Thomas. Neither of us will be able to shoulder this rail for more than half an hour."

Timothy Colegrove had certainly made himself easy to locate, because he was coatless, wearing only a white linen shirt. Though it was a fine night, it was, after all, the first of November. Trying to prove himself? Or to call attention to some planned disruption?

Amid huzzahs, the procession started up Water Street. I nodded to Colegrove, but he turned his head away as he saw me. He seemed distressed by the heavy weight on his unprotected shoulder. Betting that he'd surrender his prominent spot to a stronger lad sooner than Willett, I posted myself directly behind them.

Two lads carrying a banner inscribed "Liberty, Property & No Stamps!" arrived tardily after two blocks. When we halted for the benefit of a group of people who'd rushed away from their suppers, I held the torch up to illuminate it. As I turned back, someone was tossing a peach pit at the effigy, another a chicken bone. Whistles and jeers abounded.

The procession halted in front of the Merchants' Coffee House at Wall Street, for the delectation of the prominent individuals dining there. I saw Benjamin Leavering endeavoring to entertain his taciturn customer Lambert Colegrove. Both came out on the veranda to applaud the spectacle. After spotting his elder brother, however, Timothy Colegrove stared resolutely ahead until the crowd finally moved once again.

Marching up Wall Street, the procession grew in number and volume, until City Hall was reached. And there, the mayor and some of the aldermen were nervously waiting, flanked by four unmoving redcoats. "Halt! Stop this!" the mayor yelled. The parade marshal signaled a stop, but the crowd murmured angrily. "This is an outrage!" the mayor continued. "I cannot permit this to continue. You are desecrating the likeness of the man who is our rightful governor, the representative of our sovereign king, the sacrosanct embodiment of all authority, the—"

Whistles and catcalls drowned him out. Everyone knew he loathed Colden, but his ceremonial position required him to put up a loyal front. Inflamed by the demonstration, a DeLancey-faction alderman strode over to the rail and boldly yanked the effigy off to the ground. Unbalanced, Timothy Colegrove fell and dropped his end of the rail, pulling Willett sharply backward. The crowd screamed its disapproval, and the alderman retreated toward the sentries.

"Stand fast!" the mayor ordered. The redcoats held their ground, skittishly eyeing the crowd.

Colegrove angrily stood back up, and I feared that he would attack the alderman and touch off a riot. If he was bent on causing trouble, surely this would be a prime opportunity. Willett looked alarmed. A sturdy black sailor was a few feet away, and I contemplated simply shoving the torch into his hands if I had to grapple with Colegrove. The mob—probably two hundred strong now—continued hollering furiously at the officials, who were slowly inching backwards.

But Timothy Colegrove appeared to be restraining himself. Though he cast angry glances at the alderman, he merely dusted his breeches and rubbed his elbow. The parade marshal calmly walked back to the rail, nodded at the sailor to take up Colegrove's end of the rail, and then raised his beefy arm to procure the silence the officials were unable to command. With a torchbearer highlighting his every move, he asked another supporter to put the effigy back on the rail. Then he turned and faced the mayor. "If you'll just stay where you are, gentlemen," he said calmly—but loudly enough for all to hear, "no one needs to get hurt, and we'll be on about our business!"

The mayor's face twisted in exasperation, livid over the effrontery of a mere butcher, but he could see that any resistance might instantly draw bloodshed—his own, first and foremost. "This isn't right!" he insisted.

"Neither is the Stamp Act!" the marshal bellowed. "Proceed!"

The drummers started up again, and everyone walked ahead. The officials suffered some disdainful epithets and rude gestures, but parade deputies among the Sons discouraged the tossing of any missiles.

Timothy Colegrove simply marched along with the others, next to the fellow who'd assumed his place.

But perhaps he was only biding his time.

Reaching Broadway, the parade turned down toward the fort …

As it came into view, we could see redcoats lined up behind the parapet of the fort, well illuminated by torches, some bearing muskets with bayonets affixed, others standing grimly beside the cannons. Rumors flew as we passed across the Bowling Green, that the soldiers had been seen this afternoon loading grapeshot into the cannons.

As the marshal passed the Green, Marinus Willett signaled another man to take his place, and called a squad to follow him around the western edge of the fort—which baffled me, as there was no other entrance, and I couldn't recall any structure by the Battery save the governor's private coach house.

The rest of us continued up to the fort, and halted a few yards from its gate. The marshal called my torch forward to make sure those inside could enjoy the dummy's foolish expression. Everyone particularly relished the thought that Cadwallader Colden himself was barricaded inside, along with his precious stamps. The sound of a sledgehammer smashing wood and metal came from the western edge of the fort.

A minute later, the governor's own coach—its elegant crest recognizable to everyone—was suddenly man-hauled beside us, twenty feet from the gate. The anger was great enough that no one protested that private property had been commandeered. Willett, grinning wildly, hefted the effigy off the rail and jumped into the coach, followed immediately by my cousin Charles—out of the blue—who was inexplicably bearing a long stick with a bulbous top, covered with a sheet.

The crowd was still roaring approval of the theft of the coach, when a huge puppet—a young female with its long blonde tresses hanging down—was thrust out the coach's window toward the fort.

"Help! Help!" Charles shrieked in falsetto.

The effigy of Governor Colden was instantly on top of the female puppet. "Oh ho ho, my pretty!" Marinus bellowed, manipulating the two puppets' faces together. "Let me put my *stamp* upon you!"

"Stop, stop! You *cad*, you *cad*!" Charles screamed. He pushed the stick holding his puppet sharply upward, to knock against the Colden face.

It was a Punch and Judy show, with a twist, and the crowd loved it.

"Do not protest, my sweet! I have your *virtual* consent!" Marinus hollered.

"Oh help! I am *a-taxed*!"

"It's only *a little one*, my precious!"

"It's poxy enough for all America, you cad!"

"Just try it, my lovely! It may *grow* on you!"

"It will *ruin* me, monster!"

"But my own, 'tis your *duty* to submit!"

"Nay, you cad, 'tis my *duty* … to *whack your bollocks!*"

There was a huge thump—likely a rock slammed onto the floor of the coach—and Marinus emitted a great, petulant howl of wounded masculinity.

The laughter and applause were so uproarious, they thumped and howled twice again. Then the puppets switched positions and the female head pounded downward at the Colden face, prompting further storms of mirth. Both were then retrieved into the coach and immediately displayed out the other window, where the scene was repeated for the crowds on that side.

Eight men—including Timothy Colegrove—arranged themselves into a harness and commenced pulling the coach as the parade marshal turned back uptown. Still holding the torch high, I switched from side to side as Charles and Marinus—their voices growing ever more hoarse—repeated their puppet show over and over, adding new, ever more ribald lines as they went.

It took nearly an hour to traverse the mile up to the Common, which—now that most had had their suppers—was teeming with five times as many people as had been following us. After repeating the show thrice more as we made a circuit about the fields, we came to rest behind the big truck that Marinus had constructed in his yard, now drawn by horses and fitted out with a gallows. From the gallows hung another, even more elaborate effigy of the governor, plus one of Grenville, complete with dialogue strips. Perched next to the Colden effigy's ear was a mock-up of the devil himself, whispering fiendish advice. Scattered decoratively about were pieces of paper emblazoned with outsized stamps.

Charles and Marinus, leaving the Colden puppet lewdly atop the hapless female, finally tumbled out of the coach to great applause. When congratulated, each of them pointed to his throat and whispered, "Can't talk!" Seeing a street vendor, I shoved my torch into Colegrove's startled hands, ran over and bought mugs of ale to provide them some relief.

My worrisome charge glowered irritably as I retrieved the torch, but he stayed put with the others in the coach's makeshift harness, waiting to draw the coach back downtown.

John Glasby, his wife on one arm and Hermione Leavering on the other, walked up to me as we waited. "Quite a remarkable show, Thomas!" he said, as if surprised. "We must all pray the message will be received across the ocean."

"Indeed, sir!"

Hermione tugged him away to examine some of the detail on the gallows. "I must say, the painting of these effigies is brilliant work," I observed slyly to Adelie Glasby. "They're instantly recognizable, yet not too repulsive, and terrifically amusing. Can you imagine who painted them?"

"Why, I've no idea, Thomas, no idea who *he* was at all!" she protested, equally slyly. "Yet I must confess, I do agree with you!"

"Surely the artist is a ... *an individual* with many talents!"

"I ... couldn't say, Thomas!" She strode off to join John and Hermione, leaving me admiring her person and her art once again. I sensed she had been recruited by the Sons—Charles, of course—despite her husband's reservations. Perhaps she was slowly bringing him round.

After church bells tolled eight o'clock, the peals continued. Two black horses turned the corner out of Beekman Street, drawing a flat bed wagon draped in black bunting. As it passed to the head of the procession, men doffed their hats and all gasped and fell silent on beholding a coffin labeled *LIBERTY* on each side.

The parade marshal raised his arm and gestured to the south. The drummers beat a dead march in time with the church bells. The hearse, the gallows, the flags and banners, the coach, and the somber crowd began making their way back down toward the fort. In addition to the torches, hundreds were carrying lit candles. "I'm guessing we're two thousand strong," Charles whispered as he rushed past me toward the front.

Two thousand! I thought. *Facing what?*

Had this been a commonplace disturbance, the governor would surely have called out the militia. But Colden knew the city militia was entirely against him—as were those in the countryside and the neighboring provinces. Colden's infuriating lectures to the town magistrates, harping on duty and obedience—repeated constantly—plus his regular avowal that the Act would be enforced no matter what, guaranteed intransigence on all sides. Lacking a civilian option, he was dependent on the dangerously volatile military. There were only two hundred redcoats in the fort, and their closest reinforcements were over a hundred miles away. But they were all well armed, we knew, and the cannons were loaded with grapeshot, and there were navy ships in the harbor.

The hearse pulled away onto Beaver Street. The gallows were lifted off the truck and set in an open area of Bowling Green. The coach was pulled up beside it, and the harness was disconnected. The crowd kept streaming down Broadway, moving past the Green to the gates of the fort. I stayed behind Timothy Colegrove, who seemed fatigued by the long pull. Looking back up the slope, there were myriads of twinkling candles still gathering, joining the hundreds already ahead of us. Many a carpenter edged toward the front, carrying hammers, chisels, and saws. To dismantle the gates! Dozens of sailors pushed forward, brandishing cutlasses, pistols, and shillelaghs. To rush into the breach! Men and boys, native and foreign, white and black, drunk and sober—spoiling for a fight, the lot! I swallowed hard, thinking back on the massacre at Ticonderoga, and not wanting anything of the like to happen in my city.

Were the officers and men up on the rampart as crazed as some of those below? I shuddered on hearing that the commander of artillery was the same Major Thomas James who had vowed to cram the stamps down New Yorkers' throats!

Timothy Colegrove didn't move forward—or backward, either. I had to remind myself that, whatever happened between the populace and the army, he was my primary concern.

The parade marshal stepped forward to the gate, with torch-bearers on either side. He raised his arm and suddenly achieved silence. Then he knocked his fist against the gate! "The people of New York," he bellowed, "demand admittance to their fort!"

Ten seconds passed. "Denied!"

He pounded the doors again. "The people of New York—"

"Oh, the hell with that!" a man behind him shouted furiously. And with a roar of rage, the crowd surged toward the fort. Ladders appeared, but they weren't tall enough. A boy—one of the lads who'd worked with us yesterday—clambered over the shoulders of a tall man on the top rung and put his hands on the parapet. I cringed, fearing that an axe might separate those hands from his body, but the ladder was simply pushed over backward and caught by the crowd below.

"No!" the parade marshal was yelling. "No, no, not now!" He was joined by Sears and Lamb.

"Go ahead! Fire!" yelled some in the mob. "Fire, you damn cowards!" Insane—even though it was public knowledge that the Sons had given the redcoats clear warning that one New York casualty would be repaid by the evisceration of every last soldier.

I saw lit slow matches being held up by the gunners facing us. If the matches were brought to the touchholes, the enfilading fire would produce carnage on Bowling Green that would make Ticonderoga look like a carriage accident. Were the hands moving? Horrified, I yelled, "Stand away! Take cover!" I dashed behind the trunk of one of the trees that shade the mansions bordering the square—a pious hope in the event of a direct hit, but nonetheless …

For ninety terrorized seconds, scarcely able to breathe, I anticipated a murderous barrage. I caught one child running around, and held her, squirming, beside me. Finally I realized: despite all the provocations from both sides, they hadn't fired. We were still here—at least, as yet. I told the little girl to stay behind the tree and count to a hundred, then dared to look out. Men were still yelling curses up at the soldiers, but the hotheads inciting them to fire had backed away. The redcoats remained stolidly immobile—*waiting for orders*. I searched for my charge.

If Timothy Colegrove were trying to encourage havoc, he should have rushed forward, to goad others to scale the walls. If he was a false patriot, concerned solely with his own safety, he should have scampered far away. If he was a true Son of Liberty, he should have echoed the urgent admonitions of the leaders to stand down. But Colegrove, like most of the hundreds about him, had done nothing. He was standing pat, shaking his fists at the redcoats—just one more lamb awaiting the slaughter!

Then Willett was suddenly leading a group into the center of the

Green, carrying planks from the wooden walls of the governor's carriage house. "Quick, the bonfire!" he yelled. "We need to get the bonfire going *now!* Once we get that kindling stacked, we can touch it off!" Colegrove shook himself to join in and, forgetting my own fear of a bloodbath, I hastened to bear a hand.

Amazingly enough, the Sons' leadership did manage to pull the mob back—as soon as the wild men perceived the bonfire. It was equally amazing that no soldier had fired, and that the big guns had remained silent. Some of the less sober in our mob grumbled that the army "should've been shown what was what," but most were content that the intimidation had gone as far as it did. Cheers rose as the governor's coach was heaved on top of the blaze—poor Judy carelessly tossed in along with Punch—followed by two fine sleighs also pilfered from the coach house.

The *pièce de résistance*, however, was the gallows, and the stout lads handling it by the upright posts twice managed to swing the effigies back and forth over the flames before the figures caught.

It gave many of us mordant satisfaction to presume that Governor Colden himself was watching the event. And how charming that, in addition to the hundreds of country people, sailors, blacks, and boys in the mob, he could make out dozens of well-dressed gentlemen—*his people*—equally relishing his virtual incineration!

I surely enjoyed it and, like many, turned around, to warm my back against the November night's chill. The crowd was slowly beginning to disperse, but when I turned around again, I spotted a rowdy clutch of sailors on the northern edge of the Green. One of them—one I'd never seen before—suddenly waved his arms about and hollered, "Major James must be made to pay for his insults! Volunteers! Follow me!"

Cheering, the sailors—a few dozen strong—took off as a body up Broadway, followed by streams of boys and roughnecks. In a sudden guilty panic, I looked for Timothy Colegrove, realizing I'd not clapped eyes on him in forty minutes.

He was nowhere to be— Wasn't that he, a flash of white disappearing up at the bend in the road? I scanned the crowd once more. Not finding him, I abandoned the bonfire and took off after the phantom.

Atop the rise, at Wall Street, I looked again. In the moonlight, I could make out a mob, four or five blocks ahead, but not Colegrove. But if he were still intent on any mischief, the Sons had matters well in hand at Bowling Green, so his obvious choice would be to follow these bully lads and egg them on. I ran in pursuit. One gang split off from the others onto Barclay Street, but I couldn't see any of them when I reached it. Were they jumping over peoples' backyard fences? I stayed after the main group on Broadway.

The rump cohort turned to the west on Murray Street, and I followed, finally divining their plan. That hated redcoat chief of artillery, Major Thomas James, the very one who'd threatened to cram stamps down our throats with his sword, had refurbished an elegant residence on the Greenwich road facing Vauxhall Gardens. King Mob was bent on outdoing Boston at last!

Crossing Church Street, a block and a half away from the house, I was positive I saw Colegrove, but by the time I rounded the corner, I couldn't locate him. The screaming mob was tearing up paving stones from the sidewalk and heaving them at the house windows. Three sailors were butting their shoulders against the front door … which gave way just as I arrived. Dozens followed them inside, and immediately the sound of crashing furniture, ripping cloth, breaking chinaware, was loud and clear.

The crowd was only growing. Panting, I waved at a bewildered-looking Cyrus Mapes, who seemed stuck in the middle of it, but I couldn't spot my quarry. There was a pitch dark service passageway running alongside the house, ignored by the mob concentrated at the front entrance. Could Colegrove be in the back, plotting special mischief? The greatest chaos anyone could manage would be to start a fire. As arson could easily precipitate a general catastrophe, nothing would as thoroughly discredit the protests against the stamp tax.

A well fuddled bloke was leaning against the brick wall that surrounded the property. "Did you see a fellow wearing a white shirt go back through here?" I shouted to him.

"*Huh?* Ain't seen nobody go back there! Damned if I'd go—" He belched and swayed as he gestured at the narrow entrance. "Why? We can get in the front now. I hear that major's got plenty booze locked in his cellar!" Not for him, I'm afraid: he slid to the ground and rolled over, unconscious.

I scanned the crowd carefully again, hoping to avoid having to fumble through the passageway. Still not seeing Colegrove, however, and unable to get any sober man's attention, I reluctantly faced up to it and began feeling my way back, barking my shin on a stack of firewood, five paces in. When I emerged into a quiet, private garden fifteen yards later, there was just enough light from torches held high out in the street that I could perceive there was no one about. Oh: save another useless drunk in an odd coat, pissing on the wall of a tool shed. A cascade of feathers—ripped bedding—descended on me from an upper window. "Hey! We found it!" someone yelled inside the house.

I cursed bitterly to myself. Where *was* the man? I'd missed him again! There was nowhere to hide in the yard, so it was pointless to linger. Seeing a gate to Warren Street, barred on the inside, I started toward it, relieved I'd not have to struggle back through the passageway. But as I moved, I heard a grunt and a sudden rush of steps behind me—

CHAPTER 11

A WAVE OF NAUSEA SUFFUSED ME as I struggled again to lift my head and focus my eyes.

"Don't try to get up, Thomas!" she said.

She? Who? The benign, homely, middle-aged face finally became clear. "Aunt Janna!"

"You'll be all right, dear, if you just won't rush things!"

"What? It's daylight! How—"

"Thomas, my dear, just please lie still. You've had an awful knock on the head, and you mustn't—"

"But—"

"I'll fetch Charles, since you're talking. I still don't understand what happened. Don't try to rise, now!"

She walked out of the room. What room? I'd seen it before. The parlor, my aunt's parlor. I was on the floor, by the fireplace. But every time I turned my head, it seemed I was moving the earth to meet my eyes, not the other way around. I took deep breaths.

"Thomas?"

"Charles? What—"

"Stay still, will you!"

"What—"

"Thomas, you recollect the riot at Major James's house? You were clobbered on the head by one of the paving stones. You're damned lucky to be alive! You were knocked out and bleeding terribly when I found you—"

"I was in his backyard."

"That's right. Good, you're coherent!"

"Coherent?"

"Aye. That's a change."

"This is … your house?"

"You recognize it! My father's. I had to draft three other men to help lug you back here, then to find a barber to stitch you up. Not managed in a trice, in the middle of the— Easy, easy!"

I was attempting to thrash about to discover what he was talking about.

"Thomas, we had to shave half your head to clear the wound. Then he put twenty stitches in your scalp to stanch the bleeding. *Stop!* Don't pick at it!"

I had managed to move my arm to feel my head, which was wrapped in a bandage, and discerned an enormous lump on the starboard side. I moaned with a petulant thought that my looks might be ruined. "You brought me here last night?"

"*Last* night? It's Monday afternoon, old lad. You've been lying here, in and out of consciousness, since the wee hours of Saturday! Today's the fourth of November."

It took me half a minute to absorb the statement. "Somebody— People were throwing paving stones at the house. Someone missed and—"

"I'm afraid not, Thomas. It wasn't a *miss*. Somebody wielded that stone deliberately. The mob was still out front, in the street. Nobody went around to the back until later. The paving stone I found next to you was the only one in the yard, and you were fifteen feet from the house itself, too far for anyone to have tried to throw it at the kitchen window. Somebody was trying to do you in!"

Carefully, I pushed myself up onto one elbow, fighting dizziness. "They *meant* to—"

"Yeah. He meant to kill, Thomas, though maybe he hoped the paving stone could make it look like an accident if anyone saw him. Not completely implausible—there were quite a few other cracked heads that night. We're lucky that's all there were!"

"He meant to— I was looking for Timothy Colegrove!"

"Right. So was I. When I got there, I couldn't find him, or you. I found Cyrus Mapes, who told me he'd seen you go into the backyard five minutes before, but hadn't seen you come out. That's how I found you. You'd have bled to death or caught pneumonia from the cold, if you'd been left for an hour."

"Was it Colegrove who—"

"Who coshed you?" Charles frowned bitterly. "I don't know, Thomas.

I wonder who else, but … the fact is, I never saw him at the major's house, haven't seen him at all since the bonfire."

"I saw him on his way there. The son of a—"

Aunt Janna appeared, and I immediately moderated my language. "Mr. Mapes has come by to look in on you, Thomas. Are you feeling well enough to see him?"

"Mapes?"

"I dragooned Mapes into helping carry you back here, Thomas," Charles said. "Then he even went out to roust up a barber for you."

"He came by both yesterday and the day before. He has been most civilly concerned for you, nephew!"

"Even been civil to *me!*" Charles added.

"Well, then … yes, of course, Aunt Janna."

She was back with him a few seconds later. "Dordrecht! I rejoice to see you alert! A good day to you, Mr. Cooper!"

"And to you, Mr. Mapes," Charles said. He stood up. "But, gentlemen, you'll have to excuse me. I was just preparing to leave when Mother called me. I am tardy for a committee meeting."

"They're *still* meeting?" I ventured uneasily.

"Oh indeed. More frequently than ever. Perhaps Mapes can fill you in. He only rallied twenty minutes ago, Mr. Mapes. He thought it was Saturday!"

"Good lord!"

"Make sure he doesn't over-exert himself!"

"Oh, to be sure!" With a few more pleasantries, I was soon alone with my erstwhile colleague.

After labored inquiries into each other's state of health, Mapes said, "So … you'll be wondering what has overtaken our fair city in the last eventful days?"

Something other than personal woes to talk about, at any rate! "Yes. Yes, please!"

"That mob got out of hand, Friday night, Dordrecht. I doubt the Sons were pleased. I *know* the big-wigs weren't! Mob was just getting fired up when we carted you away. Found where he'd stashed the liquor. I haven't been back since, but I hear they were … thorough!"

"They didn't burn it?"

"Oh no. Wooden houses everywhere! Though it's a miracle the whole city didn't catch by accident, with all the drunks carrying torches! Wind was calm, thank heaven."

"God protects riotous fools and drunks?"

"Must be. Anyway, the royalist crowd—the placemen—are screaming that anarchy is reigning, and *complaining* that the army failed to fire its cannon at the crowds on Bowling Green."

"Dear Christ!"

"Right! Meanwhile, Governor Colden is getting death threats right and left—accusations that he's the chief murderer of our rights, threats that he'll be hanged on a signpost as a warning to all wicked governors ... the lot."

"I should feel some sympathy, I guess ..."

Mapes snorted. "Spare it, friend! He's trying every ruse possible to avoid handing the stamps over to the people. First, he just said he'd not distribute the stamps, he'd wait until his replacement gets here."

"He's overdue already, isn't he? Sir Henry Moore, right?"

"Yes and yes. Boats coming in are reporting bad weather out on the ocean. So Colden put the promise in writing and had it printed up. All over town on Saturday afternoon. Mr. Sears is heard, to the contrary, boasting that we'd have the stamps within twenty-four hours—"

"Oh yes?"

"But that was forty-eight hours ago. Meanwhile, Colden tried to get the navy to take the stamps off his hands, and get them out onto a warship. Went after Captain Kennedy of HMS *Coventry*." He chuckled a bit. "But Kennedy wasn't game—just maybe because he has a house on Broadway even nicer than the major's."

"Than the major's *was!*"

"Aye. Town's really, really edgy. Mr. Glasby joined a group of business principals who talked some of the merchant captains into visiting the sailors' haunts."

"To talk sense into the men?"

"Aye. Theory being, they might listen to their captains, but they'll never listen to the merchants themselves."

"How about that!"

"Seems to have helped. But then yesterday, Colden—the man's his own worst enemy!—had the soldiers spike all the guns on the shoreline battery. So they couldn't be turned around against the fort, he said."

"I bet that went over well!"

"Everyone had thought it impossible to hate him more!" Mapes said, shaking his head. "He's still trying to avoid surrendering the stamps. Walking over here, I saw another broadside from him: the same promise as before, to hold the stamps for the new governor, but this time he had the mayor and the aldermen witness his pledge."

"Won't work!"

"You're right. And because of his obstinacy, the whole city's completely terrified that hell itself will break loose tomorrow!"

"Tomorrow?"

"Guy Fawkes Day, friend! Remember? There *are* a goodly number who are talking about attacking Fort George in real earnest!"

Of course. But the fifth of November was usually just an occasion for everyone to display their perfervid anti-Romanist prejudices. "Seriously?"

"It … does look ominous! Even more than it did on Friday. I … just don't know …"

We were each lost in our private thoughts for a moment. Mine were inconclusive—save a new dread that the bloodbath avoided before might yet be in the cards. "Mapes, I'd like to try sitting up. Can you—"

He sprang to my assistance, and presently, still on the pallet, I was leaning back against the couch, with sensations not unlike sea legs. But they passed.

"Better?"

"Aye, much! Now, tell me, pray: what happened on Friday night? How was it that I got here, again?"

Mapes had been on his route home after the parade and the bonfire, when he chanced upon the fracas. As incensed at the major as anyone, he dallied while the crowd grew, until he realized no one was at home and the mob meant to destroy the place. It was about then that he noticed me—but he was hemmed in and already hoarse from shouting all evening. A few minutes later, Charles had appeared, asked if he'd seen me, and gone into the backyard in pursuit. A moment after that, he said, my cousin, having located me unconscious in the backyard, pressed Mapes and two others, whose names he never learned, into hauling me bodily across town to my present sanctuary. "How'd you manage that?" I asked.

"Someone had already gotten into the upstairs bedrooms, and was systematically destroying the mattresses. They slit them open, shook the feathers out the window, then dropped the canvas—which we used to improvise a stretcher! That's what you're sitting on. See? One of the feathers, still!"

"Well … I surely do thank you, good sir!"

"Not at all, sir! What had you been about, that evening? Why'd you ever go into the backyard? I nearly broke my leg in that passage!"

"*Ah*. Well, I was—for various reasons—in search of Mr. Timothy Colegrove."

"Timothy Colegrove? But—"

"Charles is certain that I was deliberately attacked."

"Oh, no doubt of that, I'm afraid!"

"And we have our reasons to suspect Timothy Colegrove."

"But … well, *um*—"

"What? Do you know him to see him?"

"Oh yes, he's made himself notorious at the Sons' meetings. But, *uh* … he was standing, right there, ten feet ahead of me in the crowd, when I first saw you."

"No! You sure? I didn't— He was wearing a white shirt, no coat. Hard to miss!"

"*Un uh*, he was huddling under a blanket. Filthy old, brown, moth-eaten thing—looked like he'd pulled it from a trash bin."

"Did he see me go into the backyard?"

"I don't know. But he was still right there, shivering with all the rest in the front, when Mr. Cooper asked for you. Crowd was packed in pretty tight!"

"Charles was looking for him too! Didn't he—"

"He only asked me about you. Knew that we worked together at the firm."

"Then … you're saying that Timothy Colegrove was nearby you, in the front of the house, *all* the time I was in the back? You're certain?"

"Well, yeah. Would've been hard to move anywhere if you wanted to! I was looking to shove my way out and go home when Cooper came back and said you were hurt."

"Then … Colegrove couldn't have been the one who attacked me!"

"You thought maybe he was?"

"I … yes, that's what I was thinking."

"Nah. Couldn't be, Dordrecht. 'Less he's a magician or something!"

"*Huh!*"

"Cooper—while we were bringing you here—asked me if I'd seen anything suspicious, and I said no, but … I was thinking, just this morning, and I *had* seen one man, a tall fellow, walking quickly out from the back, holding his hat so his hand covered his face. He stalked off down Greenwich Street, but I didn't think anything of it at the time. He got lost right away, with all the people coming up the street from the bonfire."

"Did you notice anything particular about him?"

"That's what I recalled this morning. He was wearing a right fancy coat—silver and maroon stripes, don't you know. Not too many of them around! And I remembered where I'd seen the like before."

"Where was that?"

"Back in August. When we got Aaron Colegrove to tear up his son's commission?"

"Oh yes?"

"The son who was going to be the lucky winner, he was wearing a coat just like that. Really stuck out, back in August!"

I fell back onto the pallet. *It was James the Missing!*

"Mother got some porridge into you, I understand?"

Charles had just returned as darkness fell.

"Yes. She's doling it out ever so slowly, even though I'm famished."

"A good sign!"

My cousin looked very morose. "Something wrong, Charles?"

He sighed heavily. "I'm very worried about tomorrow, Thomas. Really, I was even thinking … of sending you, and Mother, and Mary and her children, all out to New Utrecht."

I was stunned. "It's that bad?"

"It could be. Maybe not. We have some … real hotheads—crying for blood, the fools."

"Timothy Colegrove?"

He seemed startled. "No, actually. He's stayed quiet. Perhaps because I've been watching him like a hawk, the—"

"I had a long talk with Mapes, Charles. It couldn't have been Timothy who attacked me."

"What!"

"Mapes happened to be looking right at him the whole time I was in the backyard."

"Wait a minute! *I* didn't see him. I was right there beside Mapes!"

"He says Colegrove had thrown an old blanket over himself, to keep warm. He was ten feet in front of him, from the moment I waved to him until you came back to fetch him."

Charles simply gaped. "But then—"

"Then who did bludgeon me? He had an insight there, too."

"Told me he hadn't seen anything suspicious!"

"He remembered something just today. While I was in the back, he saw a tall man coming out and walking quickly away down Greenwich Street."

"Yes?"

"Wearing a distinctive coat, maroon and silver stripes."

Charles stared for five seconds. "*James* Colegrove!"

I nodded. "Mapes said he recognized the coat from the time you cowed Aaron into tearing up the commission."

"You think he—"

"Mustn't rush it, Charles, but … he and Timothy are the only Colegroves whose whereabouts I haven't been able to determine, at the moment Artemis was murdered, and—" I stopped dead.

"What?"

"I just … Colegrove's youngest child, Agnes, the twelve-year-old … she was returning for dinner just at noon, and said she saw *her brother*. At first, I thought she was talking of Oliver or even Gideon Boyce, but that was stupid, because Oliver was shopping for baubles and Boyce's class began at eleven. Then I assumed it was Timothy—but that's unlikely, because Timothy's been so remote Agnes would barely know him at all. So maybe—"

"Maybe it was James? Why didn't you just ask the girl?"

"Why? Oh: because my client, Miss Theodora, chose that instant to barge into the room and accuse me of molesting the child."

"Oh for god's sake! Well, but you could ask her now. When you're better, that is!"

"I could! *Um*, if I can get to her. I saw Colegrove's womenfolk leaving town in a coach yesterday morning."

"*Yesterday?*"

"Oh. *Friday* morning. I presumed they were heading for Mamaroneck."

Charles looked thoughtful. "Right. Right. What d'you think, should we pack you and our womenfolk off to New Utrecht?"

"*No!* Well, not me, anyhow."

"Your mother will blame me if anything happens to you! She was here Saturday, you know. Sent Geertruid yesterday. Everyone's been asking for you."

I was touched, but adamant. "She'd know to blame *me*, Charles, not you. And I'm … feeling stronger by the minute. I'll be walking tomorrow, I'm sure of it!"

He sighed. "Well … maybe I am overestimating the danger … It's just— When a mob gets fired up, Thomas, the Tories are right, there's no stopping them. I went by the major's house yesterday, and … the only thing left is the walls. Brick. 'A sacrifice for liberty,' they want to call this destruction! That house is a total loss."

"*Whew!*"

"And when they were done reducing the major's house and drinking up his extensive wine cellar, they weren't finished. At two or three in the morning, they attacked a couple of the bawdyhouses around on Barclay. Got most of the windows, roughed up one of the madams!"

"Whatever for?"

"Taking a stand for American virtue, I've been told. Bastards!"

Charles? "Favorite establishments, cousin?" I leered.

"None of *your* business, Mr. Dordrecht!"

"Sorry!"

"They *have* been well patronized by the soldiery, of late. Part of the excuse, but—"

There was a commotion out in the street. A large number of men were marching to a drumbeat, hollering "LIB-ER-*TEE!* LIB-ER-*TEE!*"

Then we heard breaking glass. "Oh Jesus!" Charles exclaimed. He jumped up, yelled, "Mother! Quick! The candles!" and hastily lit the candle sitting on the window sill.

The noise of the mob, deafening for the two minutes it took to pass us, finally receded.

"They assume you're not sympathetic if you fail to waste candles to illuminate your windows!" He looked after them, shaking his head.

"You're not becoming disillusioned with the cause?"

"No. Oh no," he demurred. "But … *Liberty!* Such a beautiful word! A fragile and precious word, Thomas!" He blew the candle out. "How can anybody *yell* it?"

I had a miserable night, my throbbing headache compounded by horrible imaginings of urban catastrophe, indignation over the Stamp Act, outrage at the governor's intransigence, perplexity about the murder of Artemis Colegrove, and—hardly least—fury at my having been coshed on the head. Somehow, however, I managed to fall asleep around dawn, from which I awoke, feeling ravenous and considerably better, in mid-afternoon.

Sensing that I was alone in the house, I carefully essayed hauling myself up into a standing position. After a second's dizziness, I tried a few steps, keeping a grip on the mantelpiece. Success! I tried the steps again without holding on, and only clutched the mantle when I abruptly turned about. I had done it twice again when the Cooper family returned home.

I heard Aunt Janna say, "I'll just look in on ... Thomas! You're up!"

Smiles were all around as my aunt, her husband William, Charles, my lovable cousin Mary Fitzweiler and her toddler, Ben, all piled into the room to exclaim over me. But the source of the ebullience was not merely my renewed strength. "There's brave news at last, Thomas," Mary gushed. "Governor Colden has finally agreed to surrender the stamps to the city!"

"Isn't that wonderful!" Aunt Janna exclaimed.

"High time the old fool saw sense!" Uncle William groused.

Charles merely grinned and nodded, his relief palpable.

"We're having ourselves a little celebration, Thomas," my aunt continued, "before we go out to watch the delivery. They're supposedly packing them onto carts right now. Will you be able to join us?"

I had a minute with Charles as they went off to set up. "How was it managed, cousin?"

"It wasn't easy, Thomas. He fought it to the very end. Insisted that the city corporation sign a voucher fully indemnifying the alleged value of the stamps."

"Hundreds of pounds?"

"Aye. For which we the rate-payers are responsible. But the real hold-up, I understand, was getting a response from General Gage, from whom Colden demanded a written statement attesting that his hand had been forced. Colden still dreams that the king's Privy Council will someday make him governor by right, if only he carries out their commands to the letter."

I had a moment to clean myself up before we sat down to supper, and I managed to get into the clothes Charles had acquired four days earlier, when he told Mrs. Nugent what had happened. We had a pleasant repast, at which I ate most heartily, and then set out down toward the fort, amid the largest throng of people I'd ever seen.

There were so many citizens about, we only managed to get to the top of the Bowling Green, two hundred yards from the fort, but it was enough to view the gratifying sight of the gates being opened from inside, and the first of seven carts pulling out onto Broadway.

The cheers were prolonged and boisterous. People jumped up and down and embraced perfect strangers. The accompanying redcoats were even slapped on the back! After the carts passed us, Charles and I chose to follow them, while Mary decided it was her lad's bedtime, and her parents escorted them to the Fitzweiler home.

With me leaning on Charles's shoulder for balance, we two cut across Beaver Street and up Broad, to beat the crowds for a good view of the delivery. Even so, we could get no nearer than two hundred feet away. A line of torches illuminated the entrance to the building, however, and one could make out the double rows of soldiers at rigid attention. Nerves were still taut as the first cart trundled down Wall Street. It took four redcoats to lift the crate off and carry it up the stairs. At the entry of the building, the mayor preened while Mr. Tolbert gravely signed a slip of paper; the soldiers' burden was assumed by four civilian workmen; the crate went into the building and the four workmen returned a moment later, empty-handed, receiving thunderous applause for their two-minute effort.

Wanting to be sure, however, no one left the scene until six more wagons had completed their transfer. When the workmen emerged after receiving the seventh crate, the building's doors were closed, and the rejoicing was so wild, old Mr. Tolbert and even the mayor were paraded about on men's shoulders.

"As if the mayor had anything to do with it!" Charles smirked. But he wasn't about to let the foolishness sully our enjoyment. Slowly we made our way north, stopping often to talk to friends and acquaintances. We were proceeding up Nassau Street—I had agreed to spend one more night at the Cooper home—when we came across Timothy Colegrove, who was leaning against a building just north of City Hall with a rather idiotic grin on his face.

"Cooper!" he shouted. Then, as we approached, "Oh hello, Dordrecht!"

"Good evening, Mr. Colegrove," Charles said levelly. It was apparent that Colegrove, like many we'd met, had imbibed a substantial quantity of cheer. However, unlike some, he was not unsteady on his feet; and, quite contrary to my expectation, he seemed mellowed by the booze, rather than coarsened.

"I posted myself back here while all that was going on," he asserted proudly. "I thought it'd be a good idea to make sure they weren't just taking the crates straight through to the north entrance of the building!"

"I see. And?"

"That door has stayed shut ever since I got here at four-thirty!"

"The stamps are definitely locked inside, then! Well ... that shows some initiative on your part. Excellent!" Charles was being a tad patronizing, given the obvious fact that any effort to remove the stamps from the back of the building would have been blatantly visible to the whole city.

"Just trying to help!" Colegrove said, wariness creeping into his voice.

"I'm very glad to hear it," Charles went on, "particularly as we were concerned at one point that you might not be truly sympathetic to the aims of the Sons of Liberty."

The lights of passing torches showed the emotion working in Colegrove's face. "You had doubts ... about *me?*"

"Indeed we did, sir!" Charles replied. "Much alleviated of late, but ... you must realize that your surname works against you in this regard."

"I can't help who my father was!"

"Nor can any of us, sir, but ... we can choose our employers, and I know of no other Son of Liberty who works for an arch-Tory such as Darius Gerrison!"

"How'd you find that out? You've been spying on me!"

"It's true, then?" Charles demanded.

Colegrove grimaced and remained silent.

"We wouldn't have thought of spying on you, notwithstanding your surname, had your behavior not seemed suspicious in other respects." Now there was only puzzlement. "Particularly your obstinate refusal to explain your true whereabouts on the day Artemis Colegrove was murdered!"

"Oh. But—"

I could restrain myself no longer. "*Where were you* at noon that day, Mr. Colegrove?"

His present mood was clearly fighting his customary truculence. "I ... If you must know—"

"Well, yes, man, we *must* know!"

"I was right here, in City Hall, all day!"

"Here? *Here?* Doing what?" Charles said.

Colegrove turned his head to the side once more before facing us. "I was conducting a deposition, on Mr. Gerrison's behalf."

"Who were you deposing, please? And were there any other witnesses?"

"I was deposing the navy's Captain Kennedy regarding his claim of prize money for the impoundment of the *Plover*. Mr. Tolbert and his secretary ... and his guards ... were present the whole time."

Charles had a look of complete disgust. "Kennedy arrested the brig *Plover* in Block Island Sound last summer, Thomas, and he contends that it and its cargo are wholly forfeit to the crown for violations of the Molasses Act. He stands to pocket seven thousand in prize money, of course. Not an argument that would endear anyone to the Sons of Liberty!" he growled at Colegrove.

"I hope to get a start in the legal field, Mr. Cooper," Colegrove said defensively, "and I can't be choosy where I begin. A man has to make a living somehow!" he added, to me. "And if I hadn't deposed Kennedy, Gerrison would've gotten someone else to do it!"

"I suppose so," Charles said. "But if you had told us, Colegrove, we would have been *less* suspicious of you. Dordrecht here wouldn't have been chasing after you last Friday, to his mortal peril!"

Colegrove seemed to notice my bandage for the first time. "What happened to you, Dord— Mr. Dordrecht?"

"Someone brained me with a paving stone while I was in the major's backyard, looking for you."

"But I was—"

"I know, I know."

"But ... why—"

"Somebody sent me a threatening note, three days before. I assumed it was you."

"*Me!* No! Oh no! What, because of your stupid— Because of your work for Theodora, you think?"

"It was rather preciously phrased, but yes."

"I've ... always assumed she—Artemis—was done in by a mariner— if not *the* mariner—who had a grudge against my father *and* hated his politics."

"It doesn't look likely, at this point. Tell me, have you had any communication with your brother James?"

"*James?* No, I have not. He's only my half-brother! I've never had any communication with James. Can't stand him! Peter and the girls are at least civil to me, but James is too great a snob! I presume he's still cowering up in Mamaroneck."

"Do you know of anyone else who has a silver and maroon-striped coat?"

Colegrove inhaled sharply, perhaps realizing the implication of the question. "I ... don't think I have seen— You saw it that night?"

"I was taken unawares. Someone else saw it. Saw a tall man in a silver and maroon-striped coat."

He looked stumped. "Not that I have any great love for him, Mr. Dordrecht, but ... I wouldn't have thought James would have the gumption. I wouldn't have thought he'd have any at all!"

"Perhaps you may be wrong, Mr. Colegrove."

He briefly looked queasy.

Now fighting an aching head and a strong desire to sit down in privacy, I persevered. "Another matter you refused to discuss with me, sir! You paid a visit to your father's house the day before Mrs. Colegrove was killed. What was your errand?"

"I don't think it has anything to do with—"

"Can you simply answer the question, man?" Charles said.

"You were responding to a call from your aunt Eudoxia, I understand?"

He hesitated another few seconds, then gave in. "Yes. Eudoxia wanted to know—of a sudden, and I've no idea *why*—whether my father had written a will. She said she'd asked Father to write a will before he left, and he'd agreed, but he'd never actually told her he'd done it. She knew I was working for Mr. Gerrison, and that Gerrison is Father's lawyer."

"Both James and Peter Colegrove have more legal training than you. Why didn't she ask them?"

"I don't— I'd have to guess she didn't want them to know of her request. I was quite surprised to be commissioned by her, but ... she gave me a shilling for it, so—"

"And what was the answer?"

"Mr. Gerrison categorically said no, my father—ignoring *his* advice—was intestate."

"You told your aunt?"

"Of course. That's when … I bumped into that ridic—into Artemis— as I was leaving, and she shrieked and carried on, no end! Caesar had to introduce me. She had no idea who I was!"

It was very curious. And confusing. But I sensed he was telling the truth at last, and I could think of no further questions for him.

"Thank you, finally, for your responses, Mr. Colegrove," Charles said, taking me by the elbow and turning back up Nassau Street.

"I am a patriotic Son of Liberty, Mr. Cooper!" Colegrove wailed after him.

Though the city remained tense the next day—no one knowing whether the overdue Sir Henry Moore might not prove even more refractory than Cadwallader Colden—a semblance of normality tentatively returned. Glass was swept up from the streets. Most retail shops were again conducting business—I noticed a good many marked-up prices. The fort's doors were open at their usual hours.

The wharves, however, remained deathly quiet.

On my way back to my regular domicile, I stopped by City Hall. Mr. Tolbert's domain was even more heavily guarded than it had been the week before. Soldiers demanded that I state my business, and made me wait ten minutes before two of them escorted me into his room, where his regular furniture had been shunted to the side to make room for the seven huge crates of stamps.

Mr. Tolbert, however, was still deprived of his "usual customers," and so he cheerfully responded to my query and produced the archival copy of the deposition filed on the day Mrs. Colegrove was murdered, signed by himself, Captain Archibald Kennedy, and Timothy Colegrove. He recalled that the process had begun in mid-morning and continued into the afternoon.

Thinking matters over as I walked on to Reade Street, I berated myself not only for having failed to query Timothy about the slapdash memorandum of understanding, but for again having missed the opportunity to ask Mr. Tolbert which Colegrove had seen it. *But it must have been James!* Timothy had been commissioned to investigate his sire's arrangements, and James is four years younger than Timothy. Had that paving stone knocked some of my screws loose?

Mrs. Nugent, who appeared to regard my injury as a fecund tidbit of neighborhood gossip, presented me with some bills and three letters from Theodora Colegrove.

The first, dated Friday afternoon, contained more ludicrous suggestions for clues to follow. The second, much longer one from Monday morning, related her intense indignation on hearing from her nephew, Vincent, on their return from church the day before, that I had "badgered the boy unmercifully," and demanded an apology and an explanation. The third, received only an hour before I got in, tersely commanded me to wait on her at her sister-in-law's home before suppertime this evening.

After paying my bills and effecting a few chores, I obediently walked through a calm, steady rain to present myself at the door of Irene Colegrove's Frankfort Street home. When she finally opened the door, Miss Theodora's evasive, scowling regard boded no good. "Mr. Dordrecht! It's high time, sir! I've had no report from you for over three weeks, and I specifically—"

"Miss Colegrove, it's *raining!* May I please step inside?"

For a second, I thought she'd actually refuse. Her reluctance was clear, but she allowed me inside just far enough to close the door, and remained standing. "I specifically asked you, three days ago, to explain why you so churlishly tormented my poor nephew! The lad was so mortified, he didn't even tell me of his agony until Sunday, which I think is—"

Her anger appeared to be the product of arduous cultivation. With my injured head pounding, however, I was in no mood to tolerate it. "Actually, one of the questions I wanted to investigate, Miss Colegrove, was precisely what Mr. Vincent Colegrove was doing this past Friday evening!"

I didn't really imagine that Vincent had been my attacker, but it couldn't hurt to ask, and it briefly stumped my client's flow of holy indignation. "He was right here, of course, Mr. Dordrecht. Someone had to guard this house. He and I remained vigilant against the riotous mobs until well past midnight!" She favored me directly with a frown—and noticed my bandaged head for the first time. "From the look of you, I have to guess that you were *among* the rioters destroying private property that evening!"

"As a matter of fact, ma'am, I was deliberately attacked on Friday evening while in the course of your investigation!"

She was only taken aback for a second. "*Pshaw!* I find that quite incredible, Mr. Dordrecht! Quite impossible to—"

I fear my patience was wearing thin. I elected to solicit the information

I most wanted immediately. "Can you tell me, please, when your aunt and the other ladies will be returning to the city? I have a question—"

"Father has told them to stay on in Mamaroneck until Peter's wedding. He thinks the city remains dangerous and there's no—"

I'd forgotten Peter Colegrove's wedding entirely! "When is that precisely, Miss Colegrove?"

"It's none of your concern, Mr. Dordrecht!"

"When will the ladies be back in town, please, ma'am?"

"Sometime after Saturday the sixteenth!" she hissed furiously.

Aha! "There's just one simple question that I think may finally point to a solution, if I can have but one minute with Miss Agnes to—"

Miss Colegrove's countenance assumed a most unattractive aspect. "Agnes!" she screamed. "How dare you even think of ever approaching that poor child again, sir? Haven't I made it clear that—" She stamped her foot. "Mr. Dordrecht, this is absolutely the last straw! I have repeatedly told you not to distress my family's peace of mind, yet you—"

"I am endeavoring to discover Mrs. Colegrove's assassin, ma'am!"

"And I have no report that you have ever bestirred yourself to follow up the many suggestions that I have written you! Mr. Dordrecht, I consider that we are at an impasse, and I summoned you here to tell you to your face that your services are no longer required. You are dismissed, sir! I trust the enormous sum I gave you in September will more than suffice for any expenses you have incurred."

She opened the door, and was attempting to push me outside. "Miss Colegrove, someone tried to kill *me* on Friday, and—"

"Enough, sir! Preposterous!" She shut the door in my face.

"And I intend to find out who!" I yelled.

After seething for half a minute, I took a deep breath and walked away. At least it had stopped raining.

Chapter 12

"Ah, Herr Dordrecht, how good to— Merciful heaven, what happened to you, sir?"

Still needing to calm myself after two hours' perambulation through the orchards north of town, I came into Mr. Fischl's shop in the frank hope of sympathy, as well as some new sheet of music for guitar with which I might solace myself. Since his shop was quiet, we sat down together and he brewed some tea. I explained that I had been injured while observing the protest at Major James's house. After sincere commiseration, he related his experiences and observations of the past week, culminating in the sad decline in business he'd noted. This prompted a search for a piece for me to practice; he found one by Telemann that he assured me I'd like. I was paying him for it when he said, "I suppose you've not been able to give any further thought to my problems with the ball in Marble Neck?"

Marble Neck? I was confounded.

He cocked his head. "Marmara Neck? Something like that. Mr. Colegrove's wedding, in—"

I had to grab the counter, as my head was reeling. "*Mamaroneck*, sir?"

"That's it. I still haven't—"

"The *ball* is part of the Peter Colegrove wedding in Mamaroneck?"

"Yes. You know him? His brother says it's to be an extremely lavish— Are you all right?"

I had collapsed back onto the chair, overcome by excitement and confusion. "I, *uhh*— You were saying?"

"I still haven't found anyone to play the pianoforte, and I still haven't been able to arrange the instrument's transportation."

"Oh!" I had a fit of laughing as my mind jumbled over an unexpected set of possibilities. "Mr. Fischl, I—"

"You *do* know the bridegroom, I take it?"

"Aye. His *brother* made this arrangement?"

"Yes. A strange boy, Mr. Oliver, very particular in his dress. Not at all musical, but his money's good!"

"Did he ask whether *I* had had anything to do with the pianofortes?"

"No," Fischl replied, astonished by the question. "He had only heard that they were the *dernier cri* among the London elite, and he had convinced his family that the wedding had to include one."

There was no alternative but to take my friend into my full confidence with regard to the plan I was rapidly devising. I would attend the wedding *incognito!* What better method could there be to learn all there was to know about James Colegrove than to appear as a humble servant at his brother's wedding, with all the family gathered around? There would be nothing unusual in a musician's wearing a periwig, which would cover my own hair, and even the bandage if I were still encumbered with it. With ten days of assiduous practice, I pleaded, perhaps I could after all manage a creditable performance on the instrument. And a few seconds' thought was all that was required to determine that the transportation problem was surmountable—particularly since no provincial borders would have to be crossed, and therefore the new tax would not even be expected.

Not surprisingly, Mr. Fischl had difficulty taking all of this in. He recalled the mystery of Mrs. Colegrove's unsolved murder, but couldn't comprehend how I had come to have anything to do with it. Then it took another half-hour to convey my intention to perform entirely under an assumed identity, and to persuade him to abet that intention. He let it fall that he was in possession of a cheap, uniform set of coats and periwigs that he used for such occasions, though he doubted any coat would fit me well. Finally, we looked over some of the pieces he was considering—Handel, Purcell, Pachelbel—with a view to determining whether I'd ever be able to perform them. Happily—my uncle Thomas having been an excellent teacher—he pronounced me readier than I'd thought, but still concurred that I must practice daily until the event.

Night had descended by the time I left Mr. Fischl's shop, feeling incomparably lighter in mood than I had on entering it, and suffused with renewed determination to discover the murderer of Artemis Colegrove once and for all.

My delight in my little intrigue nearly ran away with itself. I decided that I should impersonate a recent immigrant who spoke next to no English. A Dutchman, I thought at first—but decided against it on the ground that the wedding guests might well include Dutch speakers. A German, Spaniard, or Italian would be ideal, but I feared I could never be convincing in those guises. Recalling that Fischl was also fluent in French, I determined to pass myself off as one of that nationality—but a harmless *musicien*.

At first I thought to denominate myself "Candide Arouet," after my fictional hero and his true author, but then I considered that there was a surfeit of facile cleverness already abroad, and settled for "Jacques LeBrun" instead. Old Mrs. DeLancey, I trusted, would not deign to converse with a hired entertainer, but any other native French-speaker could land me in trouble enough.

On my way to Fischl's the next morning, I stopped to pay my respects to Mrs. Glasby, and asked her confidential assistance in further disguising myself—she being a mistress of all dramatic subterfuge. "A wig will do wonders, as you've never worn one," she said, "but if you pitch your voice low and we also darken your blond eyebrows, no one will ever guess." She produced a small jar containing an evil-looking brown paste, which she carefully applied with the tip of her little finger. "You might emphasize the parts nearest the nose, but be sparing with it overall." She put a hat on my head, produced a hand mirror, and I was startled not to recognize the bloke staring back!

"It might be wise to start wearing the wig and the makeup immediately, Thomas," Adelie cautioned. "What would you do if Aaron Colegrove came into Fischl's shop while you were practicing there?"

"What would I do if any of my *friends* should recognize me?"

"Indeed, it's a dilemma. Better to consider such possibilities in advance!" She lent me another jar, a cream that worked as a soap to remove the dye.

Following her recommendation, I resolved to become Monsieur LeBrun immediately on my daily arrival at the store, and to resume my own person each evening as I left. Working out the details with Mr. Fischl—and locating his wigs—took half an hour; fortunately for me, he had no customers until later.

My first test came just as I was preparing to leave that afternoon. "Ah, Mr. Colegrove!" Fischl loudly sang out.

It was Oliver Colegrove, goaded by his aunt to verify Fischl's progress in securing the musical entertainment. Fischl sat with him to describe the several pieces he was considering. I continued practicing until I noticed young Oliver's restless eyes on me, then I growled to Fischl that *"Je doit visiter le pissoir, monsieur!"* and walked out the back, where I stopped to overhear the rest of their discussion. Mr. Fischl boldly told him, "Monsieur LeBrun has agreed to play at your brother's wedding, Mr. Colegrove!" Fortunately, this aroused no curiosity.

At dusk, exhausted by both practice and pretense, I doffed the wig, cleaned my eyebrows, and started for home, looking forward to supper, a little reading, and bed.

As I progressed down Reade Street from Broadway, however, I perceived some sort of mêlée in the westernmost block. It seemed to be growing in volume and intensity as I approached. On reaching my building in the middle block, I was surprised to find Mrs. Nugent waiting for me, holding my musket and haversack at the ready. "The militia captain was looking for you, Mr. Dordrecht! Said you were to report directly!"

"What's going on?"

"It's that crazy woman, Marge Williams! Out of the blue, she attacked some old gentleman and got the best of him, and now all the neighbors have taken sides and joined in the fight. Must be her landlord!"

Ructions were nothing extraordinary on Reade Street, but this was the first time that, as a militia member, I had been called to help break one up. And the summons, I knew, was peremptory, as the town's gentry were frantic to ensure that the tenuous public peace was maintained. I gave her the parcels I was carrying, took the musket and bag, and dashed toward the fray.

Locating the captain amid the three dozen or so heaving bodies, male and female, young and old, white and black, I waved to him, and he yelled, "Just try to keep them apart!"

How, exactly? I interposed myself between two short but hefty men, literally trying to keep both at arm's length while simultaneously holding onto the musket. Consequently, both of them turned on me. One put a fist to my ear on the uninjured side of my head, which stunned me so badly, I fell to my knees. They returned to pummeling each other as I made my way back upright. "You just can't let women fight men!" howled the one. "That old buzzard's not from our ward, he's an interloper!" roared his antagonist. Two women were having at it, hollering similarly inane arguments at each other. What on earth was the original quarrel? One crashed back into me, knocking me down once more.

"Dordrecht!" the militia captain called. "Fire your piece!" When he saw my shocked reaction, he added, "Into the *air*, ninny!"

I had to move aside in order to prime the pan and ram the wadding home, and in the moment it took, I observed that I was the only one in possession of a firearm. When I finally pulled the trigger, firing high over toward the river, the recoil shook my poor noggin yet again, but it also alarmed the rioters, scared half of them away, and called more militiamen to the scene.

Town constables also arrived, and arrested five men and three women for riot. I saw the militia sergeant and two others escorting a slight man in business dress, well past sixty, away from the scene. He was leaning his head backward, holding a handkerchief to his bloodied nose. "The bitch was making all sort of wild accusations," he squalled, "and then had the effrontery to try to blackmail me with them!"

"Calm down, sir!" said the sergeant. "The judge will hear you out, never fear!"

"Calm *down*? Calm down, hell! I— What are you doing? Where are you taking me?"

"Don't let him get *away!*" shrieked a tall, thick-set, red-faced woman of thirty-some years, struggling all the while with the two militiamen pressing her back against the wall of a house. "Don't let him escape! He's a killer! He murdered her, I tell you!"

"You tell him, Marge!" one of her female neighbors shouted.

"Shut your fool trap, missus!" bellowed one of the men simultaneously. "It's no good!"

She kneed him in the groin, and started down the street, dragging the shorter militiaman behind her—earning cheers from the bystanders. "Don't believe him!" she wailed. "He stabbed her, I know he did! He killed my sister!"

Another militiaman came to the aid of the first pair and halted her progress. The sergeant and his elderly captive disappeared around the corner. The mob evaporated, its fury spent as quickly as it had arisen. I got up off the tall fellow on whom I'd been kneeling, and he dashed off without a word. "Stop this! You're spending the night in jail, woman!" the captain yelled.

"No!" she howled. "That foul old bastard did it! He killed her!"

"Oh now, now!"

"She ain't right in the head, she ain't!" a man asserted, unasked. I got a look at her, and my first impression concurred: there was something false, something furtive about all the righteous rage.

But she ceased struggling at last. Her wrists were secured behind her back. The militiamen took her arms, and started to pull her toward the jail. They turned the corner down Church Street and I, having gotten a nod from the captain, headed back for home, my brain throbbing within my skull.

"You're letting him go!" I heard her wailing. "He stabbed her over and over!"

I halted, feeling a sudden chill.

"He murdered my poor little Hattie!"

"What was all that about?" Mrs. Nugent asked. "I thought they were going to tear another house to pieces! It was Crazy Marge who started it, wasn't it?"

"So it appears."

"She's no good, that one. She'd sell her grandmother to the highest bidder!"

"Mrs. Nugent, you recall, weeks back, I asked if you knew of a Peggy Mercer?"

"Aye?"

"Could Marge be—" I answered my own question: Peggy and Marge are among many nicknames for Margaret, and women take their husbands' surnames. "Do you know if she's married?"

"Marge?" She snorted. "Oh yes. But Williams left her years ago!"

"Why do you call her Crazy Marge?"

"Not just me, everyone! It's her airs. Her snooty self-importance. Everyone knows she's a trollop. She thinks she's high-class, way better than the madams in the bawdyhouses. Just because one of her girls was married by some fool merchant, she pretends all the rest of 'em weren't ruined!"

"She was squalling that the old fellow she attacked had murdered her sister."

"What? Good lord, what'll she think of next? I'd lay odds he's her landlord!"

"What else do you know about her?"

"Lucy says she runs a gambling den. 'Ladies Only,' she says—*ha!* Which don't include the likes of *me*, you ken! No, it's only for them rich hussies what don't want their husbands knowing they play *faro* for money, just like their menfolk do!" She scrunched up her face, examining mine. "You think *she's* your Peggy Mercer?"

I nodded.

"*Oof!* I thought that Peggy Mercer was maybe your long-lost love, Mr. Dordrecht!"

No wonder she hadn't connected her to Marge!

I confronted the woman the first thing in the morning.

"I know you!" she snarled. "You're one of the damned militiamen who got me into this klink! What the hell do you want?"

Not surprisingly, Crazy Marge looked as if she'd had a bad night. The brick walls of the new jail had kept out the rain, but not the chill, and she was pacing back and forth in the tiny cell to keep herself warm. It was hard to believe that this blowsy, ungainly female could be a sister to Artemis, universally credited with at least being petite and comely. But such variation in resemblance is hardly unprecedented in families.

"Want some information, if you please, Mrs. Williams."

She seemed slightly mollified to be addressed politely. "Like what?"

I introduced myself and explained that Miss Theodora had retained me to discover the murderer of Artemis Colegrove.

"*Hmph!* Is that so? Well, I can tell you that! I've been trying to tell these clowns, but—"

"First of all, ma'am, can you tell me if you were ever known by another name?"

She was impatient, but elected to humor me. "Well, if you must know, my maiden name was Mercer, and my folks called me Peggy when I was— Is that Theodora the old harpie that's Aaron's sister? What does she care—"

"Theodora Colegrove is a daughter of Aaron Colegrove, by his first wife."

"*Huh!* Well, if she wants to know who did Hattie in, it was the old buzzard I caught last night and they let go! I saw him just walk away! They were letting him walk away as they were bringing me in here. There's no justice, I tell—"

"Who *was* the man, Mrs. Williams? He seemed respect—"

"Oh yeah, respectable enough to look at, maybe! His name's Caleb Lawson, and he's no more than a bloodthirsty murderer!"

I scoured my memory of the family chart. Caleb Lawson is the elderly husband of Colegrove's young daughter ... Prudence. Also Colegrove's business partner and second-in-command. "And you think he—"

"I *know* he killed her! He's the only one who had a motive to kill her. Everyone else loved her!"

In one respect, at least, the woman was clearly prone to delusion. "What motive would Caleb Lawson possibly have?"

"Because she'd borrowed a lot of money from Lawson's goose of a wife, and he knew she'd never be able to pay it back, and he'd have to ask her husband, his partner, for it!"

"But, Mrs. Williams—"

"And he knew that skinflint would never, ever pay up, and so he was stuck!"

"Mrs. Williams, this makes no sense at all. What possible good would it do Mr. Lawson to murder Mrs. Colegrove?"

"He was mad at her!"

"Well, I can imagine he might be. But this murder took some calculation, and anyone in Mr. Lawson's business position would have to be a calculating man, and I would think he'd at least want to wait and try to get Mr. Colegrove to redeem the loan. Wouldn't you?"

"Hattie said Colegrove doesn't trust nobody, and the partners ain't getting along!"

"Still— How much money are we talking about?"

She avoided my eyes. "Eighty pounds—Hattie said."

More than a workman makes in a year! "How on earth was it that Mrs. Colegrove needed eighty pounds? And why borrow it, rather than ask her husband for it after he returned?"

"Well, she owed it, and it was overdue, so she had to pay it up."

"How did she contract such an enormous debt?"

The woman became increasingly agitated and evasive. "Look, she gambled, mister. She gambled and she lost."

"You'd think her husband would've put a stop to it before—"

"Course he did! But then he went away. Hattie had to sneak out through the backyard to avoid the old harridans in the place."

"She told you all about this?"

"Well, yeah, she was my sister!"

I mumbled a thought aloud: "The last people I'd ever want to know about such a mortifying calamity would be my family!"

Suddenly regaining her composure, Mrs. Williams snorted with amusement. "Well, she had to, you see. It was me she owed the money to!"

"She had gambled with you, and ended up owing *you* eighty pounds?"

"Not just me, with other ladies too! We had a club, every Wednesday morning, and Hattie—" She stopped, possibly taken aback by the look of revulsion that I'm sure was on my face. "It's not what you're thinking, mister! She was old enough, and she was rich, and—"

Tenkus had never realized the "girlfriend" Artemis visited on Wednesdays was the same older sister he knew as Peggy ... who had callously allowed the girl to amass a staggering indebtedness to herself.

"So you're saying she borrowed eighty pounds from Caleb Lawson to—"

"From his wife, Aaron's daughter, who was the only one in the family she really liked. Same age, practically, you see."

"And she told you all this ... when?"

"When she paid me back." She paused, looking out through the grating on the door. "The morning she was killed."

"The regular gambling party?"

"Yeah, but she didn't play that morning. Other gals were wondering what was wrong with her."

I dare say! "So ... you think Mr. Lawson discovered that his wife had lent Mrs. Colegrove all that money, and he killed her in a fury?"

"What else?" I looked at her dubiously. "Well, I admit it weren't my first reckoning. They all said Tenkus had done it, but I knowed that was wrong. Tenkus was mad for her. I figured it had to be one of them Sons of Liberty. I don't trust them holy bastards! Took me a long while to guess it had to be Lawson."

"How did your confrontation with Mr. Lawson, last night, come to be?"

"Well, I taxed him with it, you see, and—"

"What was he doing on Reade Street in the first place?"

"He came to see me."

Colegrove's business partner traveled to the roughest section of town two nights after the worst riots ever known? "A social call, Mrs. Williams?"

"He came—all I'm saying! He came, he slapped me, and I hit him back! And I ain't apologizing if I hit him hard! It's him who should be stuck in here, not me!"

I decided I'd had enough of her, and stood, about to leave. "What happened to the eighty pounds, Mrs. Williams?"

She looked away, then shrugged. "Lost it. You going to tell them to let me out of here?"

She could have settled herself quite decently with all that money. "In your case, madam, I'm content to let the law take its tiresome course! Good day to you!"

"*Aww!*" she growled indignantly as the jailer let me out.

In a chat with the bovine jailer, before I left the building, I learned that Lawson had been released almost immediately, "because he said he hadn't done it." When I recovered my breath, he explained that the *gentleman* had given his address—William Street just north of Hanover Square—and insisted that he wanted to see a judge, because he was determined to press charges against the she-wolf for assault.

Walking south from the jail, I debated whether to interview Lawson at Colegrove's office, or his wife at their home, and decided the latter would likely produce more relevant information faster.

A stout, rather fierce-looking slave woman answered my knock at the Lawson home. I stated my business, and waited less than a minute before being admitted to the parlor, where a pretty but glum young woman—who bore a strong resemblance to the lovely Élise—nervously rocked a cradle. The slave remained standing in the room, her arms folded across her ample bosom. "Yes?" the mistress said. "What can I do for you?"

I gave my name and unblushingly announced that I had been asked by Miss Theodora Colegrove to investigate the murder of Mrs. Artemis Colegrove. Mrs. Lawson brightened considerably. "Oh, Theodora, I haven't laid eyes on her in ages! Of course, I haven't been back to church since well before Baby was born!" I was tacitly relieved that she had no inkling of my recent dismissal. "Peter told me how she'd asked someone to look into it. Do sit down, sir! He said we should be grateful for Theodora's initiative!"

As she leant forward to rock the cradle, I observed a bruise on her forearm, and that she winced with the effort. "Mrs. Lawson, I trust you know that a certain fracas occurred last night on Reade Street, and—"

"Oh!"

"It happened that I live nearby and was called, as a member of the local militia, to help preserve the peace."

"I ... see. Mauddie, can you take Baby upstairs? We don't want to wake her!" The slave gathered not only the infant, but the heavy oaken cradle as well, and carried both to the second floor.

"Your husband explained to you that he had an encounter on Reade Street with a certain Marge Williams, and that he intends to press assault charges against her?"

"Yes," she said hesitantly, her face a mask of distress and nervousness. "Caleb was in a terrible state of fury when he got home. He ... still is."

"I just now interviewed Mrs. Williams in the town jail. She asserts that your husband sought her out last night, despite the town's unsettled state. Do you have any idea what prompted such a meeting?"

She sighed, looking all about the room, as if debating whether to talk to me. Then she faced me. "I do, Mr. Dordrecht, since my husband pressed it on me after he returned home." She stood—wincing again—and walked to a bureau, from which she removed a crumpled sheet of paper with burnt edges. She smoothed it out, handed it to me, and sat back down, clearly fighting an outburst of tears.

Lawson—
You foul, foul murderer! I know all and will tell all!
See me tonight at dark, or it will be the worse for you!
Marge Williams
151 Reade

"He said it had been given to a page outside his office during the afternoon."

Blatant blackmail. No wonder he slapped her! "He saw fit to acknowledge such a missive?"

She sighed again. "My husband ... knows no fear and does not allow such things to rest."

"Was Mrs. Williams previously known to him?"

"Not at all, not remotely. The charge— He knew it had to have something to do with Artemis. There's no other ... *murder.*" She shuddered.

"Are *you* familiar with Mrs. Williams?"

"No. Artemis had occasionally said she missed Peggy, her sister, but I had no idea the woman even lived in the city."

"Mrs. Williams still asserts that Mr. Lawson must have murdered Mrs. Colegrove, because he was enraged over a certain debt?"

"*Ohh!*" she moaned. "Caleb knew nothing about it. He had no idea what the woman was talking about!"

"The debt?"

"Yes. He never missed the money at all. I ... replaced it right away!"

"Mrs. Lawson, can you please explain the whole situation for me? From the beginning?"

Again she seemed to debate assisting me before complying. "Artemis— We were friends, you see. I hardly ever thought of her as my father's wife."

One can imagine the absurdities that might present!

"Artemis came to me in tears, explaining that she had a debt that she had to repay—immediately. And she didn't have the money, and she didn't know when Father would arrive home. And she—"

"When was this, please, Mrs. Lawson?"

"The week before—before she was killed. The Thursday, I think. In the afternoon."

"Did you inquire what brought the indebtedness about?"

"Oh, I didn't want to interfere, she was in such distress!"

"Mrs. Williams said it was a matter of eighty pounds, ma'am."

"Yes, but the poor lass was beside herself. I couldn't bear it!"

I recovered my breath and pressed ahead. "So how—"

"My husband keeps some of his fortune hidden in this house, Mr. Dordrecht. Or rather, he did until this morning! And he had shown me where, in case— You know. But it was carefully secured, so he almost never took it out, you see." I nodded. "So I opened the trove and found eighty-seven pounds, and I gave Artemis what she needed, feeling certain that Father would repay me before my husband would look for it."

And this woman's name is *Prudence?* "I trust Mrs. Colegrove was relieved?"

"Oh yes," she said casually. "But it began to worry me that my husband— Indeed, the very idea *did* upset him mightily! Where was I? It preyed on my mind that Caleb might discover the funds were missing. But happily I had another resource."

"Indeed?"

"Yes, my dear brother, who was terribly fond of Artemis, and has always been the closest to me. I managed to persuade him, two days later, to recompense me the eighty pounds. I explained that Father would of course repay it on Artemis's behalf!"

Though a businessman's daughter, she was devoid of all common reason! "*Um, uh*— Which brother, Mrs. Lawson? Not young Oliver, I trust?"

"Oh heavens, no! Oliver has no practical sense!"

I swallowed.

"It was darling James! After all, he was going to be the really rich one! We were all certain his fortunes were made by Father's successful effort to get him a sinecure."

James. "James Colegrove assumed the debt, in order to—"

"In order to spare me worry, of course, and because he loved— I mean, he *cared for* Artemis, he cared for … Father's wife."

One wonders how he treated his own! "Did this sudden transfer of cash cause your brother no inconvenience?"

"Not that he ever troubled me with, sir. It was very sweet of him, don't you think?"

"Mrs. Lawson, did you know that your brother was overheard, the Sunday before Mrs. Colegrove's death, arguing with her—about money, in fact—in the parlor of the Broadway house?"

"No, I did not, Mr. Dordrecht, but—Oh goodness!—I'm sure it must have been some minor family squabble. The servants, I suppose? Really, we should all learn to live without them!"

"You never asked your brother how he managed the outlay?"

"In fact, I haven't even seen James since the day he restored Mr. Lawson's funds. He's been concerned about the dreadful mob rule of this city. I had hoped we might see him at Peter's wedding, a week from Saturday, but, *um*, we decided I wouldn't yet be strong enough to travel."

Her evasive visage strongly suggested that this had not been a mutual decision. I turned back to the original question. "So then, despite Mrs. Williams's contentions, your husband had no quarrel with Mrs. Colegrove, because he never knew the money had been purloined?"

"He never knew anything of it … until he confronted me last night." Her lips trembled slightly. "He was … very much enraged."

He beat her, I realized. Having been knocked around by Marge Williams, he took his revenge on his wife.

She saw my look and hastily covered her forearm. "It was all so ridiculous of the Williams woman, because it was impossible for Caleb to have had any opportunity for mischief in the first place!"

"How is that, ma'am?"

"Well, I remember perfectly. He gave me the news about Artemis when he got home that day. I was in the last week of my confinement, you see. Baby was born on September third. And it was so terribly hot, I was prostrate! He had heard of the murder as he left the monthly meeting of his dinner club, the Encyclopedia Club. They meet at midday on the last Wednesday of every month."

Though I'd long since discounted much of Mrs. Williams's argument, I was glad to have an easily verifiable assertion that could seal the issue.

I took my leave of Prudence Lawson, with thanks, and not without concern that her spouse might take further umbrage at her having talked to me.

Once out of doors, I recollected why I recognized the name of the men's club. On the way back to Fischl's, I stopped in what I already was thinking of as "my old office," and begged two minutes of Mr. Glasby's time. He confirmed to me that he remembered the Encyclopedia Club's meeting of August twenty-eighth perfectly well—the horrifying news of the murder had greeted the members as they left the premises. And he was positive that Caleb Lawson had been present. He had found the man extremely irritating, because he'd disrupted an earnest attempt to parse Rousseau in order to fulminate against the Stamp Act protesters.

I repaired to one of our ubiquitous cheap eateries for my standard frugal dinner—bread, cheese, and ale, with a slice of cold gammon as a treat, partaken standing up, as usual—before continuing to Mr. Fischl's shop on Pearl Street. After explanations for my tardiness, he hurried me to effect my disguise, as our fellow players were expected shortly for our first rehearsal. These proved to be two shy young brothers from Württemberg, Jens and Torsten, recently arrived nephews of one of Fischl's old friends, who were proficient on the viola and viola da gamba.

Our first readings of the pieces Fischl had chosen made it obvious that Monsieur LeBrun needed a great deal of practice. Given that my head still throbbed as I walked, however, the prospect of sitting quietly in front of a pianoforte for a few days was very welcome.

Mr. Fischl only kept his shop open for ten hours a day, so I used the hours outside to consolidate and correlate my notes, particularly in regard to the specific hours in which Mrs. Colegrove—and later, I myself—were attacked. It occasionally seemed an insubstantial exercise, given the gaping lack of report for the missing Colegrove, but I pushed myself to complete what I had.

Returning home from Fischl's on Saturday, I walked by the jail and chanced to see the jailer. "Has Marge learned any manners yet?" I joked.

"Gone!" he replied, much to my surprise. Some lawyer had appeared the day before, spent an hour in her cell, and reappeared later with a paper attesting that Caleb Lawson had withdrawn all charges against her. He couldn't remember the man's name until—after he'd described him to me—I suggested *Gerrison*. "Yeah, that's him!" He had escorted Mrs. Williams home following her release.

The rest of the story was provided by Mrs. Nugent, who'd only learned it that afternoon from Lucy, her equally gossipy friend of the next block. Marge and her incongruous escort had ignored all greetings on her return to Reade Street. She'd quickly packed two bags of goods, and the gossip had followed them as they'd walked to the New Jersey ferry. Marge had boarded it, and the man had watched it depart before turning back toward town. "What do you make of *that?*" Mrs. Nugent demanded triumphantly.

Lawson had been persuaded that *any* public connection with Marge Williams—not least the risible fact that she'd beaten him up—would work to his detriment, and Gerrison had negotiated her release in exchange for a commitment to leave the province. *That* was what I made of it.

Hardly a loss to our fair city!

Though the weather turned mild and humid the following week, the said fair city was still nervously awaiting the new governor. The harbor began to fill with idle vessels and the town swelled with idle sailors. Ship captains were still being asked to promote calm. Tense groups of men and women could be found on street corners, having heated discussions that always seemed on the verge of altercations. The relic acting Lieutenant-Governor Colden remained sequestered inside the fort.

The *Janie* was among the first ships to return to New York harbor—empty-laden. She would be ideal, I realized, for transporting the pianoforte up to Mamaroneck. Captain Ford expressed some trepidation about the Hell Gate passage, with which he was unfamiliar, but I think he was merely disgruntled at the thought of spending days moving no more than a single parcel, however valuable. Mr. Glasby was wryly amused at the hard bargain I wrung out of him on Fischl's behalf, but I was of course aware that the *Janie* had no other immediate prospects.

On the Wednesday before the wedding, eight days after Governor Colden's surrender of the stamps, his replacement stepped ashore in New York, having endured ten long, cold weeks at sea from Portsmouth. I joined the crowds greeting the man. Charles sneered that Sir Henry owed his elevation to his particularly brutal suppression of the slaves of Jamaica, as we all suffered through interminable formalities on a gray morning: the requisite number of cannons fired by sea and shore, reading of the royal proclamation of his appointment, welcoming speeches by too many dignitaries, etc., etc. Finally, the Council members took him inside where, everyone knew, the real issue of the day would be decided in private. There was an unexpected flutter of interest when Isaac Sears was invited to join that colloquy. After another hour, the happy word came out that the new governor, apprised of the vehement and unrelenting objection of the populace to the Stamp Act, had decided ... that he'd send a request for further guidance back to the cabinet in Whitehall, and make no immediate effort to enforce it. Even greater relief came the following day, when the nine crates of stamped paper Moore had brought with him were also consigned to the care of the city fathers in Mr. Tolbert's archives.

Walking back to Fischl's after all the ceremonials, I looked out at the wharf and was puzzled by something odd in the *Janie's* appearance. It took half a minute to discern it: her sails had been struck from the rigging. I walked over to the dock and learned from a crewman that Captain Ford was much alarmed by the deteriorating state of the weather. The day seemed merely rather dark and humid to me, but ... one learns to take old seamen's apprehensions seriously, and so I became anxious in turn that my careful scheme might pathetically succumb to inclement skies.

The storm—a particularly violent nor'easter such as afflicts us every few years—woke me from my slumber in the middle of the night, and crashed and poured and blew throughout Thursday.

Dauntless, my collaborators and I trudged to the store as usual. After spending an hour trying to dry ourselves out, we had a final practice, disassembled the pianoforte, and crated it up for shipment. The storm was still blustering away in the middle of the afternoon. Its force was exacerbated, I was told, by the new moon's high tide, which had flooded the King's Wharf overnight, causing terrible havoc to ships and low-lying buildings. Captain Ford arrived to inform us stoically that our original plan of leaving on this evening's tide was infeasible, and that our only chance was to depart before ten in the morning, in the hope of making the entire trip in one day. Our quartet agreed to reunite at the store at seven, to hire a carter and get ourselves and our instruments to the wharf by eight-thirty, no matter how foul the weather, just in case.

As I was about to leave, Mr. Fischl caught me. "You realize that *monsieur* forgot to darken his eyebrows?" I felt a wave a panic, imagining one of the lads pointing this out at some inopportune moment. "I don't think either of them noticed. We each had our own preoccupations today!"

At dawn the next morning, I hurriedly repacked my valise, and made my way to Fischl's through still squally weather. Rain was no longer descending in steady torrents, but in waves of lesser intensity. The temperature had dropped and the wind was not so consistently fierce. It was awful weather, in short—but an improvement over that of the previous day.

When we arrived at Peck Slip, Captain Ford, swathed in oilskins, was standing at the end of the wharf and looking outward at the gray, menacing East River. It was alive with choppy waves, spume, and the floating detritus of a major storm: dead fish, branches of trees, planks of broken docks, oars, empty crates. He was shaking his head disconsolately as Fischl and I approached. "I don't know!" he said, in answer to the question we hadn't even articulated. For another ten minutes—the churches tolled eight forty-five—we waited in a sodden agony of suspense. Finally he sighed heavily, turned to us and said, "All right!" and immediately strode back to the ship, where his crew of five men snapped to readiness. He called two ashore to assist with rigging our crate for lifting into the hold, while the other three began hauling the sails back onto the deck.

All was intense activity for an hour, during which I hardly noticed either rain or wind. When everything was ready, the two German lads were still huddled against a shed, looking at the *Janie* with complete dismay, perhaps having expected a ship as large as the one that had brought them to America. It was all Fischl and I could do to persuade them to board. "You survived three thousand miles of open ocean, and you're frightened of thirty miles in protected waters?" Fischl told me he'd said in German. I surely didn't offer the observation that negotiating tight passages in coastal waters was frequently even more perilous, and the lads boarded with the proviso that they could stay below decks, where Captain Ford would want them anyway.

At the very hour he had bruited the day before, rowers tugged us out of the slip and we raised some sail. Ford seemed glad of an extra hand even with my minimal nautical experience, and sent me to the bow to watch for traffic and "stuff in the water."

The wind, still gusty, was now mostly from the east, which made for constant work until we rounded Corlear's Hook, and constant attention as we proceeded along the shore of Long Island toward the justly feared confluence with the Haarlem River known as Hell Gate. I alerted the captain to one nearly sunken skiff off Newtown Creek, but he'd already spotted it. Just south of Hallett's Point, the northwest corner of Long Island, four ships our size were anchored in a cove. Thinking of our urgent need to get on, I was surprised when Ford elected to furl his sails and anchor as well. The other ships were launching their jolly boats—to go ashore, I presumed. I wondered if they had all gone shy of braving the Gate.

The weather had moderated, but only slightly. Captain Ford took Mr. Fischl and me aside. "It's still very rough," he needlessly informed us. "If you want to travel on today, I'll need to press you both into service." Not having any idea what he meant, we both nodded. "Mr. Fischl will stay on the deck, and will stand ready to release the sails at my command." Fischl nodded, though I sensed he had no idea what was meant. "Mr. Dordrecht, you will man the tiller of our jolly boat, which must at all times stay ahead of the *Janie*. Four of the crew will be rowing as hard as they can." I looked around and saw the crew launching the heavy rowboat that had been lying, upside down, on the foredeck.

"The *rowboat* is going to pull the *ship*, sir?"

"Oh yes. Can be done. Easier, when we're tons lighter in cargo than normal." A whistle was sounded on the largest of the other ships, and its anchor was being hauled in. "You're to follow these others up the middle of the channels," Ford instructed me. "If the *Janie* can't sail, which is likely with the present wind, we have to sweep her through." I gaped, finally comprehending what was meant. "You go ahead and get in now!"

In a daze, I obeyed. I turned back briefly, and saw a look of alarm on poor Fischl's countenance. "Make sure he really understands what you want of him!" I urged—and then carefully lowered myself down the wooden frets on the *Janie*'s side into the bobbing rowboat.

The other ships each pulled up their anchors and raised their fore-and-aft sails, and their jolly boats sped out ahead, tow-lines pulling taut. My consternation increased as I heard *Janie*'s anchor being lifted, then her sails flapping out once more, and particularly as the four sailors dropped into the rowboat in fast succession—the last two literally jumped from the deck, rocking the little craft terribly. They settled side-by-side on the two benches ahead of me, placed their oars, grunted by common consent, and started rowing. As we passed *Janie's* bow, the painter was thrown from the deck; it landed on the head of one of the rowers, who cursed, dropped his oar, gathered and coiled the line, and resumed rowing—all of which challenged the other rowers and my ability to steer. But we were soon moving faster than our charge, and I had a panic wondering how we were to tow her without the painter. Just as I was about to voice this foolish worry, the answer rose out of the briny: there was already a tow line, affixed by a bridle to the stern *behind* me.

"Mr. Dordrecht!" Lemuel, the oldest mariner, said, his voice already husky from the effort. "You hear the coxswain ahead? Call out something to keep us together!"

Faintly, I heard a man chanting, "*Pull*, two, three, and *pull*, two, three ..." Enthusiastically, I mimicked this, and we rushed forward—until we fetched our tow, which jerked us alarmingly backward. The sailors snickered as I shook with dismay.

"Save your strength, lads," the mate called from *Janie's* bow, thirty feet behind us. "You'll need it right soon, on the turn!" He waved to us cheerfully—unaccountably brandishing an axe.

I'd been so concentrated on watching the ship immediately ahead through the drizzle, I'd barely noticed we were now directly between the first pair of obstacles, rocks but a hundred yards apart. And the ships in the lead had rounded another, and turned east. Into the wind!

"Steady, lad! Keep counting," Lemuel remonstrated.

I resumed the chant, striving for concentration. The many swirls and whirlpools in the heaving water did not make it easier. The bloated carcass of a goat drifted by and was swallowed up in one.

We came up on the next islet and the ship ahead of us turned. I could hear the coxswain urging his rowers to pull harder.

"Not yet, Mr. Dordrecht!" the mate called. "Wait 'til we're where the ship *was* before you turn!" Forty seconds elapsed. "Now!"

I steered to the right. *Janie* held her course! A whirlpool caught us and threw us sharply to the left, but I managed to correct us out of it. *Janie* came round, and her sails were suddenly flapping noisily. She lost her speed as the rowboat surged ahead.

Again the tow-line fetched up, this time in earnest. We seemed to be stopped dead in the water. No, the general current was slowly forcing us on our way. But were we in control, or at the total mercy of the elements?

The four sailors, having anticipated this change more clearly than I had, strained energetically at the oars. Finally I realized it was not only the current; we—rather, the four men sweating hard despite the rain and the chill—were towing the *Janie* slowly through the strait!

A full half-hour of unrelenting toil later, we had traversed possibly four hundred yards, and the ship ahead ponderously turned to port and began to pull away from us.

"Not yet, Mr. Dordrecht!" our mate called again. "Wait until *Janie*'s in line with her, then you move!"

It won't be long now, I thought. Except it was—over five minutes more. Finally, we turned four points to the north, the sails caught a little of the wind, and the *Janie* gained some speed on her own. But the rowboat was still pulling, and the narrow channel that opened to view was a mile long. After another ten minutes, we were able to head two more points to the north. *Janie*'s sails filled on the starboard tack, and she began keeping pace with the rowboat, which now pulled only to stay ahead.

"Safe to get back on board now?" I asked the older mariner.

"Not in the bloody channel, lad! Barely ten boat-lengths wide. There's clear water just ahead."

Just *a mile* ahead! The pattern of toil continued another twenty minutes. Suddenly a man in the ship ahead of us shouted, "A gust, a gust!" Another yelled, "Look out!" A third: "My god, *pull!*"

"*Pull!*" Lemuel roared.

Captain Ford hollered, "Let loose, let loose!"

What was happening? I finally realized: the sharply freshened wind was giving renewed speed to the ships, which were quickly overtaking their rowboats.

Janie was overtaking *us!* "The other one!" Ford yelled. "Let it *go!*" *Janie* turned slightly to the left, barely avoiding running us down as she pulled ahead.

I was not the only man who screamed when the rowboat was suddenly yanked about, and found itself being dragged backward by the ship! Water was flooding over the transom, quickly filling the boat. For five awful seconds, I truly thought, *This is it!* In this evil, cold, swirling water, in my heavy clothes, I'd have trouble getting myself two hundred feet to the shore, despite knowing how to swim. God help the other men, who probably never even learned how to keep themselves afloat!

Two loud thumps sounded from the bow of the *Janie*, even as the rowboat crashed against her side. The rowboat then abruptly righted itself with barely four inches of freeboard left, and *Janie* sailed blithely away. The five of us sat in a daze, panting. "Jesus!" exclaimed one. "*Thank you*, Jesus!" murmured another.

"What … *happened?*" I cried, my heart hammering in my chest.

Lemuel was the first to recover his senses. "Mate axed the tow-line, of course," he said. "Just like he's s'posed to. Let's start bailing, lads! Steady, don't rock her!" The four of them commenced using whatever tools they could employ to remove the water that had just nearly sunk the boat.

Another rowboat pulled near to us. "You lads all right?" a man called brightly.

Oh just dandy! I thought, with mordant sarcasm. Sitting in eight inches of frigid salt water!

"We seen your trouble. Same thing happened to us, but they dropped us in time."

"We're fine, thank'ee!" Lemuel called. "But if you could fetch us that oar, we'd take it right kindly!"

They did. I hadn't even noticed that one of our oars had popped out as we'd collided with the ship. As the sailors threw water out of the boat, I hauled and coiled the useless tow-line. Just as we were completing the bailing, a whirlpool caught us and spun us twice around, pulling us perilously near to a set of jagged rocks on the Long Island shore. "Oh hustle it, lads!" I cried, and we finally got under way, rowing on toward the next bend, behind which the *Janie* had already disappeared.

After another twenty minutes, we too rounded the bend, and found our mother ship calmly waiting nearby at anchor.

Captain Ford was busy with the others as I wearily pulled myself onto the deck. "Are you all right?" Fischl asked nervously.

Was I? "How long were we in that passage? Two hours?" I asked, shaking my head. "They were probably two of the most frightening hours of my entire life!"

As my friend gaped, we heard the captain praising his men. "Good job, lads! Really, that went very well indeed!"

I started laughing, wondering, *Why am I feeling exhilarated?*

CHAPTER 13

WE ARRIVED OUTSIDE MAMARONECK just at dusk. Fortunately, given the narrow passage into the harbor, a pilot spotted us. We had to get back in the rowboat to negotiate our entrance, but by dark we were tied up safe and sound. The pilot promised to alert the house of our arrival and our plan to debark the pianoforte at first light.

We all slept very soundly.

The day of the wedding broke clear and chilly. The fall colors I'd hoped to see were gone, the recent storm having blown down the last of the leaves, which now lay everywhere in soggy heaps. It wasn't easy to darken my eyebrows in the cramped privacy of the boat's head, but I managed. Though we were all wearing work clothes, I put my wig on; Fischl and the lads were sensibly not planning to don theirs until later, when we would change for performance.

Soon after we breakfasted, a cart yoked to two oxen made its way down the hill to the wharf, driven by a nimble pair of slaves from the estate. With patient coaxing, they managed to get the beasts and the cart turned around, so it could be loaded directly next to the crane. During the half-hour the delicate operation of hoisting the instrument required, I came to assume the slaves, whose names were Gus and Tayvie, were about thirty and must be brothers.

Finally, we started on our way. It was only two hundred yards to the house, but it was up a fairly steep grade that gave the oxen trouble. Captain Ford hastily recalled the liberty he'd just afforded the sailors, and had them help pull the cart on to the house. This rural dwelling was not one of your palatial manors such as have recently been built by our more ostentatious grand moguls, but a sprawling edifice that had once been a modest farmhouse but had seen numerous additions over many years. The latest of these was our destination: an outsized rectangular room with huge, showy windows, that stuck out at an odd angle from the rest of the structure.

We were greeted at its courtyard entrance by a tall, portly, middle-aged man who seemed ill-at-ease in his formal clothes. Mr. Fischl introduced himself and thus we learned he was Edward Colegrove, manager of the estate and the bridegroom's uncle. He held the door while the two slaves and the four of us carried the pianoforte crate into the ballroom, which was festooned with white bunting and wreaths of pine boughs. On the short side adjoining the house, opposite the entrance, a table had been set up on a dais, with candles, flowers, and a small altar cross. Mr. Colegrove told us to arrange ourselves between the middle windows of the long side on our left.

Speaking to the slaves in English, to Jens and Torsten in German, and to me in French, Mr. Fischl directed the uncrating and assembly of the instrument. To attach the legs, the pianoforte had to be suspended while each leg was bolted on from below. Yours truly was lying on the floor, effecting that important operation, when a woman's voice I recognized challenged the intended placement. "Edward, what are they doing *there?*"

"I thought the center would be best for hearing, Eudoxia! Mr. Fischl says—"

"I don't care what he says, it's an absurd place for the servants! They belong back there, next to the entrance!"

"Well, we do want everyone to hear the music, Aunt," a younger male voice urged. "After all, Ollie paid a fortune to rent this thing!"

"They'll just have to play louder, that's all, James!" Eudoxia insisted. "Can't have them here. No! Move it over there!"

"They still fixing legs, Miss!" Tayvie objected softly.

"Oh yes? Well, as soon as that's done, then, Octavian!" They moved back toward the entry. "James, see that Augustus sets out the chairs as soon as they settle the pianoforte. Make sure he keeps the rows even!"

"All right, all right!"

Though the others were still holding the full weight of the instrument, I stole a few seconds to look askance at James Colegrove, my prime suspect. Like his brother Peter, his junior by a year, he was tall, well-formed, and unblemished by pox. But he had a curiously casual, diffident, disjointed air—one might even say slovenly—in contrast to the meticulous Peter. Oddly, he was wearing a rough gray osnaburg coat that contrasted sharply with his blue satin breeches, silver-buckled shoes, and freshly-powdered wig.

"Edward, has the boy gotten that ox cart out of the way?"

"I was just about to see to it, Eudoxia," the man answered wearily.

"Well, for heaven's sake, the guests could start arriving any minute!"

She walked into the main section of the house while Edward Colegrove proceeded outside, muttering, "Barely nine o'clock!" and I resumed working.

"Gus, you heard her about the chairs?" James said.

"Yassuh, I do," the slave responded.

"Right!" James Colegrove walked out the door, shaking his head.

I had an odd feeling that— Oh, he was just not what I expected to be looking at and listening to, that was all!

He certainly possessed the physical wherewithal, however—to strangle a woman or to wield a paving stone against a man.

With the legs attached, we carried the pianoforte across the polished parquet to its amended location. Catching my breath for a minute, I observed the two slaves setting out the chairs—some four dozen people were apparently expected—and tumbled to the realization that *Augustus* and *Octavian* were likely the sons of *Caesar* and *Calpurnia*. Except that, historically, they weren't! Oh, worse: historically, Augustus *was* Octavian! The bloke changed his name, right? Obviously the Colegrove clan cared more about the form of classical reference than the received actuality.

Mr. Fischl and I now had the time-consuming task of tuning the pianoforte, which was of course necessary after the jostling it had suffered in transportation. The two German lads went out for a walk.

We were not alone for long. Early guests began drifting in and out, and many stopped to indulge their curiosity about the pianoforte, as none had ever seen one before. Over and over, Mr. Fischl had to explain how it differed from a harpsichord by striking down on the strings, rather than plucking them, and how this afforded the possibility of the pleasing variation in loudness common to other instruments. "And you shall hear this, when Monsieur LeBrun, who has lately arrived from La Rochelle, plays it for us today!"

Monsieur LeBrun, affecting shyness, politely said *"Bonjour,"* and continued to concentrate on his work—all the while striving to memorize the faces and names of everyone who introduced themselves.

When we were almost finished, an hour later, two couples—the younger of whom introduced themselves only as "Edward's neighbors"—proved to be of unexpected interest to Monsieur LeBrun. After the usual five minute examination of the modern musical wonder, they retired to our side and began gossiping, at a perfectly audible volume, *in Dutch.*

"I had the oddest reaction from James, just now," the older woman said. "I was congratulating him on his horse's victory in Hempstead, and he simply turned and walked away!"

"Oh Auntie!" exclaimed the younger man. "You hadn't heard? It was Atalanta who won, but he had sold her before the race."

"Oh no, I didn't know that! My goodness, when was that? I thought—"

"Before he came here to stay. I mean, before his set-to with the radicals in the city. Late August, I think."

Monsieur LeBrun fumbled the tuning wrench. Mr. Fischl was about to complain when the former quickly put his index finger to his lips and nodded in the gossipers' direction. Fischl picked up the wrench himself and resumed working.

"You don't suppose he needed the money, do you?" the older gentleman said. "I saw Atalanta out in the paddock. She was an obvious winner. I'd have put money on her myself if I'd been there!"

"I can't imagine any Colegrove needing money!" the younger woman laughed. "Have you looked at the spread Edward is laying out?"

"Ah but, my dear, it's not Edward who's hosting this, it's Aaron Colegrove. Our friend Edward hasn't got two shillings to rub together. It's Aaron who owns this house!"

"But he's almost never here!"

"Possibly that's because he and his brother haven't gotten along, ever since he put up such a fuss about Edward's taking up with Jane and Jane being part Indian," the older man suggested.

"*That's* why they never married?"

"Aaron and Eudoxia wouldn't allow it! Would embarrass the family, they said."

"Then *he* went and married a girl one-third his age!" exclaimed the elder woman. "Heavens! Scandal doesn't matter when the rich one does it!"

"Who was that, Auntie?" the lass inquired. "Will she be here today?"

"No no, Hansje! Goodness, no!"

"That was the girl who was murdered, Hansje," the younger man said gently.

"Oh! Oh dear, yes! Did they ever catch the sailor who did it?"

Monsieur LeBrun gritted his teeth to keep himself from screaming. But he was spared further aggravation when other neighbors joined the foursome, and commenced an assessment, in English, of the destruction wrought by the storm.

The pianoforte was finally tuned to Fischl's satisfaction a quarter-hour later. The lads returned and it was time to change into our performance suits. Fischl and I walked out in search of Edward Colegrove. We found him—just as his brother's carriage, driven by Caesar in his resplendent blue livery, pulled into the yard. Out of it, dressed spectacularly, stepped Oliver, Aaron, and Peter Colegrove, followed by a lost-looking Dr. Gideon Boyce. Caesar drove the carriage on through some trees toward a long one-story structure, evidently a stables.

Eudoxia and James rushed over to join the reunion—which showed very little evidence of family affection. "Dear heaven, I thought you'd never get here!" Eudoxia stormed. "What on earth—"

"Calm *down*, Eudoxia!" Aaron replied. "Roads are a disaster, of course, after all that rain."

"You should have anticipated that! You're very late! Some of the guests are already here!"

Peter properly shook hands with James and his uncle. Oliver, attired in a yellow and white confection of a suit, copied him once prompted, and asked to be excused to refresh himself. Aaron appeared to be preoccupied with James. "A long time since I've seen *you*, lad!" he said, a hint of menace in his voice.

"Yes sir," James nervously replied. Aaron took his elbow and led him toward the small formal garden.

The reunion was splitting in several directions. Mr. Fischl caught Edward Colegrove's eye and received directions to the servants' quarters. I watched as Aaron and James continued into the garden. Fischl returned to pass on his instructions. "I'll catch up," I said. "Let me borrow your pipe and pouch!"

"I was going to have a smoke!"

"I *need* it!" I whispered, striving to convey urgency without calling attention to myself. Mr. Fischl groaned, but handed me the prop accouterments and went back inside to fetch the German lads. I pulled out the pipe, followed the father and son, and found a bench by a tree at the garden entrance where I fussed with tobacco and affected nonchalant ignorance of their conversation.

"… but I'm not ready to come back, Father," James was protesting.

"James, I need you in the city. Staying up here any longer is completely ridiculous! They might force you to make one of their grotesque public recantations, but you're not going to be tarred and feathered or anything!"

"Oh I don't know, it's—"

"Now listen to me! There are hard times ahead, and— Who's that fellow smoking there?"

Would he see through my disguise? With effort, I drew a long, relaxed pull, because Monsieur LeBrun, of course, did not understand that Aaron Colegrove was talking about him.

"Just some Frog with the musicians, Father. It's not only the radicals, Father—"

"Well what then?"

"I've been … avoiding some creditors, I'm afraid. I ran up a few expenses while you were away, anticipating—well, you know—and then—"

"I heard you sold Atalanta! Surely that covered—"

"No. And that's something else I need to talk to you about."

"James, look, I've done my best for you. Who knew the Stamp Tax would cause such a damned fuss? You've got to come back to the city with us, or—"

"Aaron, the Kempes and Reverend Peacham have arrived!" Eudoxia Colegrove broke in imperiously.

"Oh Christ!" Colegrove grumbled. "I'll be right there!" he told her. "James, we'll talk again, but you've *got* to come back!" He hurried to join his sister, and James Colegrove shambled along after them.

Monsieur LeBrun blithely enjoyed his pipe until they were out of sight.

"Ware deed ze musiciens go, pliz?" Monsieur LeBrun asked the elder Dutch-speaking guest, who was himself taking a pipe in the fresh air. He pointed me on toward the stables. "Merci, m'sieur!"

I followed a short path through trees, then went around the back of the stables, where I saw Caesar, Gus, and Tayvie sitting together, deep in conversation.

"Ze musiciens, pliz?"

They pointed to the rickety door just beyond them, as Fischl sang out, "Ici, monsieur!"

I nodded and walked inside. It was a glorified privy with some extra room for the stable's maintenance tools. My three colleagues had already changed. Fischl was fussing over Torsten's cravat. "Vite, vite, monsieur!" Fischl insisted. Jens and Torsten were babbling in German. "Il faut que—"

"*Shh!*" I suddenly commanded them all—because I was overhearing the slaves, just outside the thin walls.

Though Mr. Fischl looked exasperated—no doubt he was feeling some anxiety about our impending performance—he presently appeared to understand my problem. "Les esclaves?" he said.

"Oui!"

"Purnie still not well?" Gus was asking.

Fischl put his finger to his lips, pushed the two mystified lads out the door, and whispered, "They want us to start in half an hour, Mr. Dordrecht!" before leaving himself.

"Purnie ain't been real well since they lock her up three days!"

"Damn!"

"Don't talk that!"

"We had bag of apples to give you for her, the day ladies came, but Mista Edward say James fetch, we stay with harvest."

"Would been nice."

"Mista James no use for harvest!" They all chortled—and I suddenly *had* to talk with them.

I walked out—and they froze, doubtless confused by the look of consternation that doubtless was on Monsieur LeBrun's face. "Caesar, I—"

Now they were alarmed—as was I, when the two younger men stood up to face me. I hadn't realized how tall and burly they were.

I pulled off the wig. "Caesar, it's me, it's Thomas Dordrecht!"

Gus and Tayvie were blocking his view. Still sitting, he pushed their legs apart. "Mista Dordrick?" he said, shaking his head. "What—"

"I'm still trying to find the murderer, Caesar, but—"

"You know?" Gus asked the older man.

"Yes. He ... he help Purnie."

"But Miss Theodora doesn't want me here, so I'm pretending—"

Had I been in his shoes, looking at my oddly arranged hair, I'd have been stupefied too. I gave up the struggle to explain myself. "I heard you say something I have to ask about, and ... I haven't much time."

"He crazy, Caesar?" Tayvie asked.

"He ... no. What?"

"I actually saw you, the day of the riots, driving the ladies up Broadway. I assume you took them all the way here?"

"Here? No. Mista James meet half-way. Kingsbridge. He take ladies rest of way."

Kingsbridge is the sole bridge connecting New York island, at its northern tip, to the mainland. By road, it would be about half-way from the city to Mamaroneck. "And you?"

"I have pass, I walk back. Masta want me help guard house that night."

"That would be … a matter of many hours, each way?"

"Oh yes."

"So then … James Colegrove and the ladies would have arrived here—when?"

"Dark," Gus said. "We serve big supper."

"Then … James couldn't have— Did you get back to the city in time?"

"Just. Masta frightened. We barricade all doors."

"You and Aaron? And Oliver?"

"And Mista Peter. He come to help."

But not James, I kept thinking. "Did you stay at it all night?"

"Masta go easy 'round half-ten. Say worst over. We stay locked, though."

"Peter stayed at the house?"

"Masta want him to. But he go home."

I shook my head, my assumptions disrupted. "Oh! Another question! Mr. James sold a racehorse. Do you have any idea *why* he sold her?"

Tayvie snickered. "He need money. He bargain hard!"

"He *try!*" Gus sneered sarcastically.

"Mista Coldcastle offer him sixty-five pound. He fuss and fuss until he get eighty, then—"

"Eighty!"

"Yassuh. Then Mista Coldcastle, he run Atalanta in the race, they say he win two hundred!"

He'd used a name I knew. "James sold the horse to Mr. Substance Coldcastle, the horse dealer, in Hempstead, on Long Island?"

"Yeah," Tayvie said. "I with him, I seen him."

"He damn fool!" Gus said. Caesar tapped him ineffectually. "Well, he is!"

"When— What day was this? You remember?"

"Damn hot day—long, long trip—what *I* remember!"

"It was day we hear about Missus," Gus prompted. "When you get back."

I stared at him, willing him to tell me more.

"Rider gallop up, supper hour, just after Tayvie and Mista James get home. Say Missus got stab, she kilt. And they all coming next day for funeral."

"Tayvie, you and James traveled all the way to Hempstead, and back, with a horse, in one day?"

"Go with three horse. Come back with two."

The day Artemis Colegrove was murdered!

"Gus? Tayvie?" a man bellowed. "What the hell are you—" Edward Colegrove halted at the corner of the building, staring at me, much bewildered.

I pulled the pipe from Mr. Fischl's smoking pouch. "J'ai besoin du tabac!" I announced—my heart thumping.

For five seconds, we all gawked at each other. "Well, they ain't gonna have none!" Colegrove finally said. "Women need you three right smart in the kitchen!" he roared. They rushed off. Then he turned to me. "You better forget that smoke, monsoor! Your man's looking for you too!"

"Ah oui? Tres bien. Merci, m'sieur!" Hastily replacing the wig, I hared on toward the ballroom as fast as I could.

Emerging from the copse of trees in a state of great agitation, I slowed myself down when I perceived John Tabor Kempe standing at ease with an older woman—from her familiarity with him presumably his mother—and with two other women slightly older than himself, likely two of his four sisters. They were all conversing amiably with an imposing middle-aged clergyman swathed in *embroidered* robes. The remnants of my Calvinist upbringing cringed: embroidered with figures *in all colors!*

I shook off my objections—the embroidery was rather beautiful, actually—and deduced that this must be Reverend Peacham ... and that that was another name that vaguely rang a bell. Perhaps from some reference in a newspaper article? The two younger women escorted the elder into the hall; the priest proceeded around the hall's outside walk; and Mr. Kempe remained outdoors, greeting other guests. Of course: it will be he who will escort the bride!

Having lost all sense of time, I was anxious that I might be tardy, and was hastening toward the entrance when I abruptly turned aside, having seen Miss Theodora Colegrove just ahead, in the company of a couple slightly older than herself. She was still wearing mourning clothes. I turned away and quickly faked a coughing fit. Miraculously recovering thirty seconds later, I cautiously entered the hall.

Mr. Fischl and the two German lads greeted me with strongly mixed looks of irritation and relief. The former, however, was talking to a guest who had obviously made a commercial inquiry. "I have only two copies of the Albinoni sonata left, sir. I urge you to stop by my shop as soon as you may, because it's very popular and I'm pledged not to import anything more until the repeal!"

As he conveyed his address to the gentleman, I noted with interest that Miss Theodora had taken a seat just two rows ahead of us. "Now who is that in front of Uncle Edward, Hulda?" she was saying—her voice slightly raised to surmount the general din.

"Nous allons commencer avec le Purcell, Monsieur, dans un petit moment!" Fischl said urgently. I quickly arranged the music in front of me.

"It's Mr. and Mrs. Traphagen, Theodora—she's Lavinia Boyce's eldest child. And you recognize Mr. Pugh, of course—Marguerite's husband. Marguerite's the other bridesmaid, beside Philadelphia Kempe."

"You're not telling me the gal's name is *Philadelphia*, surely?" the man said. I deduced he must be Mr. MacGregor, husband to Hulda Colegrove.

"Indeed I am, my dear," said the latter, "but of course they're not Quakers or anything, they were all born back in England."

MacGregor shook his head in evident amusement. "I don't see a single member of the DeLancey clan, Theodora. Surely they were invited?"

Miss Theodora's face reddened. "I'm afraid the DeLanceys must all have discovered their schedules were in conflict, John." Her sister and brother-in-law looked at her questioningly. "They've not been particularly attentive since the murder and Father's controversy with the radicals. Save the grandmother, of course."

As if on cue, Aaron Colegrove entered the room from the house, with Jacqueline DeLancey on one arm and his sister Eudoxia on the other. After seating the elder in the first row, he glad-handed several of the guests, to his sister's clear annoyance, before sitting as well. Eudoxia Colegrove then waved to Mr. Fischl, and we began to play.

After a succession of chords—*pianissimo* rising to *fortissimo*, at Mr. Fischl's special direction—the listeners were unable to resist remarking the contrast aloud—the strings took over and my part in the Purcell was easy.

Surely the slaves had to be mistaken about the date! Yet how could they be? Everyone remembers what they were about when earth-shattering news arrives. Everyone recalls what they were doing when the report of the Québec's surrender was heard. Could Tayvie possibly have gone on the excursion to Hempstead on any day other than the one in which they'd learned their mistress had been murdered? And they'd hardly mistake the date of the riots, barely a fortnight past.

Could they be misleading me deliberately? Oh Thomas Dordrecht, now you're truly hallucinating! Once Caesar relieved his sons' suspicions, they'd have no motive—not that they'd have any such motive otherwise! And how would they— No, no ... *silly!*

But then, who—

Mr. Fischl poked my arm with his bow and I jerked my hands up. I'd been sustaining the last chord beyond the cutoff. "Sorry!" I breathed as he looked at me in alarm. "Sorry!" I repeated.

Agnes, Élise, and Oliver Colegrove rushed in from outside with an air of miscreant adolescent tardiness, and seated themselves in the empty last row, six feet in front of us. Élise was resplendent, I couldn't help noticing, in her finished sky blue wonder.

"Ready with the Pachelbel?" Fischl demanded nervously—altogether forgetting to say it in French. I retrieved the music and nodded.

Again, the main function of the pianoforte was just to provide the *continuo*, to fill out the chords while the strings played the melodies. Once more my mind began racing to other concerns.

James had haggled the horse's price up to eighty pounds! How would Tayvie even know Coldcastle's name if he hadn't been there? Was it really possible to get to Hempstead and back in one day? I had something I really wanted to ask the girl Agnes.

"Oh no, he's wearing *that coat* again!" Élise Colegrove lamented. She was not, of course, the only person talking over the music, just the closest to myself.

"I know, I hate it too," Oliver Colegrove snidely replied. "It's *so* George-the-Second!"

I once had a coat that I loved but everyone else hated!

I had a *cadenza* to play.

"I was hoping he was planning to wear something else, as I'd not seen it since we got here." Miss Élise said.

"Peter fetched it for him. We brought it with us today."

Coda. Finished!

I looked up. James Colegrove was standing between his brother, the bridegroom, and Gideon Boyce, wearing not the gray osnaburg jacket, but a very distinctive maroon and silver striped woolen coat.

The coat that Charles had seen James wearing during the debacle of his father's arrival. The coat that Mapes had seen leaving the major's backyard during the riots. And … *I'd* seen that coat … on the back of the man relieving himself against the wall of a shed in that backyard.

"All right, this is it! The Handel." With a big nod, Mr. Fischl started the processional.

"Mrs. James again balked at coming?" Élise asked.

"You know she can't stand the lot of us. They really should get a divorce!"

"Oliver Colegrove! Wash your mouth out with soap!"

I glanced up. Oliver smirked. The youngest sister looked steadily ahead. Reverend Peacham paraded in with much dignity. He was followed eight measures later by two young women. The pretty one was indubitably Élise's sister. The one stuck with the ungainly name was also stuck with an ungainly appearance. Finally, the province's smiling attorney general strode in, escorting a woman in an impressive white gown whose face was mostly obscured by her veil.

Oliver Colegrove at least *tried* to hide his next remark to Élise: "With four sisters who look like *that* dependent on him, it's no wonder Mr. Kempe looks ecstatic!"

"Oh stop it!" his sister replied.

What did I want to ask Agnes?

The bridal party arranged themselves in a line facing the priest, who was standing on the raised platform beside the makeshift altar.

Da capo al fine.

The plighted couple were standing in the middle, and the bridegroom's brother was by his side. The two men were identical in height and build, but Peter seemed naturally so much more correct, more precise in appearance.

And yet, and yet … *James Colegrove could not have been in New York City the day Artemis Colegrove was murdered. And James Colegrove could not have been anywhere near the riot in which I had been attacked.*

The music thundered to a noble conclusion. The assembly sat back down and the bridal party knelt before Reverend Peacham. "Dearly beloved," he began.

I wanted to ask Agnes Colegrove who she meant when she said "I'd just waved at my brother." She'd seen a brother leaving the house just before noon, yet no one else had remarked the presence of any of them. Could she—the family's most innocent and ingenuous member—have been mistaken about *a brother?*

There was a hymn. The guests sang it abysmally, as usual, notwithstanding my support for the harmony and Fischl's on the melody. Then Peacham began to lecture the pair on their marital duties.

I didn't *need* to ask the lass which brother she'd seen! I'd already learned who was where when!

Gideon Boyce was lecturing at the college.

Nathaniel Boyce was at sea, then as now.

Lambert Colegrove was inspecting his mills at Saugerties.

Timothy Colegrove was taking a deposition in City Hall.

Vincent Colegrove, the son of her late brother William, was attempting suicide in the Hudson River.

Caleb Lawson, her brother-in-law, was haranguing the Encyclopedia Club.

Oliver Colegrove was shopping in Otterby's on Beaver Street.

And James Colegrove was selling a racehorse to Substance Coldcastle in Hempstead.

I staggered upright, reeling drunkenly with a sudden, horrendous realization. Mr. Fischl's eyes widened with alarm.

"If any man can show just cause ..."

There was only one other brother, the one whose impeccable behavior bespoke the reputation for candor and veracity I'd blindly accorded him on every occasion we'd met ...

Like a perfect fool!

"Let him speak now, or forever hold—"

CHAPTER 14

⊰▨⊱

"No!"

If looks were daggers, I'd have been dead in three seconds. I threw off my wig and stepped forward.

"No!" I shouted. *"He* did it!"

Peter Colegrove roared furiously and rushed at me as I was moving toward the front of the room, his hands outstretched to grab me by the throat. Aaron Colegrove and John Tabor Kempe followed, bearing down on me with raised fists.

"He killed her! *He* murdered Artemis Colegrove!"

"It's Dordrecht!" shouted Eudoxia Colegrove, hard on their heels. "You damned, interfering scoundrel!"

Peter Colegrove caught me from behind as I was distracted to the side by Miss Theodora's shriek. Before I could break his hold, he had both hands squeezing my neck. Aaron Colegrove grabbed my lapels, bawling incoherently, and shook me violently back and forth. As I struggled for balance and breath, I saw my erstwhile client faint into the arms of her brother-in-law.

"Snake!" screamed the bridegroom, tightening his grip.

As I struggled to keep from choking, I saw Kempe bring himself up short. "Halt!" he cried. "Hold it!"

But it was another ten seconds before more sober members of the assembly wrestled the three of us to the floor, and broke Peter's hold on my neck—and mine on his father's. "Mur— Murderer!" I gasped, unheard over the raging commotion in the hall. *"Murderer!"*

Suddenly, Aaron Colegrove released my coat and looked across me at his son. "Peter?" he said, panting. *"Peter?"*

"Hogwash!" Peter Colegrove shouted. "It was the goddam sailor killed her!"

"And that's the second time you've tried to kill *me!*" I cried simultaneously, with regained breath. I pulled my fist back to strike him, but Kempe caught my arm.

"Gentlemen!" thundered the white-faced priest. "In a room consecrated for a sacrament? Stop this! For all shame, desist!"

The struggles, roars of recrimination, and general chaos persisted another quarter-minute, until Peacham bellowed "*Silence!*" at the top of his lungs.

As all looked to him for direction, he panted and whispered, "I've never had this happen before!"

John Tabor Kempe recovered himself. "I believe it is ... required to examine the arguments of anyone who disrupts a wedding?" he said.

"Yes!" Peacham agreed nervously. "Yes, that is so. We must do that!"

"No!" Peter Colegrove howled. "No, that's preposterous! Haul this cretin off to jail, and let us get on with the ceremony!"

"Lynch the snake, I say!" Eudoxia Colegrove contributed vehemently. "He's ruined ... everything!" she added when many turned their eyes upon her.

Some, obviously intent on carrying out her suggestion, placed their hands on me again. "*No!*" Kempe yelled. "Stop! *Stop!* There will be no lynching! Not in *my* presence, at least!" he added sardonically. He looked about, panting. "Do we have a room in this house where half a dozen can meet in private?"

"Of course," said Edward Colegrove. "The parlor. I'll show you."

But Kempe looked about again, fixed on the younger Dutch-speaking man, and motioned him closer. "You must be a member of the militia?" He nodded. "You know that I am the province's attorney general? I charge you: go into town, fetch at least half a dozen of your fellows, and bring them back here. No one is to leave the premises until we have this sorted out!" he proclaimed loudly. The man indicated his willingness and rushed out.

"Well, that won't take long!" Aaron Colegrove blustered over the resultant outcry.

"But this is an outrage, an *outrage!*" Peter Colegrove spluttered.

"Lead us in, please, sir," Kempe said to the host.

"Eudoxia," Aaron Colegrove said urgently, "go ahead and feed them! And have the damn musicians ... do *something!*"

"I'm going with you!" she protested.

"No!" Kempe said emphatically. "Wait. It will be best to keep this to a minimum. Just … Reverend Peacham, the bridegroom, the accuser—"

"The bride has a right to attend," Peacham said.

The bride had also fainted. Prostrate, surrounded by her mother and sisters, she was a portrait of misery. Kempe shrugged. "The bride's brother will represent her," he asserted. "We may call others as needed. Meanwhile, as I say, I ask that no one depart the premises!"

"This is *my house*, sir!" Aaron Colegrove bellowed.

"Sir, I'm *sure* you will excuse us to impress a room for just an hour!" Kempe retorted.

"It's my wife's killing he's talking about, damn it!"

"Ah. Yes, quite so!" Kempe reddened, embarrassed, perhaps, that he'd overlooked that detail. "Very well then." He took Peter Colegrove's arm. "Let us get on with it, Reverend, Dordrecht!"

Edward Colegrove led the five of us back into the house. I heard Eudoxia yelling, "Well, play something! Play *anything!*"

When Edward Colegrove closed us in, I faced four very angry men, only two of whom were making any effort to contain themselves. I took some comfort as I realized that my awareness of Reverend Peacham went all the way back to the war: he had done the pathetic Private Talmadge a good turn, and my late friend Sergeant Hannamore had spoken highly of him.

"You poxy son of a whore!" Peter Colegrove snarled, his customary reserve shattered. He looked ready to leap upon me once again.

"You have a goddam nerve disrupting—" Aaron Colegrove began shouting.

"Gentlemen! *Gentlemen!*" Peacham admonished, interposing himself in front of me. "Can we all sit down, please?" I waited until they were settled before following suit.

"Mr. Kempe," Peacham began, bringing his voice and demeanor into careful control, "we have in this situation—unprecedented in my experience—a matter of deep concern to both church and state. A sacrament of our established religion has been disrupted, and an accusation has been made that the laws of both God and man have been violated."

Kempe seemed impressed. "Indeed that is so, sir," he said with more respectful deference than I had thought possible of him.

"I propose therefore that we conduct this interview jointly. I must decide whether the service may be resumed, and you must decide if the law is to take any cognizance of this man's accusations."

"Oh for Chri— for heaven's sake, Reverend," Peter exploded, "can't you see this swine is a charlatan? He's here under completely false pretenses— pretending he's some Frog musician! *He's* the one who should—"

"I think that's a fair proposal, Reverend Peacham," Kempe interrupted smoothly. "Perhaps you would care to begin?"

"Very well. You all appear to know this fellow's name. I do not."

"Thomas Dordrecht, sir, of New York City," I said. "Your servant!"

"And how is it that you come to be here, Mr. Dordrecht?"

"Some nine weeks ago, sir, I was approached by Miss Theodora Colegrove, with whom I was previously not acquainted, and offered a substantial consideration to discover who was the murderer of Mrs. Artemis Colegrove."

"And with all the evidence pointing to a sailor—or one of the damned radicals—you dare to—"

"Mr. Colegrove, I do understand that you're upset! Please make an effort—" The bridegroom sat back, his fists clenched. "Thank you! How was it that Miss Theodora asked you to perform this odd office, Mr. Dordrecht? Perhaps we should call her in?"

"*No!*" the other three exclaimed.

Kempe cleared his throat. "I presume it was at my suggestion, Reverend," he interjected. The priest's eyes widened considerably. "I had … reasons. But, *um*, perhaps rather than detailing them or demanding an explanation of his disguised and uninvited presence today, it might be expeditious to demand Mr. Dordrecht's explanation for disrupting the service?"

"I see. Very well. And what *is* that, Mr. Dordrecht?"

They couldn't guess? "I could hardly remain silent while Miss Kempe allied herself to a murderer, Reverend!"

John Tabor Kempe squirmed uncomfortably as Aaron Colegrove thundered, "Preposterous! Simply preposterous!"

"Could you not have offered this objection some time ago, Mr. Dordrecht? It appears positively … *mischievous* to wait until such a juncture to—"

"With respect, Reverend, I came to the conclusion only seconds before you asked whether cause could be shown. Until that—"

"I don't believe what I'm hearing!" Aaron growled.

"Until just an hour ago, I was almost completely convinced another party altogether had committed the crime."

"Oh fine, *fine!* And just who was that?" Aaron demanded.

"I no longer suspect the individual, sir!"

"It's a fair question, Mr. Dordrecht," Kempe said.

Very well. "I came to Mamaroneck largely persuaded that Mr. James Colegrove had murdered the victim."

Three faces were agog with shock. "*James!*" Aaron wheezed. "You thought *James* murdered Artemis?"

"I learned but half an hour ago that he could not possibly have been in the city that day. He spent the entire day traveling from Mamaroneck to Hempstead, and back, in order to sell Atalanta, his racehorse."

"And how'd you find *that* out, *eh?*" Peter Colegrove demanded angrily. But he restrained himself when he realized he was the only one objecting to my exoneration of his brother.

Five seconds passed in silence. "Perhaps, Mr. Peacham, I might more directly explain why I believe it was Peter Colegrove who murdered her?"

Peter Colegrove's objection was silenced by the priest's raised hand. "Mr. Kempe?" Peacham inquired.

Kempe was perhaps recalling the history that had led him to suggest me in the first place, and he was looking extremely uncomfortable. "It might be— If you can keep to the point, Dordrecht!"

"But—" Peter was now silenced by his father, though the latter was still frowning at me, not him.

"Thank you! When Miss Theodora gave me this commission, I had to discover who had the capability to commit the crime, who had the opportunity ... and who might have a motive."

Again Aaron couldn't restrain himself. "No one had a motive against poor Artemis, you dolt! It was *me* they were attacking, and I wasn't even here to defend her!"

"I would prefer to hear Mr. Dordrecht without interruption, Mr. Colegrove!" Peacham asserted authoritatively. Colegrove sat back, fuming. "Go on, sir!"

"First of all, the murderer had at the least to know the layout of the house and the yard—the folly, the privy, and what rooms were located in the rear of the building. But more importantly, he needed intimately to know the schedules of the eight individuals living there at the time."

"Eight?" Aaron interrupted. "There were only six!"

"I include the two slaves, Mr. Colegrove."

"Oh."

"When eight individuals are coming and going through the same house, only a rare occasion might present itself for a confrontation that would not be observed. Such a moment occurred that day—as the murderer realized it would. It of course follows that the murderer's own schedule had to permit him the time to commit the deed.

"Also, the murderer had to be physically capable of subduing a frail but healthy young woman. This eliminates the one resident of the house who was constantly present, Mrs. DeLancey, who was bedridden at the time."

"Oh for— for heaven's sake!" the elder Colegrove grumbled.

"Now, why could it *not* have been an intruder? Not even a mad intruder, a crazed Whig radical so intent on inflicting harm on the wife of the prominent Mr. Aaron Colegrove that he was careless of his own detection and escape? Well, the main problem is that this is an extremely far-fetched narrative. If the murderer was simply a madman, how do we account for the posted political slogan? If he was motivated by fanatical politics, how do we explain the extraordinary foolhardiness of attacking a large, unfamiliar household in the middle of the day? Furthermore, the felt anger of the moment was more likely to be visited upon Governor Colden, Captain Kennedy, or Major Thomas James—as we recently saw—rather than the spouse of the then out-of-sight-out-of-mind Aaron Colegrove. Mrs. Colegrove *had* infuriated many with her quip about stamping out the Sons of Liberty—but the major had inspired far greater passion by threatening to cram the stamps down everyone's throat."

"Artemis was making some stupid joke?" Aaron moaned, bewildered. His son and Kempe nodded uneasily.

"So the question becomes, of the people who were familiar with the house *and* were aware of everyone's daily habits, who had the opportunity? Who could have committed the crime during the three-quarter hour interval from eleven forty-five, when the delivery boy from Martin's grocery observed nothing amiss, to twelve-thirty, when Oliver Colegrove discovered a brutalized corpse?

"Let's dispose of the favored villain first: the mariner Henry Tenkus. I tracked him down in September, before he shipped out. He had known

Mrs. Colegrove three years ago, before she was married, and returned to the city this past April expecting that she would espouse him. Disabused of that hope, he took advantage of her husband's absence to meet with her on several occasions, and repeatedly urged her to abscond with him."

"The fiend! The bounder! I'd have shot him for *that!*"

Kempe scowled him into silence.

"Though their usual tryst was in a tavern, Tenkus visited the house itself at least three times, most notably on the evening before the murder. On that occasion, Mrs. Colegrove definitively rejected him, but he left without offering any violence. The slave Caesar was a direct witness to this, and others of the family were present on the upper floor. Immediately after that rebuff, Tenkus imbibed so much liquor that he did not wake from his stupor until he was arrested the following afternoon."

"But still—" Peter began.

Kempe sighed with irritation. "Mr. Dordrecht is quite correct in this particular. The grand jury heard five credible witnesses testify to the sailor's incapacity! You really cannot question it!"

"Could he not have contrived to get another sailor to act in his stead?" Aaron demanded.

"The publican in question," I responded, "told me Tenkus did not appear to have any close comrades, and also had already gone through the bulk of his funds. When he arrived that evening, he immediately began drinking hard, so I think the idea that he might have explained the situation to another, whom he then paid to commit murder, is beyond plausibility."

Would they finally concede the Tenkus issue? Both father and son looked as if they were desperately trying to imagine another angle—but they remained silent.

"So the question of the necessary opportunity becomes a process of elimination of the many individuals who were familiar with the household." From my waistcoat I retrieved the notes I'd made on this subject, which I'd kept close for days.

"The first three may surprise you. Mr. Vincent Colegrove had—"

"*Vincent!*" Aaron exclaimed, his eyes bulging with disbelief. His son affected to shrug.

"Mr. Vincent Colegrove had paid many visits to the house over the summer, always spending the bulk of his time with Mrs. Colegrove. He appears—"

"Did you know about this?" Aaron demanded of Peter.

"I knew he had visited once or twice," was the evasive reply.

I had to turn my head, wondering how many times I had swallowed lies from the man. "Vincent appears," I continued, "to have developed a Platonic affection for Mrs. Colegrove, born of their mutual love of poetry, and—"

"*Ugh!*"

"And he too, while quite ignorant of the sailor's advances, was hopeful that Mrs. Colegrove would abscond with *him*."

"*Oh!*" The head of the Colegrove clan exhaled furiously, slamming one fist into the other and shaking his head.

"He too was aware that his grandfather was soon expected to return, and also made his final plea on the day prior to the murder. He too was refused. He was emotionally devastated, and spent the hours during which the murder occurred the next day attempting to drown himself in the Hudson River. I have some corroboration for the hours at issue."

"Oh, you're *sure* of all this fantasy?" Peter Colegrove said sarcastically.

"Yes." I looked to Kempe. "I have names, the locations, and the hours of the day."

The attorney general arched his eyebrows. "Go on, then."

"Mr. Timothy Colegrove—" Both Aaron and Peter groaned loudly. "Timothy came under my suspicion for some time, not merely because he is openly partial to the radical faction in the city, but because he too had appeared in the house on the day before Mrs. Colegrove's death."

"Timothy was in the house?" Aaron said wonderingly.

"He was running an errand for his aunt, Miss Eudoxia Colegrove. In the process he inadvertently startled Artemis Colegrove, causing her considerable alarm, because she didn't even recognize him. However, despite his own obstinacy, I've learned that he spent the hours of the murder on a legal errand for Mr. Darius Gerrison, for whom he works as a petty clerk." Both Aaron and Peter stared in disbelief. "He has ambitions in the legal field and hopes to acquire an education in this way.

"A most unexpected individual," I continued, "was vehemently accused of the crime just last week: Mr. Caleb Lawson. Given his membership in the family for the past two years, he arguably could have acquired the requisite familiarity with the household."

"But ... *Caleb?* Prudence's Caleb? My business partner?"

"Yes sir. He was accused by a Mrs. Marge Williams, formerly known as Miss Peggy Mercer, who is the elder sister of Artemis Mercer Colegrove."

"Damn! I *told* Artemis never to see that wretched woman again!"

"She … appears to have disregarded your wishes in that case, sir."

Aaron Colegrove was looking ready to faint. "Are you quite well, sir?" Peacham asked.

"Yes yes," he responded testily. "Let's … just … go ahead."

"Without explaining Mrs. Williams' muddled reasoning, her contention can be easily dismissed, because Mr. Lawson was observed at mid-day on the twenty-eighth participating in a meeting of the Encyclopedia Club."

"*Hmph!*" Mr. Kempe shifted about in his chair.

"The two slaves," I continued, "could, like all slaves, be plausibly imagined to have grievances against their mistress. And the woman Calpurnia had in fact created a voodoo doll, a female with straw hair, which she employed as a pin cushion."

"*Ugh!* Dear heaven!" Peacham breathed.

"She was accused of the crime and in fact incarcerated for several days last month, until the fact that she had been observed by three individuals, working in the front rooms of the house, washing windows and mirrors on a ladder, made it impossible to conceive that she had been simultaneously engaged in slaughter in the backyard. The man Caesar's hours are also accounted for: after exercising Mr. Colegrove's horses in the morning, he spent the mid-day hour shopping for the family at Martin's grocery."

"Are you done with this absurd catalog yet?" Peter Colegrove demanded testily. His nervous gestures increased when the priest and the lawyer grimaced.

"Suspicion of many people who were familiar with the household can be quickly dispensed with. Dr. Gideon Boyce had come that morning—and for three mornings past—to bleed Mrs. DeLancey, in accordance with medical practice. He departed at approximately ten-fifty, in order to conduct his daily course at the college, beginning at eleven sharp.

"Mr. Lambert Colegrove was inspecting his mills up-river, in Saugerties, that whole week. Miss Theodora and Mrs. Irene Colegrove were together at the latter's home, occupied with Captain William's younger children. Miss Eudoxia was at Fort George, enjoying her regular invitation to tea from Mrs. Colden; she returned to the house around ten minutes past noon, and went to her room, the curtains of which were still drawn against the morning sun. Miss Agnes and Miss Élise were in school that morning. The former returned around noon; the latter, shortly after Miss Eudoxia. Mr. Oliver Colegrove was, following regular habit, taking a constitutional walk about the Battery with his two friends, Virginia and Edward Ramsay. They had stopped for some time in Otterby's emporium before parting company on Nassau Street at twelve-thirty. Mr. Oliver returned to the house for dinner, entering through the yard and discovering the body."

Mr. Peacham sighed, looking dazed. "Mr. Dordrecht, this seems very comprehensive, but I'm afraid my contact with the family has been somewhat sporadic over the years, and—"

I pulled out the family chart and handed it to him. "Perhaps this would help, sir?"

"Ah! A genealogical map, is it?" he said aloud. After perusing it a minute, he passed it to Mr. Kempe. Peter Colegrove looked discomfited.

His father seemed far more exercised. When Kempe passed the sheet to him, he snatched it away. Aaron Colegrove looked me in the eye, pointedly tore it up, and threw the pieces onto the floor. "It's not your business to put your nose into my family relations, Mr. Dordrecht!"

Fortunately, I had long since committed it wholly to memory. "Not all families suffer a murder, Mr. Colegrove!" I replied. Peter Colegrove nervously retrieved the scraps and placed them on the hearth.

Peacham had forestalled a shocked and furious objection to the destruction from Kempe. He allowed a few seconds for tempers to abate. "I presume you are not finished, Mr. Dordrecht?"

"No, sir. As I say, when I arrived here this morning, I had been mostly persuaded, for the last ten days, that Mr. James Colegrove was the murderer. Until November fifth, if I had any prime suspect, it was Mr. Timothy Colegrove, on account of several instances of obstructive and mendacious behavior. But I then discovered and verified that he was fully occupied at the moment Mrs. Colegrove was killed—and also at the time I was attacked on November first."

"You were *attacked*, Mr. Dordrecht?" Kempe said, arching his eyebrows.

"Or you were just injured while merrily participating in a lawless riot, *eh*?" Peter sneered.

"I was *attacked*, Mr. Kempe." Without comment, I pulled aside the hair I'd carefully trained to the right, to expose the still-livid wound. "But, *um* ... to return to my suspicion of Mr. James Colegrove: his continuing absence from the city, first of all, suggested more than concern that he might face abuse from the radicals. Also, some men I spoke to believed they had seen him at the scene of the riots. And most importantly, on the Sunday before Mrs. Colegrove was killed, he was overheard, arguing with her in the parlor about money. I can't boast that I discovered the substance of this argument through any ingenious deduction. I fortuitously happened to get a call, as a member of the militia in the West Ward, to help suppress a set-to on Reade Street, last Thursday evening. A near-riot was initiated when Mrs. Williams physically attacked Mr. Lawson. Not knowing either party, I became interested only after order was restored, when I realized the woman was Mrs. Colegrove's sister, and she was accusing Mr. Lawson of the murder. I interviewed her the following morning—she was jailed for assault—and learned that she assumed Lawson had murdered Mrs. Colegrove because his wife had lent her the eighty pounds she needed to repay her gambling debts."

Aaron Colegrove's jaw dropped open. "*Eighty* pounds? *Gambling?*" he choked out.

"That was the figure, sir. Under pressure to pay, she turned to her closest friend in the family, Prudence Colegrove Lawson, who located the funds in a secret cache that only she and her husband knew about. However, Mrs. Lawson thought better of it later, and cajoled her brother James into assuming the debt, thus making Mr. Lawson whole. Mr. Lawson never knew the money had been taken, and was completely dumbfounded when the Williams woman attempted to blackmail him.

"James Colegrove, meanwhile, quarreled with Mrs. Colegrove after he realized that he too had foolishly overextended himself in a weak moment. He saw that he wouldn't be able to hold off his own creditors—who undoubtedly realized better than he did that his anticipated income as a tax collector was unlikely to materialize—and so he rushed back here to convey his racehorse to Hempstead for sale. He returned to the city with the family, after Mrs. Colegrove's funeral, only to face the same mob his father faced at the wharf on his arrival from England. His reluctance to revisit New York City, I surmise, has more to do with unwillingness to confront his creditors than fear of intimidation by the Sons of Liberty.

"There's one factor more, which I'll return to, but we are inevitably left with the one Colegrove whose genteel manners and poised, helpful responses I inherently trusted: Mr. Peter—"

Peter Colegrove stood up, raging. "Must I be made to endure this calumny another minute? If you were a true gentleman, Dordrecht, I'd call you out for a duel, but I know you for a petty mountebank, so if you gentlemen are determined to hear this out, you'll excuse me if I decline to—"

Kempe was also on his feet, standing athwart Colegrove's path to the door. "You'll recall, sir, that I gave orders that no one was to leave the premises? I trust the militia is now on guard to ensure that command. I would recommend that you sit this out, so that you may refute it completely, as I imagine you intend. *Don't you?*"

Peter Colegrove's face worked horribly as he struggled to master himself. "Yes. Of course!" He sat down again, crossed his arms over his chest, and gritted his teeth in exasperation. "Very well!"

Kempe nodded to me.

"Peter Colegrove knew that all he had to do was to answer my questions in an honest and straightforward manner, because most of the time, he could tell the exact truth without concern. He of course knew the house intimately, and he'd observed the schedules of its current residents precisely over the summer. He knew Henry Tenkus had been pursuing Mrs. Colegrove. He could easily have learned that young Vincent was besotted with her—and as easily pretend he had no idea. He knew she had infuriated the town's radicals, and that that faction included Timothy Colegrove, who was deeply disaffected from the family. He knew—having overheard it beside her—that the slave Calpurnia was terrified by Mrs. Colegrove's plan to separate her from Caesar, as a wedding gift to himself and Miss Kempe. He knew—from the same incident—that James Colegrove was angry with Artemis, and he knew the sordid reasons for that anger.

"In short, he knew that any investigation of the crime would discover many plausible suspects to focus upon before anyone would ever think of *him*. And he was exquisitely correct in that assumption!

"Now let's consider *how* he did it. He said that he had gone to his own abode after studying in the library, about ten-fifteen. He encountered Dr. Boyce as he left. But he lied: he did not go directly home. He probably sat in Sweet's, the public house just across Broadway, watching the comings and goings. He knew that Caesar was occupied with his chores, that the girls were in school, that Miss Eudoxia was paying her social call, that Mrs. DeLancey was indisposed, and that Mr. Oliver was perambulating the Battery. He knew Artemis Colegrove herself would depart through the back for her weekly rendezvous with her sister, and that she'd return the same way before noon.

"So he waited. Dr. Boyce left the house around ten-fifty, affording himself just enough time to reach the college by eleven. Oliver Colegrove left a few minutes later to join his friends in Bowling Green. Peter then watched the slavewoman's movements carefully through the windows, and picked a moment when she'd be most occupied to quietly re-enter the house. I presume he first took refuge in the library. He could always say he had forgotten something if she happened to discover him. At some later point, he proceeded out into the yard, possibly noting the bowl of blood Calpurnia left in the washtub, waiting to be emptied. When the delivery boy knocked on the gate, he quickly hid himself in the privy. Had Mrs. Colegrove chanced to return during the delivery transaction, she might still be alive!

"But it was a few minutes later that she did return. The slave was back on her ladder in the front rooms, and the boy had proceeded on to the Van Brunts' house. Mrs. Colegrove may have been surprised to find Peter in the garden, but she would hardly be alarmed ... until he struck!"

Peter Colegrove was finely executing a mummery of barely suppressed righteous indignation, and now rose to protest. Kempe, however, again ordered him to restrain himself. Then he turned to me. "How could it be that Mrs. Colegrove was not moved to scream for assistance at this juncture?"

"Because she was not attacked with a knife, sir. She was strangled—as Peter Colegrove just now attempted to strangle me!"

After a second's hesitation, Kempe rejoined, "Oh come, Mr. Dordrecht! The coroner averred that she was stabbed to death, that there was blood all over her person and the floor of the folly."

"We have a contrary medical opinion, sir, one that was not officially recorded—because his invitation to the inquest was not forwarded."

"I had nothing to do with that!" Peter Colegrove exclaimed defensively. Kempe and Peacham looked at him dubiously.

"I refer of course to Mr. Colegrove's stepson, Dr. Gideon Boyce. Dr. Boyce was recalled to the house after the corpse was discovered, and arrived within twenty minutes. His observation was that Mrs. Colegrove had been throttled, the stab wounds were inflicted post-mortem, and the blood was not actually hers. My supposition is that, after he strangled her, the murderer inflicted the knife wounds in order to make it appear to be a crime of passion; then he posted the radical slogan—prepared well beforehand—on the arrow of the statuette, in order to make it seem to be a political crime. I think the idea of pouring the blood over the corpse was an inspiration of the moment."

"Fantastic. Utterly fantastic!" Peter Colegrove exclaimed sarcastically. But his father was quite pale.

A thought occurred to me that I quickly dismissed as too circumstantial to raise. The victim normally wore her hair up, secured with combs. The hair had been discovered loose—incidentally covering the marks on her neck—and the combs were found, not strewn about the yard, but in an orderly pile. Who but the fastidious Peter Colegrove would have arranged them thus?

"Good lord!" Kempe breathed simultaneously. "But wait: how could the coroner—"

"It was a general observation that the coroner was deeply inebriated, sir."

Kempe shook his head to the side, hissing to himself. "Why didn't Boyce—"

"You'll have to ask him yourself, Mr. Kempe. My impression is that the man is excessively modest, and—"

"*Ohh!*" Kempe moaned with frustration. "Well, let's finish with you first! What else have—"

"We must consider *why* Peter Colegrove would decide to commit such a heinous crime. First of all, he had recently been made aware of a fact that only the adult females of the household had guessed, which is that Artemis Colegrove was with child."

"She *what?*" Kempe said.

"Dr. Boyce's estimate is that she was five months along, and—"

"I knew that, of course," Aaron Colegrove said calmly. "She wrote to me."

His son looked ill. "But nobody in town—"

The senior Colegrove shrugged. "I'd always told her I'd want to make the happy announcement myself." Peter Colegrove was staring at him with hatred. "Considering the sensibilities of … that is …"

Kempe and Peacham both shook their heads.

"Well, as an obvious consequence of Mrs. Colegrove's reticence and her husband's lack of acknowledgement," I observed, "speculation inevitably arose whether the child might have been fathered by Henry Tenkus, who was first seen shortly after Mr. Colegrove's departure.

"Peter also knew," I continued, "as we all do, that both ocean travel and childbirth are very hazardous callings, and he made it his business to find out what his father's intentions for his considerable fortune were, in the case of fatal accident. Miss Eudoxia had also been concerned about a will, and—"

"There is no will, I never wrote a will," Aaron Colegrove stated.

"And your closest relatives did not know whether you had, or had not, sir," I added. Kempe glared at him, appalled. "Miss Eudoxia asked James Colegrove to investigate, soon after Aaron's departure. James inquired of Aaron's partner, Caleb Lawson, who said there was no will. He also enquired of Mr. Tolbert, at the city archives, and was dismissed with the same answer. When Miss Eudoxia later realized Mrs. Colegrove was with child, she became doubly anxious, and asked Timothy Colegrove to pursue the matter directly with Mr. Gerrison, her brother's chosen solicitor. Timothy reported back that Gerrison affirmed there was no will—and he and Miss Eudoxia left it at that. But Peter Colegrove, having learned from Miss Eudoxia and Mrs. DeLancey that Mrs. Colegrove was expecting, took it upon himself to visit the town archives, where he persisted with the question, as I also did. Thus, we each learned that Aaron Colegrove had indeed never written a will—"

"That's correct, I never—"

"Well, for heaven's sake, man," Peacham expostulated, "if you're traveling across the Atlantic, and—"

"However, there was a paper, dating to the year of his second marriage, that could be legally construed as a statement of intent."

"*What?*" Aaron Colegrove exclaimed. He seemed genuinely mystified.

I pulled my copy from my waistcoat, and Colegrove snatched it away. "This is a *copy*, Mr. Colegrove. The original is in Mr. Tolbert's safekeeping. There would be no point in destroying this!"

"But this is— This is ancient history, Dordrecht! This is twenty-five years ago. I'd forgotten all about this!"

Kempe pulled the sheet from his outstretched fingers, read it, and shook his head. "It would nonetheless prompt a stupendous legal wrangle, Mr. Colegrove. I'm amazed that Oliver DeLancey and his father permitted such a folly!" He passed the paper to Reverend Peacham.

"And consider, too, gentlemen," I added, "as I imagine Peter Colegrove did, what the consequences might have been in the plausible eventuality that Aaron Colegrove did not survive his travels, and Artemis Colegrove did not survive childbirth, *but the infant—whose paternity he doubted—did!*"

Kempe took the paper back and read it again. "In that sad case, it could be argued that the intent would be to leave the real estate to Lambert Colegrove, specific amounts to the issue of the Boyces, the entire commercial empire to the orphaned infant … and *nothing at all* to the surviving children of the second marriage."

Aaron Colegrove was red-faced. "But that's ridiculous, Kempe! This was foisted on me by old DeLancey all those years ago. Surely it would never be—"

"Mr. Tolbert would of course bring it forward in any probate proceeding, sir. How much weight the surrogates would give to it—impossible to guess."

"And of course," I added, "if Mr. Colegrove were taken by shipwreck, and both Mrs. Colegrove and her infant survived, they would together inherit the commercial enterprises."

Peter Colegrove was glaring at his father—who spotted the glare and was repelled by it. He had the presence of mind not to call further attention to himself by speaking.

"In addition, Peter Colegrove, along with most of his relations and many residents of the city, had come to view Artemis Colegrove as an embarrassment and a detriment to their future. Her—"

"No!" Aaron protested. "How? How could anyone—"

Peter Colegrove faced away from him. Even Kempe was squirming.

"Her unfortunate political jests, her pretensions to high status, her quarrel with her neighbor, on top of the fact that most people could not endure the fact that she was younger than her husband's grandson—"

"Well, that's nobody's goddam business!" Aaron shouted.

"Perhaps so, sir, but it nevertheless prejudiced people against her—and you and your family in general. And then Peter realized she was leading the sailor on, flirting with Vincent Colegrove, meeting her disreputable sister against her husband's command, running up gambling debts she could never repay, and suborning other family members for loans … and decided *he* would have to take charge of the situation, knowing that neither James Colegrove, nor Lambert Colegrove, nor even Aaron Colegrove himself, would ever do so. My conjecture is that he started planning his actions after overhearing the confrontation of James and Artemis on the Sunday evening, assessing that his best chance would come on Wednesday morning."

Peter Colegrove was bristling. The others were struggling to assimilate my contentions.

"It was not a political crime," I added. "It was not truly a crime of passion. It was a highly calculated, arrogant crime with a fundamentally mercenary motive."

Peter Colegrove seemed to recover his poise. "I shall be suing you for defamation, Dordrecht!" he announced coldly. "You haven't a shred of evidence to prove these fantasies. There can't be any evidence because I was nowhere near the house from ten-fifteen until Aunt Eudoxia summoned me back after twelve-thirty. This is all supposition—a grand fiction that would make Cervantes or Fielding blush for shame!"

Ha! An overt lie. He'd hung himself! I stared back at him, unflinching. After a few seconds, I continued, ignoring his outburst. "Having executed his crime with such care and precision, he was, in contrast to the rest of the family, courteous and effusively helpful on every occasion wherein I spoke with him. An elegant *act!* However, I do believe that, by the end of last month, he'd come to regard my efforts as a threat, and was looking for a way to dispose of me—as he'd successfully disposed of Mrs. Colegrove. Again, he looked for the most propitious moment, and realized a chance might come during the protests. Perhaps the army would even open fire on the populace and do the job for him! But when there was no massacre, he left the family home around ten-thirty that evening, contrary to his father's urging to stay, and went to his own lodging. He went there solely to change into his brother James' coat—the very memorable coat James Colegrove is wearing today, which Peter brought with him from the city this morning. He donned that garment, set out around eleven p.m., and followed the crowd noise to the home of Major Thomas James. He was in search of me, just as I was, at that juncture, in search of Timothy Colegrove. Quite fortuitously, he discovered me alone in the backyard of the house, seized his opportunity, and struck me from behind with a paving stone—an attack that disabled me for four days, and which I am very lucky to have survived."

"More fantasy!"

"No one saw him, though a man of his height and build was seen hurriedly leaving the yard of the house shortly after I went into it. And the unique *coat*, which had become infamous on the occasion of Aaron Colegrove's raucous reception, was definitely noticed. But it could not have been James Colegrove, because James Colegrove was *here*, having arrived at nightfall after escorting the Colegrove ladies from Kingsbridge."

Aaron Colegrove looked ill.

"The inference is inescapable," I confirmed relentlessly, "that he deliberately wore his brother James' coat ... in case anyone might see him. That's precisely why I was concentrated on James Colegrove until today."

"No! No!" Aaron wailed. I almost felt sorry for him.

"Now I have to concede that no one directly observed Peter Colegrove committing either crime, but I submit it could only have been he. And I further submit that he just now perjured himself in front of you when he asserted he was nowhere near the house at the fatal hour."

"How so, Mr. Dordrecht?" Kempe said. "That could be very important."

"There is a witness ... you will not wish to call ... right away."

"Oh come, sir!" Aaron blustered—suddenly recovering some hope. "What could—"

"May I write?" I pulled out my pencil, and wrote on a blank page of my notebook: "The child Agnes saw 'her brother' leaving the house as she returned from school at noon. It could only have been Peter."

I tore it out and handed it carefully to John Tabor Kempe. "Oh," he said.

He handed it carefully to Reverend Peacham. "Oh," he said.

Kempe stood and motioned the priest to join him in the far corner of the room. They whispered together for two minutes as Aaron, Peter, and I stared breathlessly at each other. Finally, Kempe went to the door, opened it, and was gratified to find an armed militiaman. "The generality of guests are free to leave or stay at their host's pleasure," he announced without preliminaries, "but I desire the family members to remain. The wedding is"—he looked to Peacham, who nodded—"at the least, postponed. Please send four militiamen to this room directly."

The man saluted—rather smartly for militia—and hurried toward the banquet hall. Kempe turned back to us, crossed his arms, and simply waited.

The four men arrived, pursued by several inquisitive others. "You two"—he gestured to the two in front—"take Mr. Dordrecht to another room, close the door, and *see that he stays there*. You lads, take Mr. Peter Colegrove to a different room and do the same. I expect we'll be half an hour." He turned to the patriarch. "And now, sir, we truly do need privacy."

"But—"

"Ask Dr. Gideon Boyce to come to us, please!"

Peter Colegrove and I were each unceremoniously taken by the arms and pulled out of the room. I saw his father walking the other way, with Miss Eudoxia screeching at him. But all I heard was, "This is all your fault, Theodora!"—and my client's shriek.

———◈———

It was forty-five minutes later when Kempe opened the door. "Mr. Dordrecht is at liberty to go," he told my guards, "and you lads are dismissed, with thanks." In response to three queries, he added, "The other men have arrested Peter Colegrove on suspicion of murder and attempted murder, and have taken him to the town's lock-up, from which he will tomorrow be removed to the city under armed guard."

The two militiamen boisterously departed. "Both Dr. Boyce and Agnes Colegrove confirmed everything you asserted, Dordrecht," Kempe said rather sadly. He looked very shaken. "The lass was very brave!" He sighed. "If you'll excuse me now, I must look to my sister, who is probably in an extreme state of distress."

I nodded, and he started toward the great hall, but stopped and turned back at the entryway. "Remind me," he said with a twisted smile, "not to invite you to *my* wedding, Dordrecht!"

Rather stupefied by the realization that John Tabor Kempe was actually making a jest, I only smiled and shrugged in return.

Suddenly feeling as though a great weight had been taken from my shoulders, I presently followed Mr. Kempe back into the reception hall. Fischl and the two German lads were playing a string trio.

Most of the guests were still there, but the orderly rows of chairs were all askew, and it seemed that many people were just now deciding to take their leave. The Kempe family was standing to one side, the erstwhile bride weeping profusely on her brother's shoulder. The older woman broke away from them and came to me.

"Mr. ... Dordrecht, is it? I am Abigail Kempe, the mother of the bride, and—" She briefly seemed at a loss for words. "Like his late sire, my son absolutely refuses to discuss any case that is open before the courts. But ... again as with his father, *I* can always sense what he's thinking. And ... if what John is thinking is proven true, then you have spared my daughter a life of shame and misery, sir, and for that I shall always, always be grateful!"

"Ma'am, I—"

She held up her hand to indicate that no more needed to be said, and returned to her flock.

Fischl and the lads finished their piece as I drew near. Fischl smiled broadly as he acknowledged the scattered applause. "Well, Monsieur LeBrun! You've had quite a day!"

"Indeed!" I sighed. "What— Where's the pianoforte? Have you already crated it up?"

"Yes … because I *sold* it! One of the neighbors fell in love with it—even though it was me playing and not you." He pulled me close and whispered in my ear, "One hundred twenty pounds. We're rich!"

Another weight off! "Congratulations, Herr Fischl!"

"Congratulations, Meneer Dordrecht!"

Sensing our elation, Torsten played a quick victory *cadenza*, prompting chuckles.

Edward Colegrove joined us, looking as bewildered as ever. "I think you gentlemen may pack up and leave at any time, now. I'd … really prefer to have this all over and done with!"

Fischl had some questions for him, but a pleasant-faced middle-aged lady whose name I couldn't recall was seeking my attention.

"Mr. Dordrecht? If I might beg a moment of your time, sir?" she said, urging me to the side for greater privacy. "I am Hulda Colegrove MacGregor, sir, Theodora's older sister, sister to Lambert and Timothy, and to the late Captain William; and this is my husband, John." She indicated the man shadowing her.

"Your servant, ma'am, sir!"

"I want to— Theodora spent much of the hour in which you were closeted with Reverend Peacham and Mr. Kempe explaining to us who you were and what was going on, and … I gathered that she has treated you very badly, sir, and I wanted to apologize on her behalf. I'm sure she—"

"That's not at all necessary, ma'am! The quest became my own, you see, and— Is she all right?"

"I've made her lie down, Mr. Dordrecht. She was recovering fairly well until … until father attacked her yet again!"

"Old brute!" John MacGregor grumbled.

"Theodora and I have forever had disparate opinions of our parent, Mr. Dordrecht. I have made my peace with the fact that there's only duty, no love, between him and me. Theodora … hasn't. Oh … when our mother died, you see, and father married the widow Boyce, twenty-five years ago now, Lambert and William were finishing their education. I was fourteen, Theodora was seven, Timmy was three—and there was a baby, Edna. Well, father packed the four of us off here to Uncle Edward and Jane, in February of that year, to make room for Mrs. Boyce's children. Caesar drove us in the open sleigh. I was trying to shelter Tim all the way, and Theodora the baby. But the baby was dead when we got here. I've … never quite forgiven father for that—but Theodora's never forgiven *herself!*"

"Oh. I … see," I said uncertainly, wondering if that could explain her desire to discover the murderer … without "disrupting" her father's *routine.*

"I shall insist that she sojourn a week with us in White Plains. Even though our house is somewhat of a bedlam, with five children, she needs urgently to spend time apart from her usual situation."

"That sounds like an excellent plan, Mrs. MacGregor!"

Warmed by my agreement, she babbled on. "At one point, Theodora was talking of forming a grammar school for girls. Irene's two youngest are the right age, now. I hope she will put her energies into that project, you see!"

"I'm not sure we should encourage her toward an enterprise that cannot really be afforded, Hulda!" her husband murmured uncomfortably.

"Oh but it must be, John! Or— Oh, well, she needs something to aim at, you know." She looked suddenly embarrassed. "Oh I beg your pardon for detaining you, Mr. Dordrecht! You must have—"

"Not at all, ma'am!"

"Thank you for your forbearance! Well, we must see if we can rouse her and get her out of here."

After exchanging goodbyes, I turned back to Mr. Fischl—and suddenly realized I was famished. "Is there any food left?"

"No. And we didn't get any, either! They kept us playing the whole time."

"*Gad!* Not a morsel?"

"And I saw Captain Ford just twenty minutes ago. He says, since we don't have to return the pianoforte, we can leave immediately, and we could get to City Island tonight, where we would wait for the morning tide to take us back through Hell Gate."

"Oh my! Well, I guess we'll have to go hungry, then."

Tayvie, grinning broadly, broke away from straightening the room to join us. "We have big bag food for you!"

"Oh!" Fischl exclaimed. "It was very thoughtful of Mr. Edward to save some for us!"

"Not Mista Edward!"

"It wasn't *Miss Eudoxia*, surely?" I couldn't help interjecting.

"No. *Caesar* save for you!" Observing our perplexity that a slave would undertake such an initiative, he added, "Caesar very happy man."

Gus brought out an enormous bag of food—and a jug of cider. "You take bag and jug if you want."

The German lads were all but drooling. Fischl seemed mystified. Tayvie looked directly at me. "No wedding, Mista Dordrick—no wedding *present!*"

CHAPTER 15

To Captain Ford's great satisfaction, we reached the busy anchorage off City Island, which some land developer has recently purchased and is promoting as a great port to rival New York City—*Best of luck, mate!*—just at dusk. Finally, we dove into the bag of food the slaves had set aside for us.

Though we were all exhausted after our demanding day, it was only seven o'clock or thereabouts when we could gorge ourselves no longer. The night was chilly but clear and dry—and the three string instruments promptly came out. I was more than happy to listen, as the effort of trying to explain what had occurred to the German boys was a strain—particularly when Fischl himself was befuddled by the Colegrove clan relationships. However, within five minutes of their starting to play, rowboats from two nearby ships, each bearing gifts of food and liquor, had rafted themselves onto the *Janie*.

Despite the presence of eleven men and two women singing and drumming at full volume, I fell asleep sometime before the party was over.

One boatload of guests was off a sturdy bark out of Providence, bound for the city, and they volunteered to tow *Janie* through the worst of the Hell Gate passage. They had their sweeps out in the morning, but we were able to rely on the tide, the tow, and the continued calm weather. Still, there was one moment, when the bark slowed down, and the *Janie* got caught in a whirlpool. She lurched directly toward a rock awash, unable to gain steerage … only to feel the towline pull taut at the last instant, jerking us back into the center of the channel. All the sailors' faces had briefly looked panicked, but promptly displayed utter assurance that they *knew* there had never been any real danger.

Without further incident, we docked at Peck Slip in the middle of the afternoon.

It wasn't until Monday evening that Charles caught up with me, treated me to supper, and demanded the whole story. "So Peter Colegrove had managed everything perfectly," I summarized, "and very nearly succeeded."

"Save for you!"

"Save for his half-sister, and the fact that some people rather object to murder!"

Charles smiled. "Similar to our cherished Prime Minister Grenville, who thought out his new revenue measure in every detail—save that some people rather object to being robbed!"

We both chuckled at that. "Did you know that Kempe has already had Peter Colegrove indicted?" he asked.

I didn't. "Already?"

"Not wasting any time. I think he's infuriated by his sister's humiliation and eager to wash his hands of the entire Colegrove family. Officially, he's recused himself and turned the prosecution over to his associate, but you can sense that he's pressing the matter. And he always was a Livingston man at heart," he added.

The Livingston faction, the DeLancey faction, and the radicals are the chief contenders in New York's messy political struggles. The only matter they can all unite on is loathing of Cadwallader Colden and the tiny cadre of high Tory placemen and military officials who actually support the Stamp Act.

"I hear the Sons of Liberty honored Governor Moore with a bonfire on Friday night?"

"*Yup!* Minimal common sense being so very rare these days, we thought a celebration was in order! But we have a long way to go, Thomas, before we're rid of the Stamp Tax. We've neutralized the officials and sequestered the stamps themselves, but now we're faced with the next problem. Which is, how do we get our commerce and civic life started again *without* the wretched things? The Livingston lawyers are all atwitter that, since the tax is officially law, nothing but nothing requiring legal paperwork may take place without them, and everyone will just somehow have to *wait*. The DeLancey merchants are quivering in terror lest the grand imperial system, on which all America is alleged to depend, should come crashing to a halt."

"Well—"

"Not to mention the various preferments and special privileges they happen to have accumulated over the years."

"And what—"

"It's not as if both factions—and all the rest of us—haven't ignored the navigation acts and the trading with the enemy rules whenever it suited us, for the whole century since New Amsterdam became New York!"

"What are the radicals proposing, then?"

"We are proposing that all civil business should proceed exactly as it did just one month ago, with contracts, deeds, bills of lading, books, newspapers, and *playing cards*"—Oh, the sarcasm was getting thick!—"being issued without Parliament's unconstitutional stamp!"

"And let Whitehall make the most of it?"

"And let Whitehall make the most of it!"

Could I endorse such risky defiance? Was there any alternative?

"We're at a perfect impasse, Thomas. No one wants the stamps, no one believes in the stamps, yet we're too timid to budge without them. But until we do move without them, our whole economy has ground to a halt, and heaven help us get through the winter!"

"What can I do, Charles? I have some funds, but I am now completely without employment and therefore, *um*, available."

"You and multitudes of others, Thomas! The ships that come back in are going to have to dismiss their sailors onto the streets, because they won't be able to depart again. If *that* doesn't make our big-wigs shake, I don't know what will! But ... we can all keep the pressure on. As occasions arise."

"Rely on me!"

"We shall!"

The next morning, I complacently ruminated upon my newfound status as an unemployed gentleman of leisure *of sorts*, debating whether I might return to my old boarding house on Chambers Street. These fantasies were brought up short when Mr. Fischl informed me there was a delay to be expected in the payment for the pianoforte, as the purchaser was suffering a delay in obtaining receivables from *his* customers. *Thrift* will have to continue as my mainstay.

The following day, voluntarily responding to a request from Mr. Kempe heavily larded with overtones of public duty, I spent eight hours cloistered with his subordinate, a Mr. Ebling, detailing everything I had learned, inferred, and guessed about the murder of Artemis Colegrove. I was relieved to find him perceptive and articulate, particularly when he told me the case would be tried the following Monday—and would I please attend *that*, too, also *gratis*?

I had three days' work from Mr. Fischl, because the man who bought the pianoforte finally admitted that Fischl had been right to insist that it would have to be tuned again after it was moved; unfortunately, my two days' travel and one day of work also had to be provided on credit.

The trial of Peter Colegrove was a tense, but anticlimactic affair, managed with great thoroughness and aplomb by the ambitious Mr. Ebling. Although several members of the Colegrove family were called as witnesses, only Theodora and Timothy were present as spectators—another sad reflection on the family loyalty.

Neither spoke to me, of course.

I was called only to testify regarding the attack on myself, as were Charles Cooper, Cyrus Mapes, and—the one surprise of the day—Aston Wilkes, a freedman who asserted under oath that he had positively recognized Peter Colegrove, wearing his brother's coat, at the riot at the major's house. "*Hoo*, he scoot outta there early, like the Old Nick were chasing him!"

After two hours' deliberation, the jury pronounced the defendant guilty on both counts, and he was sentenced to hang. The only person moved to tears by this decision was Theodora Colegrove, who was grudgingly consoled by her brother Timothy.

At a tavern, later, Mapes wondered aloud, "What the devil was that black fellow doing there, if he wasn't busy ransacking the major's house like everyone else?"

I recalled that Aston—then with no surname—had been a slave of the city corporation three years before, attached to the constables.

"They freed him a year and a half ago," Charles informed us. *Omniscient, as ever.* "He now works as a night-soil collector—officially."

There was a pause. "*Un*-officially?" I asked.

Charles smiled. "Who's ever going to notice a quiet black workman's presence on the periphery of a riot? I'll lay odds either Kempe or Colden himself had paid him to make careful note of *everyone* who was present that night—never expecting that it would prove useful in a murder trial. If they had dared to prosecute the rioters, you can bet that our Mr. Aston Wilkes would've come forth with the names!"

The day after Colegrove's conviction, the Sons of Liberty called an open meeting of the town, to discuss the instructions that should be given to the town's representatives in the provincial Assembly. While common enough in New England, such a meeting was actually unprecedented in New York, and both the Livingston and the DeLancey factions were horrified to see this epitome of anarchy on the march. Charles got me to post some handbills announcing the event, many of which were torn down not an hour later. When the meeting was held despite this interference, the factions maneuvered a call for a *committee* to draft the memorial to the Assemblymen. They had a slate of committee members at the ready, who were accepted, and who—to the great annoyance of Sears, Lamb, Willett, and Cooper—instructed the town's Assemblymen to pursue no more than yet another humble *petition* to the crown.

Undaunted—and perhaps to reassert their spirit—the Sons confronted the arrival the next day of a bloke my age who was a grandson of both Stephen DeLancey *and* Cadwallader Colden. He'd been so sanguine as to accept a stamp distributorship while in London, in alleged ignorance of his countrymen's detestation of same, and was met with the same aggressive reception that Aaron Colegrove had faced in August. Needless to say, he too tore up his commission.

And the very next day, some two hundred of us lugged fifteen miles into Queens County, to harass one Zachariah Hood. Hood had been the designated distributor for the Province of Maryland, until his outraged neighbors had pulled his house down and he'd fled to Fort George. However, it grated on opponents of the Stamp Act everywhere that he'd never formally renounced his commission and had quietly retired to the sleepy hamlet of Flushing. *Ha!* No longer! Accosted by fire-breathers from the city, Hood had capitulated at last.

The Sons' leadership allowed a few days' rest—which I spent mostly in the New York Society Library—before reasserting the pressure on the first Monday of December by seeking out James McEvers, he who had quietly resigned the tax collector's commission for New York, after the Boston riots, but before anyone in New York had asked. Months later, he was *asked* to make a formal, public resignation. Unsurprisingly, he did.

The Sons repeated the performance the next day with none other than

James Colegrove, who had finally returned to work in his father's office. Timothy Colegrove excused himself that day—and I elected to watch quietly in the background. James Colegrove—again wearing his notorious striped coat—appeared as unaware as ever of the public ramifications of his hoped-for sinecure. Neither he nor anyone else made mention of his brother Peter.

Leisler's Ghost—I know who *that* is, *ha!*—had a letter printed in the paper, insisting that so far from granting Colden any compensation for his coach and sleighs, he should be personally assessed for the damage caused by spiking the cannons.

Perhaps it was this relentless defiance by the radical partisans that stiffened the spine of the Assembly, which delivered a startling response to General Gage, the commander in chief of all the military in North America. Gage had demanded that the province build new winter quarters for his troops in New York City. The Assembly flatly refused, arguing that existing barracks in Albany ought to be perfectly acceptable. Amid our general rejoicing, Marinus warned, "But don't dream for a minute that we've heard the last of *that!*"

Philadelphia merchants had recently concocted a ruse that New York now copied: the port functionaries were persuaded—admittedly under some pressure—to issue un-stamped cockets and manifests to departing vessels ... along with formal certifications that this illegal procedure was necessary because stamps were—*somehow*—just "not available." One of the first ships to take advantage of this subterfuge was my dear old *Dorothy C.*, which had returned on November seventh from Jamaica, and had been reloaded, mainly with lumber and barrel staves, for Barbados.

I joined my old colleagues at Peck Slip to wish Captain Trent and his crew godspeed as they were among the first to pull out on December fifth. The entire waterfront went into shock twelve hours later, when she and others returned, having had shots fired across their bows by the British navy. The infamous Captain Kennedy, chief of the New York station, had deemed the certifications inadequate, and forced the ships back. Kennedy became a prime object of public obloquy, especially detested because, unlike all others of rank in the navy, he was American-born. It was a reaction that could never have happened but five years ago: this captain of "our" navy was looked on as a *traitor*.

The Sons next took the legal profession to task. The civil courts had been closed since November first, and this was grinding even the domestic commerce to a standstill. The lawyers were rightfully concerned that, if the government persisted with the tax, any contracts, leases, or deeds issued without stamps would be retroactively invalidated and, further, that *they* would be considered liable for malpractice. The radicals, seconded by the business community at large, were impatient to break the logjam of delays.

That Friday, the relentless Sons called another public meeting, to urge a remonstrance upon the lawyers, citing the hardship their position was causing the community at large. They were joined by an unexpected ally: Captain James DeLancey, Jr., as conservative a mercantilist as they come. "No," Charles asserted, "he hasn't had a change of heart, just a change of tactics. It's a sally against the Livingston faction … but we may as well be grateful!"

The lawyers had their own bonanza a day later, when news arrived that Whitehall had reversed its own ruling in a notorious case that had aggravated them to a man for three long years: the Privy Council had arbitrarily overturned a New York jury's guilty verdict in a local criminal case, outraging every New York lawyer but Cadwallader Colden.

Perhaps that remote but now-foreclosed option had been sustaining the condemned Peter Colegrove. I was told he broke down after hearing of it, and blubbered his way to the gallows on Monday morning. I declined to attend, not lured by the deep personal animosity that I'd felt against the murderer of Daniel Sproul. I felt only the cold, empty satisfaction of assurance that justice, according to our law, had been done.

I spent more days in the library, working on my French by reading essays of La Boétie and Montaigne.

After I plodded home through the first big snowfall on Wednesday evening, Mrs. Nugent presented me with a missive from Theodora Colegrove.

December 11

Mr. Dordrecht:

I desire to speak with you. The nave of Trinity Church is open and generally quiet in mid-afternoon. I should appreciate it if you would meet me there tomorrow at three o'clock.

When I arrived, Miss Colegrove was on her knees in prayer. Standing in the side aisle, waiting for her to finish, I noticed she had finally foresworn mourning attire for a patterned purple, even though the traditional six months had not yet elapsed. Seeing me, she sat back, raised her veil, and indicated that I should join her. Her face, though still troubled, was surprisingly bereft of its usual bitterness. It occurred to me to think that the woman actually *could* be pretty, were she to put her mind to it.

It was a full minute before she spoke. "Do you think that justice was done this past Monday, Mr. Dordrecht?"

"When Peter Colegrove was hanged, ma'am?"

"Yes. I did not see you on the Common."

You did attend? You surely know how to torment yourself, madam! "I have no doubt that it was he who murdered Artemis Colegrove, ma'am. As for justice, we are all taught that our human mechanisms are but clumsy excuses for divinity."

Her face worked briefly as she fought off tears. "I—" She opened her purse and extracted a small bag that obviously contained coins. "Here!" She thrust it at me. "You've earned this."

Having accepted her dismissal a month before, I hadn't been intending to demand payment, but … *yes, I had.* "I thank you for your custom, Miss Colegrove." I quietly put the bag in my coat pocket.

"Events have forced me to reconsider my life, Mr. Dordrecht—to search my soul, as they say."

"The events of the last months would have sorely tried anyone in your position, ma'am."

"Perhaps." She was lost in contemplation for a minute. "I do trust that you—and the jury, of course—were correct in affixing blame, but— Oh, I suppose we must all rest content with our own fallibility, in regard to justice."

"We do what we can, ma'am."

"Yes." She sighed heavily and rose. "I thank you for coming, sir. I do appreciate it!" Without offering her hand, she turned and made her way to the aisle.

Caressing the bag in my pocket, I bit down on an impish urge to say, *Well, hell, lady, not half as much as I do!*

I did catch her attention again before she walked away. "If I may say so, Miss Colegrove, your purple gown is most becoming!"

One could tell she didn't intend to—but she blushed and smiled shyly before retrieving her composure and walking out of the church.

A strange—strangely noble—woman, I thought, making my own way out.

But she was not satisfied with the justice rendered!

The snowfall somehow brought it home: defying the Stamp Tax was going to be a long, hard slog for everyone in New York, for everyone in America. Though the riots of November First now seemed like so much ancient history, it was unlikely the news would even reach our antagonists in Parliament before another month. Then months would be required for them to dither over repealing it, and for that news to travel back. Notwithstanding the unanimity with which the tax was detested, we could anticipate a grim winter of tension and deprivation.

Me, I was materially much relieved. My client had paid in full as originally agreed. When the new owner of the pianoforte would do the same—and when the second one was sold—I would be a fellow of some means, perhaps able to strike out in business on my own.

But until then … The very next day—it was Friday the thirteenth, no less—my old chum Uzal Parigo, boatswain of the *Dorothy C.*, appeared on the doorstep, begging to be allowed to sling his hammock in my room. The boarding houses were filling up with becalmed sailors, he explained, and rates were soaring. "I pay you what I did pay them before, right?"

"Look, Uzal, my room is tiny!" I protested. I led him up the stairs to prove it.

"It *enormous!*" he exclaimed. "This all for you?" He must have noticed my dismay. "Only 'til ship sails!"

My landlady was disgruntled as much by his being a sailor as his being dark-skinned—not that there weren't plenty of black residents in our humble neighborhood—but she was mollified by an extra sixpence a week, and the fact that Parigo instantly ingratiated himself with her children.

Though I was haunted by Miss Colegrove's dissatisfaction, and knew the public situation was still dire, and knew the Sons of Liberty would always welcome another body to swell their visible ranks, I now withdrew to the library—which was at least relatively warm and quiet. But after ten days of blessed peace, I was more than happy to receive an invitation to dine at the Leaverings', not having seen any of my friends for weeks.

Being Anglicans, they tend to make almost as much fuss over Christmas as my family do over Sinterklaas. Hermione had festooned her parlor with gay sprigs of pine and cheerful red ribbon bows. Charles enjoyed speculating how much Reverend Henry would have been scandalized—but without his usual fratricidal rancor. Conversation first ran to everyone's troubles with the city's situation. When I explained that Parigo had already exhausted his ready funds, and was attempting to earn his keep by doing odd jobs for Mrs. Nugent, the Glasbys announced that they had taken in Mr. Fox, first lieutenant of the *Dorothy C.*

While the ladies made last-minute arrangements for our supper, we men groused about the political quandary. Governor Sir Henry Moore, a hero last month, had already sacrificed much of his popularity by declining to issue "letpasses"—personal certifications from the governor that stamped manifests could not be issued. "He's like all the other royal governors," Charles asserted. "He was convinced America would succumb within days, the instant we endured a financial sacrifice. They were all persuaded they had designed the perfect, irresistible means to remedy Britain's financial problems."

"But what are we ever to *do*, Charles?" Benjamin Leavering demanded. "You saw the letter in the last *Weekly Post-Boy*, complaining that our vessels are ready for sea, but are blocked up in harbor, as if we were besieged by an enemy?"

"Well … surely you heard that one of DeLancey's ships managed to give Kennedy the slip the other night?"

"It managed to elude the British navy?" John exclaimed.

"It was a dark night. But I wonder whether most of the navy feels its duty toward the Stamp Act as ardently as Captain Kennedy does. They surely don't care to find hundreds of idled merchant sailors in the town rubbing shoulders with their own."

John Glasby looked at his partner and sighed. "Do you think we—"

"We'd never be able to convince Captain Trent to attempt something like that, John. He has settled notions of what an upright man may do, and he was mortified to have *Dorothy C.* ordered back into port. Our options are very limited."

John changed the subject, grumbling, "Well … whatever we do, I'm not sure that burning the effigies of public officials will be any help!" Some such incident had occurred the week before.

"We only burnt members of the Privy Council, John!" Charles objected lightly. "Nobody close to hand. We left Moore and General Gage and even Cadwallader Colden alone."

"The town was rife yesterday with a rumor that the radicals were about to attack City Hall to destroy the stamps," Benjamin said worriedly.

"But they *did not*, sir!" Charles protested. "The rumor was completely unfounded!"

"Well, there hasn't been much luck with the lawyers," John complained. "The radicals presented their vaunted memorial to them, but I still can't rewrite the lease on my family's property in Westchester."

And so it went, until the ladies called us in for supper, and politics was banned for the oddly more cheerful subject of the resolution of the case of Artemis Colegrove. After recounting the sequence of revelations that had led me to disrupt the wedding—an episode they found both entertaining and disquieting—I mentioned that Miss Theodora was apparently reconciled to the fact, and had at least settled her account with me.

"That young woman has real promise, if she can only break away from her father and her aunt," Hermione Leavering asserted. "Since you told me what her sister had told you, Adelie and I have made a point of seeking her out at church."

"I think her idea of a grammar academy for girls is wonderful," Adelie said. "If only she had the funds! John, could we not contribute something toward—"

"We must be *very* careful with all charitable requests, Adelie! There's no point in our becoming as pressed as Mr. Fox or Parigo."

"Some ladies in Massachusetts are urging their fellows to re-learn the spinning of yarn," Charles observed. "The Sons promote it ... as a patriotic gesture, you see ... to reduce American dependence on British manufactures ..."

Everyone looked at him blankly. "Have *you* ever spun yarn, Charles?" Hermione asked darkly.

"No."

"Right. Come to me with that suggestion after you've spent a few days at it, my dear!"

Conversation drifted among disparate topics. I recounted the ups and down of the purchaser of the pianoforte. Benjamin speculated on the reaction of English merchants to the American boycotts. Adelie wondered whether anyone could be entertained by a production of *King Lear.*

A wisp of an idea came to me, and my mind wandered, trying to keep hold of it.

Finally, Benjamin, who was looking very tired, observed aloud that *I* looked tired, and the party began to break up. Now possessed of my inspiration, I volunteered to assist the ladies in clearing the table.

Alone with Hermione and Adelie in the kitchen, I blurted it out. "I have a favor to ask, ladies! Would you be free tomorrow morning, to pay an odd social call?"

"I was planning to get my marketing out of the—"

Hermione caught the intrigue. "A *social* call?" she exclaimed. "Why on earth would you need *us* to pay a social call? On Christmas Eve?"

I smiled, abashed, but not wanting to prejudice the event. "A call on two nefarious miscreants! I may need your ... *protection!*"

For three seconds they both regarded me with skeptical bemusement. "Adelie, is my hearing going?" Hermione said. "I thought I just heard this tall, healthy young man requesting the *protection* of two frail—one rather elderly—females."

"You heard perfectly, ma'am! And ... how can we refuse?"

"Duty calls!" Hermione affirmed.

Following our rendezvous in the vestibule of Trinity Church, we made our way at ten-fifteen across Broadway to the Colegrove mansion. Adelie rapped the knocker.

Calpurnia answered. "Good morning, ladi— *He not allowed!*"

"Would you kindly tell Miss Colegrove and Mrs. DeLancey that Mrs. Benjamin Leavering and Mrs. John Glasby and *a gentleman* are here, on a charitable mission?"

"They don't want—" the slave whispered in protest, as my two friends pushed past her into the hallway. I tried to convey a reassuring smile. "But—"

"We are of course already acquainted, as fellow members of the Trinity parish," Hermione explained. Adelie confidently pointed toward the stairs that led up to their sitting room. Calpurnia wrung her hands nervously, but presently started up the stairs.

"What *is* it?" we heard Miss Eudoxia snarl.

Hermione and Adelie followed the slave without invitation.

"Guests, ma'am!" Calpurnia mumbled. "They—"

"Mrs. Leavering! Mrs. Glasby! To what do we owe this unexpected—" She stopped dead on seeing me in train. The two of them were settled on their respective couches with their respective disagreeable pets. Clearly wishing she could flee, Calpurnia arranged three of the Chippendale chairs in a row facing the ladies and the windows onto Broadway. Eudoxia, instantly deciding against refreshments, waved the slave away as we settled ourselves.

"We come on a mission of Christian charity," Adelie piously began, "to learn if—"

"*So!*" Mrs. DeLancey loudly and furiously interrupted. "You have insinuated this viper back into our home!"

My friends took this in stride, but it was now obviously my call to proceed. "There are some questions that are as yet unanswered, madam, which—"

"Was not my nephew's execution enough of an *answer*, Mr. Dordrecht?" Eudoxia Colegrove demanded.

"I am thinking of other matters, Miss Colegrove. For example, it appears that Peter Colegrove was first impelled toward his criminal folly when he realized that Mrs. Colegrove was with child." Stubborn stares abounded. "*How* did he come to realize that, do you know?" Chins were thrust forward in silent defiance. "It's not something you'd expect the likes of Peter to observe independently ... and yet it of course it bore strongly on the entire family's future."

The obdurate glares persisted. "I also wonder that no one had sanctioned or even remarked Mrs. Colegrove's regular but unexplained absences from the house. Did it never occur to you that she might be seeing the sailor? Or her sister, in defiance of her husband's prohibition?" There was no need to wait more than two seconds. "Or perhaps the young woman was deliberately being allowed enough scope to hang herself, as it were!"

"Mr. Dordrecht, you're quite insupportable," Miss Eudoxia fumed. "I should have a constable summoned to evict you!"

But you won't—because you want to know how much I've learned!

"I wonder whether Artemis Colegrove independently conceived the idea of giving Calpurnia away to the new bride—or whether someone else first made that suggestion to her, perhaps to generate friction in the household?" Again—stony silence. "At any rate, the voodoo doll pin-cushion did not fly by magic into the cookie canister where Oliver would surely discover it during the hour in which I had scheduled a visit. How, I wonder, did it ever get there?"

"Well, *I* had nothing to do with *that!*" Miss Eudoxia vehemently asserted, slamming her fist on the arm of the couch so strongly that the cat jumped out of her lap and hid. Mrs. DeLancey grimaced at her with frightening intensity, her teeth bared. The feckless little spaniel essayed a growl.

"I wonder if it was only in the absence of the patriarch that you realized that it was Peter, not the eldest son James, who could best be relied upon for foresight … and for ruthlessness in action?"

"You conceive that Peter Colegrove's careful manners were but a pose?" Adelie asked, after ten seconds without a response.

"I believe they were ingrained, ma'am, but in most people they are habitual as a matter of consideration for others, whereas—"

"*Calculation!*" Hermione averred.

"It would seem so, Mrs. Leavering," I agreed. "At any rate, I speculate that some in this household guessed early on that he was the murderer. What else could explain the failure to forward notice of the inquest to Dr. Boyce?"

"*I* had nothing to do with *that!*" Mrs. DeLancey avowed.

"A simple oversight!" Miss Colegrove declared. "Nothing more."

After an interval of shocked disbelief, Mrs. Glasby said, "Are you suggesting that these ladies directly inspired the crime, Mr. Dordrecht?"

"Oh, I don't think so," I said, slowly looking from one to the other. "The murderer had his own motives, his special grievances, and an unshakeable belief in his exquisite dexterity in action." The two eyed me warily without comment. "However, they certainly were neither horrified by, nor sorry for the act. And—much worse—they would have been perfectly content to see the innocent Henry Tenkus—or their own slavewoman—swing for the crime!"

Both my friends pulled their shawls more tightly around themselves. "In fact," I continued, "Miss Colegrove had even enlarged, under oath, on Tenkus' alleged threats against Artemis as though she'd been present at their last encounter." Miss Colegrove furiously shook her head as Mrs. DeLancey clucked her tongue with righteous disapproval.

Another interval of silence ensued. "Do you imagine that they might have suggested the attack on yourself, Mr. Dordrecht?"

"Again, not directly, Mrs. Glasby," I replied. We were speculating about the two women almost as if they weren't even present—yet they were angrily absorbing every word. "But I am certain they were made nervous by my efforts, and would have communicated their concern to Peter Colegrove. It's he whom I suspect of authoring the anonymous threat. But they did make an unexpected effort to ingratiate themselves, by buying these very chairs from my uncle's store, and then they brazenly tried to suborn me by dangling the lovely and shallow Miss Élise in front of me."

"*Oh my*, Mr. Dordrecht, what a tribulation for you!" Adelie said, smiling to herself. "But the actual attack?"

"They were well away, almost a full day before, and no one could have anticipated how the evening's events would unfold. But one thing I doubt they'd ever have approved: they may have winked at throwing the blame for Mrs. Colegrove's murder on the sailor or the radicals, but Peter Colegrove deliberately wore *his own brother's coat* when he ventured out toward the *mêlée* at the major's house." Both the women shuddered. "No, they only learned of *that* after he was accused at his wedding!"

It took Miss Eudoxia a minute to regain her strength. "Mr. Dordrecht, these are all slanderous assertions, for which you have not the slightest proof! We shall sue you for defamation, sir!"

"*Will you*, Miss Colegrove? Will you insist that everything just said be repeated in a public court? I admit that my speculations can never be proven according to strict rules of evidence, and I see no compelling reason why they should ever again be aired outside of present company."

"It's shocking, however, how gossip does get around in our busy little town!" Adelie observed innocently.

"And the damage it can do is horrendous," Hermione added.

The five of us stared at each other for half a minute.

"All right!" Mrs. DeLancey snapped. "What do you want?"

"*Want*, ma'am?" Hermione said. "Did we not announce that we are merely soliciting for a charity on the occasion of this holy season?"

"The object of our effort does not even know we are soliciting on her behalf," Adelie said. "But we've learned that Miss Theodora Colegrove has conceived the excellent notion of starting a grammar school for girls, and might well do so, save that she lacks the necessary funds. She of course devoted the largest part of her personal savings just recently, to ensure that your family's honor was secure, never imagining that the threat might have come from within."

"If she could now be made whole, ladies," Hermione observed, "perhaps she could once again contemplate a future project."

"How much was it?" Miss Eudoxia spat out.

Adelie forestalled me from replying. "I understand it was thirty pounds, ma'am!"

"Thirty *pounds*! Good lord."

"Of course, that would only restore her to the condition she enjoyed last summer. Now I would venture that if you were to subscribe for thirty pounds *each*"—Adelie paused, as we savored their discomfort—"that would make her sufficiently confident to go forward!"

Both of them gaped in disbelief.

"Well," Hermione said, rubbing her hands together, "we merely wanted to put the idea in front of you this morning, ladies. But I'm sure you can see what a splendid addition to our town it would be!"

"And how fine to have the Colegrove family name associated with it!" Adelie added, rising.

"I do believe she needs just the slightest encouragement," Hermione said. "And we shall be eager to hear that she has gotten it, *in the very near future!*"

Adelie indicated that Hermione and I should precede her down the stairs. "Good day to you, ladies! We wish you joy of the holy Christmas season!"

Sacred holidays notwithstanding, I returned to my studies in the library—but with a lighter heart.

The travails of the continent, and of our city, continued apace. Another rumor circulated that City Hall would be invested by a mob seeking to burn the stamps. A crowd milled about in front of the hated Captain Kennedy's home, obviously contemplating mayhem—but the house still stands. Other officers of the navy have been accosted on the streets with raised fists and angry curses.

More interestingly, Charles tells me two representatives of the New York Sons have been dispatched up to New England, in the hope of creating formal alliances among the patriotic militias of the various provinces.

On the afternoon of the thirtieth, I was startled to find John Glasby beckoning to me across the library's reading room. He urged me to allow him immediately to stand me for a tipple. Whether thirst or curiosity compelled my agreement, I dare not say.

John came directly to the point. "Several more ships have successfully departed in the night, Thomas! In fact, they've not caught a one."

"Well, fine, then. You can put her to sea without violating the merchants' agreement!"

"Ah. Save that our worthy Captain Trent is *spooked*, Thomas. The ordeal of being forced back into port sits perhaps more heavily on his mind than it does that of others."

"He told me three years ago that he was on his fourteenth reading of the Bible, so I—"

John was mouthing the word *fourteenth*, in wide-eyed amazement.

"—So I don't wonder how he takes it to heart."

"*Uh*, yes. But I've simply got to get that ship on its way, Thomas. In addition to all the lumber, there are two hundred barrels of flour and four hundred of cider just sitting in it."

"Won't the navy have to come in to winter quarters soon?"

"Yes. And half the harbor will instantly make a break for it. But how soon? There's been relatively little ice floating down the Hudson thus far."

"Ah."

"I've got an idea, Thomas. Benjamin likes it, but I haven't yet proposed it to Trent. Conditions will be almost perfect tomorrow night. The ebb will begin around ten-twenty p.m. It is likely to be dry but overcast, which should dampen the brightness of the last-quarter moon. And of course—"

"It will be New Year's Eve!" we both said together.

"Aye. If their lookouts have been casual most nights, recently, perhaps—"

"*Dorothy C.* should be passing the fleet off Staten Island just around midnight!"

"Exactly. But Mr. Fox suggested one further inducement. A ruse, actually. We get someone to pose as the vessel's supercargo, and—"

Uh oh. "To *pose* as a supercargo?"

"Until she clears the last of the shoals and the sentinels in the Lower Bay."

"What good will that do anybody?"

"None at all, except, we hope, to mollify our stubborn Captain Trent! It could be claimed that the supercargo is responsible for all the ship's stores, you see. Trent may see through the ruse, but he just needs a tiny push to convince him the navy would not hold him or the ship responsible, and we feel certain there's no real concern in the first place."

"*Uh huh*. And who do you have in mind to—"

"*You*, of course, old lad! Who better? You should be back home within twenty-four hours, and we'll give you three days' pay."

That wasn't the reason I was grinning.

"And you'll have your very own chance to tweak the lion's nose!" John added pointedly.

"Softly! Softly, lads!"

Parigo didn't really need to remind them. The sailors were united in their desire to get their craft past the navy ships anchored off the northeast shore of Staten Island.

"Two more miles, worst be over!" Parigo said. "That one a merchant," he observed, pointing at the barely-visible outlines of a ship, possibly a hundred yards away to starboard, on which two dim lights burned feebly.

The very light breeze was, happily, from the northwest, ensuring that *Dorothy C.* had some steerage over the tide. "South southwest by south, watch lest she jibe," Captain Trent whispered to Mr. Fox at helm.

"Aye aye, sir."

Shortly thereafter, the wind dropped to nothing, but the slackening tide kept us moving south. At five a.m., however, the current changed, and slowly began setting us back toward the Narrows. As my anxiety grew again, the sun rose on another overcast morn ... and brought the relief of a soft westerly breeze with it. Half an hour later, the fellow on the masthead—*Oh, he hadn't frozen to death, that's good!*—reported a sail to the southwest. "Heading toward us!" he reported two minutes later.

"Warship?" Trent called, raising his voice a little, with no one in proximity.

"Too small, I think. No, it's the pilot, the pilot!"

After another half-hour, the pilot boat pulled next to us, and a grizzled old fellow deftly clambered up our side. "Morning, Enos!" he crowed. "Safe so far!"

"Aye, so far, Jeptha," Captain Trent responded. He nodded to the south. "Who's out there?"

"Just *HMS Minerva*. Headed east, last we saw her. I think we should keep near the Jersey side."

"Fine. You take her!"

The breeze smartened up as we passed Sandy Hook and proceeded down the coast. The topmasts of *Minerva* were sighted around ten o'clock, but she held her course and passed out of sight to the north. "I think you're fixed, now, Captain Trent," the pilot announced as the sun approached its zenith. "Out of *all* dangers!"

"I thank ye, sir!" Trent gave orders to heave-to—to arrest progress while holding the ship's heading into the wind—as the pilot signaled his boat to approach.

"Too rough to climb down, now, Enos!" The wind was kicking up substantial waves.

"Aye. Rig the chair, please, Mr. Fox!"

"Parigo's already working on it, sir."

Trent addressed the pilot. "You understand, you're to take this lad back with you?" He nodded toward me.

"We are? Ever been in a bosun's chair, my friend?"

"Oh yes, when we were moored at Saint Eustatius, I—"

"Not between two ships in open water?"

"Oh. No."

"Ah. Well, has to be done. Live and learn, *eh?*"

Thinking my transfer into the smaller boat might be rather fun, I didn't understand his hesitation. With both boats hove-to, Parigo tossed a light line down to the pilot boat; that line pulled back a thicker one, which was rove through pulleys at the crosstrees of both ships' masts. A two-foot plank was then suspended horizontally with a bridle to the heavier line, and two guy lines were attached at the connection point, one of which was passed to a crewman whose torso was strapped tightly to the mast of the pilot boat. "Right!" Jeptha announced. "I'll go first, show you how it's done."

"Very good, sir!" I said, making cheerful farewells to the *Dorothy C.*'s crew. The austere Captain Trent completely astonished me by *winking* as he shook my hand.

Then I noticed that the pilot was being *tied* onto the plank. "Hang on *for your life*, lad!" he warned. "Ready!" he shouted.

I moved to the gunwale to watch … and gulped. The two ships were parallel, some fifteen feet apart, but both were rolling from side to side ... *and not together.* The crewmen on both boats hauled in several feet, raising the chair ten feet. But then the boats swung toward each other, and it dropped six feet in a second. Then it bounced back up. A foot at a time, Parigo let the line out, and the pilot boat crew hauled in, other crewmen struggling with the guy lines to prevent the chair from crashing into the hull or rigging of either boat. After two minutes in which my heart nearly stopped three times, Jeptha was grabbed bodily by the man strapped to his mast. Untied from the chair, he stepped free and jauntily waved at Trent. The chair was hauled back to our side, and lowered to the deck ... for me.

I looked at it, petrified, wondering how much a pleasure excursion to Barbados might run me. "It all right, Tom," Parigo said, grinning. "Won't drop you!" He pushed me toward the chair and tied me into it. "Give regards to Mrs. Nugent! You ready?"

Unable to get the word out, I absently inclined my head. Suddenly I was in the air, swinging wildly in every direction. Fortunate that half a day had elapsed since I'd last eaten! The chair started moving out over the roiling ocean, and the two ships each swung outward, yanking me so sharply up that the bridle went slack for an instant. Then they swung inward, and I would have smashed against *Dorothy C.*'s hull, save that the pilot's alert crewmen hauled in sharply on the guy line. After bouncing twice more, my feet touched the deck of the pilot, and the arms of the crewman strapped to the mast were clutching me as another untied the safety gaskets. I was gasping, ready to weep with relief, and simultaneously laughing. My knees gave way and, pulling on the jack line, I crawled aft to the little boat's cockpit. I managed to get myself upright just in time for an almighty slap of cold, salt ocean spray to hit me in the face.

"Well now, that was easy enough, wasn't it!" Jeptha exclaimed, pounding me heartily on the back.

Still bereft of air, I merely nodded and turned to watch the proceedings. Parigo had already retrieved the chair and lines, and the two boats were moving apart.

She's going south! I thought enviously. *And I'm going back to winter!*

But as I waved to them, I considered our parting in a more philosophical light. They're off to engage in the noble free trade of our great Atlantic world, bringing and exchanging urgently needed goods in either direction—honest goods that sustain and enhance life. And they've avoided the damned impost unjustly claimed against them, too! *Ha!* I smiled to myself, chuffed to have played a small part in this one vessel's liberation.

"We're headed back to Sandy Hook, Mr. Dordrecht," Jeptha said. "About two hours, I'd guess."

"Could you possibly leave me in Gravesend or Sheepshead Bay, sir?"

"Well out of our way, lad!" I dug a silver half-crown out of my waistcoat and proffered it. "Ah," he said, accepting, "Not *that* far out of our way!"

On the familiar two-mile trudge through snow from Gravesend Bay to my family's home, happily anticipating the surprised welcome I'd receive when I appeared amid the town's New Year's Day celebrations, I had opportunity to contemplate the ups and downs of my life in the year 'sixty-five, now history.

I hadn't established myself in business. I hadn't managed to get married. If I ever get paid for the one pianoforte and sell the other, I'll be well ahead—but that's thanks largely to my completely fortuitous emolument from Miss Theodora Colegrove. One can hardly rely on such prodigies, and I really ought to avoid such distractions in the future, and concentrate on my true calling!

A foolish speculation nonetheless captured my whimsy that, try as I might, I couldn't dismiss out of hand. Were I ever again offered a commission like Miss Theodora's, *would I accept it?* Preposterous. *Preposterous*, but … well, *perhaps*.

After all, I hardly felt the poorer for my adventures!

Other than nearly being killed, that is.

I clambered over the Ligtenbargs' great stone fence, and was cheered to see smoke wafting from the chimneys of *The Arms of Orange* in the fading light.

A much more sensible concern occupied my home stretch. Would we ever get the Stamp Act repealed, I wondered. Surely—*surely*—we would, in time! The British merchants I had met would never tolerate the wholesale loss of American business. If we can just hold firm through the winter, I thought, the government will have to see reason, repeal its encumbrances on us, and reinstate the felicity we long enjoyed before the war as a productive and free province of Great Britain's empire.

Best to maintain our optimism on that question!

Best to maintain optimism always, I say.

About the Author

Jonathan Carriel possesses a BA and MA in History from New York University. He lives in New York City and has spent decades supporting computer networks in each of its boroughs. As a recreational sailor, he has cruised the United States east coast and the Caribbean, sailed from North Carolina to St. Thomas, traversed the English Channel and the Aegean Sea, and crossed the Atlantic.

Photo by Margery Westin

Exquisite Folly is his fourth novel, continuing the series of Thomas Dordrecht mystery and adventure stories that began with *Die Fasting, Great Mischief,* and *If Two Are Dead.* Each story takes place in the context of a specific historical year in the turbulent second half of the eighteenth century—the decades of the industrial, American, French, and Haitian revolutions.

He invites his readers to visit www.JonathanCarriel.com, where they will find further material to pique their curiosity about the era, in addition to maps, photographs, genealogies, and text expanding upon these fictions.

Printed in the United States
By Bookmasters